THE OLD GIRLS' NETWORK

JUDY LEIGH

Boldwood

First published in Great Britain in 2020 by Boldwood Books Ltd.

Copyright © Judy Leigh, 2020

Cover Design by Debbie Clement Design

Cover Photography: Shutterstock

A CIP catalogue record for this book is available from the British Library.

Paperback ISBN 978-1-83889-563-1

Large Print ISBN 978-1-83889-562-4

Ebook ISBN 978-1-83889-564-8

Kindle ISBN 978-1-83889-565-5

Audio CD ISBN 978-1-83889-557-0

MP3 CD ISBN 978-1-83889-558-7

Digital audio download ISBN 978-1-83889-559-4

Boldwood Books Ltd
23 Bowerdean Street
London SW6 3TN
www.boldwoodbooks.com

Dedication: To Big G

1

Barbara thought she must be dead. She could remember exactly what had happened, right up to the last second. She was rushing up the path to the little terraced house, fixing her sights on the familiar green door, number eighty-six. Then she recalled feeling strange, a little bit as if she had floated above her own head for a moment, or was hovering outside her body. She wobbled, the dizziness a thick haze behind her eyes as she stared at the smooth paint of the front door, leaning forward to steady herself. Then she slipped. The earth fell away, the sky turned upside down, and the air seemed to whirl from within her, emptying her lungs.

Dying wasn't as painful as she'd imagined it would be, and she didn't feel the bump when the back of her head hit the stone step as she toppled down three more to the ground. Dying was surprisingly easy, in fact: it was just the regret she felt, the sense of missed opportunities, as she tumbled. Her eyes rolled back in her head and that was it. She'd had a fairly long life, but she hadn't done nearly enough with it. She was glad that she'd served for most of her working life as a secretary in the Air Force. She was proud of the order and rigour she'd brought to the job. And she'd never broken the law or been in debt. Barbara's life had been exemplary. Spotless even. But it had all been a bit dull, that was the problem. She'd never behaved badly enough. She'd seldom taken risks. She had never really let go, danced on tables, shouted from the depths of her lungs in quiet libraries. She'd never taken life by the throat, flirted with danger, or even flirted with men. She was a spinster, for goodness sake. But at least she wasn't a virgin. That would have been too hard to bear at the final gasp.

Of course, Barbara knew that, had she lived, she'd never have become a wild party animal; she wouldn't have become the centre of attention, the admired ringleader – she wouldn't even have been very popular. So what was her biggest regret? She had no family of her own now, no one except her sister. In a flash, like her life tumbling before her eyes, Barbara knew she hadn't been a good sibling: she'd never really defended Pauline, looked out for her or even spent quality time with her. She wasn't sure she even liked her very much. Perhaps that was her biggest regret. But it was too late now that she was dead. Death would be a great disappointment, though. She wasn't ready to go yet, and she'd only just realised it.

She'd had all the warning signs beforehand and ignored them, in her usual determined, obstinate way. Three weeks ago, she'd been a little light-headed and breathless when running up the stairs. She'd had to hang on to the walls, almost knocking down her favourite photo of herself, smiling in uniform, posed at her desk aged twenty-six. Her hair had been a mass of fashionable curls tied back, restrained beneath the cap; her body slim inside the smart uniform.

Then, a fortnight ago, she'd been desperate to take off on the two-week early spring break to Suffolk with Green Sage Holidays. But it had all been far too stressful. The coach trip had been dull and stuffy, most pairs of seats occupied by retired couples; she'd had nothing to interest her during the journey except a frivolous book and the pointless chatter of the driver over the microphone. The hotel had been plain and lacklustre, the food bland, as bland as the other holiday makers. All those sedentary pensioners with their afternoon cups of weak tea, listening to Frankie Vaughan singing songs about the moonlight, and their non-stop chatter about knitting patterns when she'd wanted to go outside in the brisk air, hiking along the coastal paths.

Barbara wondered what she had been expecting, but the holiday hadn't delivered anything. She'd set out in the early morning wind and trekked along a muddy path for three miles, dragging a complete stranger behind her, a poor woman called Dorothy, who moaned about her bunions and about being a widow and how hard it was to go on holiday alone. Barbara had to turn back long before she was ready.

Barbara might be seventy-seven, but there was life in the old girl yet. And yet, suddenly, sadly, now there wasn't. She had slipped down the steps in a faint, a suitcase in each hand, her heart beating too fast and then – nothing. White lights blazed above her. Blindingly white, like the angels at Damascus. Heaven? Surely not – Barbara didn't believe in heaven, so of course it didn't exist. White ceilings. A person in shining white clothes, with a halo around her head. Barbara groaned. 'Who are you? Where am I?'

A firm voice replied. 'Try to rest. You're in the hospital, Mrs Harvey.'

'Miss,' Barbara grunted and fell back into drowsiness. At least she wasn't dead, not yet.

When she opened her eyes, she was aware of a young man in a white coat moving around the room. He was writing something on a clipboard, peering across at her slyly. Barbara called out, 'Hello.' She was surprised at how croaky her voice sounded. She tried to sit up, and immediately she felt better. She tried her voice again, deliberately adding boom to it. 'Are you a nurse?'

She frowned at the young man. He couldn't be more than twenty: he still had teenage spots on his cheeks. He had dark hair, large ears, and huge hazel eyes. She couldn't read his name badge. He coughed and murmured something back. Barbara had no idea what he'd just said. 'Speak up, can't you, young man?' Her voice had almost regained its resonance.

'The doctor is come soon,' he muttered in an accent which could have been Italian or Spanish, and then he shuffled away. Barbara put a hand to her head. There was a rounded bump on the crown, a tender spot, presumably where she'd fallen. Her shoulder ached a little, but otherwise she felt fine. She gazed around her. She was in a small hospital room. Overhead there were fluorescent lights, blinding white against a blank ceiling. The paint on the walls was pale and grubby. Next to her bed there was a cabinet with shelves. She wriggled around in the bed to see if there was anything of interest in the rest of the room. There wasn't. She breathed out. At least she wasn't in a populated ward. She had been in hospital once before, in 1953, to have her tonsils out. She had been thirteen; they'd put her in a ward full of sallow ancient women, all trussed up like Egyptian mummies. She had hated it.

She pushed back the starched sheet which held her body tight as a shroud, and swung her legs across the bed, testing her feet against the floor. She felt better. The dizziness had gone. She glanced down at herself; her bony arms stuck out from a pale night dress, a flimsy one that had seen better days and wasn't even fit for a jumble sale. It had small white flowers on it, the print a relief in the pale blue material. Barbara thought it was ghastly and raked the room with her eyes for her own clothes. She sighed, a sharp, irritated exhaling of breath: her clothing was presumably folded away in the shelved cabinet, probably not tidy and certainly unwashed. She fixed her eyes on a sash window, heaved herself up and away from the bed and moved across the room to look outside.

The window frame was dingy, the paint chipped. She gazed out, across at buildings, roofs: a supermarket sprawled on the other side of the road and cars were crawling along, stopping at red traffic lights and inching forwards. She assumed she must be on the third floor. The sky was pale grey, sombre and cloudless, a cold March day. She folded her arms and sighed again. She longed for some fresh air. The room was too warm and unbearably stuffy.

The door opened behind her and a woman walked in, wearing a white coat, her light brown hair clipped back into a roll behind her head. She was fair skinned, freckled, probably in her thirties. She gestured to the end of the bed. Barbara sat down facing her and said 'Hello.'

The woman in the white coat didn't smile. She had a serious frowning face. 'Mrs Harvey?'

Barbara didn't smile either. 'I'm Miss Harvey. I can't abide this "Ms" business. It's neither one thing nor the other, is it? Are you a doctor? When can I go home?'

The doctor clipped the stethoscope into her ears and approached Barbara, making a soft humming noise and muttering, 'I'm Dr North, and I'm here to check you over,' then pulling the low neck of her blue robe to one side, listening to her heart beat. Barbara was unimpressed. The doctor hadn't asked permission or even spoken to her properly. She forced her lips together in a grimace.

'I'm perfectly well, Doctor. I don't know what I'm doing here. This is just a waste of both our time.'

Dr North frowned, put slim fingers to Barbara's wrist and seemed thoughtful. She picked up the clipboard and turned to one side.

Barbara said, 'Well? I'm waiting, Doctor. When can I go home?'

The doctor met her eyes. 'You are in your late seventies. You've had a fall. You were suffering from hypotension.'

'I agree with you on the first two counts, Doctor. I know how old I am, and I know I had a tumble. Why don't you just tell me that I'm all right now and I'll go straight home?'

'I'm afraid that's not possible yet. There are many reasons for low blood pressure. We need to run a few tests.'

Barbara leaned forward, chin thrust out, as if she was about to argue with someone who had sold her shoddy goods. 'What reasons? What tests?'

The doctor's face remained impassive. She clearly lacked the ability to feel any emotions. Barbara thought she should be able to show empathy, at least, in her job. She wished she wasn't wearing the silly pale robe. She'd be more dignified in clothes and certainly the doctor would be able to tell that she wasn't to be argued with if she had on a tailored suit and some court shoes, her hair properly brushed and not flattened at both sides by the pressure of the pillow.

'Hmmm.' Dr North was thoughtful. Barbara folded her arms. For the first time, the doctor met her eyes. 'You had a fall, Barbara. It has to be checked out thoroughly. At any age, but particularly with the elderly.' She ignored Barbara's glare. 'We have to make sure there are no underlying factors: heart problems, endocrine problems.'

'My heart is fine. And my endocrine system functions perfectly. I'd been on holiday, overdoing things a bit. Now I'm back I can put my feet up.' The doctor was paying no attention, so Barbara tried again. 'I can sit at home drinking tea and reading pointless romance novels.'

'Is there any one at home who can be on hand? A partner? Children?'

'I have no children, Doctor,' Barbara said between clenched teeth. 'And as for a partner, I loathe dancing. If you mean, do I have a husband or do I live in sin with a man or a woman, the answer is no, I'm by myself.' Doctor North's face remained immobile so Barbara added, 'I prefer it that way,' just for clarity.

The doctor nodded, like she was dismissing an irritating child. 'We'll run a few tests. You'll be here for a couple of days. Is there anyone we can contact?'

Barbara thought of Pauline, how she might panic, take the first train from Somerset and then fly into the waiting room, all fumbling fingers and flushed cheeks, her voice high and shrieking, flapping her elbows like a chicken and causing an unnecessary fuss.

'No. No one at all.'

The doctor nodded again and moved to the door, pressing the handle, then she was gone and Barbara was alone. She stared down at her bare feet, the long legs dangling below the hemline of the thin robe. She put her hand to her face and felt her skin, normal, a little dry, slightly warm. She fingered the slate grey curls, once raven black, cut sensibly to cover her ears, the soft fringe, the tiny pearl earrings. She was stuck in hospital, with nothing to look forward to except routine tests which she was sure would tell her what she knew already. She'd been too busy and yes, perhaps she needed a rest. But there was nothing at all wrong with her. She was fine. And, thank goodness, she was definitely not dead, although she'd feared she had been when she'd stumbled.

Barbara remained on the bed for a moment, stretching out her calves, considering her options. She felt hungry. And a cup of tea would be nice. She'd stay in the hospital, tolerate the pointless tests and then she'd make some plans. She had already thought about what she needed to do; she'd decided the moment she had fallen down outside the green door of her home, number eighty-six. This was her life and it needed taking by the throat. She had things to do, to resolve, to put right. She wasn't sure exactly how she would do it yet, but she would make plans. She'd have time to think about it over the next two days.

She found the bell at the end of the wire by the side of the bed and she pressed it hard. Soon a nurse would come running in, perhaps the young man with the teenage acne. She pressed again, allowing the bell to buzz for a long time. She hoped he'd know where she could find a decent cup of tea.

2

The late March wind blew around the corner so fiercely, Pauline almost tottered over as she carried her basket of washing. From this part of the garden, she could see the lane that weaved in front of her property. Beyond it was the new neighbours' house. They'd moved in a few days ago – she'd seen the removal vans – and Pauline wondered if she should go over and introduce herself. But she decided she'd let them settle in first. She stared across the fields and there in the distance was Winsley Green, nestling between the woodlands and the hills: she could see the church spire, the cluster of houses and a few shops. She could walk there in twelve minutes but it was usually easier to drive, although the lanes were narrow and she was often forced to back up or to pull in for a large farm vehicle. Len from Bottom Farm would always let her through, but most people would glare at her and wait for her to edge back. Pauline hated reversing.

The clothesline that hung just out of reach above her head was fraying and the ancient wooden prop with its two-pronged end was splintered. But this was the best drying space in the garden; gusts funnelled around the corner, blasts of fierce air, and a duvet cover would fill like a sail and dry in an hour. Pauline struggled with the weight of the wet laundry, but she was used to dealing with strenuous chores by herself now, leaning into the buffeting wind to haul up two towels, a blouse, a pair of jeans, some white underwear and her bedding. The washing flapped in the air, a tall ship borne out to sea, as she hoisted the prop to its fullest height and balanced it upright. She put her hands on her hips and thought about the underwear. She probably ought to buy a new bra. A lacy one might be nice, rather than the two-in-a-pack old plain design. She giggled at the thought of herself in racy red underwear and stared across the farmer's field. Spring was approaching and there were already ewes grazing, with their lambs huddled against them for warmth.

Pauline thought for a moment, then she turned her back to the wind as it blew her hair, wrenching silver strands from her hair clip and smothering her face with dancing threads. The breeze was so cold her skin tingled, and she paused for a moment to breathe the chill air, allowing it to fill her lungs.

'An icy wind from the north. Change is in the air.'

She nodded like a wise country woman, although she didn't think of herself as being particularly wise. She could smell the sweet scent of spring, and with it the promise of summer's warmth, new beginnings.

'Change is always good,' she reassured herself.

Then her eyes caught a twitch in the grass: a black rump, a swishing tail, just a yard away. There was a flurry of paws and a swift lurching movement. Two green eyes met hers, narrowing. Between the cat's claws something wriggled: the cat gripped the shrew in its mouth and faced Pauline defiantly; a thin tail and two feet dangled from one side and an immobile head with tiny ears on the other. Pauline muttered to herself.

'That's Derek, isn't it? So, where's the other one?' She swivelled her head a few inches to the right and, as she had thought, there was the other cat, the brother, all black with white paws: Clive. Pauline chuckled and waved an arm. 'Go on, you bad boys. Get out of here. Go home.'

Derek stared at her, just long enough to make the point that he had no respect for humans whatsoever. Then he sauntered forward, dropped the dead shrew at her feet and ambled away. Quick as an arrow, Clive bounced forward with slits for eyes, growled at Pauline, snatched the shrew in his mouth and bolted after his brother. Pauline smiled.

'No wonder everyone round here calls them the Feral Peril. I'm sure Dulcie doesn't know what they get up to when they come down here. She thinks they're both little angels.' She picked up her washing basket and headed towards the back door. She deserved a cup of tea and a homemade cupcake, the fudgy ones she'd made yesterday.

The kitchen was warm, the womb of the house, the air swelling with the rich scent of baking. Pauline settled the heavy kettle on the Aga and moved to the Welsh dresser, reaching for the tea caddy. It was in its usual place, next to the photo of her daughter Jessica with her horse. Jessica was in her late forties now; she and her partner were living in New Zealand. The photo of her smiling daughter was next to the urn inside its box: next to Douglas. She had not moved it for two years. She wasn't really sure what to do with the contents. She could hardly scatter them on the floor of the local pub.

She touched the smooth surface of the box with her fingertips, thinking how she had seldom brushed his cheek with the same tenderness when he was alive. His name and dates were engraved on the metal. Douglas John Pye. 1938–2017. It had become a marriage of habit, a routine, but she'd loved him in her own way. His retirement had suited Douglas more than it had Pauline. He'd led his life the way he'd wanted: he was gregarious and sociable, and Pauline had been in the background. Douglas was always laughing, happiest when he was in the local inn, a whisky in his hand, chatting to other men. A man's man.

She'd worked in an antiques shop before Jessica came along. She'd loved it but Douglas had wanted her to stay at home, so she'd been there with a fried breakfast and a full sandwich box in the morning, and a substantial supper when he'd strolled home at night. He'd worked in an office, filing insurance claims. A sedentary lifestyle was no good for a man.

The dripping tap interrupted Pauline's thoughts. She shuffled over to the sink and used all the brute force she had in both hands to turn the tap off. The drip persisted and Pauline shook her head. The tiles were cracked around the window, the wooden frame was rotten. There was so much to do. She poured her tea, carried it to the scrubbed oak table and sat down, reaching for the cake tin and fingering a chocolate cream fudge square. She sipped tea and munched her cake, deep in thought.

She and Douglas had moved here just over three years ago. She'd loved Winsley Green from the first moment she arrived, and they'd said it would be their last home, their most comfortable, the country idyll. The little three-bedroomed cottage was cosy, in need of some TLC, but it would be perfect when it was finished, like something from a glossy magazine about perfect rural lifestyles. Pauline remembered with a sigh. Douglas didn't make it through the winter. He'd been in the pub, the Sheep Dip, drinking a single malt with the locals. By all accounts he was on his fourth when he fell down on the flagstones and died where he lay. His heart had stopped. A kind doctor had told her much later that Douglas had had a pulmonary embolism; he probably hadn't felt a thing.

Pauline had felt alone and empty. Her elder sister Barbara had come over from Cambridge to stay for a week, but she hadn't helped. Barbara had said that at least Douglas had died the way he'd have wanted to, with a glass of malt in his hand, and he hadn't suffered. But Pauline was left behind, suffering. She was alone and the house was badly in need of renovation. It was all so sudden, and at first she'd no idea how to pick herself up, or where to start. She'd spent those days after his death sitting in stunned silence. Then, gradually, she started to occupy herself with small things: cleaning, tidying, trying to become independent. The locals were friendly, always offering a neighbourly word or a carton of free-range eggs, and two years had passed slowly, but she was coping. The house was cold.

Some days had been better than others; for the first few months, it had been too easy to retreat into herself and she'd been glad of the distraction from the local residents, who would call in whether she'd asked them to or not, and would help themselves to coffee or tea and fudgy cupcakes. She hadn't seen Barbara for a while, though. Barbara had said that Winsley Green was a terrible place, either too remote and lonely or full of gossips and busybodies; she'd go out of her mind if she had to stay in such a backwater for long.

Pauline smiled. She was coping well now. She missed Douglas but she was made of strong stuff. Winsley Green was her home now; the community surrounded her like a warm blanket. She belonged; she'd become part of the fabric, part of the thick stone walls of the cottage, a small spoke in the hub of the community. The locals were lovely, like a second family.

Pauline wiped crumbs from the corner of her mouth and swiped the last morsels of cake from the wooden table into her hand, then into the bin. She picked up the empty teacup and took it to the sink, placing it below the dripping tap. At least the water wouldn't go to waste. She leaned against the Belfast sink and wondered what to make for lunch. She'd treat herself to something nice and nutritious, like homemade soup and crusty rolls.

She picked up the radio and fiddled with the switch; she'd listen to Radio 4. A friendly voice in the room might lift her spirits, which had started to sag a little today. Pauline glanced at the silver urn again. The Sheep Dip would be open now, Oskar and Justina pulling pints and chatting to the customers. A log fire would be burning in the huge hearth and, if Douglas were still alive, it was likely that's where he'd be. The dripping tap would still need fixing; the window frame would still be rotten.

Pauline was pulled from her thoughts by a resonant banging sound: someone was at the front door, heaving the huge horseshoe knocker. She wiped her fingers on a teacloth, dabbed a hand over her hair where the strands had come loose, and rushed down the hallway to open the heavy door. Len Chatfield filled the doorway, his square shoulders broad inside a tight jacket, the fabric torn and dirty. His blue eyes stared at her from beneath grey wavy hair. His face was ruddy, wind-ravaged, whiskers blooming from the lower part of his cheeks, and he looked anxious.

'Pauline...'

'Hello, Len.' Pauline offered him a warm smile.

'Brought logs,' he muttered in his crackly accent, nodding behind him at the Land Rover. 'I'll put them in the woodshed for you, shall I?'

Pauline nodded. 'That's nice of you, Len. But spring's well on the way. It's late for logs. Still I suppose they'll come in useful for next winter.'

'No.' Len's face clouded with further anxiety, his curling eyebrows moving upwards. 'Weather will turn next week. It'll come cold again before summer is here proper – it'll come icy, snow even, mark my words.'

Pauline met his eyes. Neither she nor Len spoke for a moment, then she said, 'Thanks, that's kind.'

Len brought his lips together, wiped his face with the back of his wrist. 'Ah, yes, right. So, I'll put them in your woodshed for you then, Pauline.'

She fingered the neck of her jumper. 'Thanks, Len.' Her eyes met his: a thought came to her. 'Would you like a cup of tea?'

'No.' He shook his head fiercely, as if a bee was buzzing against his nose. 'No. Best be off. Things to do. Lambs. Sheep. Tractor.'

Pauline nodded as if she understood. But she didn't really understand how Len Chatfield managed to find time to bring her gifts. He was a busy man; he owned Bottom Farm and many other fields around the village, and of course he was always working, daytimes and even into the late evening. She wondered how they coped up at the big farmhouse on the hill, Len and his son Gary, who all the neighbours said should be married and gone now he was in his thirties. But perhaps he didn't want to leave his father, in his seventies, a widower of some twenty years, or the farm where he had worked since he was a boy.

Pauline studied Len's strong features and wondered how well he cooked for himself. Of course, he could easily kill a chicken with his bare hands but she had no idea how he managed with basic meals from day to day. Pauline reached out and patted his arm.

'Thank you, Len.'

He grunted, his cheeks ruddier than ever, then he turned and ambled back to the Land Rover, lifting out two sacks filled with bulky logs. He heaved the sacks towards the wood shed, where he pushed the door open and deposited the logs on the floor. He strode back to a Land Rover parked by the gate without turning to look back. Pauline watched him go, noticing his square solid back in a thick checked shirt, the steadiness of his stride. He swung himself into the Land Rover. She waved as he drove away down the lane, but his eyes were firmly on the road. She was alone again. Pauline sighed.

A gust of wind swirled the grass of her front lawn and she saw

Derek decapitating a sparrow. She closed the door with a clunk and wondered if Len was right, if the weather would change. It was almost midday. She'd hoover the lounge, lay a fire for later and perhaps she'd have a little snooze in the afternoon. The phone started to trill in the kitchen. Pauline disliked phone calls; it usually meant that she had to do something she didn't want, or talk to someone she'd rather not. It might be the surgery reminding her about a routine appointment; double glazing salespeople; life insurance. And she'd heard stories about all these scammers. She breathed into the receiver.

'Hello?'

Barbara's voice boomed back. 'I'm coming to visit, Pauline. The day after tomorrow. There's nothing wrong with me but I've been in hospital and they've told me to take it easy so I'm coming to you for a rest.'

Pauline frowned. 'Well I'm not sure you'd like...'

'The train arrives on Thursday at one thirty. Of course, it doesn't come as far as Winsley Green because you haven't got a station there, so you'll have to pick me up in Taunton. One thirty sharp.'

'But how long will you stay? I'll have to get the spare room ready and do some shopping. I haven't got any vegetables in...'

'Oh, never mind about that.' Barbara's tone was irritable. 'Just be there. I've no idea how long I'll be staying. The woman next door will keep an eye on my little place.' There was a pause and when her voice returned to the earpiece, Barbara sounded strangely cheerful. 'I'm actually looking forward to the break. Do you know, Pauline, we might even enjoy ourselves.'

Pauline pulled a face: she wasn't sure. She could imagine Barbara in Douglas' favourite chair in the lounge, her feet up, sipping the Christmas sherry while Pauline rushed around obeying orders.

'Barbara—'

'That's settled then. Thursday, Taunton station. Don't be late.'

Pauline wondered if her sister was pausing to smile or to clench her teeth, then she heard her add, 'There's a dear girl. Goodbye.'

Pauline put the phone back softly into its cradle and stood still for a moment. She wondered what the next few days would bring. Barbara was coming to stay, and she had no idea for how long. She breathed in, pushed back her shoulders and tried a smile. It might be nice seeing Barbara again; it would certainly be pleasant to have another person in the house, another voice. But Barbara could be quite difficult.

Pauline considered for a moment and resolved to be positive. They were sisters, after all, both in their seventies now: it was about time she tried again to close the gulf between them: Barbara couldn't do it. She was by nature a little prickly and Pauline thought it might be the right thing to do, to try to connect. They were the only local family either of them had now, after all, Jessica being so far away.

The word *family* made Pauline frown thoughtfully. Most sisters usually had something in common; there was usually an opinion they shared, a hobby, a memory. But not Pauline and Barbara. They couldn't be more different. It would be an interesting challenge though, to try to befriend her unfriendly sister.

Pauline moved to the sink and began to dry her teacup. She stared out of the window at the bleak grey sky. Len had been right – there would be ice, cold in the air, even a storm coming. Pauline expected the worst.

3

Barbara was not enjoying the journey. The carriage from Cambridge smelled of stale cheese which she believed came from the perspiration of too-closely-seated unwashed bodies. The man who sat hunched opposite her had a laptop on the table and it hogged the entire space, so there was hardly any room for her small handbag. Then a teenager in the seat across the aisle continued to chatter on her phone about her disastrous shopping trip, despite the fact that it was the quiet carriage. After five minutes, Barbara was forced to tap her on the shoulder and point to the sign, but the young woman continued to gabble about tacky handbags and over-sized leopard-print onesies.

Barbara spent the rest of the journey thinking about Pauline. As a child, she'd always called her younger sister 'Pud', a clumsy attempt at an affectionate abbreviation, but when Pauline became a slightly pudgy adolescent, the nickname had made her cry. Barbara smiled: it was even more appropriate once she became Mrs Pye. Mrs Pudding Pye. But it hurt her sister's feelings each time she slipped into the childish pet name. Barbara decided she'd try her best not to upset Pauline this time. Now was about mending a fragmented past; about closing the distance that had developed between them, due to neglect, due to not noticing the passing of time, having little or no practice at being proper sisters. She brought her lips together in a straight line: so far, she hadn't had much success. But she would try harder now. They didn't have much in common, though. Pauline was a widow, all alone now her daughter was in New Zealand. Barbara wondered how well her sister coped, living in the sticks so far from civilisation.

It was a shame about Douglas. Barbara was not sure how happy their marriage had been, but at least Pauline had married. She'd had a child, Jessica, who had completely enveloped her for eighteen years. Then Jessica looked for a new opportunity and found it with her husband and young family, working with horses abroad. Barbara remembered Pauline and Douglas, first married, a white wedding, Pauline in a stiff ivory dress. The memory dissolved and she recalled herself as a young woman, brisk and slim, attractive in her uniform, remembering the warm feeling that came from the first hesitant glances of admiration from a dashing young officer.

But that was behind her now. Her heart had hardened and that was all for the best. Pauline would have to do the same now she had no one left to love apart from a daughter who lived abroad. Barbara knew that her sister wasn't the type to jet off to New Zealand twice a year; she'd have to be resilient, on her own for most of the time, contented with phone calls on a Sunday. Barbara thought her sister was far too sensitive for her own good.

On the platform, Barbara placed her case on the ground and stared at the sign which hung down from the iron rafters of the station. The train would arrive in forty-five minutes at platform seven. When she had bought her ticket and chosen to go via Reading, she'd noticed that the change of trains did not include a wait. A female voice over the speakers announced that there were unforeseeable circumstances and the connection would be delayed. There was no apology, no regretful tone, just a flat statement of facts. She inhaled, breathed out sharply. She wouldn't be in Taunton until after half past two. Pauline would be kept waiting.

Barbara had invested in one of those mobile phones that young people carried all the time, but she rarely used it. She'd rather talk to people directly. Besides, they were complicated things with small buttons, and she didn't have the patience to mess about with it. It was at the bottom of her handbag. Barbara wondered if she should use it now. Pauline had one: she could ring her and say she'd been delayed at Reading.

A slim man in a high-visibility jacket walked past, ginger hair sticking out like sprigs of hay from his cap. Barbara accosted him as he drew level.

'Excuse me. Are you a railway man?'

He was pale faced, a few red dots of acne on his nose. Barbara decided he must be a teenager. His mouth had an unpleasant sneer.

'I'm a customer service assistant, madam.'

Barbara extended herself to her full height, easily five feet ten inches. 'Well I'm a customer. And I'd like to know what's holding up the service. Why is the train to Taunton delayed for so long?'

'Problems on the line, madam.'

Barbara sniffed. 'I didn't think it was Santa Claus. What problems?'

The young man seemed to notice her for the first time. His eyes were expressionless, like those of a cod in a fish shop window.

'I think there's a body on the line, madam.'

Barbara gasped. 'What? A dead one? That's a thoughtless thing to do. Can't someone just take it away?'

The young man shrugged. 'Matter for the police, madam. And forensics. I expect the front of the train will need cleaning.'

Barbara's eyes widened. 'But what about my journey to Taunton? I am being met at the station.'

'I expect there will be an announcement there, to tell people the train is delayed.'

'That's really not good enough.'

A smirk played around his thin lips, below the beginnings of ginger facial hair. 'It's the best I can do, madam.'

Barbara watched him walk away. She shook her head briskly. Pauline would be fretful by herself at the station in Taunton. A stiff gust of wind whipped around the corner and buffeted her full-on, making her catch her breath. It was icy cold. Barbara wondered if she should find customer services and lodge a complaint. Instead, she took out her phone and squinted at the buttons.

* * *

Pauline hauled up the engine cover at the back of the ancient Volkswagen, checking the oil, wiping the dipstick carefully with a paper towel. The journey to Taunton was fifteen miles, and she didn't want the engine to seize up because she'd run out of lubricant. She walked around the yellow car and inspected the tyres. They seemed all right: they weren't flat. She had enough petrol. The journey would take her twenty-five minutes, so she had plenty of time, especially now Barbara's train was running late. She hugged her jacket around herself; there was ice in the wind this morning. Her fingers were cold as she took the car keys from her pocket.

'Yoo-hoo, Pauline.'

Down by the gate, a woman was waving through the open window of a white Fiesta. She stopped the car by the gate and wriggled out. The woman was very slim, with short red hair in a pixie cut, bright green jacket and red skirt, orange tights, clumpy heeled shoes, in her late thirties or early forties.

'Are you all right, Pauline? Has the car broken down? Do you need a hand?'

Pauline grinned. 'No, I'm fine. Dizzy. Just—'

The woman bounded over, her face creased in a huge smile, her legs fast and flexible as a Labrador's.

'I wondered if your car wouldn't start. I have jump leads in the Fiesta. Mind you, I have no idea how to use them.' Dizzy pushed a hand through her long layered fringe, three shades of red, orange and burgundy. 'I only carry them so that I can pretend to break down occasionally and ask a handsome strapping man to help me. Of course, it hasn't worked yet. I either get crabby pensioners or hearty women from the WI who tell me I should learn to do things for myself.' Dizzy chuckled, oblivious to the fact that Pauline had been receiving a pension for well over ten years.

Pauline shrugged. 'Well, maybe they are right, Dizzy. Maybe it's good to be able to do things for ourselves. I wish I'd been brought up to be a bit more practical at basic tasks.' For a moment her face was sad. 'I've learned to be independent and do a bit more for myself nowadays.'

Dizzy's forehead creased. 'Oh, I'm sorry. Pauline, I didn't mean to...' She grabbed Pauline's arm, patted the coat sleeve and grinned. 'I'm on my way to Thorpe. I've got a job there. Some woman I've never met before rang last night – she wants a complete restyle.' She scrutinised Pauline's hair, the soft roll on top of her head, the loose waving strands. 'You must let me do yours, Pauline. My rates are good. I could make you look like a new woman.'

'Oh, I'm fine, Dizzy...'

'So,' Dizzy appeared to have forgotten she had a hairdressing appointment in Thorpe, four miles away. 'Tell me all about your new neighbours from across the road.'

'I don't know them yet.' Pauline looked towards the neighbours' house. 'They only moved in last week. I haven't met them. I saw them when the removals van arrived. She's in her forties, I suppose, the woman – dark hair. He has glasses, same age as his wife, same hair colour.'

Dizzy rolled her eyes. 'I must pop round there, offer my services. She might benefit from a good cut and blow dry. Or him, a nice tidy-up. And I'll do the kids cut-price, if they have any. Do they?'

'I've no idea. Look, Dizzy, I'm sorry – I have to leave soon. I'm picking up my sister from the station in Taunton – she's just phoned me with a third update on her arrival time.'

Dizzy beamed, her eyes shining. 'Is she coming to stay? I didn't think she'd been here since you moved – what – it must be more than three years ago now?'

'That's right. She's been twice, once for our first Christmas. She stayed for a day or two. She was bored, I think. Then she came just after Douglas died and managed to tolerate me for three days. I don't think she likes the country life.'

'Why is she coming, then?' Dizzy's hands flew to her mouth. 'She won't stay long.'

Pauline nodded. 'I expect not.'

Dizzy patted her on the arm and gave a little skip. 'You mustn't miss yoga, the day after tomorrow in the village hall. You are coming, aren't you?'

'I wouldn't miss it.' Pauline's eyes shone. 'I always look forward to it.'

Dizzy turned. 'I'll see you there then.' She walked four paces away, then twisted back. 'Bring your sister. It might do her some good.'

Pauline watched Dizzy slide into the Fiesta, following it with her eyes as the car shunted away. She chuckled softly. 'It might be an idea. It could help Barbara to chill out. On the other hand...' Perhaps it was the word chill, or the bite in the gust of wind, but Pauline shivered inside her jacket. With a heart heavy as stone, she flopped into the Volkswagen and started the engine.

Two hours later, Pauline gripped her keys, opened the oak front door and stood back to allow Barbara to walk in with her case. Barbara stopped stiffly in the hallway.

'Smells damp in here, Pauline. Very musty.'

Pauline was conscious that plenty of fresh air was sweeping into the house, cold air with a touch of ice, and that she had put the radiators on full especially to welcome Barbara into her home. She shut the door with a heavy thud and made her voice light.

'I can't smell anything.'

'I suppose you are accustomed to the damp. It's in all these old houses. That's why I live in a cosy little modern terrace.'

Pauline murmured, 'Soulless places,' under her breath, then put an arm on her sister's. She hoped a warm gesture might be a positive start; it might begin to close the gap between them. 'Let's go and have a cup of tea. I need one.'

'Good idea. But I'll need to take my bag up to my room first and put my things away tidily. I like everything in order.' Barbara glanced at Pauline's hand on her arm and her eyes glittered. 'And I'll need the loo. Tea always goes straight through me.'

Pauline shook her head and led the way to the kitchen, hurrying forward like a broody chicken: the quicker she could seat Barbara at the table and fill her mouth with tea and cake, the less her sister would be able to speak, to complain about the house. Pauline considered her home through Barbara's eyes: musty, damp, old, in need of renovation. Pauline wondered if her sister saw her the same way: a lonely widow, past help, crumbling, incapable of keeping up her own home. She folded her arms, determined she'd show her that she was independent and in charge of her own life. Barbara wouldn't stay for long but, while she was here, Pauline was certainly not going to put up with any of her nonsense, that was a certainty.

* * *

Barbara considered the spare room, the double bed with its soft duvet with a colourful picture of the Buddha on the front, the smooth matching pillows. She frowned, observing the rounded doorways, iron latches, low black beams. She moved to the window and held out a hand; she could feel a breeze blowing through, and thought of her own neat bedroom, half the size of this vast room, with triple glazing and a tidy built-in wardrobe. She folded her clothes into the heavy wooden drawers, glancing at her looming reflection in the mirror of the dark wardrobe. She moved to the fire-place, turning her back to the old mantelpiece, and shivered as a draught whirled around her hips and up her spine to her shoulders.

'This place is so cold.' Barbara said the words aloud, wondering how Pauline could survive in such a draughty house. Even now, just standing in the room with its one small radiator on full, Barbara's fingers were rigid. She folded the last of her underwear, pushed the winceyette night dress under the matching Buddha pillow and thought that a cup of tea would be very pleasant. At least the kitchen had an Aga. It would be warm there.

4

'You don't have to come with me, Barbara. There will be lots of people there. You mightn't enjoy it.'

'What makes you think I won't? I'm flexible for my age.' Barbara glanced up from the chair at the kitchen table and smirked at her own joke. 'Physically and mentally.'

'I don't mean that. I mean, I've been going for over a year. I know all the people at yoga – all the villagers. They might not be, you know, your sort of people.'

'There you go again, making assumptions. What are you trying to say, Pud? That I'm not the sociable type?'

'Pauline. I hate being called Pud.' She took a breath, determined to be assertive. 'You're the only person who's ever called me that and it's not my name. And I didn't mean to imply that you're antisocial, it's just that—'

'When I was on holiday in Suffolk recently, I went out hiking and made a new friend, a woman who came with me on the coastal paths.'

'Oh yes?' Pauline raised her eyebrow in disbelief. 'What was her name? Was she young?'

Barbara shrugged. 'My age, I suppose.'

She couldn't remember the woman's name: Doris, Dorothy? Barbara had been walking in front most of the time, surging ahead and trying to ignore the woman's pleas to go back and the complaints about her raw bunions. She forced a smile.

'I make friends easily. You never know, I might even like yoga. I might be good at it.'

Pauline looked at her sister in the purple baggy t-shirt and the well-worn jogging bottoms she'd just borrowed, which reached her calves. She turned away and muttered, 'I doubt it,' then raised her voice. 'Come on then – let's get going. Yoga starts in half an hour.'

'We're far too early.'

Pauline grabbed her keys and her jacket and moved towards the front door, pretending she hadn't heard. After all, it was her house, her friends, her yoga class.

Barbara had insisted they walk into Winsley Green, despite the chill in the air. She maintained that it was a crisp April day and that a stroll would be good for them both. She added that Pauline needed the muscle tone. Pauline said nothing, although she was piqued: she thought her muscle tone was fine for a woman of seventy-five. They arrived in the village, Barbara surging ahead and Pauline strolling several paces behind, five minutes before eleven o'clock when the class would start.

A stone sign on the brickwork proclaimed that the village hall had been built in 1947. It was dilapidated now; a dull grey two-storey building used for all purposes from the Guides' meetings to the local am-dram group's twice-yearly productions, usually an Ayck-bourn comedy and a pantomime. The sash windows were rotten, the paint flaking and the window panes dirty. Inside, in a little cloakroom, several women were sitting on narrow benches, taking off their shoes and wriggling bare toes. One woman stood in the centre of the space: a petite woman in her forties, dark glossy hair tied loosely on the top of her head. She opened her arms in a gracious gesture.

'I've put the heating on full. All the radiators will be lovely and warm in a few moments. It's quite cool today, so I thought we'd feel the benefit of the ancient central heating system.'

Pauline grasped the woman's hand, smiling. 'Hayley. Nice to see you.'

The woman hugged Pauline. 'I'm so glad you could come. And who's this?'

Pauline stepped back and waved her sister forward, but Barbara was there already, clutching Hayley's hand and shaking it firmly.

'Barbara Harvey. Miss Harvey. Pauline's sister. I've come to try the yoga.'

'Welcome. I'm Hayley Choy. Please take your shoes off and come into the hall. I'll find you a spare mat.'

Barbara turned. Pauline was in conversation with a woman she called Dizzy, who was waving her hands and whispering something about someone being in the family way. Barbara frowned: it obviously wasn't Dizzy, she was too slim and too old – at least forty. Barbara thought she was a little brash and her hair was far too lurid for a woman of her age, her fringe a stripy concoction of red, orange and burgundy; she wondered why Pauline seemed so at ease.

Barbara felt a light pressure on her shoulder and saw a round faced woman smiling at her, her cheeks dimpled, with a wide mouth and good teeth, a cascade of black curls, slightly greying at the temples. Barbara stared into the twinkling hazel eyes and glowered. 'Hello?'

'Hello – you're Pauline's sister, Barbara. I'm Chrissie Drake, the local vicar. It's lovely to meet you.'

Barbara noticed the vicar didn't let go of her hand and didn't stop grinning. She waited for the obligatory phrase about becoming one of Chrissie's flock while she was staying in Winsley Green.

Barbara had no intention of visiting the church. She made her lips into a thin line.

'I don't do God.'

Chrissie Drake smiled. 'What's important is that God is always ready to "do" us. But never mind that now. I'm all revved up to do yoga. Revved? Get it?'

Chrissie Drake chuckled. Barbara remained disinterested, but the vicar didn't seem to notice, her voice full of enthusiasm. 'I must introduce you to everyone after the session.'

Barbara felt a hand on her back, guiding her to the open doorway. She stood firm: she wasn't about to be shepherded inside by a woman of God. Chrissie took no notice, bringing Barbara's attention to the people in the room.

'There's Dr Natalie – she and her husband are GPs – she has some good news – the patter of tiny feet is due in September, I believe. Over there is Yvonne from the village Post Office.'

Barbara gazed at the doctor, a young woman with dark hair who had just relaxed in a lying down position, and then at an older blonde woman with rosy cheeks who was unrolling her mat. Chrissie kept talking and waving her hand.

'Over there is Dulcie and there's her neighbour Phyllis. As yet, we haven't found a way to bring them together, but I'm sure God has something up His sleeve.'

Barbara looked from one angry-looking elderly lady to the other, both busy at opposite ends of the room, rolling out mats and staring furiously at each other and then away, and she shrugged. 'They hate each other?'

Chrissie nodded. 'They don't buy into the Love Thy Neighbour idea, shall we say.'

'What is wrong with them?'

'Cat problems, mostly.' Chrissie shrugged. 'Dulcie's cats, the Feral Peril, are a bit of a local liability. And Phyllis and Dulcie used to go to school together – they were best friends but time has changed all that.'

'How petty,' Barbara muttered. 'I'll never remember all these names anyway.'

Hayley appeared at the door; her face serene. 'Please come into the space. We're ready to start.'

Barbara took the blue mat offered to her and marched to the back, sitting down. She stared around – the older ladies, clearly well past eighty-years-old, one wiry and the other plumper, were still eyeballing each other viciously. They certainly wouldn't be good recruits for a hike around the hills with her. Barbara wondered what these old ladies managed to achieve in yoga. Phyllis was propped up with cushions and Dulcie moved sharply but with deliberate effort.

She glanced at the yoga teacher who was writing something down on a piece of paper, and the young doctor, who appeared to be asleep. Barbara couldn't remember either of their names. Then at the front, there was Pauline and the woman with orange and purple hair, whom Barbara knew instantly that she wouldn't like. On one side of her was Chrissie, the crazy vicar, who was sitting cross-legged, her eyes squeezed, shut: she appeared to be praying. The blonde woman on the other side of Barbara glanced over and winked.

'I'm Yvonne.'

Barbara nodded curtly. 'From the Post Office. I know.'

She decided she couldn't be bothered to introduce herself. The yoga teacher, Hayley, was playing some soothing music on a portable CD player and everyone was now lying down. Barbara stared around her, at the filthy windows and the grubby finger-marked walls that clearly needed a coat of paint.

Hayley had lit a joss stick, so Barbara coughed loudly to make it clear that the smoke was an irritant. Hayley beamed across at her and gestured that she should lie down. Barbara frowned: she thought she was here to do yoga, not to go to sleep, but she leaned back and closed her eyes. The music was reminiscent of waves ebbing and flowing and there were soft sounds, the chattering of dolphins or the gentle calls of gulls. Barbara breathed out and let the music wash over her, the sickly-sweet smell of incense, the warm heat from the metal radiators, and she began to drift. It was as if she was floating, her limbs numb, her mind at peace.

Suddenly there was a silence, no sound at all; the stillness jolted her awake and she opened her eyes. Everyone else was standing up, stretching long arms into the air and Barbara sat bolt upright, about to ask crossly why no one had woken her, but Hayley's sweet voice chimed, 'Nice to have you with us again, Barbara. Take your time, don't rush. Join us when you're ready.'

Pauline turned and smiled across at her and Barbara scuttled to her feet, making a short sound to show she was exasperated at being allowed to sleep through the beginning of the class. Hayley resumed the session, lifting her arms in the air and sweeping them down to her sides. Everyone else was doing the same, Phyllis still seated on her mat propped with cushions. Barbara copied, wafting her arms around as fast as possible, thinking the whole thing reminiscent of primary school PE but with ill-fitting borrowed jogging bottoms instead of baggy navy knickers. She did her best to follow everyone else, but it all felt somewhat pointless. There was an exercise where everyone sat down and twisted round, and Hayley ran around the hall putting more cushions behind Dulcie and Phyllis. Barbara wondered why they chose to take the class: their bones kept cracking, a sort of stereo percussion popping, and at one point she was sure Dulcie passed wind.

Hayley's soothing voice pulled Barbara from her thoughts.

'We're going to revisit Warrior Two now. So, take up the first position. Stand in Tadasana, exhale, step forward so that your feet are about three or four feet apart.'

Barbara had no idea what to do, so she copied Yvonne. Hayley moved softly around the room, helping Phyllis into position.

'Now raise your arms parallel to the floor and reach out to the sides.'

Hayley appeared discreetly next to Barbara, supporting her arm, smiling. Barbara scowled: she'd thought she was doing well enough by herself. Hayley moved back to the front.

'Exhale and bend your left knee over the left ankle, so that the shin is perpendicular to the floor. Anchor yourself strongly. Well done.'

Barbara glanced at the other women. They were all facing a huge window, their arms stretched out, waving in the air like a bunch of flapping flamingos, balanced precariously on the front foot. She made her body into some sort of scarecrow position, copying Yvonne. Hayley seemed pleased with the class.

'Now, turn your head to the left and look out over the fingers. Exhale. Relax in the position now. Think of yourself as Shiva the warrior, solid and grounded. You are Virabhadra with a thousand heads, a thousand eyes.'

Barbara managed not to make a comment, although she felt silly and thought the pose was daft. The thousand eyes were turned on the grimy window. The room was silent. She thought she heard someone wobble behind her. Dulcie passed wind again. Then an almost-naked young man in tight jeans filled the windowpane, a chamois leather cloth in his hand. His face was serious as he swished water onto the window and rubbed the glass. The cold clearly didn't bother him: he was working strenuously, his body gleaming with sweat.

The thousand eyes of Virabhadra took in the shape of the young man, his broad shoulders, his long damp curls, his bare chest. The eyes gazed at the perspiration that shone on his torso, the tangle of hairs that appeared to extend beyond his flat stomach and at the taut muscles in his arms. The eyes moved in unison back to his stunningly beautiful face, with its high cheekbones, soft lips, dark eyes beneath strong brows.

The young man in his mid-twenties didn't seem to notice the gaze of several enamoured Shivas or their concentrated examination of the water droplets that were running down his neck and across his naked chest, onto the waistband of his denims. He had no idea that the warriors in the room were assessing his physical talents and imagining the level balance of his straddled legs below, unfortunately out of view.

Suddenly someone from the front, probably the woman with the hair in various shades of scarlet, muttered, 'Oh my God – just look at him.'

Another voice whispered, 'Amen to that.'

Barbara wondered if it was Chrissie the vicar. Then there was a crashing sound, and all the warriors synchronised a turn of their heads in the opposite direction, to stare at Phyllis, whose knee had given way; she'd come hurtling down onto her mat. Hayley called, 'I'm here, Phyllis. Everyone, please just sit down and take five.'

Dutifully, the women had collapsed down and their gaze moved in perfect synchronicity back to the window. The young man had gone, and they were staring at a clean window and a thousand gleaming droplets of water. Yvonne leaned over to Barbara and whispered, 'Who on earth was that?'

Dr Natalie sat upright on her rug. 'He's the new odd-job man. He's done the windows at the surgery. I think he's from Milton Rogus.'

'Mmm.' The sound of pleasure came from the red-haired woman next to Pauline. 'He can do my windows any time.'

Hayley helped a loudly protesting Phyllis into a comfortable position and was fanning her with a sheet of paper. 'I'll make sure Kostas isn't on window cleaning duties at this time next week, shall I?'

There were murmurs of good-natured disapproval and Pauline turned around to smile encouragingly at her sister. The yoga had made her feel relaxed, expansive and strong: she was enjoying the company of the local women, happy to feel a part of a powerful group and the Kostas incident had made her smile. She wondered if it had melted some of Barbara's frostiness; it would be a good thing if she'd started to feel at home, accepted by the people of Winsley Green, part of the community. Pauline imagined the prospect of Barbara making friends in the village during her stay. That, in itself, gave her a warm feeling of success.

But Barbara was still staring blankly through the window, a perplexed look on her face. Yoga was definitely not for her. She wouldn't go again. She was confused by life in this village, where women met to share an activity, to laugh together and to gaze in rapt admiration at a man cleaning windows.

She had to admit, he was easy on the eye. But everything was all so different from her own life in Cambridge, where she took holidays in order to meet people and spent the rest of the time by herself, reading, hiking, listening to the radio. It was all very strange, an alien lifestyle. Yet something was stirring inside, from a place which felt familiar yet distant and neglected, and as she thought about Pauline and her yoga friends, she wondered if she had been missing out on something quite important.

5

Pauline lay awake that night, wondering if it had been a good idea to welcome Barbara into her home so readily. Of course, they were sisters, family, and Pauline wanted somehow to try to close the gap between them that had stretched over the years. They were both in their seventies now: she'd hoped Barbara would have mellowed. But she might never change.

That evening, she'd made them a delicious dinner, opened a bottle of wine and chatted nostalgically about their childhood. She'd reminisced about their parents, her beloved father, a holiday in Bournemouth, and for a moment she thought the ice was beginning to melt. Then Barbara had said she didn't like overcooked potatoes; she remembered the weather in Bournemouth had been dismal that week and now, all these years later, look where they were now: both alone and both old.

Pauline clamped her lips together in the darkness: if Barbara became too difficult, she would simply ask her to leave. After all, it was her home. She closed her eyes and dragged her thoughts to the summer. It was always fun in Winsley Green during the summer;

cricket matches and dancing and fetes. She smiled and drifted into sleep.

During the early hours the temperature plummeted, and it snowed heavily. When Pauline woke at eight, someone was banging on the front door. She pulled on her dressing gown and padded downstairs. She pushed the door open onto a rigid bank of drifted snow. Shivering, she stared into the bright eyes of Len Chatfield. He had a huge piece of mobile farm machinery parked by her gate, a sort of tractor with a digger at the front.

'Len?'

He nodded, rubbing his whiskers with a flat hand. 'Expected snow today. Cleared the path for you. Thought you might need to get your car out, drive into Winsley Green, get groceries. Brought you this. Not much left in the shops.' He stretched out a stiff arm, clutching a carton of milk. 'Panic buyers got most of it already, I reckon.'

Pauline smiled and pushed a hand over her hair, still in its clip and dishevelled. 'You were right about the snow in April.' They stared at each other for a moment. 'Well, thanks, Len. That's thoughtful. How much do I owe you?'

'Oh, no...' he began and was cut off by a shrieking voice behind Pauline.

'For goodness sake, shut the door. It's like Siberia in here as it is.'

Pauline shrugged. 'Ah, Len – my sister, Barb—'

Barbara pushed forwards, stood behind her sister, her hands on her hips, and stared at Len, taking in his shabby overcoat, the carton of milk and the digger at the gate.

'I must say, they go to all sorts of lengths here to do the milk round. Well, come in if you're going to. Don't freeze us all to death.'

Len pushed the milk into Pauline's hand. 'No. No time. Got work to do. Sheep. Lambs. Digger.' He turned and shuffled away, his boots making deep prints in the pure snow.

Barbara boomed, 'How very strange. Why on earth do they make the farmers deliver milk around here? And in cartons too. It's quite incredible. And he's cleared the pathway for us. How useful.'

'He's a nice man.' Pauline murmured to herself, watching him clamber into the tractor by the gate. She eased herself to her full height.

'Right, Barbara. Let's make a fire in the wood burner, get a good blaze going and have some breakfast.'

* * *

The snow stayed for three days. Pauline spent most of the time in the kitchen cooking, humming to herself as she worked while Barbara read a book about hiking in the Lake District. On the fourth day, a Thursday, the soft snow became dirty slush, and life in Winsley Green returned to its normal routine. The shops had bread and milk again in large supplies and cars swished up and down in the roads, their tyres turning sludge into murky water which gurgled down the drains. The skies were bright; the buffeting wind a reminder that winter had stayed too long. Buds pushed out from bark and stems, sticky sap smelling sweet and a golden sheen illuminated fields and trees, promising warmth. It was mid-April and spring had finally arrived.

* * *

The Jaguar F-type in British Racing Green was motoring briskly down the M5. Bisto huddled in the passenger seat and glanced at the driver, a smart young man in a peaked cap, frowning, concentrating on the road. He must be in his thirties; clean shaven, a rounded determined chin, fair hair like silken corn sticking out beneath the cap around pink ears. The young man had been very kind, offering him a lift from Swindon to just beyond Taunton, which was as far as he was going.

Swindon. Bisto squeezed his eyes shut and when he opened them, he glanced down at his clothes, mud-stained and unkempt. He hadn't had a shower in several days and he hoped the young man's rakish aftershave would conceal his own sweaty stench. Bisto rubbed a grubby hand around his bristly chin, scratching his four-day growth with dirty nails. He pushed fingers through his mane of white curls. He badly needed to use a comb, but he had nothing. No suitcase, no toothbrush, no wallet. He'd lost it all. If only, he thought, and a sigh shuddered from him. It was a lifetime full of 'if only'... it had all worked out differently to the way he'd hoped.

He shouldn't have drunk the two pints of Guinness on the ferry from Dublin. He'd been chatting to a pleasant young couple and dozed off. When the steward woke him up, the boat was almost empty and his rucksack was gone, containing his wallet, his rail tickets and the paperwork for the ferry to France. He was lucky that his passport and iPhone had been in the inside pocket of his jacket. He'd texted his son Barney that he'd hitch a ride to the ferry port and then ring him – they'd sort out a ticket from there. But he'd never made it as far as Plymouth.

The weather had been awful – drifting snow, blizzards, intense cold. He'd waited ages for a lift from Manchester, been dropped not far from Birmingham. It was then he'd slipped over on the ice into a mound of mud and slush, ripped his jeans and become soaking wet. Two hours later, a lorry bound for London picked him up and he realised he'd miss the ferry, so he'd asked to be dropped off at Swindon.

He'd stopped in Swindon to see Randeep. They'd worked there together twenty years ago, but as usual Bisto had lost touch, put things off, not sent a card or a text for – how many years? Too many. It wasn't that he didn't care – he did, but memories brought so much pain with them. Then suddenly he was filled with an urge to see his brother-in-law, to hug him, to see the familiar smile and to ask for help. He'd hoped Randeep and his wife would be at the same address; when he knocked, Ruchi had answered the door and not even recognised him.

Bisto sighed. How would she have known it was him? He was bedraggled, dishevelled, old. Ruchi, always so beautiful, her eyes shining, told him that Randeep had died five months ago. Bisto had cried there and then, wept bitter tears for Randeep and for his other loss, the funeral in Dublin last week, still too raw in his throat and chest to speak about or to comprehend.

Ruchi had asked him to come in; she'd offered a meal and he should have asked for a bath and to borrow an old coat of Randeep's. But he couldn't. He was sad and miserable, and he was too filthy and unkempt to go into their house and tread his soiled boots on the plush carpet. It didn't seem right after so many years of forgetfulness and besides, it brought the pain of Nisha's death back again. He still thought of his wife, every day, and it had been years now since she had passed.

Bisto had mumbled that he'd be in touch soon and turned away. That night he'd slept in the bitter cold under a tree near a service station. He'd thought he deserved no better. Damp with dew and shivering, ice in his beard, he'd been offered a lift as far as Taunton by the kind man in the Jaguar who was buying petrol.

A gentle voice brought Bisto from his thoughts. '... and we're nearly there now. I'll drop you in the main street, shall I?'

Bisto nodded. 'Fine, yes. That would be fine.'

The young man kept his eyes on the road. 'And how will you get to Plymouth? To the ferry? You have a place in France, you say?'

Bisto wiped his grubby face on his grubbier sleeve, noticing the dirt engrained in the fabric of his jacket and the fabric of his skin.

'Yes, I have a place in the Loire. My son is there. Sure, if I hadn't lost my wallet and tickets...'

The young man slowed the car, stopping by an old village hall. 'This is as far as I go now. I live at the end of that long drive.'

'Well, okay – thanks, then.' Bisto grabbed the door handle, then as an afterthought he held out his hand to the young man, who was instantly dismayed at the sight of the grime embedded in the lines of his palm. The young man took his hand and squeezed it.

'Nice to meet you, Mr—?'

'Mulligan.' Bisto pulled his hand away. 'Bisto Mulligan.'

The man met his eyes with sparkling blue ones. 'Well, I'm sorry to hear that you lost your wallet, Mr Mulligan. It sounds as if you've had a horrendous time in Dublin.'

Bisto scrutinised the open expression and he knew the man didn't believe him. 'I lost the wallet and my luggage and tickets on the ferry to Liverpool.'

The young man gave a cheery smile. 'Well, I hope you won't mind if I offer you something. May the luck of the Irish be with you and with me too. Here you are.' He tugged off his cap, ruffled a hand through the silky blond thatch and took out his wallet, fingering two twenties and pushing them into Bisto's hand.

'God bless you,' Bisto mumbled, a saying that owed more to the Catholic priests of his Dublin schooldays than his own faith.

'I hope it will help you get back home. There's a number eleven bus across the road which will take you to the station at Taunton.' The young man smiled again, a charming grin, boyish and good-natured. 'I'm Hugo Garrett, by the way.'

'Pleased to meet you. And very many thanks to you indeed, Hugo, for your generosity.'

Bisto slithered from the Jaguar, watched it glide away, and waved his hand towards the fading throaty sounds of the engine. His hand held two notes. Forty pounds. He could afford a ticket for a bus, and maybe a train, even a sandwich. He turned to cross the road and a sign caught his eye, swinging in the wind on the side of a large white house with a thatched roof. The sign showed a picture of a cartoon sheep, all smiling face and curly wool, holding up a pint of beer. The sign proclaimed the place was called the Sheep Dip Inn. He rubbed a hand to his eyes. The last few days had been some of the worst of his life. Bisto screwed the twenty pound notes in his fist and muttered beneath his breath.

'The hell with it. I fancy a quick gargle. A fool and his money are soon parted, eh, Bisto?'

A tall man with neatly cropped dark hair and a t-shirt which proclaimed it was BEER O' CLOCK was wiping glasses behind the bar. He was probably in his forties. He was talking to an attractive woman of the same age, her hair in a long chestnut plait, wearing a dark shirt and denim dungarees. The man had an accent Bisto couldn't recognise. He leaned on the bar and caught sight of himself in the long mirror behind it, a short scruffy man in his mid-seventies, his white hair thick and curling over the collar of a putrid blue jacket. Bisto knew he looked like a vagrant. He snorted softly to himself: he was a vagrant right now. There was no other word for him, except perhaps tramp. Or drifter. He wiped his nose; the nostrils were damp and his fingers came away wet.

The man behind the bar turned to the woman. 'Justina?'

Bisto scrutinised his own face in the mirror again. His eyes were shining, circled with dark rings, from the cold and the lack of sleep. He had an uneven grizzled beard. His breath tasted funny in his own mouth. The woman leaned forward against the bar, languid and sleepy.

'What can I get you?'

Bisto noticed she had a slight accent, similar to the man's, but he couldn't place it. 'I'll have a half of your Murphy's.'

The woman shrugged and selected a clean glass from above her head. The man was watching him carefully.

'Are you just passing through, friend?'

'Well, you'd be about right,' Bisto nodded. 'I have a château in France. I'm on my way there now. I just thought I'd stop for a quick one before I'm off again.'

The man raised an eyebrow; he clearly thought Bisto wasn't telling the truth and Bisto wasn't surprised. He glanced down at himself, unkempt and dirty. He groaned – his outside appearance was nothing to how dreadful he was feeling inside. The woman handed over the beer. Bisto grasped his glass and made his way over to a dark corner, making himself comfortable in his seat before he supped the top from the Murphy's.

He gazed around the bar. There were two people seated separately. One was a young man with neat dark hair and a full beard, sitting on a stool sipping coffee. The other was a woman with long grey curly hair, perched over a laptop, a glass of red wine on the table. She wore little round glasses and tapped the keys delicately. Bisto thought she looked like a studious fairy. He nodded over to her.

'Hello,' he murmured. 'Are you writing poems?'

She shook her fluffy hair and turned piercing grey eyes on him, quizzically, like a Siamese cat. 'It's a novel, actually.'

'A novel, is it?' Bisto sipped his beer. 'And are you famous? Have I heard of you?'

'You may have.' She wriggled in her seat, a sort of provocative curling of her body. 'I'm editing my next bestseller. I'm Tilly Hardy.'

'Pleased to make your acquaintance, Tilly. I'm Bisto Mulligan.'

'Bisto? That's an unusual name.'

Bisto chuckled. 'I was always sniffing up at my mammy's cooking when I was a snapper, a face like the kiddies in the gravy advert. She gave me the nickname herself.' For a moment, he became pensive, then he tipped the glass to his mouth. 'Can I get a lady writer a drink, Tilly?'

She made a face. 'I'm just a writer and no, thanks. This Shiraz will last me. I have just this one passionate scene to edit and then I'm finished and off home.'

Bisto stood up, plucking his glass from the table. 'This didn't last me five minutes. I'd better slow down.' He ambled to the bar, plonking his empty glass in front of the barman. 'Same again, will you, friend?'

The barman remembered what he had ordered, pouring Murphy's without a word. Bisto caught the eye of the dark-haired bearded man seated on the stool, finishing his coffee. Bisto leaned over and called out, his voice too loud. 'Can I fill your cup for you with another one of the same?'

The dark-haired man shook his head. 'Thanks, no. I'm on my way back to work in a moment. I just popped over for a quick shot of caffeine.'

Bisto lifted his glass. '*Sláinte.*' He glugged a mouthful and smacked his lips. It was warm and homely in the bar. 'So, you're on your lunch break? What is it that you do?'

The bearded man drained the dregs from his cup. 'I'm a GP. I share the local practice with my wife.'

'Doctor, eh?' Bisto's eyes twinkled. 'You sure I can't buy you a scoop? It can't be easy, the both of yous being doctors in one house.'

The man met his eyes, his own a little misty, then slid down from the stool and picked up his bag. 'Thanks, no. It'll be just me soon. My wife's about to go on maternity leave.'

Bisto sipped his Murphy's. 'Ah, a kiddie on the way eh? Oh, that's grand. I remember when I ... ah.' He gazed into the murky swirl of his glass.

Bisto watched the bearded doctor walk away and a feeling of sadness stuck in his throat. He turned back to the barman with the cropped hair, wondering where the pretty woman with the chestnut plait had disappeared to. Then he lifted his glass carefully and slunk back to his seat in the shadowy corner. The novelist Tilly Hardy had gone. He thought about the last few weeks in Dublin, and everything that had happened. He'd been smartly dressed then, he'd had money, but he'd carried a heavy pain in his heart that still hadn't left him. He finished the last mouthful of beer, taking a long draught and enjoying the taste of bitterness on his tongue.

6

Pauline put her hands to her ears, but she could still hear Barbara's voice drifting from the little conservatory.

'I like proper brown bread, soft bread. Not the rough old stuff with bits of grains in it that you bake here. And couldn't you just buy some margarine? Butter is so cloying.'

Pauline washed the potatoes in the Belfast sink, watching the muddy water drain away down the plug hole. She raised her voice. 'I thought you came here to sort out your blood pressure, Barbara. You're not doing yours or mine any good.'

Barbara stalked in and plonked herself down at the kitchen table. 'That cold old conservatory needs ripping down, all the rotten wood burning and a proper one building in its place.'

'Douglas was always going to build a timber garden room. He said it would be lovely to look out on the garden on a Sunday in summer with a tipple and read the papers.' Pauline sighed.

'A UPVC one, clean and white, with proper double-glazed insulation.' Barbara clamped her lips together. 'And I need to buy an electric blanket. I'm freezing in bed at night.'

Pauline busied herself with scrubbing the potatoes. They were clean already, but she wanted to keep her hands busy and her thoughts occupied or she'd be tempted to say something blunt in reply.

Barbara hadn't finished. 'I don't suppose I can buy an electric blanket in Whimsy Green.'

'Winsley Green. I have a hot water bottle you can use.'

Barbara was aghast. 'I'll get chilblains.'

Pauline dried her hands. 'All right. Let's go into the village and buy a few things. I need carrots anyway.'

'Oh, not stew again, Pauline. I can't bear it. My bowels are all out of sorts...'

'I don't want to hear it, Barbara.' Pauline snatched the keys from the hook shaped like a piglet on the kitchen wall. 'Are you coming or not?'

'Of course I'm coming. I can't leave the organisation of the evening meal to you. Tonight we'll have chops.'

'I can't afford chops.'

Barbara put her hands on her hips. 'Well you should get your fancy farmer man friend to bring you a nice bit of pork.'

Pauline caught her sister's eye and stared at her, offered her best smirk then turned on her heel and marched out.

* * *

Bisto blinked hard as he came out of the dark into the brightness of the spring day. It was almost two o'clock and he had some money left in his pocket. He decided that the publican was a nice man. Oskar and his wife Justina had been a bit distant at first. He could understand why they might have been suspicious: he was a new customer and he didn't look or smell his best. But they'd supplied him with two glasses of beer in exchange for his money: it was a fair deal. Now he'd find the shelter of a tree in the sunshine and snooze for the afternoon, then he'd get on a bus for Plymouth with the change. He had enough. He smiled and sauntered across the road.

He didn't see the car coming. The noise of screeching breaks and another squeal, higher and more alarming, had filled his ears first, and then his own voice, a sudden yell of shock. His head hit the ground hard and he felt the gravel embedding itself in the skin of his hands and face. The world swirled and became a little fuzzy. He breathed out and lay very still.

'My goodness, Pauline – you've killed him.'

'I didn't see him. He just stepped out in front of me.'

'Well, I doubt very much he'll be stepping out anywhere again.'

The two women bent over him. Bisto squinted through one eye. His entire body hurt.

'He stinks of booze. He's obviously drunk so it wasn't completely your fault, Pauline. If you weren't such an erratic driver...'

'He's not moving, Barbara. Ring for an ambulance. Let's get him to hospital.'

Bisto opened his eyes. He had no intention of going inside a hospital ever again. He sat upright, blinking at the ladies' anxious faces peering at him and grinned.

'I must have died and gone to heaven. All the angels here are beautiful ladies.'

He gazed from one face to another. A pleasant looking woman, a soft expression in her eyes, silky silver hair in a roll on the top of her head; a frowning woman with strong features, a bony frame inside a woollen coat, with steel grey curls and intense, intelligent eyes. He put a hand to his head. He was dizzy, confused, as he stared from one to the other.

'No worries. I'll be fine in a little minute. I just fell over.'

'Can you stand up?' Pauline held out a hand.

Barbara loomed over him. 'Put him in the car. Let's take him to Taunton, to the hospital.'

'No, I don't need a hospital. I'll be just dandy.' Bisto tried to heave himself up and he yelped in pain and tottered back. 'I think I've hurt my ankle – and my head.'

Barbara's voice boomed loud and clear. 'Ring 999, Pauline. At once.'

Pauline pushed Bisto's trouser leg up, ignoring the grime on his leg, easing off his shoe and sock. His foot was filthy, long toenails curling like talons. His ankle was already swelling. She sighed.

'You should have this x-rayed. It might be broken. Oh, I'm so sorry, Mr...'

'Mulligan. Bisto Mulligan.' He struggled to stand, wobbling, and grasped Barbara's arm, leaning heavily against her. 'Can you find me a good wooden stick? I'll be on my way.'

Barbara was indignant. 'Are you a tramp?'

The impact had blurred his vision – or perhaps it was the pain, the knock to his head. Bisto wasn't sure, but he heaved himself up to his full five feet five inches and huffed.

'I'm not looking my best today, believe me – I've had a few setbacks but I'm on my way to France. I have a château in the Loire.'

Barbara laughed one single harsh sound. 'Oh, what a perfect pack of lies. I can see what you are. You're a vagrant.'

Pauline put her hands on her hips and stared at the man. He was clearly in pain. He was not drunk, but she saw something in his eyes that moved her: vulnerability, sadness. She immediately felt sorry for him. She put a hand on his sleeve.

'Can you get into the car? I'll take you home. I have a friend who's a GP and she'll come over and take a look at your foot. Maybe you'd like something to eat.'

Bisto looked hopeful. 'A whisky'd be nice. Medicinal. Just for the terrible pain.'

'Are you sure, Pauline? Do you think it's safe? Taking a man like this into our home and we're two defenceless women...?'

'I've always been a good judge of character, Barbara.' Pauline stared at her sister, determined to do things her own way. 'He's hurt and in pain. And you and I aren't defenceless.'

Bisto's ankle was very sore. His head was pounding. He leaned his weight against the two women and lurched towards the old Volkswagen Beetle.

'It's yous two who've banjaxed me, not the other way around.' He narrowed his eyes at Barbara, breathing beer fumes in her face. 'And as for you, you mad ould boot, I'm frightened to my death of you already.'

* * *

An hour later, Bisto was sitting back in Douglas's comfy armchair, a malt whisky from Douglas' drinks cupboard in his hand, groaning in pain as Dr Natalie touched his bruised ankle with light fingers and examined the raised lump on his head. The doctor sat upright, brushed dark hair from her face and sighed.

'You ought to have an x-ray on the ankle.'

Bisto sipped his drink and grunted. 'I'm fine, really. Just let me sit for half an hour and I'll be on my way.'

Natalie's forehead puckered. 'You have a bump on your head. And you can't just go off with your ankle in this state. Rest for a while. It's best if I don't strap it up. A few days in hospital might do you good.' She stood up slowly. 'You can't hobble on that, given how swollen it is.'

Pauline folded her arms and looked at Bisto. He was curled in the seat, wide-eyed, like a bewildered child. She would be happy to take care of him for a day or two: it would be no trouble. 'It was my fault, Natalie. I have a spare room...'

'Don't even think about it, Pauline.' Barbara folded her arms tightly.

Natalie patted Bisto's arm. 'You do need to rest the ankle. I'm a bit concerned about the bump to your head too. You are a little concussed. If you notice double vision or any other new symptoms, call me at once and we'll get you an x-ray.' She pressed her lips together. 'I suppose, Pauline, you could give him a ride into the village later for an evening appointment with my husband? How about having a little ride to the surgery later, Mr Mulligan?'

Bisto pushed out his arm, holding the glass towards the doctor. 'Oh, I remember now. Your ould fella's a doctor too. I met him in the pub. Nice sort. But I don't know about a ride to the surgery.' He suddenly chuckled. 'Seems like you're the one who's been doing all the riding, Doctor.' He gestured towards her belly. 'You and your man had a very good ride, so it seems, and now you've got a kiddie on the way.'

Bisto turned to Barbara, who was appalled, mouth open, her hands to her face, and laughed. 'Mind you, I wouldn't ride the ould one here if she had pedals. But you're a bit of all right, Pauline. Stick another glassful in there, will you?'

Barbara huffed, turning away. 'In the kitchen, Pauline. We need to talk. Now.'

Without thinking, Pauline let the third-full bottle of Scotch drop into Bisto's open hand and followed her sister out of the room. Natalie gave Bisto an anxious glance, and trailed after the other two women.

It was warm in the kitchen; the Aga was on and a kettle was reaching a soft boil, the spout gently whistling. Pauline reached out automatically and moved it to a cooler spot on the plate.

Barbara was in full swing. 'He's not our responsibility. He should go to one of those places where they look after the homeless.'

Natalie shrugged. 'He needs temporary care, that's for certain. He really needs someone to keep an eye on him for a few hours – he's concussed. I'm sure the ankle's just a sprain but I can take him to the hospital – or I could call someone to come and pick him up. Mario's on surgery duty again tonight. I can ask him to try to fit Bisto in.' A smile twitched across her mouth. 'After all, they've met already, in the pub.'

Pauline put her hands on her hips. 'No. I knocked him down. It was my fault. He's obviously terrified of hospitals. I'll look after him here, watch out for concussion and how the ankle progresses just for a day or two until he's able to move a little bit, and by then I'm sure we can find a relative or someone he knows to come and collect him.'

Natalie made a humming sound. 'I wouldn't advise putting him up here...'

Pauline had made up her mind. 'Just for the night. You could come and see him here tomorrow, Natalie, or I could bring him down to the surgery.'

Barbara was aghast. 'But he's drunk. And so rude.'

Natalie sighed again and Pauline squeezed her arm. 'I'll keep him here overnight. We'll make a decision tomorrow.'

Natalie nodded her head. 'All right. Just for tonight.'

'It's an awful idea. He could murder us in our beds, Pauline.'

Pauline turned to her sister, her face set. 'He can hardly move. Look at him. He's just a frail old gentleman who's lost his way a bit. Besides, you heard what he said – he's not really likely to wander into your room.'

Barbara was still taking the comment in as Pauline brushed past her and hurried back to the lounge. Douglas' armchair was empty. And there wasn't much left in the bottle of Scotch, resting on the chair arm. Bisto had gone. Pauline breathed out, wondering how he was managing to walk on his swollen ankle, when she heard Barbara breathe a sigh of relief behind her.

'Well, thank goodness for that. He's on his way. We won't see him again, I hope.'

Pauline swung round, about to say something about Barbara being heartless, when Dr Natalie appeared, standing just behind her, her face anxious.

Pauline's thoughts turned to Bisto. She had knocked him over and she'd wanted to make amends. It would have been the decent thing and she was frustrated that the opportunity had passed. Besides, she had taken to him: he seemed good company: he was warm hearted and he had a sense of humour, which was more than she could say for her complaining sister. She was about to snap at Barbara, to say something rude, but her conscience intervened. She decided to put space between her and her sister before she commented on her lack of compassion. She strode over to Douglas' drinks cupboard and found a bottle of wine.

'Right. I'm off out. I'm going to take this to the new neighbours' house, to say hello and welcome. It's what good neighbours do. I haven't introduced myself yet.'

Barbara stood up straight. 'I'll get my coat.'

'There's no need, Barbara. I'll go alone. I'm sure you could stay here and make Natalie another cup of tea. I'll only be gone for ten minutes – the house is just across the road and down a little path. You don't need to come. In fact, I'd rather go by myself. I haven't met them yet and I don't want you upsetting them.'

Barbara watched as Pauline rushed past her, the bottle clutched in her fist, and was gone. She exhaled, a little surprised that her sister could be so impolite. She'd have words with her when she came back, and explain that it wasn't appropriate to berate her in front of the GP. Barbara turned to Natalie.

'I'll make you that cup of tea, shall I? I'm sorry about Pauline.

Knocking the tramp down has obviously affected her a little more than I thought. Perhaps a chocolate biscuit will sort her out when she gets back. I think we have a packet of bourbons in the cupboard. And perhaps while the tea is brewing, you could tell me if there is anything of any cultural interest whatsoever to be found in this desolate little village.'

7

Pauline was feeling unhappy that the little man had limped away. She'd liked him immediately; she'd found him amusing and she'd been sorry for him, not to mention feeling a little guilty as it had all been her fault. She crossed the road and pushed open her neighbour's gate. A dark-haired woman was in the garden, busying herself with something in front of the open garage door. She was bending over a large cardboard box, pulling out implements and laying them on the floor. Pauline saw a shiny new trowel, a pair of shears, gardening gloves and a roll of wire. She called out, 'Hello,' and raised the hand carrying the wine.

The woman's face was expressionless. She stood up and stared at Pauline. She was in her forties, probably; she had dark brown hair, pale skin, a sombre face, attractive, yet there was something aloof about the way she held herself, as if she was untrusting. She had on tailored jeans, heeled boots, a cashmere sweater and an expensive-looking jacket. Pauline thought she was far too smart to be emptying grubby boxes in the garden. She smiled and waved the bottle again.

'Yoo-hoo.'

The woman frowned. 'If you're selling anything, please go away. We're new to the neighbourhood and I'm not interested in buying anything.'

Pauline laughed, a light trilling sound. 'Oh, no. I'm your neighbour. I brought this.' She brandished the wine, held out her other hand towards the woman. 'I'm Pauline Pye from the house across the lane.'

The woman took her hand tentatively, held it for a second as if obliged to make a polite gesture. Pauline handed the bottle to the woman who gazed at the label with interest and then murmured, 'Thank you. That's kind.'

Pauline wondered if everyone in the family was teetotal; if she'd just made a mistake. She took a deep breath. 'So, how are you settling in?'

The woman pulled a face. 'It's so difficult. My husband was keen to buy this house. I just think we've taken on a lot of work. The people who lived here before have let it get into a bit of a state.'

Pauline brought her lips together. Henry and Catherine, who'd lived there before, were in their eighties; delightful people, welcoming, church-going – great friends of Chrissie the vicar, and they'd always kept their house and garden immaculate. She nodded hopefully. 'Are you planning to make big changes, then?'

The woman stared into the distance, seemingly not interested.

'I think there's a lot to do.' She seemed to notice Pauline for the first time. 'I'm Julia Darby.'

Pauline grinned. 'I hope you'll be happy here.'

Julia didn't look happy at all. 'Oh, I so hope I will. I was very happy where we were before, in Bath. It's such a lovely place, fantastic architecture. This place is so – well, it's like the back of beyond, isn't it?'

'It's a great community, Winsley.' Pauline put on her most positive face. 'Everyone is so nice, so helpful. We have a really good neighbourhood. Everyone looks after everyone else. You'll make friends so easily.'

Julia shook her head. 'It's been a gamble, selling our lovely house and coming here.'

'You won't regret it. I've been here for a couple of years and I love it. Everyone is so nice, so decent. There isn't a single bad thing to be said about the local...'

Pauline stopped and stared across the garden. A little man in tattered clothes had limped onto the flower bed and was tottering, confused and bewildered, as he approached a rose bush. Pauline pressed her lips together to stop a giggle as she saw him fiddling with the zip of his jeans.

Julia turned to her with an expression of horror. 'Is that your husband?'

Pauline waved her arms apologetically. 'Oh, no, no. He's a tramp... He's just had a drink with me. I knocked him down in my car this morning.' She stared at Bisto, whose face was clearly baffled. 'He bumped his head. I'm not sure he knows where he is...'

Six feet away, behind the rose bush, Bisto was adjusting his zip. The dirty material of his jeans sagged, falling to his ankles. There was a moment's silence then there came the persistent gush of a steady stream of liquid.

Bisto sighed. 'Ah, nothing like a good pish, is there?' He tottered forward, staggering beyond the rose bush, clearly confused, then his feet encountered the material wrapped around his ankles and he fell headlong.

Pauline put a hand to her lips to conceal a smile. 'I'm so sorry...'

Julia's mouth was a perfect circle. The women locked eyes for a moment, then their gaze moved back to Bisto, who was wriggling on his front like a snake in the grass.

'Ah well...' his voice was muffled by the earth beneath his face, but the tone was full of good humour. 'It was the Scotch, I think.

One too many. Hey, give us a hand here, will you? I swear I have thorns from the rose bush stuck in my mickey.' He groaned and twitched. 'I can't get up.'

Pauline shook her head at her neighbour. 'He's concussed, clearly – and he's sprained his ankle.'

It was the best excuse she could think of. She mumbled an apology and rushed over to the scruffy little man who wriggled in the grass, his pink bottom stuck in the air like a pale peach. She attempted to cover a giggle with one hand and held out the other. She'd take him home now and put him in a nice clean bed in the spare room to sleep it off.

* * *

Pauline and Barbara were in the kitchen, Pauline leaning against the Belfast sink and Barbara resting her back against the warmth of the Aga. The smell of toast and hot frying oil lingered in the air, and two empty plates were on the wooden table, with left-over smears of fried egg and crumbs of brown toast. Barbara glared at Pauline, who shrugged and turned to stare out of the window. Two blue tits hovered next to the coconut she'd hung at the bird feeder, and then a woodpecker fluttered down, its pointed beak pecking furiously at the fat. She turned back to Barbara.

'He's been asleep since yesterday afternoon. I thought I'd take him some breakfast up this morning. He must be hungry. I don't think he ate anything at all yesterday.' As an afterthought she added, 'Poor man. He was tired out.'

'He was drunk.' Barbara folded her arms. 'I can't believe you had to pull his trousers up for him and half-carry him back here.'

Pauline grinned. 'I've seen a naked man before...'

'That's not the point.' Barbara looked away and frowned. 'He shouldn't be here at all, that's the point. He's filthy, messing up your clean bed, stinking out the house with his sweaty smell. He had urine down his trousers.'

'I put his clothes in the wash.'

'You should have burned them, Pauline. They are just infested rags.'

Pauline shook her head. 'The jacket had been expensive once. The shirt too. They are drying out on the line now. I'd have offered him something of Douglas' but I gave them all away after he...' She let out a slow sigh. 'I took them to the charity shop. Douglas' clothes would have swamped Bisto anyway.'

Barbara wrinkled her nose at the mention of his name. 'I hope you'll come to your senses today and dump him at the hospital. Let the experts patch him up and send him on his way.'

'I certainly will not.' Pauline raised her eyebrows, remembering how grateful he had been as she'd tucked him under the duvet in the spare room, how his eyes had closed in sleep almost immediately, like a soothed child. He had been in pain and exhausted. 'He was apologetic, thankful and polite. I've taken quite a shine to him.'

'You're too soft, Pauline. That's your trouble.'

'And you are just too callous, Barbara.' She couldn't help the next words. 'You've always been like that. Selfish.'

Barbara snapped her head towards Pauline, her chin jutting out. 'He's taking advantage of your good nature. Whereas since I've come here to recuperate, all you do is argue with me.'

'In fairness, Barbara, you are the one who's being argumentative.'

'I certainly am not.' Barbara folded her arms, tucking in her chin. 'I've been the voice of reason, trying to protect you from what is clearly an awful error of judgement. But you won't listen to me, will you? Oh no. You've become stubborn, Pauline. Since Douglas died, I think you have probably become lonely and you're just grasping at straws to stave off the feeling.' Pauline shot her sister a horrified glance and Barbara smiled, triumphant. 'You'll even hang on to a filthy vagrant, Pauline, if it means you have a bit of company.'

'That is utter rubbish, Barbara. It's my house and I knocked the poor man over. He's incapacitated. He needs to rest. And besides, he's very pleasant.'

'I'm being honest for your own good. You are getting on a bit now, and you're vulnerable. Even losing your grip a bit, I dare say.'

Pauline flushed, her face tingling at her older sister's hypocrisy. 'How dare you? Barbara, you're a guest here and since you've arrived, you've been bossy and controlling.'

'I have not.'

'You have. And I wish you'd stop it. If you can't be nice, you can just go back to Cambridge. You're welcome to stay, but I do wish you'd just – well – chill out.'

Barbara gasped. 'Chill out? Are you mad?'

'I think she has a point, to tell the truth.'

A voice came from the doorway, a gentle gravelly lilt, and the sisters turned together to see a short man standing in front of them in a baggy blue nightgown that fell past his knees. The buttons, once fastened up to the neck, had been undone, exposing a mass of white curly chest hair.

Barbara put her hands to her mouth. 'He's wearing my nightie.'

'It suits him.' Pauline grinned.

Bisto shrugged. 'I found it on your bed. I was starkers when I woke up this morning.' He gazed from Barbara to Pauline. 'I was completely poleaxed yesterday. After the Scotch I was totally wrote off. I have a hell of a headache on me this morning. But I promise, it was a one off. It won't happen again.' He paused and his eyes twinkled. 'So, which of you lovely ladies stripped me naked and had your wicked way with me?' He raised his eyebrows at Pauline, then stared at Barbara. 'I really don't mind which of yous it was. Or both.'

Barbara breathed in. 'As if we'd be that desperate.'

'I took your things and washed them, Bisto.' Pauline smiled. 'They are outside drying. I'll get you some breakfast and then I'll see if they are ready to wear.'

'That's very kind, Pauline.' Bisto hobbled over to the table past the Aga, brushing against Barbara. She could see the pale colour of his skin through the flimsy material. He plonked himself down, scratching the white curls on top of his head. 'I could eat a whole house.'

'Toast and scrambled eggs, then?' Pauline held out a hand, almost tempted to ruffle his hair, but she thought the better of it. 'How do you like your coffee?'

'It'd better be black and sweet this morning.' Bisto winked at her. 'Thanks. You're a good woman, Pauline.'

Barbara heaved herself as tall as she could against the Aga and took a deep breath. Bisto clearly appreciated Pauline's kindness so she thought she'd try to be slightly pleasant. Her words came out grudgingly. 'I hope you're feeling better. How is the swollen ankle this morning?'

'Ah, not good, Barbara. And my head's pounding. I've only just managed to see straight. Yesterday I thought there were two of yous – that's enough to frighten any man to death, that's for sure. But I'll be out of your hair today. I'll find a good strong stick to lean on and be on my way...'

'You're welcome to stay for a day or two. It's the least I can do.' Pauline poured eggs in a frying pan, easing Barbara out of the way with her shoulder, a gentle movement. She couldn't help smiling. Bisto's natural warmth was a perfect foil for Barbara's frostiness. Her instinct had been right. With Bisto here, Barbara's presence would certainly be more bearable. Pauline wondered if her sister might even develop a sense of humour.

The eggs began to sizzle, and Barbara picked up the steaming kettle to make coffee. Pauline had her back to Bisto, but her voice was determined. 'You can have a bath after breakfast and we'll see how your ankle is. Based on that, you can stay until it is better, and that is that. We'll say no more about it.'

Bisto leaned back in his seat and sighed. It occurred to him that he had hit the bottom. After the events of the last few weeks, he felt empty, devastated – he'd lost so much that was dear to him. And now he'd lost his dignity.

'That's very kind of you, Pauline.'

He met Barbara's frown and winked. She twisted away, crinkling her nose, and dumped a mug of black coffee in front of him, the liquid splashing onto the wooden table.

Bisto pulled a pained face. 'To be honest, the ankle is a bit swollen this morning. And I've a lump on my head the size of the mountains of Morne.'

Pauline turned to him, a wooden spoon in her hand, and she giggled. 'It'll heal, Bisto. Which is more than I can say for the feelings of poor Julia across the lane. She was mortified by the sight of your naked flesh, watching you urinating on her rose bush. I think you'd better apologise later.'

Bisto nodded. 'I drank too much. I didn't show my best side, did I? I'll tell her I was completely ossified. I don't remember a thing. I'll pop over later, will I, and lay a bit of charm on her?'

Barbara stared at Bisto, his short frame wrapped in her blue filmy nightie, a fork and knife held aloft in each fist as Pauline placed a plate of eggs in front of him.

'Charm?' Barbara made a light scoffing noise. 'I think it will take a lot more than that, Mr Mulligan.'

Bisto met Pauline's eyes with his china blue ones. His voice was soft. 'Ah, thank you, Pauline. Truly. I'm very grateful.'

'My pleasure, Bisto.'

She grinned, pleased with herself as she watched him tuck into his breakfast. Already, she thought, the icy air was beginning to thaw in the house. She had been right about Bisto. She liked his sense of fun and she suspected there was a lot more to him than first met the eye. He could stay as long as he liked.

———

8

Barbara stretched out on her bed, breathed in steaming coffee from her mug and stared at the open page again, but the words blurred. She'd read the same sentence three times without realising it. The room was still chilly despite the creamy midday sunshine that shone through the window and left a buttery yellow slice of light on the Buddha duvet.

Pauline had gone off to yoga again, promising to do a bit of grocery shopping afterwards in Winsley Green. Barbara hadn't felt at all sociable; she'd decided she'd stay in the privacy of her own room and read her book, an interesting sensible piece of non-fiction by an intelligent man called Malcolm about how to achieve success. Barbara had been attracted to the idea that it took ten thousand hours of dedicated practice to become really good at something. She sighed and closed the book, the hard cover enclosing the pages with a soft thud as she dropped it on the covers of the bed. She'd had much more than ten thousand hours of life and she still hadn't worked out how to make it a success, not really.

Bisto slept for most of the time. He'd been here for over a week now and it was only yesterday that he'd made an effusive apology to the disgruntled neighbour whose roses he had violated. Natalie had prescribed lots of bed rest, fluids and pain relief for his concussion, and he'd certainly been resting a lot, although Pauline had limited his fluids to water and tea. He was probably still in bed now, at almost one o'clock in the afternoon, although he'd appeared for a dinner of bangers and mash last night, but he'd seemed quiet and he hardly ate anything. Barbara was puzzled: it may have been her fault, his reticence. Perhaps she'd asked too many questions over dinner: where he lived, why he was a tramp, if he had any family.

He'd told her he was seventy-six years old, from Dublin; that he had a son, and she certainly thought she'd overheard him talking on his mobile phone to someone after dinner in his room. She'd heard a few words: 'I'll be leaving soon,' and, 'not so great,' but she wandered away from his door when she heard Pauline's footfall on the creaky stairs. Barbara still felt a little guilty; Pauline's face had been disapproving when she'd told Bisto that people were tramps because their mother hadn't shown them enough love during childhood. Bisto had turned away, and she felt she must have struck a nerve, something that rang true for him. Perhaps no one had ever loved him at all.

Barbara wondered if she should try harder to be more like Pauline, but she'd never been one to offer sympathy. Her own mother had been straight-laced and strict, never hugging the girls and rarely praising them. Barbara had idolised her mother, copied her in all respects, down to her severe hairstyle and sensible clothes.

Pauline was Daddy's girl, cuddling up on his knee, babbling about trivia, kissing his wonky nose and laughing, but Barbara had kept herself busy, well-ordered, at a distance. She'd neglected Pauline even then, pulled away from her sister's gentle embraces and sweet-natured chatter. Emotions were pointless; they were for weak and foolish people. Love was one of those things that blinded everyone: you thought you were deliriously happy and then suddenly you weren't. Barbara decided it was the same for Pauline now. Even though Douglas had been far too thoughtless, too socia ble, too obsessed with his own hobbies to give his wife his full attention, Pauline had clearly been shocked by his death; it had shaken her routine and left her alone. And Bisto was clearly alone too. Barbara wondered again if she'd hurt his feelings and resolved not to do it again.

Perhaps if she'd spent ten thousand hours trying to connect with her emotions rather than seal them up and hide them away, she'd have been better at relationships and therefore happier. But she doubted it. She'd tried once, tried very hard for several years, to capture and keep the elusive happy-forever-after feeling that had made her skin tingle beyond belief, with a man she'd been very much in love with, who'd said he loved her too. She remembered their secret times together, him sitting on the edge of her bed at the bedsit, his arms around her, the beautifully strange shape of his feet and his knees, the comforting smell of his warming flesh next to her own trembling body.

Barbara instantly felt cold; loneliness wrapped its arms around her now, hugged her too close so that she shivered and shrank into herself, staying separate, safe. Perhaps she should apologise to Bisto, try to be pleasant to him. She thought of his shrunken frame in her nightgown the morning after he had arrived, his stubbornly hairy chest peeking through the fabric, and the swollen purple of his injured ankle. She recalled the way he looked at her, the curling of his lip. He clearly disliked her. And he'd be gone soon, so it was pointless attempting to be too agreeable or to form some sort of friendship. Barbara didn't form friendships as a rule. She had herself, and that was all, and it was all for the best. She picked up her book and stared at the merging words on the page, wondering if she should observe Pauline's behaviour more. After all, Bisto had taken to her sister very quickly.

The click of keys in the door and the sound of cheerful voices at the bottom of the stairs made her sit upright. It was Pauline and someone else, a woman. Barbara listened carefully to the excited babble, then she heard Pauline raise her voice. 'Barbara? Are you in your room? Come down, will you please – I'm making lunch. We have a guest.'

Barbara saw Pauline at the bottom of the stairs, the front door closing behind her. She was wrapped in a warm jacket, her cheeks gleaming. The woman with hair in various bright colours was with her, a wide smile on her face, carrying a shopping bag. Barbara could hear the annoying woman's voice ringing out, too brash. 'Such a shame he wasn't cleaning the windows again this week. I was hoping we'd get a glimpse of his gorgeous Greek god body. He's called Kostas, you know. He's from Crete.'

'He's certainly handsome.' Pauline patted the younger woman's arm. 'I think most of the class were craning their necks throughout the entire yoga session in case he came back. I wonder what he's doing, Dizzy, in Milton Rogus?'

'He's doing odd jobs, staying in lodgings. I spoke to Yvonne in the Post Office. She had him round to do her windows and found out about him. Apparently, she and Tamsin spent the whole time watching his bottom go up and down the ladder.'

'How silly. He's just a man.' Barbara stood firmly on the bottom step. In her roll-neck jumper, dark slacks and sensible shoes, she towered over the other two women.

Pauline giggled. 'It's harmless fun. And he's very classically good-looking.'

Dizzy agreed. 'Yvonne was saying she hopes Tamsin and he might get to know each other. Yvonne said she'd love to have him as a son-in-law.'

Barbara grimaced. 'It's not the wisest criteria to select a relative, is it? By how good their posterior appears as it bobs up a ladder?'

Dizzy ignored her. 'The thing is, Pauline, Tamsin needs someone besides her mum to help her look after the baby. He's six weeks old and keeps them both up all night with his yelling.'

Barbara guffawed. 'Sounds like any sensible man would steer clear of that situation. Who'd want to take on a woman with a child?'

Dizzy gaped at Barbara. 'No one knows who the father is. Tamsin won't say. I don't think even Yvonne knows.'

Pauline smiled. 'Well, it can't be the handsome Kostas. He's only just arrived in the area.'

'I'd love to know who little Harley's father is though.' Dizzy's eyes were wide. 'I don't know who Tamsin was going out with last year, but the child is blond, like Tamsin and her mother, so it's hard to tell who the father is. Unless it's Hugo Garrett – he's blond. Tamsin spent a lot of time last year at the manor cleaning and doing various jobs. It could be Hugo. He's young, and handsome – and rich.'

'Well, Hugo seems to be away a lot, in London on business.' Pauline ignored her sister, who was becoming more irritated, gazing around the hallway at cobwebs and making an intrusive tutting sound. 'I doubt it's Hugo. He's very dignified. But I suppose it could be.'

Dizzy's face shone. 'Perhaps Harley was the result of an uncontrollable night of passion. I mean, maybe one night when Tamsin had been up there cleaning or something, maybe Hugo lured her into one of the many chambers in the manor house and had his wicked way... or maybe Tamsin appeared in the doorway in an apron and white cap... and not much else.'

Barbara sighed loudly, her face screwed up with irritation, and prodded the woman's arm that carried the shopping bag. 'I can't remember your name.'

Dizzy ran her hand through her long scarlet and orange fringe. 'Dizzy Blackstock, mobile hairdresser. I do everyone's hair around here. You should let me do yours. You have a very simple style at the moment and the colour could do with sorting out. If I had my way, I'd soften the shape; maybe run a little streak of burgundy through the fringe.'

'You'll do no such thing.' Barbara's hands flew to her face. 'I think there are enough people around here looking like Christmas trees as it is. You have a funny name – Dizzy. Is it a nickname, something the locals call you because you're empty-headed?'

Pauline opened her mouth to protest but Dizzy merely giggled. 'No, not at all – It's short for Desiree.'

'Well, that completely clarifies it. There is no way I'd let anyone touch my hair who's been named after a potato.'

'Barbara,' Pauline took a deep breath. 'I've invited Dizzy for lunch. It's just beans on toast but—'

'I've brought us all cream cakes too...' Dizzy breathed.

'You're welcome to join us, Barbara.' Pauline frowned. 'Where's Bisto?'

'Still asleep, I think. I've really no idea,' Barbara sniffed.

'I'm longing to meet him, Pauline.' Dizzy clutched her shopping bag to her chest. 'Is he handsome?'

'If you'd find a stunted decomposing gargoyle handsome, then I suppose he could be.' Barbara brushed past the women. 'And yes, I'd like lunch.'

She led the way to the kitchen and shoved the latched door open. Bisto was standing with his back to them at the Belfast sink in jeans and a t-shirt. His feet were bare. He had a spanner in his hand and was intently manipulating something over the draining board. He turned around and beamed at the women. 'Oh, I've got three lovely women today. Which of yous would like to give me a hug first?'

'Are you drunk?' Barbara sniffed the air in the kitchen suspiciously.

'I haven't touched a drop.'

Dizzy offered her widest smile and extended her hand. 'It's so nice to meet you, Bisto. I'm Dizzy.'

'And so am I, with love. You're a looker. Well, I could certainly get used to the craic here. So many lovely looking women.' He winked at Pauline and she smiled back. 'By the way, Pauline, I couldn't stand the noise of the ould tap dripping, so I fixed it. I hope you don't mind.'

'I'm delighted. It's been in need of a good screw for ages.' Pauline caught Dizzy's twinkling eyes and blushed. She leaned over and patted Bisto's arm. 'How's the ankle and the head? You were so tired yesterday. I was worried about you.'

Bisto lifted his foot and inspected it. 'The head's completely better. My rainbow-coloured ankle is coming along fine. A few days' more rest now and I'll be out of your hair.' His eyes shifted to Barbara. 'I'm sure you'll be pleased to see the back of me.'

'Not at all, Bisto.' Pauline intervened, turning towards the cupboard, searching for cans of beans. 'In fact, talking of hair, Dizzy here is a superb hairdresser. I've asked her if she could sort you out – give the curls a trim. What do you think?'

Bisto beamed. 'Maybe she can sort the whiskers out for me while she's at it? What do you say, Dizzy? Can you make me look even more handsome?'

Dizzy moved over to Bisto, rubbed a flat hand over his chin and through his white mane. 'I'm pretty sure I can. Yes, we'll have you looking like George Clooney by the time I've finished with you.'

He chuckled. 'I'd rather be Bisto Mulligan again, but maybe that's another story.'

He thought for a moment about the man he'd been, his good reputation, a respected professional; a man who was liked, who was once loved deeply, and how the events of the last few weeks had gone so badly wrong he'd let it all slip away. He'd never imagined he could sink so low, but grief had hit him hard again.

Now here he was, looking like a vagrant, imposing on the kindness of a good woman like Pauline Pye. He saw Barbara frowning at him. She clearly had no idea how his life used to be. She'd seen only the man he'd become. Bisto drew himself up to his height and winced, then adjusted his balance to the good ankle.

'I'm looking forward to a spot of lunch, Pauline. That'd be grand.' He glanced at Barbara, who was standing with her arms folded and her jaw set. 'Babs, me ould love, you wouldn't get me a chair to sit on, my ankle being so badly bruised and sore? And I'd love a cup of tea, if you could see your way to wetting the teapot.'

Barbara turned her back and found him a hard-backed chair which she dragged in his direction, a frown on her face. She moved over to the Aga and tested the weight of the kettle, shifting it onto the hottest plate, reaching for the big brown teapot. Dizzy was already chattering to Bisto, flirting, telling him how she'd make the most of his lovely curls by layering the cut and how she'd like to leave him with a bit of hunky designer stubble. Bisto chuckled; Barbara could hear Pauline joining in, laughing, calling for the cream cakes to be placed on a dish. She thought they were all silly, giggling about nothing, but a thought rattled in her mind: it would be nice to be popular. Barbara's shoulders rose until they were level with her ears.

She realised she was grinding her teeth. She was the odd one out again. She decided, even if it took her another ten thousand hours, she'd never learn to indulge in the pointless social chit-chat so many people seemed to find so normal, so pleasant. She breathed out slowly. Everyone else's conversation seemed so silly, so superficial. So why was she feeling left out and unwanted? She almost wished she could be like Pauline: happy, confident, easy in others' company. Her ears filled with the sound of the whistling kettle and she lifted it carefully and poured hot water onto the tealeaves for all she was worth.

9

It was Saturday morning and the VW was lurching down the narrow road, windows open, a cheery radio voice chattering and playing pop music. The sky was cloudless, the deepest blue, and the air was warm with promise. Bisto smiled, dapper with his stylishly trimmed curls soft around his ears, just how he liked it and more like his old self. He had borrowed a green silk scarf from Pauline, his old jacket and jeans had come up clean in the wash and Dr Natalie had kitted him out with a pair of crutches to help him move a little more independently. He felt happy – his self-respect was starting to return and his heart felt lighter. He sat with his sore ankle stretched out in the front of the car, Barbara hunched in the back, frowning, while Pauline drove them all into Winsley Green, to the May Fair on the village green. Bisto was looking forward to it. There would be people to meet, dancing and something to wet his whistle. He leaned forward and peered through the windscreen as Pauline parked the car next to the kerb.

Pauline helped Bisto to slide from his seat, heaving him onto his crutches, and she gazed towards the village green where a maypole stood, twisted with bright ribbons. It felt very pleasant now, going to village events, no longer alone, a solitary widow, but in the company of others. She was delighted to see that Bisto's eyes were wide with joy as he gazed at the scene, and even Barbara looked intrigued. The May festivities were in full swing: several little girls in white dresses with coloured sashes sat on the grass, some drinking lemonade from small bottles, some chattering and laughing. As they walked to the green in front of the pub, Pauline saw several people she recognised, and she waved to them. A few craft stalls and a food van had been set up around the green; the air was filled with the heavy scent of frying onions. A man dressed as a hobby horse galloped past.

A chubby man was dressed in leafy green: even his bushy beard was sprayed a shade of avocado and he wore a tattered suit made from pieces of material, all different shades of emeralds and pastels, sage and olive and bottle green, and a crown of ivy on his head. Several other men were clad in white, with rainbow sashes across their chests, bands around their knees heavy with little bells and bowler hats on their heads, stuck with yellow and blue flowers. They clutched glasses of cider in their hands, in various stages of fullness. Bisto licked his lips.

Barbara stared at Pauline. 'Has everyone here lost their senses? What exactly is going on?'

Pauline was about to say something about celebrating the beautiful spring weather but a woman with a wide smiling mouth and cascading dark hair, greying at the temples, rushed over and grabbed her hand. Pauline chuckled. Chrissie's face was painted green, decorated with brown squiggles and she wore a flowery garland round her head, an emerald skirt and an olive blouse.

'Good to see you, Pauline. We're having a great time. The dancers were lovely, twelve little girls. You've just missed them.' She extended a hand and smiled warmly behind the lurid green makeup. 'Barbara, isn't it? Good to see you. I hope you're enjoying all that Winsley Green has to offer.'

Barbara wrinkled her nose and was about to say, 'It hasn't much to offer at all,' then glanced at her smiling sister and thought better of it.

Chrissie turned to Bisto. 'Hello, I'm Chrissie Drake, the vicar of St Jude's. We haven't met.'

'Bisto Mulligan.' He beamed at her. 'I have to say, you're a little late for St Pat's Day, but it's nice of you all to dress up just for me.'

Chrissie's face was puzzled for a moment then she trilled with laughter. 'Ah, you're so funny. I've heard all about you – you're a friend of Pauline's. Welcome.'

Bisto took her hand. 'This is a grand place you've got here. Good to meet you, vicar.' He appeared to notice someone sitting a distance away on the grass. 'Ah, will you excuse me? I've just seen someone I know.'

Pauline watched, secretly pleased with the progress of his sore ankle due to her ministrations, as he swung away on his crutches towards a woman with fluffy grey curls who was seated on the grass, playing a guitar. She had wound a string of little flowers in her hair and she wore a long colourful dress. Bisto heaved himself down beside her and they began to chat. Pauline wondered where he had met Tilly Hardy before. She turned to Chrissie.

'Have you ever read any of Tilly's books?'

Chrissie shook her head. 'No. I expect they are too racy for me. Modern romances. I believe she's very good though.'

Barbara shrugged. 'I don't like romances. I think they're for the feeble-minded.'

The vicar made a loud braying noise. 'I do like your sister, Pauline. She has such a lovely sense of humour.' Chrissie didn't notice the exchange of glances and Pauline's gentle hand on her sister's arm. She waved an arm. 'Shall we have a stroll around?

There are a few lovely stalls – one which sells divine fudge. I'll treat us all. And I've seen Yvonne and Tamsin with the baby – they're at a stall selling lemonade, and Dizzy is around somewhere. Let's go and find her.'

The three women wandered through the crowds. A few yards away, Bisto stretched his ankle out on the grass, clapped his hands and grinned. 'Lovely. You have a great voice on you, Tilly. I haven't heard "Blowin' in the Wind" for a long time.'

She closed her eyes for a moment. 'I like to keep my creative abilities well-oiled.'

Bisto nodded. 'Me too.' He glanced across at the pub. The doors to the Sheep Dip Inn were open, the doorway crowded with the men in white clothes and the flowery hats. His throat was suddenly dry.

'Do you sing, Bisto? Perhaps we could duet together? Do you know "Scarborough Fair"?'

'I can play a few instruments, for sure, but I sing like a stuck hog.' He grinned. 'Especially when I've been on the sauce.'

He was thoughtful for a moment. He had a little money, the change from the money Hugo had given him: he could offer to buy her a drink. He'd contacted the bank several days before, been through the long routine security checks and a replacement debit card would arrive at Pauline's address at any time. He'd feel a lot better about life if he had access to his money, if he could pay his way again and treat everyone around him to a drink or two. After all, his bank account had always been healthy. Until then, once his last few pounds had been spent, he'd need to use his wits.

'I don't suppose you fancy a swift gargle?'

Tilly blinked for a moment. 'Oh, you mean a drink? It's a little early for me. But what a nice expression – at first I thought you meant singing.'

Bisto sighed and pulled himself to his feet, leaning on the

crutch. 'Well, I'm going to have a wander. Nice to see you again, Tilly. Maybe we can catch up later.'

Tilly smiled and began to strum. As Bisto wandered away, he heard her soft voice straining to reach the notes of 'Dirty Old Town'.

As he swung his crutches across the green in the direction of the pub, Bisto passed a lemonade stall. A blonde woman in her forties in jeans and a white t-shirt smiled at him and he nodded back. She was pouring pale liquid into plastic cups and she called across.

'Best Somerset lemonade? Fifty pence?'

Bisto shook his head. 'Ah, no thanks, I'm after having a glass of the black stuff.'

'You're the man staying with Pauline. Bisto, isn't it? She's told me all about you. I'm Yvonne, from the Post Office.' She held out a cup. 'Have this one on the house.'

'Then I will.' Bisto took the cup and glanced at the young girl holding the baby. Her eyes were drowsy, her blue dress dishevelled, but she held herself in a way that seemed unaware of her good looks. Her hair was long, blonde, tangled in the baby's pudgy fingers. The child had her silky hair and huge blue eyes. Bisto finished the lemonade. 'Nice babby you have there.'

The girl turned to him and half-smiled. 'You wouldn't have said that at four o'clock this morning. He was yelling at the top of his lungs – he wouldn't go off to sleep, bless him.'

Yvonne took the plastic cup from his fingers. 'Colic, I think. Poor little chap.'

Bisto held out his arms to the younger woman. 'May I?'

The young mother frowned for a moment and then passed the baby to Bisto, who took the child in one arm, wobbling on the crutches. 'Handsome little fella. What's his name?'

The girl yawned and smiled. 'Harley. He's seven weeks old.'

'You're a lovely little man, Harley. But you've been doing a lot of yelling.' Bisto held the baby close to his chest. 'They say being calm and keeping the babby warm helps. But I'd reckon this little feller would benefit from some old-fashioned gripe water now.'

He handed the baby gently to the young woman, who seemed surprised. 'How do you know that?'

Bisto shrugged. 'Ah, well. I know a few things about kiddies. I had one of my own, Barney. He's got two grown girls now. Gripe water worked for them all...'

Yvonne poured herself lemonade and one for her daughter. 'There's a chemist in Thorpe. Perhaps we should take Harley and get him some gripe water. You never know – it might just help. Thanks, Bisto.'

Bisto tugged his crutches beneath his arms. 'I'll be seeing you, Yvonne,' and lunged towards the Sheep Dip Inn. On the way he passed two old ladies who were arguing. Both were bent over, their eyes locked together and their faces inches apart. One of them had stockings around her ankles and she was screaming about a cat that should be put down. The other thinner one threatened to pull the first woman's hair out at the roots. Bisto winked at them.

'Well, ladies, how are ye doing? Good to see you're enjoying the Mayday craic.'

They paused, turned to gape at him, then resumed their argument, the first old lady loudly threatening to punch the other's lights out. Bisto chuckled and dragged himself to the pub. His foot was a little sore and if he could persuade someone to buy him a pint, it would ease the ache. But the pain in his heart was the worst thing at the moment. Holding the baby had unsettled him, scraped the scab off an old wound, and it was too painful to bear. Past images of better days, when he'd been busy and happy and in love flooded back and filled the space behind his eyes.

He shivered; his skin cold as gooseflesh. Bisto decided a small drink might dispel the grief. He was in charge now – he wouldn't overdo it. He'd just have the one, or maybe two. He approached one of the men in the white clothes with the bells and sashes and flowery bowlers, tapping him gently on the arm.

'So how does a fella get a gargle around here, friend?'

The young man was tall, in his late thirties, with a thatch of ginger hair under his dark bowler. He tilted his hat back, scratched his scalp and gazed at Bisto.

'We've got our drinks on the house today, mate. There's a free bar for Morris men. May Day tradition.'

Bisto leaned on his crutches and pressed his lips together. He needed a pint and nodded in understanding: there was a way.

Barbara sipped lemonade from a disposable cup and stared around her at the people who all seemed to be enjoying themselves. She had to admit that she was puzzled. Everyone was having a good time, oblivious to the fact that they were making fools of themselves in odd costumes and green faces. She wondered why she didn't feel the same way; she'd certainly feel awkward with her face painted a lurid colour, but no one else seemed at all perturbed. They were all simply talking and laughing as if their ridiculous garb was the most normal thing in the world.

She watched Pauline, cool and confident, taking everything in her stride and tried to remember the names of the people she'd spoken to in the last hour: Yvonne from the Post Office, who was singing Bisto's praises about the way he'd taken an interest in baby Harley; Chrissie the Vicar; now Dizzy, who was trying to persuade Pauline to book Kostas to clean her windows. The Greek divinity was currently lying in the grass, languid and long in tight jeans and an open-necked white shirt, chewing thoughtfully on a blade of grass.

'Look at him, Pauline. Imagine him cleaning your windows at the cottage. It would be worth what it costs just to see him framed behind the leaded light windows.'

Pauline glanced at Kostas just a few feet away; he ran a hand through his curls and stretched out his arms, his eyes half-closed like a sleepy cat's.

'I could ask him, Dizzy. The windows could do with a shine now the summer is here. I can see every smear of dirt and bird poo.'

Dizzy grabbed her arm. 'I'll ask him for you, shall I? Or at least, I'll make a bit of small talk first. Find out if he's single.'

On the grass, Kostas rolled over on his front, shaking his mane, oblivious to the women's glances. Barbara tutted.

'He's just a man, for goodness sake. Anyone would think there was something special about him.'

Dizzy rolled her eyes. 'Just look at him, though!'

'We're all looking, Dizzy.' Pauline chuckled, running a hand over her hair, tucking the wisps back into the loose bun. A broad-shouldered man was approaching them, in his seventies, striding like a giant. A younger man in his thirties, handsome but surly, with dark hair and thick eyebrows walked at his side, his shoulders rolling as he moved, his elbows sticking out as if he was looking for a fight. The young man spat on the floor as Len Chatfield said, 'Hello, Pauline.' He glanced at Barbara. 'Hello.'

Pauline offered him a wide smile. 'Hello, Len. Good to see you. Are you having a good time?'

Len rubbed his chin. 'Just here for a quick visit. Sheep waiting in the fields at home. Got things to do.'

Barbara met his moving eyes. 'Do you have any decent meat you could bring round for my sister? I'm sure it would be nice if she had some proper pork.'

'Just sheep right now.' He moved his huge shoulders beneath the grubby coat. 'I can bring a rabbit though if you want one.'

'Oh, no thanks, Len.' Pauline put up her hands like a shield. 'It's fine. Barbara is staying with me at the house for a while. I don't think she'd like to eat rabbit...'

Barbara wrinkled her nose. 'I certainly wouldn't. I like my meat properly butchered and hygienically packaged in a supermarket.'

'Come on, Father.' Len's son's face became even moodier. 'I got a couple of ciders waiting for us at home.'

Len smiled at Pauline; his mouth awkward. 'Better go then. Right, Gary. Land Rover's in need of diesel.'

Pauline watched the men walk away. Barbara's voice cut through her thoughts.

'The farmer is dull enough, but his son is completely ignorant.'

Pauline closed her eyes. 'He lost his mother as a boy, I think.'

Dizzy suddenly became animated. 'Len and his wife thought they couldn't have children – they tried for years then, after they'd given up, Gary came along. She adored him, Elizabeth did. She died when Gary was ten. It was hard for him – he used to get up at four in the morning to help on the farm before school, then afterwards he'd be in the fields, late into the night. He's never been very sociable. He has done so much for his dad on that farm though. Len would be lost on his own.'

Barbara shook her head. 'Is anyone safe from the gossip in this village?'

'It's a caring community, Barbara.' Pauline gave a soft smile. 'That's what I love about it.'

'Oh, will you look over there?' Dizzy pointed over to Kostas, who had levered himself up from the grass to shake hands with a lean blond man in a tweed jacket. 'He's talking to Hugo Garrett now.'

'What a distinguished looking man,' Barbara observed, taking in the jacket and the smartly creased trousers. 'He looks as if he could be in the military.'

Dizzy was staring openly. 'It's Hugo Garrett from the manor house. He's probably offering Kostas a contract to clean all of those big windows. You've missed your chance there, Pauline.'

The blond man was giving instructions, waving his hands in an authoritative way and Kostas nodded unhurriedly, as if he understood, before both men walked away together. Pauline wondered what time it was: they must have been at the green for almost two hours.

The grass was bathed in warm sunlight, and big crowds were gathering outside the pub. Two young men were coming towards her, both in the Morris men costumes. One of them held out his hand.

'Hello, Pauline.'

'Hello. It's nice to see you. Barbara, this is Andy Priddy from Milton Rogus. And this is my sister, Barbara.'

'Hello, Barbara.' Andy Priddy was tall, in his mid-twenties, the build of a rugby player, short brown hair neatly cut and a lean handsome face. He pointed to the skinny young man with a mischievous smile and dark hair almost to his shoulders, a few years younger than himself. 'This is my cousin, Jack.'

Dizzy preened. 'They are carpenters. They did a lovely window frame for my aunt last year. I told them you had a few jobs that needed attention in your house. I hope you don't mind.'

Pauline shook their hands. 'I have lots of things that are crying out to be done in my little cottage. My husband and I intended...' Pauline sighed and thought for a moment. 'Well, that was then, but it doesn't matter now. The thing is, I don't have a lot of money.'

Andy Priddy nodded; his face troubled. 'Oh, I wasn't touting for business. It's just if you ever needed...'

Jack butted in, '...any work needing doing, then please do give us a call first.'

'Here's our business card.' Andy pressed a crisp cardboard rectangle into her palm. 'We do good rates.'

'Thank you. I'll remember that.'

Pauline watched them walk away. Jack was laughing his head thrown back, and Andy was talking animatedly. She thought of the window frames badly in need of repair, how the cold air seeped in and turned the air in the rooms to ice. She thought of the broken tiles, how Douglas had had plans to renovate the whole place, make it beautiful, and finally add a garden room in place of the old wooden conservatory.

Barbara was indignant. 'Really! On a day off, a Saturday, trying to persuade pensioners to part with what little they have...'

'They are nice young men,' Dizzy insisted, smiling. 'I think Kostas must be taking all the trade away round here. Apparently he'll do all sorts of odd jobs.'

A commotion over by the pub made them turn their heads. A drum hammered loudly and the three women saw a burly man in a bowler hat crowned with flowers wedged over a thatch of ginger hair, banging an energetic rhythm. Dizzy flushed a deep pink and whispered. 'It's Kevin Carter. I've known him for years. He's a hedger. He's won prizes for it.'

Barbara had no idea what she meant. Andy Priddy and Jack chased back to join the other men in white with colourful sashes and leg bands, who were ringing small bells and shouting. A dozen men formed a circle and raised their arms in unison. The crowd pressed closer to watch and the three women joined them. A holler went up and a concertina burst forth with a sprightly tune. The men lifted sticks in the air and began to dance, clacking a rhythm in time to the drum and rattling the bells on their legs, their heels high behind and in front of them. The music became louder, insistent, and the men's dancing was more energetic and bold. A fiddle joined in and the men twirled and whooped, leaped and dipped in perfect synchronicity.

The crowd cheered and clapped as the men formed a perfect archway, raising their sticks at the sky. The clap became louder and the Morris men stomped their feet and rang a jangle of bells in the air, building up to an expectant crescendo. Then a yell split the sky and a little man in white, bells around his legs and a bowler hat crammed hard on thick pale curls came swinging forward on crutches, his legs waving high, a smile on his face.

With bravado and panache that could only have come from a pint of the black stuff, the man flung the crutches away from him and hopped round in a circle, waving Pauline's green silk scarf in the air, cheering and howling while the Morris men shook their bells at him. The crowd roared, applauded, and Bisto bowed, waved his arms, bowed again even lower and then slipped and fell flat on his face.

10

Bisto sat in a streaming column of warm sunshine in the old rickety conservatory, his leg elevated on a cushion, sipping strong tea and eating a crumbly fudge brownie. He was feeling pleased with himself. His bank card had finally arrived at his 'temporary' address and he now had access to his funds. He'd persuaded Pauline to take him into Taunton so that he could buy himself some new clothes and he'd treated her to a pleasant lunch. Then, on the way home, they'd stopped off at a DIY outlet to buy a few items and this morning he'd replaced the broken tiles and started the repair to the window ledge in the kitchen. It was going well; Pauline would be pleased with him. He had to admit, she was a good sort. He liked her, her mischievous humour, her good nature and her kindly smiling face.

She'd told him she enjoyed having him around the house and insisted she was in no hurry for him to leave. Dr Natalie had seen his ankle again and was convinced it was only a sprain now; it was still puffy, purpled with bruising, but he could move it a little, hop around on one foot and even put his weight on it tentatively, with the help of his crutches. But, as Pauline said, it was a long way from being better, so he'd probably stay another week, maybe even two.

He had the feeling Pauline liked him too. She was a perceptive woman: despite her sense of fun and kindness, she was strong-minded, certainly no pushover. He'd help her around the house as a way of saying thank you. Of course, the grumpy ould one wasn't pleased. She'd gone to read her book upstairs in her room, where she spent a lot of her time. Bisto wouldn't have been surprised if she'd decided to go back home to Cambridge.

Bisto stretched out on the rattan chair, sighed and stared through the window. He gazed across the garden at the tulips waving in the light breeze, pushing the grass to one side. A black cat rushed across the lawn, over the narrow road and into the garden of the house opposite. Another cat, identically black but with white paws, followed it. Bisto could see the neighbours' cottage, the tiled roof and magnolia rendering, the newly blossoming roses in the garden where he'd urinated and fallen over. He hadn't seen the neighbours since he'd apologised, over a week ago. Bisto decided the woman across the lane wasn't the friendly type.

He sighed again, a contented purr. He'd made some new friends in the pub. Kevin Carter, the ginger-haired hedger and Morris men leader, had bought him a couple of drinks since his outstanding dance performance at the May Fair. He was on first name terms with Oskar and Justina of the Sheep Dip Inn and he'd been chatting to both Tilly Hardy and the nice man from the manor, who had given him a lift here in the first place. Hugo Garrett had bought him a drink and seemed very keen to spend time chatting in the pub. Furthermore, he'd been stopped by Yvonne from the Post Office yesterday, who'd hugged him and thanked him for recommending the old-fashioned gripe water.

Apparently, little Harley had howled all the way to Thorpe, where the chemist had procured a bottle of pale liquid and muttered, 'There's not much call for this nowadays.' Harley had grudgingly swallowed a spoonful, pulled a face and slept through the night and after several doses, he only cried briefly for a feed. Yvonne had promised to buy Bisto a bottle of something for his troubles, at which point he squeezed her arm and said he was partial to a drop of Irish whiskey.

He closed his eyes and the warmth seeped through them and into his brain like heated milk, and he began to snooze. He was feeling relaxed and heavy-limbed. Then, all of a sudden, he was conscious of someone nearby, coughing, standing stiffly. He blinked. A tall figure was looming over him, hands on hips, peering down. He blinked up at Barbara and his face creased into a grin.

'Well, what's a fella to do, when he's woken from his sleep by an angel?'

Barbara sniffed. 'I suppose you're going to spend all day lazing in here, are you?'

Bisto heaved himself to a sitting up position and waved an arm towards his elevated ankle. 'I'm nursing an injury, so—'

'You'd started to mend the window frame in the kitchen. I thought you'd like to finish it today. It's half three. A job left unfinished is—'

'—is a job I can finish tomorrow. I've time, plenty of it, on my hands at the moment.'

'Too much time if you ask me.' Barbara continued to glare at him. 'I mean, you're still here.'

'I didn't ask you, Babs. But you'd give me your opinion anyway.'

'Bisto.' Barbara sat down deliberately on the other rattan chair and leaned forwards. Bisto closed his eyes in anticipation. He felt sure he knew what was coming. 'Bisto – if that's really your name. I wonder if we could have a brief chat.'

Bisto offered her a smile. 'Are you capable of such a chat, Babs? A brief one? And will I get a word in edge-wise?'

She ignored him. 'Bisto. When you first came here – how many weeks ago? Too many. I wasn't very keen on it.'

'Really? I'd no idea.' Bisto pulled a mock-surprised face.

'I thought you were taking advantage of my sister's good nature. You should have gone to hospital. Or to a place for the homeless, whatever those shelter places are called. Your coming here was both ludicrous and ill-advised. I told Pauline as much.'

'Ah, I'm sure you had your say.'

'But Pauline doesn't listen. Now, I know she won't ask you this, but I will. I'm not afraid to call a spade a spade.'

Bisto winked. 'As Oscar Wilde might've said, I've never spent much time working with spades.'

She glared at him. 'Well, perhaps you should have.'

He chuckled. 'Bit of a stereotype that, Babs, the Irish navvy. Outmoded long ago and I think just a little bit racist—'

Barbara wasn't listening. 'So, I think you owe us an explanation. You're a tramp but you've read Oscar Wilde? You have an expensive mobile phone, yet you apparently lost everything else and you're homeless. You clearly drink far more than you ought, and you wouldn't be here at all if it weren't for my sister's sweet nature. Now you appear to have money – you treated her to lunch yesterday, she claims, and you bought yourself a new wardrobe. How did you finance this spending spree exactly? Have you robbed someone? Exactly what sort of conman are you, Bisto?'

The smile faded from Bisto's face. 'I'll be out of your hair soon enough. I have funds to go back home now.'

Barbara gave a triumphant yell. 'Oh yes, you said you have a castle in Spain or France or somewhere imaginary in Europe? So, what's the full story? Why are you here at all?'

'Where?'

'In England. In the south-west. In my sister's house, for that matter.'

Bisto closed his eyes briefly. 'I'm passing through.' He met her eyes, his blue ones a little misty, hers angry and glaring. 'I've had a difficult few months. Some things happened and, well, I ended up here.'

'How did you lose your wallet and your bank card? Gambling, I suppose?'

Bisto heaved a sigh. 'Ah, if you like, then yes – believe what you will. It's no skin from my nose.' He shook his head. 'Where's Pauline?'

'In the kitchen, making that heavy stuff she passes off as healthy bread.'

Bisto shook his head. 'Her cooking is grand. It reminds me of my own mammy's baking, how she stood at the stove making soda bread and potato cakes when we were kids and...'

'And so where is she now, Bisto? Your own mammy?' Barbara's tone was sarcastic, cruel. 'If she's such a good cook, why aren't you there with her and all the brothers and sisters you claim to have in Dublin? What happened? Did she throw you out? Too drunk, were you? I expect that was it. And is that why you are a tramp, drifting around England with a ridiculous sob story about a château in France, trying to live off the good nature of unsuspecting old widows, just like the parasite you are?'

Barbara stopped and put slim fingers to her mouth. She'd only meant to stick up for Pauline's interests; she'd gone too far. Bisto had slumped down in his chair, staring straight ahead. There was a single tear trickling down his cheek. She heard him take a deep breath.

'It's like you said, Barbara. Every word of it's the truth. I'm not much good for anything.'

Barbara suddenly felt the heat leave her body and she was cold. The moment had thrown her. She was expecting an off-the-cuff joke from him, a swift retort, an argument even. But she was watching a little man, his face twisted in pain, who was clearly flattened by what she'd just said. She wondered what to say to him now, how to make things better. She didn't know.

The thought occurred to her that Pauline wouldn't have been so forthright; she would have known in advance that such words would hurt his feelings. She ought to try to remedy matters. She simply said, 'How's your ankle?'

'I'm on the mend,' Bisto wiped his face on his sleeve. 'Don't you worry about me. I'll be on my way soon enough now. Don't give it another single thought.'

'Bisto...' His name hung in the air and the space between them was cold. Barbara felt awkward, uncomfortable. She turned; she'd go back to her room, to her book, and say no more about it. She'd only been trying to protect Pauline. She glanced at the little man again; she'd clearly exposed a deep-seated wound and, judging by his face, he was still suffering. She breathed in. She was about to say sorry, but the words wouldn't come. She would try harder next time not to say hurtful things but, for now, she'd just leave.

A moving figure in the corner of the garden caught her eye. A dark-haired woman was rushing towards them. She reached the conservatory door and pounded on it with her fists. Her face was a replica of Munch's painting of *The Scream*, her mouth stretched wide and her arms flailing by her face. Bisto struggled to his feet, reaching for his crutches, but Barbara had opened the door.

'Hello?'

Bisto called out. 'It's Julia from across the lane, isn't it? Will you come in?'

Julia's face was pallid. She ignored Bisto, seizing Barbara's arm. 'Come. Come at once. Something's... in my kitchen. It's horrible. Really horrible.'

Barbara pulled back. 'Whatever is the matter?'

'Come quickly.' Julia was leading the way over the lawn to the little fence and the gate that led to the road.

Bisto was pursuing her, swinging on his crutches. Barbara assumed there was a dead body involved, the woman was so troubled, so she called out, 'Pauline. I think there's an emergency at Julia's. Come and help,' and rushed after her.

In the kitchen, Pauline was wiping her hands on her apron. She pressed her lips together, smiled and turned to the door: she had her suspicions about what had happened.

Barbara arrived at Julia's house first, following the neighbour who led the way through the narrow hallway, past a living room with oak beams and a fire blazing in the hearth to a huge farmhouse kitchen. Barbara noticed how modern the interior was compared to Pauline's antiquated cottage; Julia had a stainless-steel cooking range, smart blinds, a pale table and upright fabric-covered chairs.

Bisto lurched through the doorway and Julia hurled herself at him, grabbing his arm. 'There.' She pointed to the corner, to the floor at the far end of the kitchen. 'Look, there.'

Barbara saw it and gasped. Her initial thought was that she would immediately be sick. She was rooted to the spot, shocked, her stomach lurching towards her throat. There was a black cat crouching over what had once been a fluffy rabbit. But now it was headless and the cat had hauled its entrails, stretched like bright bleeding sausages across the floor. There was blood spattered everywhere, long streaks of red where the rabbit had fought and lost, then had been dragged across the pale tiles. The cat hunkered down, fur and meat in its mouth, and gave a low growl.

'Do something,' Julia begged.

'I think there's not much to be done for the poor rabbit now,' Bisto suggested.

Barbara felt the earth spin and she leaned against the granite work top, letting her head droop onto her hands. She heard Julia screech 'It's not my cat.'

'Well, I hope it isn't your rabbit either, to be sure,' Bisto offered.

'Do something,' Julia howled even louder.

Barbara did something. She couldn't help it. She threw herself forward and retched. Thankfully it was a spasm and she wasn't sick on the expensive tiled floor.

Tears filled her eyes. She desperately needed to sit down and have a glass of water. There was a creak of crutches and Bisto was beside her.

'Don't worry, Babs, you'll be all right.'

'Pass me a bin bag.' The commanding voice was Pauline's. Barbara peeked and saw her standing in the doorway; Julia rushed to a cupboard, banging a door. Pauline's voice boomed. 'Shoo, go on, Derek, out you go. Psssst!'

Barbara felt the rush of air as the cat sprang past her. Bisto was patting her arm. 'You're all right, Barbara. Just breathe normally. Little light breaths.'

Pauline was in charge. 'Give me the bag, Julia. I'll clear it up. It's only a bit of meat.'

Barbara was conscious of squeezing her eyes closed together and then she was shaking like a leaf in an icy breeze. She heard Pauline bustling about, the sound of scraping or cleaning or scrubbing, and a bag being closed together and swung aloft.

'Don't worry, Julia. It's quite a common occurrence around here for Dulcie's cat to hunt things and bring them into people's houses. I wouldn't' be surprised if the other cat, Clive, isn't out on the grass with the rest of the poor rabbit.'

Barbara heard the sound of splashing. She opened her eyes. Pauline was washing her hands beneath a running tap. There was a black bin bag ominously perched by her foot. Bisto handed her a full glass and Barbara put the cooling water to her lips.

He held on to her arm. 'Here, Babs. You'll be feeling better in a little minute.'

Julia's face was pale as parchment. 'Peter, my husband, isn't here at the moment. My daughter's at school in Wells during the week. I'm all alone here in this place. It's awful.'

Pauline patted her shoulder and her voice was soothing. 'Country life, I'm afraid. Best to keep your back door shut, Julia. The Feral Peril are busy this time of year – there's a lot of hunting to be had among the fauna. The rabbit was only a young one.'

Barbara shook her head and glanced nervously around her. The cat, Derek, had gone, as had the spreading carnage. The space was clean and shiny as if it had never happened.

'Thank you, Pauline,' Julia breathed, her dignity returning.

Pauline smiled kindly and gathered up the bin bag. 'I'll dispose of this, shall I?'

'I'd be very grateful.'

Pauline turned to the door. Bisto, a crutch beneath each arm, was attempting to shepherd Barbara towards the way out. Barbara's face was distraught, a sickly unnatural grey, and she didn't object as Bisto leaned his shoulder against her as they moved out of the house and through the garden.

Pauline watched them go, the bin bag grasped in her hand. Behind her, Julia closed the door with a thud and Pauline thought she heard a key turn in a lock. She followed Bisto and her sister to the narrow lane and watched as they crossed. She stood still for a moment, listening. The heavy ticking sound of an engine in the distance became louder and she watched as Len Chatfield approached on his heavy tractor, pulling a trailer full of something that could be animal feed.

The farmer's eyes met hers. Pauline smiled, wiggled her fingers in a little wave but Len stared ahead, his eyes on the road, and drove past. He had clearly seen her, but he hadn't acknowledged her greeting. Pauline frowned. Len had seemed distinctly unhappy; she'd seen it in his expression. Something was wrong. She resolved to ask him next time she saw him. She didn't want distance to develop between them; she knew how hard it was to try to bridge a gap.

She thought immediately of Barbara. Her sister was struggling with country life: in Julia's kitchen she'd been wan and weak at the sight of the rabbit. There was a vulnerable side to her, a softer side Pauline had never seen before. It was a good job Bisto had been standing by: she'd been right in her decision to ask him to stay. He was the breath of fresh air that blew away Barbara's stuffiness. Then she thought of Len on his tractor, his eyes avoiding hers. With a sigh, she swung the bag out in front of her and marched across the road that led to her house.

11

Another week had rolled by and the sunshine illuminated Pauline's garden, making the blossoms bright and sweet-smelling. Pauline had planted a few seeds: beetroot, squash and cucumbers. She had organised a little herb garden of terracotta pots, nurturing seedlings of basil, coriander, chervil, dill, lovage and parsley. Barbara was helping her, proclaiming that she couldn't stand being indoors on such a lovely day, although Pauline suspected that her sister was giving Bisto a wide berth. They'd hardly spoken since the incident with Derek and the rabbit; although Bisto had shepherded her home, Barbara was clearly avoiding him.

Bisto spent his days either snoozing happily in the old conservatory or doing a few odd jobs around the house. He'd replaced three window ledges on the ground floor and installed a cleanly varnished wooden sill inside the kitchen, sealing the window and disposing of the rotten wood that had previously held water when the rain seeped in.

Pauline's idea of Sunday lunch at the Sheep Dip had two purposes: she wanted to thank Bisto for his invaluable help around the house and she intended that the three of them would sit down together for a treat and share a meal. Justina and Oskar were famous for their Sunday carveries and Pauline had just finished a hearty nut roast. Bisto had chosen the same dish and had eaten every scrap, but Barbara was pushing a slice of beef around on her plate. She'd hardly touched the vegetables. Bisto sat back in his seat, rubbed his belly and reached for his half-finished pint of Guinness. 'You should have had the nut roast, Barbara. It was just the ticket.'

Barbara wrinkled her nose. 'I don't see the point of a nut roast. Why would anyone want to roast nuts and smother them in gravy?'

Bisto smacked his lips. 'Well, I couldn't be happier. My food was delicious, thank you Pauline.' He leaned back in his seat and smiled. 'I couldn't be more content.' He thought for a moment, staring out of the latticed window. 'I remember someone very close to me once did some research into a condition called synaesthesia. Have you heard of it?'

Barbara pressed her lips together. 'Isn't it something to do with children seeing things in colour?'

Bisto was delighted. 'It is, Babs. I met someone who thought the number eight was pure yellow. Well, I often wonder what it would be like to see feelings in colour. I mean right now, here I am having eaten a lovely meal with you two ladies and I'm wondering, if the feeling was a colour, what would it be?'

'Brown,' muttered Barbara, folding her arms across her chest.

'For me it would be silver. Like the shimmering silver lining of a rain cloud.' Bisto seemed pleased with himself. 'And you, Pauline? What would your colour be right now at this moment in time?'

'A lovely rich shade of purple. Or the green of spring grass.'

A young woman in her late teens appeared at Pauline's elbow. She had long dark hair pulled back in tight plaits and a sweet dimpled face. She wore a black skirt and a white blouse, and her manner was efficient and pleasant.

'Hi. Did you enjoy the nut roast, Pauline? Can I take your plate?'

'It was lovely, thank you, Claudia. Tell Justina and Oskar it was delicious. How are the A levels going?'

Claudia picked up the plates, watching Barbara push away her uneaten beef. 'Yes, great, thanks. I'm hoping to go to Bristol next year to do Modern Languages.'

'Your parents will miss you,' Pauline smiled. 'You're a breath of fresh air.'

Claudia beamed. 'Can I interest you in the dessert menu?'

Barbara shook her head, but Pauline sat up straight. 'Yes, please. I'm sure we can all manage something.'

Bisto gave Claudia his most disarming smile. 'The roast nut dinner was deadly.' He saw Claudia's furrowed brow and added, 'I'm just saying, it was delicious. I could eat it all again.'

'I've no appetite,' Barbara said.

Pauline reached over and patted her hand. 'The country air will help you get it back. You'd become run down, I think. You will feel so much better after a good rest and a few more weeks here. You are going to stay a little longer, aren't you, Barbara? I mean, there's no rush to go back to Cambridge.' She gazed from Barbara to Bisto and back at her sister, relishing the warm geniality of a good meal and company. 'I'm surprised how much I'm appreciating having visitors. I'm used to being by myself and doing everything for myself but I'm enjoying having house guests. You're welcome to stay a bit longer.' Pauline glanced at Bisto. 'Both of you.'

'I can stay another week, I expect. I just think that my house might need airing and...'

Pauline put her hand on Barbara's arm and left it there. She was feeling a warm glow, effusive and generous: she was showing her visitors a pleasant time. It felt good to be expansive and bountiful: it was certainly better to have people to share life with than being alone, and Barbara certainly needed some joy in her life.

'The village blossoms in the summer. Do stay on. We'll have a lovely time.'

Bisto stood up, tugging at his shirt. 'Excuse me a minute, Pauline. I have to go to the jacks. Can I get you both a drink on the way back?'

'Not for me,' Barbara blurted, without meeting his eyes.

'I have the car outside, Bisto, so I'll make this small glass of red last me. Barbara might have a half of what you're drinking, though. Guinness is full of nutrients, isn't it? I'm going to order a pudding.'

'Oh no, I couldn't, Pud. I mean, Pauline. You know I don't drink. Nothing more for me.'

'You need to live a little, Barbara. Shall I order you a pudding, Bisto?'

'Pick me something out, something sweet.' Bisto winked. 'Like the pair of yous.'

He lumbered away, his stick making a rhythmic clanking on the wooden floor. Barbara turned to Pauline. 'I just don't understand that man.'

'How can you say that, Barbara? He's a model of generosity.'

Barbara leaned closer. 'He worries me a little. After all we know hardly anything about him except that he's Irish and he's a tramp.'

'He's a good man.' Pauline's face shone. 'And I expect there's much more to him than we think. He is quite a fascinating conversationalist. He knows about synaesthesia. He's clever, funny and well-travelled.'

'I expect that because he's a vagrant, Pauline, he has plenty of time on his hands.'

Pauline chuckled and shook her head. 'No, I was thinking about it. When he arrived, I agree he looked unkempt. But I noticed straight away, his jacket is expensive. And he's quite sophisticated and quite distinguished. There's much more to Mr Mulligan than meets the eye. I'd love to know what his background is...'

'You sound like a fan, Pauline.' Barbara pulled an unimpressed face. 'He's not my type – he's not very tall.'

'I think he's nice, Barbara. You should chat to him – get to know him better.'

'I don't see the point.' Barbara wrinkled her nose. 'He'll be on his way soon. And the sooner the better as far as I'm concerned.'

She chewed her lip and thought about what she had just said. The images of Bisto fixing the tap and the tiles, grinning at them and making jokes over breakfast came to her. Barbara wondered if she shouldn't try to be positive, a little more like her good-natured, popular sister.

'Well, I suppose he has been useful around the house.' Barbara sighed. 'And he has a sense of humour – that's probably more than you can say for most men.'

Claudia positioned herself next to the table, a little notepad in her hand. 'What can I get you all?'

Pauline wriggled in her seat. 'The cheesecake looks nice...'

* * *

Bisto emerged from the gents, glancing around the bar. He was searching for his new friend, Kevin Carter, the ginger-haired hedger, who had bought him drinks. Bisto hoped he could return the favour now he had money. But Kevin was nowhere to be seen. It was half past two and the bar was almost empty but for a few quiet drinkers whom Bisto didn't recognise. He leaned against the bar and waited for Oskar to finish serving a moody looking young man, who stared at him briefly, then clutched two glowing pints of cider and moved to a table in the corner, where a large square-shoul-dered man was sitting.

Bisto smiled at Oskar and ordered a pint of Guinness, a half for Barbara and a fruit juice for Pauline. He leaned on his walking stick while he was watching Oskar pour the Guinness, the creamy top tippling over the edge of the glass. Oskar grinned as he worked. 'Well, you seem to be very settled here now, Bisto. I expect Pauline is looking after you.'

'Oh, the ladies are both wonderful,' Bisto beamed. 'I love them both. Grand ladies they are, Barbara and Pauline, the pair of them.' He chuckled good-naturedly. 'I could stop here for ever and no mistake.'

A sullen voice from the back reached his ears. 'Now that *would* be a mistake, if you ask me.'

Bisto turned to see the young man taking a slurp from the glass of cider, sitting next to the older man, both glowering in his direction. He half-turned, leaning against his stick.

'And why would that be?'

The young man didn't move, his glass firmly clutched in his hand.

'We all know what you are. An Irish tramp, taking advantage of Pauline Pye and her sister. You should go back where you came from.'

Oskar raised a finger. 'Now Gary – I don't want any trouble.'

'I'm just saying,' the sulky man muttered. 'There's us locals who's been here years and we don't like to see strangers coming here and taking advantage of our neighbours.'

Bisto paid for his round, took a sip of his Guinness and walked over to the cider drinkers, a smile on his face.

'Look friend, I don't want to offend you. Can I buy you both another one of those?'

Gary picked up his cider and fixed hard eyes on Bisto. The older man leaned forward and scratched his whiskers, his voice low and determined.

'See, you aren't welcome. If you know what's good for you, you'll get gone and quickly too. This village don't want the likes of you.'

His face was inches from Bisto's. 'Pauline Pye is a friend of mine and I'm very partial about what happens to her. So why don't you just get on your way back to Ireland or wherever it is you've come from and get out of Winsley for good.'

Bisto stood still. 'I'm only staying here while I...'

The tall man leaned forward. Seated, he was almost the same height as the stooped Bisto. 'I just said. You're not welcome...'

His son's eyes glinted. 'I reckon Father's right. And a lot of other people round here might think so too.'

Bisto swallowed a mouthful of his pint, put it carefully back on the bar, clutched his walking stick and staggered to the door, his heart suddenly thumping in his ears. The light of the sunshine hit him in the face and he blinked hard. He stepped out into the brightness and stood very still. He wondered if that was what people were saying about him, that he'd taken advantage of someone's kindness. He closed his eyes for a moment. Didn't his own mammy say that about him? *Bisto, you're too single-minded – you think of nobody but your own self, to be sure.* Yes, she had said that to him, and not so long ago. He put his hand to his head and stood still for a moment, swallowing hard.

Bisto wiped a tear from his cheek and staggered forward, leaning heavily on his cane. His feet were taking him down the road, hobbling away from the pub. He had no idea where he was going or what he would do, but he didn't want to hurt Pauline and he didn't want the local folks to think he was taking advantage of her good nature. And hadn't Barbara already accused him of exactly that? She was a good woman really, Barbara – perhaps she was right. Pauline was good-natured, lovely, and, by staying with her, Bisto was allowing others to think she was weak, a pushover. He couldn't allow that to be said about such a generous, kind-hearted woman. Shame made his cheeks tingle and he put his head down and walked with a lumbering gait.

'You've been blind, Bisto,' he muttered to himself. 'Blind and stupid, thoughtless and selfish again.'

He recalled his mother, and then his brother-in-law Randeep in Swindon, remembering how Ruchi hadn't recognised him at the door, how he'd neglected to contact them in years. He was not a good person – he was selfish and inconsiderate; he took advantage of others and then he neglected them. He sighed and felt the sad wrench of parting; he'd just started to feel at home in the village, to make good friends, but he should have known that would be a mistake. It would be better for everyone if he was on his way again. He passed the sign announcing the village as Winsley Green, limping as fast as he could towards a clump of trees in the distance. He'd stick out a thumb at the next car that passed and ask for a lift. It wouldn't matter where.

* * *

Pauline pushed away the remains of cheesecake on her plate and stared around the restaurant area of the pub for the fourth time, her eyes moving to the steps down to the bar. There were a few diners finishing their meals, but there was no sign of Bisto. It was ten to three; his dessert was untouched. He'd been a long time in the toilets. She met Barbara's eyes.

'Do you think he's all right? Perhaps he's slipped over on his ankle?'

Barbara shrugged. 'I expect he's found someone to chatter to. You know what he's like. Perhaps someone has bought him a drink.'

'I don't know.' Pauline frowned. 'Look, I'm going to pay for lunch in the bar and see if he's waiting for us in there.'

'I'll come with you.' Barbara reached for her jacket.

Oskar was wiping glasses. The bar was almost empty apart from Len Chatfield and his son, who were sitting in a dark corner clutching the remains of their pints of cider. Pauline smiled in their direction. Len picked up his glass and swallowed the dregs without returning her gaze. Oskar offered her the machine and she put in her bank card.

'It was a lovely lunch. We all enjoyed it. And Claudia is so nice. She's such a credit to you, Oskar.'

The barman smiled. 'She's a good girl. She works hard. Justina and I have never had any of the teenage troubles with her that you hear other parents complain about.'

Barbara stood tall. 'I expect there's still time. I mean, these universities are a source of anxiety for parents, aren't they? All the illegal drugs and rampant sex and all-night rave-ups.'

Pauline saw Oskar's face cloud, so she grinned. 'I think it sounds like just what young people need – the chance to grow up in a safe environment and study a subject they love. I wish I'd gone to university instead of working in an antique shop when I left school.'

'I was in the Royal Air Force,' Barbara proclaimed. 'I was a secretary. I loved it. They couldn't have managed without me.'

Pauline put her bank card in her handbag. 'Oskar – you haven't seen Bisto, have you? He came through here a moment ago?'

Oskar shrugged and ran a hand over his neatly cropped dark hair. 'He bought drinks and left them on the bar.' He pointed to an almost full pint of Guinness, a half pint and an orange juice. 'Then he rushed outside.'

Pauline's concern made her voice tight in her throat. 'Has he gone? Where?'

Oskar sighed. 'Perhaps you'd better ask Len, Pauline.'

Pauline swivelled round just as the farmer was leaving his seat. He dragged himself to full height and faced her, his already ruddy face darkening, and exhaled.

'I only told him what he needed to hear.'

Pauline felt her heart thud. 'What did you say, Len?'

Gary's voice chimed in. 'Father was only thinking of you, Mrs Pye. He done the right thing, telling that tramp to sling his hook.'

Over her shoulder, Pauline heard Barbara's voice boom. 'He did what? He had no right to interfere.'

Pauline moved towards Len. 'What exactly did you say to him?'

'I told him the truth.' Len muttered, his eyes shifting away from Pauline. He was clearly embarrassed. 'I said he was taking advantage of a lady's good nature, living in your house and sleeping there and goodness knows what sort of man he might be. I said he should go away back to where he come from and leave you alone.'

'Father said it just like it was,' Gary added. 'He done you a good turn, Mrs Pye.'

Pauline breathed out. 'Len, you shouldn't have said that.' She felt tears prick her eyes, the back of her throat constricting, and angry words flew from her mouth. 'You have been a stupid man. Stupid. I am so... so cross with you, Len.'

Barbara watched her sister as she actually stamped her foot and rushed from the pub. Then she paused, took in Len's shamed face, his neck bent forward, and Gary's aggressive stance, his elbows pointing away from his body, and she turned on them both, loyalty uppermost in her mind.

'My sister is absolutely right. You've poked your noses in our business and it wasn't your place to do so.' She moved forward, then turned back with a flourish, proud of the fact that she had supported Pauline. 'Bisto has some good points. He's fixed the leaking tap. And you've interfered, which makes you just silly men.'

Outside the pub, Pauline had started up the VW Beetle. Barbara squeezed in beside her. 'What's happening? Are we off home now?'

Pauline turned sharply. 'No, we're not. We're going to look for Bisto. He can't have gone very far. We'll catch up with him and bring him back.'

12

It had rained heavily all night, the wind battering against the windowpanes. The temperature had dropped outside. Pauline had hardly closed her eyes all night, worrying about where Bisto had gone, and where he might be sleeping. She and Barbara had driven around for three hours after they'd left the pub, trying to find him, and Pauline had phoned Dizzy, Chrissie the vicar, and Kevin Carter, asking them all to keep an eye out for him, but no one had reported any positive news.

Wide awake in the small hours of Monday morning, she had thought about Len Chatfield, how he'd sent Bisto away, and her blood boiled with the injustice of it. Then the image of Len's kind eyes, his concern for her, piqued her and made her feel a little guilty for the words she had used. She'd called him stupid and she'd noticed his eyes widen with the hurt of her remark. Then she thought of Bisto again and was buffeted with the full force of anxiety. When sleep came it was fitful and troubled with snaggled dreams she couldn't remember.

The next day, she woke at six o'clock and hurried downstairs to the kitchen to find Barbara already there, drinking tea, perched on a chair in her winceyette nightie. Pauline reached for the kettle and poured hot water into a mug of instant coffee. She rubbed bleary eyes.

'I'm still so worried about Bisto. I hoped he'd come back in the night.'

Barbara sipped her tea, her forehead anxious. 'Shall we go out again and have another look?'

'I was thinking of maybe calling the police? Just in case...'

Barbara sighed. 'He could be miles away by now. Anywhere.'

'I'm just so cross.' Pauline clenched small fists. 'He was doing fine here. He was happy and we were all getting along so well. Then Len Chatfield had to intervene. I can't imagine what he was thinking about, telling Bisto he wasn't welcome?'

Barbara eyed her sister for a moment and shook her head. 'Perhaps it's a case of the green-eyed monster?'

'I don't know what you mean.' Pauline turned her back and reached for the breadknife, hacking huge slices from a loaf. 'Bisto can't walk properly yet. There was so much rain outside last night – he could have frozen to death. He didn't even come back to pick up his things or say goodbye...'

Barbara's chair scraped as she moved over to her sister and put her hands on Pauline's shoulders. She felt a strange surge of sisterly warmth.

'We'll find him. Let's have a slice of toast, put our coats on and then we'll set off to the village. We can ask the vicar to help, or Dizzy, and maybe the nice man up at the manor house, the distinguished young chap will lend a hand. We can form a search party to find him.' An idea came to Barbara. 'We should tell the farmer to come out and help us to look. And his miserable son. After all, they are to blame. They should help to find Bisto.'

Pauline turned and suddenly hugged her sister, her face flushed with gratitude. 'Thanks, Barbara. You're being so nice. I'll ring Chrissie as soon as we've had breakfast.'

Their eyes met and they both smiled and reached for their mugs at exactly the same time.

By seven o'clock, the Reverend Chrissie Drake had arrived, businesslike in jeans and a huge jumper. She had just gathered the sisters around the table to plan a route to look for Bisto, and decided that she would phone the local constabulary and hospitals, just in case, when there was a banging on the front door. Pauline heard a voice call, 'It's only me,' and Kevin Carter's ginger head appeared around the corner as he rushed into the kitchen, an anxious expression on his face. He was dressed in a heavy jacket and appeared to be in a hurry.

'Pauline, I heard about Bisto going missing.'

Chrissie answered for her. 'I know, Kevin. We're planning a huge move to find him today.'

'I just popped in to say I have a job in Thorpe this morning, but I'm going to drive through the back lanes and see if there's any sign of him. Then I'll take a detour up on the Blackdown Hills and look around there.'

Pauline offered a weak smile. 'Thanks, Kevin. I'm so worried.'

Kevin winked and his face broke into a grin. 'I heard you gave Len Chatfield a good rollicking. Poor bloke's looking a bit mystified – he was in the pub last night and couldn't work out what he'd done wrong.' Kevin winked. 'Don't worry, though. We'll find Bisto.'

Barbara sighed. 'He could be on a train or a ferry to somewhere far away already. Gone to stay with someone else, perhaps?' She thought for a moment. 'Or he could have found a pub...'

Kevin shook his head. 'He's a lovely fella. Great company. I think he's hit on hard times, though, from the things he's told me when we had a few jars together.'

'Why? What has he said?' Chrissie's brow was raised in concern.

Kevin grunted. 'Confessional talk, Chrissie. Can't reveal it. A confidence between him and me.'

'Of course,' Chrissie chimed.

'Well, I'll be in touch.' Kevin scratched his ginger thatch. 'Must be off now, Pauline. I see you have new neighbours, by the way. I've just seen the man across the lane leaving for work in a nice new BMW, wearing a stylish suit. He had a teenage girl with him in a smart uniform, carrying a violin case. Have you met them yet? All right, are they?'

Pauline chewed her lip. 'Can't say I've met the family. Julia seems nice; although I'm not sure she's ideally suited to country life.'

Barbara remembered the scene in Julia's kitchen, and she was about to add, 'Neither am I,' but she thought better of it. She was impressed by the way the villagers were rallying round Pauline. Kevin had dashed from the room on his way to work and Chrissie was assembling troops, on the phone to Dizzy.

'You are going where? Oh, yes, it's a good idea to ask Yvonne to mention it to people in the Post Office. No, don't bother Tilly – she'll be too busy working. Oh no – I'm not sure going to find Kostas will help, though, but if you really think he might have seen Bisto on his travels... no, Dizzy, best to come round here first, if you can spare the time.'

Pauline was thoughtful. 'Should I ring Natalie and Mario at the surgery? Just in case they've heard something?'

Chrissie shook her head. 'I saw Mario yesterday in church. Apparently Natalie was having a lie down. I think she's feeling the effects of pregnancy.'

Barbara had no idea what Chrissie meant: having a baby was what most women did – it was normal, it happened all the time, like delivering the post or boiling an egg. What could be the problem? She decided not to say anything. It was sometimes better to change the subject.

She piped up, 'Shall we all go out now? To see if we can find him outside the village? If we all go in different directions, we could cover a wide area.'

Pauline was already pulling her jacket on. 'Come on, then – let's make a start.'

They arrived at the front porch, Chrissie leading the way, Barbara struggling into an old jacket of Pauline's that was far too short in the arms, when Pauline called out, 'Oh look. It's Hugo, isn't it?'

A Jaguar F-type in British Racing Green had stopped by the gate. Pauline gazed past the distinguished man in a tweed jacket, a scarf knotted around his neck, dark sunglasses and thick blond hair, to a small older man huddled in a blanket, his eyes focused ahead, shining, his face expressionless.

'Bisto.' She rushed down the garden path, through the open gate to the passenger side of the car, hauling the door open. 'Bisto, it's so good to see you. We've been so worried...'

Bisto turned to her, blinking. His clothes and hair were drenched, his face was drawn and tired; his skin had a bluish-grey tinge. He forced a smile.

'It's the angels come to take me to heaven, is it?'

Hugo stepped from the car. 'Chrissie, nice to see you.' He hugged the vicar briefly, then turned to Barbara. 'And you must be Pauline's sister?'

Barbara took his gloved hand. 'Barbara Harvey. Pleased to meet you, Mr...?'

'Hugo Garrett. It seems I've found Bisto for the second time.' Barbara's expression was puzzled, so he added, 'I gave him a lift to Winsley in the first place. Then this morning, I got myself up early to drive to London and I passed him sleeping in a hedge, a couple of miles from the M5. He'd obviously been trying to find a lift and slept there all night.'

Pauline was supporting Bisto, with Chrissie helping her on the other side. She hugged the little man, who leaned against her, weak and baffled.

'I'm so glad you're back here. We've been worried, Bisto.'

'Let's fix him up with a good breakfast and a hot bath,' Chrissie suggested. 'We can sort everything else out afterwards.'

Barbara turned to the charming blond man and gave him an effusive smile, determined to show that she shared Pauline's generosity.

'Do you want to come inside and have a cup of coffee?'

Hugo extended a hand. 'Thank you, no. I'm already late for my London appointment.' For a moment his blue eyes were anxious, then he smiled at Barbara. 'Lovely to meet you, Barbara. I do hope you'll stay with us in Winsley for a while. It is a charming place, such nice people.'

'Thank you.' Barbara blushed and was immediately furious with herself. Hugo didn't appear to notice her awkwardness.

'It might be an idea to persuade Bisto to pop into the surgery and see Mario or Natalie at some point,' Hugo smiled, then slid back into the green Jaguar, raising a gloved hand in farewell.

Barbara nodded, wondering why she felt so uncomfortable talking to the polite young man. But she knew instantly. He reminded her so much of another young man, one she'd known years ago, someone who'd meant a lot to her once. Someone she wanted to forget about.

* * *

Bisto rubbed aching eyes and leaned back in his seat. He knew full well the appointment had gone on much longer than the expected eight minutes. Dr Mario Silva scratched his thick beard.

'There's no harm done. You have a clean bill of health. But thank you for sharing your story with me, Bisto. It can't have been easy for you.'

Bisto wiped a hand across his brow. It came away damp. He felt warm in the doctor's surgery, warmer than he'd felt since Sunday lunch time.

'It's been a tough time, to be honest. I hit the bottom like never before. The first time, after I stopped working twenty years ago, I was close to breakdown when my wife died. I knew I had to change everything and start again. I thought I'd be all right once I moved away and I held it together for a long time. I was happy and things were going well. Then – as I told you, I had to come back to Dublin for the funeral and I realised how much I'd let things slide. By that time it was too late and the grief hit me again.'

Dr Mario leaned forward. 'Do you find a drink helps you to forget?'

Bisto chuckled. 'Oh, I know when to stop. The odd pint helps me feel sociable. Since the embarrassing episode with Pauline's neighbour's roses, I've counted the units carefully.'

'You need to deal with the grief you've suffered, Bisto.'

'What do you suggest, Doctor?' Bisto stretched out his aching ankle. 'You're right. I have to make some changes. It's about time. I can only go back up again, for sure.'

'I know you don't want to take antidepressants and it's completely up to you.' Mario met Bisto's eyes. 'What about counselling? It'll definitely help and it's confidential, but you know all that already. If you're staying with Pauline a little longer, then I can recommend someone you could see privately.'

Bisto sighed and considered the doctor's words carefully. He nodded.

'I'll stay a little longer. I'm sure Pauline won't mind. And I'll rest my foot and do the counselling and I'll make myself useful about the house. After all, it's up to me to sort myself out.' Bisto held his hand out and Mario shook it. 'I mean, Doctor, the yo-yo of life may go up and down, but isn't it my own fingers that control the string?'

13

Bisto spent the next few days resting. Pauline insisted on bringing his meals on a tray, up to his room or in the conservatory, always with a smile or a little pleasantry. Even Barbara brought him sweet milky coffee and lent him a book about how ten thousand hours of practice could make you really good at something. Bisto gave a short laugh and joked, 'I must be the world's best drinker, then. I've had way more practice than ten thousand hours.'

On the Thursday, he'd attended the first private counselling session with a young man called Joe Parry in Taunton, seated in a cold room high on the top floor of an old building that was in desperate need of renovation. Joe was nice enough; a quietly spoken man in his early thirties, thinning brown hair, a wide smile and a range of qualifications from Dundee, but he didn't say very much. He encouraged Bisto to do the talking, but Bisto didn't really want to tell him anything. Joe Parry nudged him with questions about his childhood in Dublin, his five siblings, his parents, and Bisto treated the session as a tennis game, determined to knock back the balls, close down any conversation with a joke and avoid saying anything of any real importance. He was not looking forward to the next session the following week.

But on Saturday morning, Pauline stomped into his bedroom at eight o'clock, two eggs on toast and a cup of coffee on a tray, and announced, 'Good morning, Bisto. It's June the fourth. Do you like cricket? We're going to see a game in the village today.'

Bisto had never liked cricket. He'd played it once or twice in Dublin and once he'd been in a team with Randeep in Swindon for a charity match, but he didn't see the point in it. Randeep had loved it, he'd been a talented player, a skilful batsman, but Bisto always thought of himself as too short, too slow and too uninterested in anything other than the drinking that could be done during a match as a spectator. He sat up in bed, thinking of a well-stocked beer tent, and grinned.

'That'd be just grand. Thanks, Pauline. I love the cricket. I'm looking forward to it.'

Barbara wasn't looking forward to it, although, as the three of them reached the cricket field in the village, she had to admit it was a glorious day for a match. The grass was neatly mowed; there were tables out in the open, people sitting around with cool drinks, wearing bright clothes and sun hats, while the whole picture was illuminated in blinding sunlight. Barbara thought it was just like a watercolour painting. But she still didn't like cricket. When it was on television, she turned the channel over to something more sensible such as a documentary or a nice old film about one of the wars, starring John Mills or Richard Attenborough.

Pauline pulled her from her thoughts by pointing out a few people she knew: Kevin Carter was standing with his wife and an auburn-haired small child in a frilly dress: he would be captaining the Winsley team. The Priddy cousins, Andy and Jack, were already on the field with bats and a ball, Andy practising his skills. They were smart in white trousers and shirts, white hats and little sleeveless jumpers. Pauline said that Andy would captain the Milton Rogus team; they had won every year for the past thirteen years and took their game very seriously. Bisto noticed that Justina had set up a small beer tent at the far end of the field and, with a garbled excuse about needing to have 'a chat with yer man', he took off at a fast pace, leaning on his cane.

Barbara remarked through thin lips, 'That's the last we'll see of him today.'

Pauline merely smiled and gazed around at the spectacle. There was a hum of excited chatter from the observers, bubbling anticipation. The scoreboard was in place, Winsley Green at the top, as they were hosts, and Milton Rogus below, a blank space for the score. Chrissie the vicar was attempting to talk to two old ladies who were sitting several feet apart from each other, their deck chairs facing in opposite directions. Barbara recognised Dulcie and Phyllis from yoga. She studied them for a moment. Both at least well into their eighties, Dulcie was the slimmer, shorter one with winged glasses. Phyllis had tightly curled white hair. They both wore dark clothes and had no hats on their heads, which Barbara thought was unwise in the heat. She'd brought one of Pauline's; a huge turquoise straw hat with a rose in navy blue fabric, to go with her pale blue slacks and jaunty navy jacket. Pauline had worn a simple white cloche hat and a white jacket.

There were several men wearing cricket whites, talking energetically to each other, presumably discussing tactics. Barbara identified several of them: Oskar from the pub, Dr Mario, Gary Chatfield and, in the centre, Hugo Garrett from the manor house. Dr Natalie was sitting in the shade reading a book, her legs crossed, wearing a diaphanous pale skirt. A few feet away, Tilly Hardy was doing exactly the same thing, wearing a floaty purple hippy dress, round sunglasses and an orange wide-brimmed hat.

Then Barbara noticed Dizzy sidling up to a man who was lying on his back, stretched full-length on the grass. He was dressed in a sleeveless cricket jumper and white trousers. He sat up slowly, smiled at her, ran a hand through his dark curls and adjusted a pair of sunglasses. Barbara watched as Dizzy began to giggle. Kostas chuckled at her joke and put an arm on her shoulder. Then Dizzy noticed Pauline and waved her hand.

Pauline was staring at a man she hadn't seen before, smart in his cricket whites – dark-haired, in his forties, slim. He was talking to Julia from across the lane, so Pauline assumed it was her husband. Julia caught Pauline's eye, but ignored her friendly wave. She returned to the conversation with her husband, spoke a few firm, hurried words to him, and then twisted away, walking briskly in the direction of the exit.

'That was Julia, your neighbour,' Barbara observed. 'She's a strange one.'

'She looks so unhappy,' Pauline murmured.

Then Dizzy arrived, grabbed her in a hug and began to wave her arms around, her face illuminated in an ecstatic expression of bliss.

'He's playing for Milton Rogus, Pauline. Looking perfect in his cricket whites. Have you seen him? I mean, I don't really care about the game, I just want to look at him.'

Barbara frowned. 'Who on earth are you talking about?'

'I think she's referring to Kostas,' Pauline laughed.

The three women stared in the direction of the Greek god, impeccably dressed, his hands on his hips, sunglasses lodged on the top of his head, staring into the distance. Dizzy sighed. Barbara shook her head beneath the huge hat.

The three of them found a table with four chairs and sat down, deciding they would buy a drink later. Dizzy was still chattering about Kostas' obvious talents. Barbara settled back in her chair and picked up her book; she'd almost finished reading about how people became an expert after ten thousand hours of practice and how it made them outsiders. Barbara wondered if she was such a person. She'd always considered herself a little different. But being exceptional was a high price to pay for not being able to integrate with other people. Sometimes, she thought, it would be better to be gregarious, pleasant and simple, like Pauline. She put down her book and resolved to copy her sister and to try harder.

A shadow loomed across the table and she stared up into the blue eyes and ginger thatch of Kevin Carter. His face was twisted in an expression of urgency.

'Hi Pauline, Barbara. Hello, Dizzy, how are you?'

Dizzy immediately snatched up Barbara's non-fiction and buried her nose in it, as if she was reading avidly. Pauline smiled at Kevin.

'We're looking forward to the match. I hope you're going to lead Winsley to victory.'

Kevin pulled a face. 'Not much chance of that, with the Priddy boys playing for Milton Rogus. But we have a problem. We're a man down. Timmo Jackson's found himself a girlfriend and he'd rather be out with her than supporting his team.'

Barbara leaned forward. 'Why don't you ask one of the women? I'm sure there are plenty of athletic women in Winsley – what about you, Dizzy?'

Dizzy shoved her head closer to the book, her face reddening. Kevin pursed his lips. 'Old-fashioned village rules I'm afraid. We need a man, urgently.'

Barbara thought she heard Dizzy mutter, 'Don't we all,' from behind the open pages. She shrugged. 'Well, we don't have an answer for you, I'm afraid, Kevin.'

'I was hoping Bisto would help us out.'

'He still has a sore ankle,' Pauline shook her head. 'I'm not sure he'd be able to score many runs.'

'He'd be useful when we're fielding. Anything is better than nothing.' Kevin scratched his wiry ginger locks. 'Do you know where I can find him?'

Barbara brayed: it was a ridiculous question. 'In the beer tent. If you hurry, you might catch him while he can still stand upright.'

Kevin turned away and hurried in the direction of the tent. Barbara grabbed her book back from Dizzy. 'What's the matter with you?'

'This is an interesting looking book.' Dizzy was flustered.

'Bisto is borrowing it when I've finished with it. He's already halfway through it. I let him have it when he was in bed for a few days. But you're welcome to it afterwards.'

'Thanks,' Dizzy mumbled. She'd already lost interest. She'd caught sight of Tamsin and baby Harley a few yards away. Tamsin's blonde hair was loose, the light breeze blowing it across her face, and she wore a white shirt and a short denim skirt. Baby Harley was asleep on her shoulder, a little rosebud mouth and rounded cheeks visible beneath a white sun hat. Tamsin was talking to one of the cricket players, a tall athletic young man with brown hair.

'Tamsin's chatting up the opposition.'

Pauline followed her line of vision. 'That's Andy Priddy. He's a nice young man.'

'I'm not sure any man would want to take on a woman with a baby,' Barbara observed.

'I wonder. Perhaps he's secretly the father?' Dizzy turned to Barbara; her face still flushed. 'I always thought it was Hugo Garrett though. Tamsin works up at the manor house sometimes, cleaning and helping when he entertains.'

Barbara noticed Hugo Garrett, smart in his cricket whites, talking to Gary Chatfield, clearly engrossed in an animated conversation that involved waving of hands. She assumed they were talking business and she shouldn't intervene. Her eyes moved to the beer tent; she could just make out two figures, one limping slightly, the other urging him forward. Barbara guffawed; Kevin had found his extra man. Bisto, reluctant and unskilled, was going to be part of the match. This was suddenly going to be much more interesting.

Dizzy was still watching Tamsin and Andy Priddy. 'Do you think the baby looks like him? I'm sure Harley has Hugo's colouring.'

Pauline shook her head. 'I'm sure Tamsin wants to keep the details to herself.'

'But I'd love to know, wouldn't you?' Dizzy noticed a woman approaching them; a blonde in a blue miniskirt, identical to the one her daughter was wearing. She wriggled in her seat. 'Hello, Yvonne.'

'Mind if I join you?' Yvonne perched herself in the fourth seat, next to Pauline. 'Claudia is going to bring us a jug of Pimm's and some glasses. I thought it would be nice.'

'I don't drink,' Barbara grunted.

'I do,' Dizzy giggled. 'We were just saying what a nice couple Tamsin and Andy Priddy make.'

Pauline patted Yvonne's hand. 'The match is about to start. This should be exciting. Come on, Winsley!'

The men were taking their positions. Two clear teams moved across the grass. Winsley were to bat first. Kevin Carter shook Andy Priddy's hand. Barbara observed that the Milton Rogus cricket uniform was neater and whiter than the dingy kit sported by most members of Winsley Green. Milton Rogus were smarter and sharper almost to a man. Even Kostas, who was currently sporting a white peaked cap over his dark curls, looked impressively professional compared to the bedraggled Winsley side.

The Winsley team were lining up to bat as Claudia arrived with a jug full of bright pink liquid loaded with sliced apples, strawberries and peaches, and several glasses. Barbara thought it looked refreshing, just like a soft drink, so she accepted a glass. She swallowed a mouthful of sweet liquid and gazed back at the players.

Only Kevin and Hugo seemed to have any idea what to do. Dr Mario was waving energetically and beaming at Natalie, showing very little interest in the game. The neighbour, Peter, held his bat with a degree of confidence and behind him, Gary Chatfield seemed bored, moody and truculent. The rest of the team milled about with a demeanour of no interest at all. At the back of the line of men, some distance away, was Bisto, clad in cricket trousers that were far too long for him and which dragged on the ground, a cricket vest that came almost to his knees, leaning heavily on his cane. He was staring around himself, looking extremely confused. Barbara giggled and topped up her glass of Pimm's. This was going to be fun.

14

Barbara closed her eyes and let the streaming sunlight filter golden rays through her lashes. She felt relaxed, pleasant and strangely soft around the edges. Breathing deeply made her want to sigh and she stretched her limbs and exhaled, making a long luxurious sound. The floppy blue hat kept the top of her head in the shade, but her face was bathed in warmth. A flourish of clapping and a few cheers broke the silence and made her blink her eyes and sit up. 'How are we doing, Pud?'

'Pauline,' Pauline reminded her gently. 'And we are doing surprisingly well. Our neighbour is batting at the moment – he's Peter Darby and he's just scored some excellent runs. I think we have Milton Rogus worried.'

'When is Bisto batting?'

'He's next up, I think,' Dizzy suggested, her eyes roving around the cricket-white clad men. 'Oh, just look at Kostas now. He's got his shirt off and he's sitting on the grass, glowing in the sunlight. What a hunk.'

'He's not playing much cricket, that's for sure,' Yvonne

remarked. 'But he's the best excuse for fielding I've seen this afternoon.'

'I hope Bisto will be all right.' Pauline was watching the little man, sprawled on the ground with both feet sticking out, scratching his white curls. 'He doesn't look ready for this.'

'He can't be worse than Gary Chatfield. What a terrible innings. Andy Priddy bowled him out first go.' Yvonne adjusted dark shades. 'We haven't seen anything of Len here today. That's unusual.'

Pauline pressed her lips together and stared out into the distance, wondering sadly if Len had gone to ground since she had called him a stupid man in the pub. She'd spoken a little harshly and it pricked at her conscience and wouldn't go away. Yvonne reached for the quarter-full jug of Pimm's.

'Pauline's just requested another one of these – who wants to finish the last of this one?'

'I'll have some,' Dizzy grinned but Barbara was already holding out her glass.

She clutched her cool drink in her hand and took a deep draught, leaning back and closing her eyes. She liked the way her body felt wrapped in the chair, almost merging with it. She sighed and let the fruity sweetness of the drink soak into her tongue. She was glad she'd come to stay at Winsley Green after all. Her sister had some nice friends and the relaxing rest was doing her good, just as the doctor had ordered. She wasn't missing her terraced house in Cambridge and the slight guilt she had been feeling this morning at leaving it empty had miraculously melted away in the sunshine. It occurred to her that she might be mellowing a little: she wasn't sure.

Barbara recalled that when she'd retired from the Air Force over fifteen years ago, she'd spoken about the intention of leading an energetic life and making new friends. She'd succeeded partially; she'd been busy, trying a variety of new activities, joining clubs and offering to take on new responsibilities. She recalled how the man who ran the local walking group, an ex-Scout leader himself, had reacted a little crossly when she'd suggested that they start earlier on their coastal walks and finish later, that the routes selected were somehow inadequate for the serious walker. She'd tried to make friends at the art class, but she thought the art teacher in her orange floral leggings lacked rigour and clarity in her instructions.

'Just draw what you feel' didn't cut it for Barbara, especially when faced with a naked woman whose body was far too lascivious to commit to paper without the drawing resembling pornography. Of course, Barbara had spoken her mind and moved on to another class.

The years brought new classes: Introduction to Spanish; Pottery with Sue; Stained Glass Windows for Beginners; Singing for Positivity; Understand Your Personality. Barbara had tried them all, approaching the first session with enthusiasm and gusto, intending to become one of a community and to offer her many skills readily, but she'd seldom enjoyed anything or made friends. There had been an older man called Stanley Allenby who'd tried to befriend her during the Gardening in Containers class ten years ago, but he was clearly only seeking a replacement for his wife who'd run off with the teacher of Plastering for Fun, and Barbara found his attentions and his regular need to wipe his nose on the back of his hand annoying.

She sighed and brought the glass of fruity liquid to her lips. She hadn't made many friends; they hadn't really been her type. In fact, they belonged to two quite distinctive types: the boring ones who clung to her for direction and the bossy ones who seemed aloof and unwilling to get to know her. Barbara didn't mind, really. She'd carried on regardless, trying out different things. Over the last few years, she'd spent more time at home. It wasn't her age. She was seventy-seven but, thankfully, she was still fit and, apart from the dizzy spell that had landed her in hospital when she'd over-exerted herself, she was doing fine. She would slow down when she was ready.

But she had to admit, the delicious Pimm's had made her feel so floaty and relaxed that she might even become used to the steady pace of country living. Pauline was right on this count at least: Winsley Green seemed a pleasant place.

There was a sudden noise, like a cow in pain, and Barbara allowed her eyes to flicker open. The sound increased: it was a loud booing, replaced quickly by a ripple of laughter. Barbara sat up. 'What happened?'

Dizzy was giggling into her hand, but Pauline's face was anxious. 'Look at Bisto.'

The little man was sprawled on the ground flat on his face, his cane in front of him, his arms outstretched.

'He fell over.' Dizzy's eyes were full of tears and she was spluttering with laughter.

'I hope his ankle's all right.' Pauline stood up to get a better view. 'Bisto came up to bat. Andy Priddy bowled him out first go and, as he rushed forward, he stumbled and fell over his long trousers flat on his face.'

Bisto had scrambled to his feet and was bowing to the crowd, who were now cheering him. He raised his arms, a cane in one hand and a bat in the other, and attempted a little jig before falling on his bottom, to be rewarded with another rapturous cheer.

'He's clowning about,' Yvonne mumbled. 'We won't get many runs like that. Oh, look. Dr Mario is up to bat now.'

Barbara glanced over to the beer tent. 'Do you think I should buy us another jug of this lovely pop? I can see we're running low.'

Dizzy scrambled to her feet; her forehead and nose had turned salmon pink beneath the red hair. 'I'll go, shall I, Barbara?'

'Bring two jugs.'

Barbara handed her a ten pound note from her purse and settled back in her seat, watching Dizzy strut across the grass in spiky heels, not directly heading to the tent but making a definite detour in the direction of the mound of grass where Kostas sat, his legs stretched out, nonchalantly sucking a blade of grass as the ball sailed over his head. Dr Mario had scored his first run.

By the end of Barbara's next glass of Pimm's, the teams had changed sides or ends – she wasn't completely sure which, but it meant that Kevin Carter had enjoyed a brilliant innings and Winsley were finishing on a high. Milton Rogus had started to bat and Kostas was in first.

She watched him, poised with the bat as if someone were taking snapshots of him as the centrefold of *Cricketer Weekly*. He stood still, smiling, arm muscles flexed, long legs in the white trousers that were rolled over his knees, then he ran a hand through dark curls, tilted his head back and turned, offering his profile. He posed again, bat raised aloft in muscular arms, as the bowler Peter Darby launched a ball and it flew straight past him and smashed the wicket. Cheers filled the air and Barbara assumed it must be good for Winsley, so she clapped and refilled her glass. Kostas grinned and sauntered away, the bat dropping from his fingers onto the ground. Jack Priddy stepped up to bat next and Barbara filled her mouth with sweet Pimm's and a soft slice of peach.

The glorious June warmth enveloped her face and body and lifted her gently. She began to snooze, conscious of the trickle of applause in the distance. The deep blue canopy of the sky above her warmed her face with the orange rays of the sun. She frowned, breathed deeply, a little snuffle in her nose, and relaxed. It occurred to her that lying in the sun with the sugary taste of fruit juice on her tongue would be the best way to die. She was filled with a feeling of not caring about anything at all, like a light balloon buffeted on a breeze, with no interest in what direction it floated or landed.

When she had fallen down on her front doorstep, over two months ago now, she'd thought she'd died and, while she was in hospital, she felt twinges of remorse at the many missed opportunities in her life. Now she felt no regrets at all; just a comforting, numbing warmth, like lying in a warm bubble bath or being lifted on a gently rocking wave. She was happy. Death held no fear for her now, although she'd probably live many more years in good health. She wasn't afraid to be alone.

A thought tickled behind her mind and stuck. She hadn't wanted a partner, or someone to love. Robert had put paid to that, perfect Robert with his thick blond hair, his green eyes and his lopsided smile. Robert, whom she'd loved unconditionally: she'd promised to wait for ever, despite the fact that she could only see him when he could find excuses to get away. She'd trusted him and, afterwards, she'd vowed she'd never trust another man. Heartbreak came at too high a price and being alone was safer: by herself, she was sure of the rules; her heart was secured behind the bars of a cage and only she held the key. That would be the way of it for always.

But Pauline was alone now and, after many years of not wanting to visit her with a jolly but tedious husband in tow, Barbara was beginning to enjoy her sister's company. She thought about Pauline for a moment and was surprised at the warmth that lifted her lungs in a deep sigh. Pauline was strong, independent, coping well with living by herself, but she must feel the loss; Douglas was dead and, even though he hadn't been very interesting when he was alive, Barbara thought he must've been better than nothing at all for her gentle, gregarious sister.

Pauline seldom saw her only child Jessica, who was grown up, in her late forties now, overseas in New Zealand with her husband and children. She and Douglas had travelled there several years ago and Barbara recalled Pauline saying that she'd sobbed until her heart broke on the plane on the way home to the UK. She said she felt like she'd left the best part of herself behind; her womb had been wrenched and was empty, aching and would never repair itself. Barbara had snorted and thought that it was a silly thing to say.

She'd said that aloud to Pauline. 'What a silly thing to say, Pud. You are too sentimental.' Yes, she had said that. Barbara knew now that she had been thoughtless.

It was no wonder she and Pauline hadn't been close. But now she was bathing in a liquid emotion not unlike love. She was happy and floating and her eyes were closed, her heart singing, her fingers tingling, a strand of curly hair tickling her cheek. It was a very pleasant feeling and one she wanted to hold on to; she longed to remain buoyant and cocooned in this ambient happiness that tasted of fruit juice and melting peaches. Her eyelashes filtered bright sunlight and she blinked and eased herself upright. Her glass was empty, and Dizzy filled it again as she extended her hand.

Barbara murmured, 'Where are we?' Yvonne, Dizzy and Pauline were sitting forward, not unlike the three wise monkeys, thought Barbara, and a laugh spluttered through her lips. She swallowed more Pimm's. 'What's so interesting?'

Pauline didn't take her eyes from the cricket game. 'Andy Priddy's in to bat and he's doing well. It's getting close between Milton Rogus and us now. A few more runs and they'll beat us. He's scored lots of runs already – Kevin's bowling the best he can, but Andy's on a roll.'

Barbara shook her head. Her vision cleared for a moment and misted over again. Pauline's words made no sense. 'So Whimsy are fielding?'

Dizzy murmured. 'It's on a knife edge. We're going to lose.'

Barbara didn't understand. 'So where's Bisto?'

Dizzy pointed into the distance, where Bisto was sitting in the grass, his long cricket trousers rolled above his knees, focused on massaging his ankle. 'He's fielding, or supposed to be. I saw him a minute ago looking in the other direction, towards the beer tent.'

'He's not the athletic type,' Yvonne grinned.

'I imagine his ankle is sore,' Pauline suggested, her eyes full of sympathy.

Barbara leaned forward, sitting up straight and staring ahead; all four women were poised on the edge of their seats, glasses in hand, as Kevin Carter scratched his ginger head, then rubbed the ball on his white clad thigh and took two steps back. The four women held their breath as Kevin ran forward, hurled an arm in the air and let the ball go in a perfect arc towards Andy Priddy. Andy raised his bat and walloped the ball, and the four women turned their heads in perfect synchronisation as the ball flew through the air, past Bisto, and rolled into a mound of grass.

There were shouts of, 'Get the ball, Bisto,' and other phrases less delicate, not befitting the English sport, and Bisto raised himself languidly, grinned, limped forward, picked up the ball, studied it for a moment and then tossed it carelessly a few metres from Kevin.

'This is it,' Dizzy whispered. 'If Andy makes two runs now, they've won.'

Kevin prepared to bowl again, repeating the magic ritual of rubbing the ball against his thigh. The four women each held their breath as he took a little skip and then ran to Andy Priddy, hurling the ball hard. The Milton Rogus batsman leaned forward, lifted his bat and walloped the ball into the air, starting to run immediately. The ball soared high, against a backdrop of perfect blue sky, held its curve and then began to drop. Below, Bisto was taking a swig from his flask. The ball plummeted downwards, and the crowd yelled 'Bisto!' with one voice.

Bisto glanced up, surprised at the huge object that was hurtling towards his eyes. He lifted a hand and raised his palm over his head, to stave off the missile. By some miracle, it landed with a loud plop in his hand and he yelped as he fell over onto his back, holding the ball high in the air. His ankle twisted beneath him.

'Caught out!' Dizzy screamed and Pauline was on her feet, cheering and clapping. Yvonne leaped up, joining in the chant of, 'Bisto! Bisto! Bisto!'

Barbara gazed around her, and, for an instant, she wasn't sure what had happened. Then she swallowed the last mouthful of Pimm's and threw herself to her feet, yelling, 'Bisto is the champion!'

At once, she couldn't feel her legs. Her knees buckled and her thighs were useless, soft as jelly beneath her. They folded like concertinas as she hit the ground and rolled flat on her back. Pauline gasped, bending over her immediately, her face contorted with shock.

'Barbara? Barbara? Are you all right? Yvonne, fetch Dr Mario.'

Barbara was still for a moment, her blue hat crumpled beneath her head, then her eyelids flickered open and her mouth moved. Her face twitched, contorted and she began to laugh. Her laughter became a snort then a cackle, and she was rolling on her back in the grass, her legs pedalling in the air.

'Barbara?' Pauline loomed over her as Barbara's eyes watered. 'Barbara? What is the matter?'

Barbara's voice raised in a howl; her face creased with delight. 'I've never had so much fun. Cricket is wonderful. Pauline, help me back up to the seat and get me another jug of that lovely fruity pop. We need to celebrate.'

15

Bisto shifted his weight from one buttock to the other, wriggled in his seat and stretched out his foot, encased in a sandal. The ankle still ached a bit, even though it was eight weeks since he'd sprained it. He had twisted it again during the cricket match two days ago. Barbara hadn't shown him much sympathy. She'd been more interested in the Pimm's than his display of athleticism, although, he had to admit, the catch had been a pure fluke. He shook his head – Joe's soft voice was buzzing in his ears. 'What did you say, Joe?'

Joe Parry ran thin fingers through his sparse brown hair and replied in a hushed voice. 'We were talking about your family.' He met Bisto's eyes and assumed an expression that was somewhere between patience and pity.

Bisto shrugged. 'Sorry, Joe. I was somewhere else for the minute. My family?'

Joe breathed out slightly, not enough to show irritation. 'You were one of six children? In Dublin?'

'That's true. I still am. Well, I would be, but they're all gone now, except for my brother Pat in Canada and my sister Noreen in

Australia, and I haven't heard from her for almost a year, so she might be gone too.' Bisto glanced at the ceiling, remembering.

Joe breathed quietly for a while. Bisto glanced at the clock. He only had ten minutes left. He'd be able to procrastinate for most of that time. Already, he'd managed to say very little about his father who'd died when he was fourteen and nothing at all about his mother, having told three anecdotes about his Uncle Barty's fondness for the black stuff and his grandfather's eightieth birthday party in a two-up-two-down terraced house in Crumlin.

Joe's voice interrupted his thoughts. 'Tell me about your wife, Bisto.'

Bisto thought Joe's voice was soft as cotton wool but his questions were sharp as barbed wire. He laughed. 'Which one?'

Joe made a low humming noise, not unlike an electrified fence. 'We can do them in a chronological order if you like.'

Bisto shrugged. 'My first wife, Maeve. Barney's mother. Lovely woman, she was. She had the face of an angel but she'd a temper on her, though.'

'Did you love her?'

Bisto squirmed in his seat. 'Love. It's an interesting concept that one, Joe. You're a married man, I suppose? You know about the vagaries of love?'

'I'm not married. So – we were discussing Maeve...'

'No, I don't think I did love her. Love, no – maybe lust, at first, ah yes, it was all true lust.' Bisto guffawed. Joe was staring at him. 'She threw me out when Barney started university. I wanted to get away as far as possible, so I took up a job in Swindon and met Nisha. That was real love. But the time factor kicked in there, didn't it?'

'I don't understand.' Joe wrinkled his brow.

'I was married to Maeve for twenty years when I lived in Dublin. We had our boy, Barney, and that kept us together for a while and anyway I was always at work. I was only with Nisha for eight years, in Swindon.'

Joe's face took on a sad, hangdog expression. 'What happened to you and Nisha, Bisto?'

Bisto closed his eyes, remembering the beautiful face, the spill of long hair and the tendril that always hung over her left eye, the strand of hair he'd brush from her face with gentle fingers. He remembered Nisha's laughter, her small frame, her shining brown eyes. Then it came to him, the image of her face on the pillow, her lids closed for the last time, her face the unnatural colour of milky tea, and Randeep tugging him away, crushing him in strong arms while he howled against the pristine white coat.

'She was just fifty years old.' Bisto glanced at the clock. It was almost one. 'Well Joe, it's time I was going. Pauline will be waiting outside. There are double yellow lines...'

Joe stood up slowly, pressing a hand against his damp forehead before offering it, outstretched, to Bisto. 'Right, shall I see you next week, same time, Bisto?'

'I'm not sure, Joe.' Bisto turned to go.

'Perhaps you'd like to write something down for me to read? A memory that you think is particularly significant. Something special, something you find difficult to speak about, something deep and precious to do with your feelings. Your mother or Nisha, perhaps?'

'I'm not one for writing things down all that much, not now.' Bisto grinned. 'I always had to write everything down when I...' He paused. He was saying too much. 'Ah, well, that's it then. Maybe I'm done with the counselling now. I'd hit the bottom hard but maybe it's time for me to find my own way up. I need to get my dignity back, and become the old Bisto again. I think you've helped me take the first few steps to realising that. Thanks. Thanks a lot, Joe.'

* * *

The sun streamed through the cottage windows and the savoury smell of lunch hung in the air. It was well past two o'clock. Pauline had made everyone some cheese on toast and mugs of tea. She led Bisto into the narrow wooden conservatory where plants were lined up on the painted shelf. The small cane sofa was empty except for the pale green cushions. Barbara was sitting in a wicker chair with her eyes half- closed. Bisto chuckled.

'Been sucking on the Pimm's again, Babs?'

Barbara closed her eyes. 'I was resting... oh, the rarebit smells lovely, Pauline.'

Bisto took his plate and limped to a seat. 'I'm starved. Thanks Pauline, love.'

'I'm sorry we're all so squashed in this little conservatory,' Pauline muttered. 'It's only really big enough for two people.'

Bisto took a mouthful of toast. 'Ah, but it has a great view onto the garden and across to the road. You can see all the plants and flowers, the apple trees and gravel drive and the fishpond from here, and then it looks out on to the scenery up the hill.'

'And Julia's house beyond the lane,' Barbara remarked. 'We haven't seen much of her, though. Do you think she's depressed? Perhaps she's gone on holiday? Or perhaps she's just left?'

Pauline shook her head. 'She was hanging washing outside this morning. I couldn't get her to wave back or notice me. I think she's on her own once Peter's gone off to work.'

'What does he do?'

'No idea, Barbara.'

'He must be doing well for himself, Pauline. That's a very expensive car.'

'Mmm,' Bisto was chewing the final morsel of toast. 'It's the last day of June today. I was just thinking...'

Pauline glanced up, alarmed. 'Oh no, Bisto. You can't be ready to leave yet – your ankle will take another week or two, surely...'

Bisto wiped his mouth. 'No, I was thinking... you've been so kind, putting me up here. How about I sort out this old conservatory for you?'

Barbara raised her eyebrows. 'It certainly needs a tidy and a good vacuum. There are cobwebs and dead flies...'

'No, I mean sort it out properly.' Bisto's face cracked into a smile. 'I'll knock it all down, even the dwarf wall, and build you a garden room – all oak wood and big panes of glass. I've the money. My way of saying thanks.'

Pauline looked alarmed. 'Isn't that a bit specialist, Bisto? I mean, it would take a lot of time...'

'I've rebuilt things before – I renovated parts of my château. I can do it in eight weeks, including removing all the rubble.' Bisto nodded. 'I'll build you a really nice garden room. It'll be done by the end of August. And then I'll go back to France.'

Pauline's face was flustered, so Barbara said, 'It needs doing correctly.'

Bisto was on his feet. 'Then you can be the boss, Barbara. I'll do the labour and you can be the forewoman. After it's finished, maybe it'll be time for us to go home, the both of us.' He winked at her and she sat back in her seat, shaking her head.

Pauline looked at Bisto and then back at Barbara. She was enjoying the fact that there were happy voices in her house after so much silence; there were people sharing her food around the table, smiles and laughter and she was the host, the centre of the home, the heart of it all. Bisto's presence, his mischief and lightness, was a perfect antidote for Barbara's frostiness. Barbara, Pauline knew, would be much more abrasive and difficult to spend time with if the little man wasn't around to thaw the ice. Pauline extended a soft hand.

'It's a lovely idea, Bisto. You have a deal. Barbara?'

Barbara shrugged. 'It's much longer than I'd intended to stay. What about my house?' She wrinkled her nose. 'Well, all right. It will certainly be an experience, being the forewoman. And after all, I do know how to be in charge.' She turned stern eyes on Bisto. 'But I won't allow any slacking. Or sloppy workmanship.'

Bisto saluted her. 'You're the boss, Babs.'

'We can start on Monday,' Pauline smiled, triumphant. 'This afternoon, I'm going up to the hill outside the village to see Dulcie and her neighbour, Phyllis. I have some fudge cakes to take up and I want to check how they are doing. You can both come with me if you want.'

Barbara wrinkled her nose. 'Those two grumpy old ladies,' she muttered. 'Cantankerous old biddies.'

'It'll be good craic,' Bisto muttered. 'How about a bit more of the cheese on toast before we go, Pauline?'

* * *

Dulcie lived on the outskirts of Winsley Green, her tiny cottage perched at the end of a long path. Pauline knocked at the old brown door, although it was ajar. The paint was flaking and the smell of mould came from inside the house. Bisto and Barbara stood behind Pauline as she clutched two small chocolate tins to her chest. They waited in silence for a while, then Pauline knocked again. A small lady with bandy legs and winged glasses emerged into the hallway and her voice reached them, creaky as a rusty hinge.

'Pauline, is that you? I wasn't expecting visitors. Well, you'd better come in. I can make a pot of tea.'

The kitchen was tiny, with a small ancient Aga in the corner and a black kettle hissing on a top plate. The room was cluttered with small ornaments, knick-knacks and faded photos in dull silver frames. Dulcie scuttled around, pouring strong orange tea into cracked white china cups.

'Don't often get visitors... very nice of you to bring me the cakes. I do enjoy the fudge... not too harsh on my teeth.' Dulcie grinned and she didn't appear to have many teeth. Her hair was pale and her scalp showed through, a light pink. 'I'm ninety-eight,' Dulcie smiled and immediately scrabbled into her armchair and began sucking on one of Pauline's fudgy cakes.

'My own mother was a similar age – you're looking well, Dulcie,' Bisto murmured and sipped his tea.

Barbara pushed her cup away; she was not going to drink something that looked as if it had come straight from the inside of a leaky radiator. Pauline appeared not to notice the awful tea or the mess in the kitchen, the crumbs, the half-finished meals on cracked plates, empty cellophane wrappers and something on the floor that looked like discarded dingy underwear. Barbara wrinkled her nose and turned to Bisto, who was making Dulcie cackle with his compliments, telling her she was a fine figure of a woman for her age and he was sure she'd been a great looker – well, she still was, even now. Barbara sighed: Bisto could spout some rubbish, but it seemed to amuse Pauline.

Dulcie started on her second fudge cake, wriggling back into the softness of her tattered chair. There was a drawn-out sound like fabric ripping. It was quickly followed by a putrid smell like rotting garden vegetables. It wasn't the creaky chair springs. Dulcie had passed wind. Barbara turned her nose away, but Pauline was still chattering about the delicious free-range eggs Dizzy sourced from her mother in Thorpe when Dulcie's chair made a second tearing sound. Barbara tried not to breathe; the room stank like a sewer. Then Dulcie cried out in delight.

'Here they are, my babies.'

Two ragged cats slunk into the room, one black, the other

similar but with white paws. The black cat eyed Barbara suspiciously then showed her its fangs before springing on Dulcie's knee. The old lady kissed its flat head with pursed lips, making her voice soft and sonorous.

'Derek, my love. Come and sit with Mummy.'

Derek appeared not to mind Dulcie's noxious smell; he bedded himself on her knee and was immediately joined by the other cat, who pressed white paws against Dulcie's bony chest and made space for itself next to the first cat.

'Clive, my darling boy.' She smiled at Barbara. 'They are brothers, you know. They are the joys of my life.' Dulcie made the ripping sound again and grinned. 'My boys, my babies.'

Barbara stood up. 'We should be going, Pauline.'

Bisto grinned. 'I'll just finish this lovely cuppa.' He swallowed the dregs with relish.

Pauline clasped the second chocolate tin. 'I'm going to drop some fudge cakes off with Phyllis now.'

'Oh, no – don't do that.' Dulcie waved an arm above the cats on her knee, who were purring, eyes closed. 'She'll probably enjoy them. I'd hate for that miserable old cow to enjoy anything.'

Barbara pulled a face. 'That's not very neighbourly.'

Dulcie squeezed her lips together as if she'd just sucked on a lemon. 'She hates my cats, doesn't she, my boys? She's a nasty piece of work, Phyllis. We wouldn't cry if she dropped down dead, would we Derek, Clivey?'

Pauline moved over to the old armchair and hugged Dulcie. 'We'll see you soon; I'll bring you a pie; the apples on my trees are ripe now. You like Bramleys, don't you?'

Dulcie nodded, rubbing a bony hand over Derek's spiky fur. 'We all love Pauline's cooking, don't we, Derek? You like a nice bit of cakey, too.'

Barbara marvelled at Pauline's warmth and kindness,

wondering how her sister could stand being so close to an old woman who smelled of putrid farts. She was longing for the fresh clean summer air as she turned to the doorway. Leaving Dulcie's cottage was like emerging from the Black Hole of Calcutta.

Across a narrow path, behind a tall hedge, was Phyllis' small cottage. Pauline noticed with a wry glance that Phyllis had filled the hedge with a roll of barbed wire, that she had set several broken beer bottles on her brick barbecue, and that there was a huge wooden sign with the painted words 'KEEP YORE FILTHEY ANIMALS OF THIS PROPPERTY'. Phyllis' cottage was dingy, the yellowing rendering cracked and the windows grimy. Barbara was about to knock on the door, dismayed at the cobwebs that hung in every corner and the huge deceased spiders that hung black and brittle with protruding legs, but Pauline shook her head.

'She won't be in the house. Phyllis will be in the caravan. It's summertime.'

She led the way past a narrow garden brimming with flowers: sweet peas, geraniums, nasturtiums; there was a mass of vibrant colour everywhere. Phyllis' caravan had been a pale colour once but now it was dingy grey, leaning to one side. Where the wheels had been, it was propped up with breeze blocks. Phyllis came down the steps to meet them wearing a vast floral dress and rolled down stockings that hung around her ankles. She eased herself forward heavily on a knobbly walking stick and chuckled.

'Hello, Pauline. I see you've brought all your family. Give me a hand – we'll sit outside.'

There was a small plastic table with three dirty chairs by the side of the caravan. Pauline helped Phyllis in to one of the chairs. Barbara smoothed her jeans and sat on the ground, deciding it was definitely the cleanest place to be. As Bisto sank into a rickety seat, Phyllis turned to Pauline.

'Be a dear and pop into the caravan. I've left Stinger on the table. Can you bring him out for me, please?'

Barbara watched Pauline disappear into the caravan, hoping it wouldn't tip over while she was inside. She half-wondered who Stinger was, and hoped it wouldn't be another nasty animal like Dulcie's cats. Bisto offered Phyllis a cake and she helped herself to two, chewing with her mouth open.

'Pauline is such a good cook. I hear you're staying with her, young man. She's a good sort, but she could do with a proper man about the house.'

Bisto beamed. 'We've just been after visiting your neighbour, Dulcie.'

'Oh, she's no neighbour of mine.' Phyllis rubbed stubby fingers through her wiry hair and frowned. 'Dulcie and her Feral Peril. I have no time for any of them.'

'She looks good for ninety-eight, for sure.'

Phyllis stared at Bisto. 'She's not ninety-eight. We were in the same class at school together and I'm not yet ninety-three. She always lied about her age, that one. She'd knock ten years off until she got to eighty, then she added ten on, for sympathy. No, young man, don't believe a word of what she says. She's a born liar. It's me you should all be worried about, not her. Me, with my terrible aching hip and the doctors won't do a single thing. Arthritis, it is, and I can hardly get about now...'

Barbara closed her eyes. The sunlight was bright and her eyes had become sleepy. A bee buzzed in a sweet-scented flowerbed and Barbara wrapped her arms around her knees and laid her head down. From the corner of her drowsy eyes, Barbara noticed Pauline walking gingerly down the caravan steps carrying a long-barrelled gun. She sat upright, a gasp in her throat. 'Pauline?'

Bisto watched the old lady grasp the gun from Pauline. He took in Barbara's shocked expression and smiled.

'Sure, that's an old-fashioned air rifle you have there, Phyllis. I suppose it's for shooting the vermin, is it? Rats?'

Phyllis turned to him and set her teeth, gripping the rifle. 'Stinger, that's my name for him. And yes, I have him to shoot rats. But that's not the only thing I keep him for.'

Bisto shrugged. 'Maybe a rabbit or two? Or a pheasant in the autumn time?'

'Cats.' Phyllis spat the word. 'Those damned cats next door. One day, I'll have them both, you can be sure of that.'

Pauline's voice was soothing as she patted Phyllis' hand. 'Dulcie loves Derek and Clive, Phyllis. They aren't so bad.'

'They kill all my wild birds.'

Phyllis huffed through her nose, raised the air rifle and aimed it at her barbecue where several broken beer bottles had been lined up. She closed one eye and gazed down the barrel, a position that made her resemble a cowboy in a Wild West drama, and squeezed the trigger. A whiplash shot rang out and one of the bottles splintered, glass shards tinkling to the ground. Phyllis reloaded, fired another, shattering a second bottle with a crack shot. She turned to Bisto and snarled. 'If Dulcie lets those cats roam about on my land, they may not return alive.'

Pauline covered a smile with her palm and Barbara met her sister's eyes, her own horrified and wide. Pauline winked at her.

'It's just rural ways, Barbara. There's really nothing to worry about. Phyllis won't harm the cats.'

Barbara was mystified by Pauline's calmness, her lack of surprise. She folded her arms across her chest and huffed loudly. 'Rampant cats, smelly-bottomed neighbours and Granny Clampitt shooting beer bottles off the barbecue with a rifle? It was never like this in *Country Life Magazine*.'

16

Pauline crossed the road, clutching the bunch of flowers in her hand. As the blooms fanned forwards and back in the breeze, the fragrance wafted in front of her nose and she sighed. Although it wasn't yet ten o'clock, the air was already warm and the turquoise sky was cloudless. It was going to be a hot day and she was glad of the loose yellow sleeveless frock that swirled below her calves and allowed cooler air to tickle the backs of her knees. Her hair was freshly washed and loose, silver strands shifting around her sun-pinked cheeks.

She wondered briefly if she might see Len Chatfield passing in his tractor. He'd stopped calling round to the house since she'd been cross with him in the pub over his attitude to Bisto. There had been no knocks at the door, no fresh vegetables, no chatting on the doorstep, not for a while now. And she was anxious to see him, to put his mind at rest. She shouldn't have been angry with him and called him stupid; he was a protective sort of man; he hardly knew Bisto and he had only been concerned for her wellbeing.

The idea flitted into her head that she could invite Len round for dinner. He and Bisto might get on famously and even Barbara wouldn't be able to resist his laconic charm and honest generosity. It would be nice to see him again and, Pauline thought, it was up to her to build bridges.

The image of the four of them sharing a meal made her giggle, a thrill of excitement. She approached the gate to her neighbour's house. The lawns were neatly clipped and the hedges trimmed, but Julia Darby was nowhere to be seen. Pauline rang the front door-bell, and listened while the light chimes resonated inside the house. She waited a little longer.

The sweet peas still in her fist, Pauline followed the path around to the back of the house and called, 'Yoo-hoo. Anyone at home?'

As she turned the corner, she saw a young woman lying on a lounger, a paperback novel in front of her face, who immediately glanced up, wide-eyed and nervous, like a colt. Pauline guessed she was about eighteen years old. She was wearing sunglasses, a strappy white vest top and a short, layered skirt, her long slim legs stretched out in front of her. She had no shoes on her feet and her toenails were painted black. Pauline beamed, to make the girl feel more at ease and said, 'Hello. Lovely day, isn't it?'

The girl huddled back into the seat, scrutinised Pauline's long floral dress and frowned. 'We're not buying anything.'

Pauline took a breath. That was exactly what Julia had said when they'd first met. The girl was so like Julia in appearance too.

'I'm your neighbour – I was looking for Julia.' Pauline held out the flowers. 'I brought some sweet peas. My garden is full of them.'

The girl was still frowning. Her abundant dark hair was tied in a loose knot on top of her head. She was pushing some large sunshades onto the bridge of her nose.

'Mummy's having a lie down. She's not keen on cut flowers. They give her migraines. Besides, I have hay fever.'

'Oh,' Pauline was disappointed. 'I'll take them back home then.' The girl had lifted the book in front of her face. Pauline noticed the title: *The Runaway Virgin*. She smiled. 'You must be her daughter? I'm Pauline Pye, from across the lane.'

The girl raised an eyebrow. 'That's a funny name. I'm Ava Darby.'

Pauline sniffed the sweet peas and then pushed them behind her back. 'Have you broken up from school already?'

Ava wiggled her toes and sighed. 'Study leave. A levels.' She covered her nose with *The Runaway Virgin* and Pauline stifled a smile.

'So, what A levels are you studying?'

'Music.' Ava shrugged, as if the rest was unimportant. 'English Lit, Philosophy.' She waved the novel as if to prove her point. Pauline decided it was time to leave.

'Oh, well. I hope your mum feels better soon.' When Ava didn't respond, she added, 'I'm just across the way if you need anything.'

Ava peered over the top of her sunglasses. 'Daddy will be home later. With a bit of luck, she'll have cheered up by then.' With an air of boredom, she flicked through the pages of her book.

Pauline smiled warmly. 'Good luck with your revision.' Ava made no response so Pauline turned towards the gate.

At the roadside, she heard a familiar ticking of a distant engine and she waited, poised to greet the driver, as the noise became the louder rumbling of farm machinery. Len approached, his tractor pulling a trailer of something that resembled dirty hay, and Derek rushed across the road chasing a rabbit, the wheels missing his tail by inches. Pauline waved the flowers at the farmer. 'Hello, Len.'

Len Chatfield was hunched in the cab, wearing a checked red shirt with the sleeves rolled up and denim jeans. She smiled in the direction of the wavy grey hair and the huge whiskers below the ruddy cheeks and waved again. 'Len, hello.'

He stared blank-eyed at the road ahead, refusing to avert his gaze although Pauline was sure he must have seen her. They hadn't exchanged a word since the time he and Gary had spoken so sternly to Bisto in the pub: she was certain now that he'd been avoiding her. Pauline was determined that Len shouldn't pass by without at least acknowledging her with a wave or a nod. She wondered if she should throw herself in front of the vehicle, suffragette-style, to grab his attention. The wind buffeted her legs and lifted the skirt of her buttery floral dress into a wide bell shape, but Len didn't turn. The tractor trundled past, the trailer shuddering behind, shedding shards of straw, and Pauline breathed out, a little indignant.

'Well, fancy not even waving to me,' she said aloud. 'I wanted a chance to talk to him.'

Back at her house, Bisto was in the process of demolishing the ancient conservatory. Pauline smiled at him, watching him bent over, hard at work, lifting a hammer and bringing it down on the rotten wood with a crash. He was wearing a white vest, pink shorts to his knees, sandals and a straw hat. She put her hands on her hips.

'Cup of tea, Bisto?'

'You're all right for the minute, Pauline. Maybe later. I'm on a roll here. And the ankle's bearing up well. I hardly feel a twinge, now.'

Pauline nodded and went into the kitchen. It was cool and dark inside and, as she pushed a window open, the fresh air blew across her face. She put the sweet peas into a small vase, added tap water and stood the flowers on the clean wooden windowsill Bisto had made. She was still secretly troubled by Len's reticence and was determined he wouldn't get away with avoiding her again. An idea had come to her. She opened a cupboard and took out flour, salt, a mixing bowl. She would make an apple pie or two. Behind her, she heard light footfall as Barbara came into the kitchen. 'Good morning, Pauline.'

'Help yourself to coffee and toast for breakfast, Barbara. I'm making apple pie. You've slept in this morning.'

Barbara exhaled, irritated. 'I'd have slept in longer but for that infernal banging nose. I take it Bisto has started work.'

Pauline stifled a smirk. 'You'd better check. You're his boss, I believe.'

Barbara was filling two cups. 'I'm taking him a cup of tea. Not out of kindness, mind you. Or weakness. I just want to see how he's getting on.'

After lunch, Pauline had made two apple pies, crimped and freshly sugared on top; one was cooling under a light tea towel. She announced in her most innocent voice, 'I'm off to take one of these to Len Chatfield's. He likes apple pie.'

Barbara picked up three plates, despite Bisto not having finished his sandwich. 'Where is the farm?'

'On the Thorpe Road. Bottom Farm is about ten minutes' walk the other side of Winsley Green. I'll take the car though. I won't be long.'

'I'll come with you, Pauline. It might be interesting.'

'Oh, there's no need, Barbara. I'll be fine.'

Bisto stood up, stretching his arms into the air. 'Perhaps I'll come along too. To keep you company. I can work later on, till about eight. I thought I'd pop down the pub after that, to exercise the ankle a little bit. It keeps it in good working order.'

'Exercise the throat, you mean,' Barbara suggested grimly.

'I want to catch up with the boys,' Bisto grinned.

Pauline waved a hand. 'I can go to Len's farm by myself... I'll be fine.'

'Nonsense,' Barbara huffed. 'You need company. It's a farm, for goodness sake – all those wild animals roaming around. There might be dogs, too.'

Bisto chuckled. 'Plenty of savage animals out there on farms,

Barbara. You want to be a bit careful – you might find yourself mauled by a chicken.'

Barbara slipped on a jacket and reached for Pauline's blue straw hat. 'I'm just being sensible.'

Pauline rolled her eyes. She didn't want company. 'Really – I'll be fine...'

'Come along if we're going.' Barbara urged Pauline forward with a firm nudge and she almost dropped the apple pie. 'Perhaps we could buy a joint of beef for dinner, maybe some fresh milk?'

Pauline shook her head, clutched the pie to her chest and reached for her car keys. She hoped Len would be still having lunch and not out on his tractor. She had plenty to say to him, and she'd rehearsed her speech perfectly, although she hadn't bargained on taking an audience with her.

Twenty minutes later, Pauline's watch proclaimed that it was well after midday. The sun was a blinding yellow beam through the windscreen as she pulled up outside the farmhouse. A few feet away, Derek and Clive were nibbling at a dead mouse in the dirt, Derek flinging the corpse into the air on the end of his claw. She lifted the pie from where she had placed it on Barbara's knee and slid out of the car. Both Len's Land Rover and Gary's old blue Ford Escort were parked nearby, so Pauline hoped Len was home as she picked her way towards the front door, Bisto following close behind and Barbara bringing up the rear, complaining about the dusty ground spoiling her shoes. Pauline stopped. She could hear male voices coming from the nearby stables. She could make out the low rumble of Len murmuring, then Gary's voice rose, complaining.

'I think they're in here,' Pauline suggested, forging ahead.

'Oh, I love horses,' Bisto grinned. 'I've a few nags myself at home, in France.'

They turned in the direction of the huge ramshackle building where two horses were housed. One, a fine horse with a shiny black coat, stuck his head out of the half door of the first stable, waving his mane. It was General. The second stable, a vast wooden building, belonged to Gary's horse, Ruby. The door had been pulled closed. Pauline knocked on the stable door and called out, 'Hello. Can we come in?'

It was dark inside the stable. Pauline blinked. Dust particles floated in front of her eyes, illuminated in a slice of light from a high window. Gary had his mobile phone in his hand, his face creased with anxiety. Len was hunched over, his hands in his jeans pocket, his expression puzzled. He glanced at Pauline, who was holding the cloth-covered pie. He stared at her for a moment, then gazed awkwardly at his boots.

'Hello, Pauline. We have a problem. Mare in labour but no foal has come yet. Rang the vet but she's not here.'

Bisto and Barbara stood either side of her as she glanced at Ruby, who was lying on the straw on her side, her flanks covered with a film of sweat. Gary's eyes opened wide. 'The vet's on her way. Ruby started in the night – I found her at six this morning. She's not right. The foal should be out by now.'

Barbara put her hands on her hips. 'What's that red thing sticking out of her bottom?'

'The foal can't come out. It should only take a few minutes after this stage.' Gary growled. 'Something's wrong. Where's the bloody vet?'

Len shook his head. 'Jill Maynard's over in Yarbury Huish. It'll take her half an hour from there – it's all country lanes.'

Gary's face crumpled, as if he was about to cry. 'I'll lose Ruby and the foal if Jill's not quick.'

'What's that?' gasped Barbara. She gazed, horrified, as a long spindly leg emerged from Ruby's rear end, followed by another.

'Has she been pushing for a long time?' Bisto stared at Gary, who shrugged and seemed confused. 'Gary, has she been like this for a while, your mare?'

Gary nodded. 'Vet's on her way though.'

Bisto frowned. 'I've got horses at the château, a couple of mares. I was brought up around horses. I think I've seen this sort of thing once before.'

Gary snorted with disbelief. Bisto rubbed his chin thoughtfully. 'I'm sure the foal's head and neck are bent backwards. It's stopping the delivery. We ought to do something to help the poor mare out.' Bisto moved to Ruby and bent over her.

Pauline clutched the pie to her stomach. Barbara turned away; the thick smell of straw and sweating horse was making her feel decidedly sick. Bisto breathed in sharply.

'Gary, give me a hand to get Ruby up.' He put his head close to the chestnut horse and patted her neck gently. 'Come on now, there's a good girl. It's up on your feet for you. We'll take a little walk around the stable, will we now, Ruby?'

Gary glared at Bisto. 'You leave her alone, you stupid bugger. She's having a foal. You'll kill her.'

Bisto shook his head. 'Listen, Gary. We need to get the mare up and walking to reduce the pressure of the foal in the birth canal and encourage it to fall back into the uterus. It's clear she can't push it out as it is. Honestly, I had a mare just like this once, in my own stables. I saw the vet do it and it saved her and the foal. Give me a hand, will you, for her sake?'

Gary hesitated, mouth open, unsure. Len shuffled over to Bisto, his shoulders hunched and awkward. 'I'll help.'

They gently encouraged Ruby to her feet, Len clucking with his tongue as Bisto spoke softly. 'Come on, Ruby, girl. Your foal has flipped itself into the wrong place for delivery. Let's take a little walk round the stables now, will we? Good girl. It might get your little one back into position.'

Ruby lumbered softly around the straw. Barbara held her breath, staring at the red bag-shaped protuberance from the mare's rear and the gangling limbs of the foal hanging helpless. She stared at Pauline.

'How does he know that? The horse looks very unwell to me. I mean, how can it walk with all that stuff in its bottom?' Pauline clutched her sister's arm and squeezed her eyes shut.

The noise of a car engine arriving outside made Gary turn, then he rushed into the sunshine, his voice raised in complaint to someone who'd just slammed a heavy car door. A soft female voice replied, then a blonde woman rushed in, Gary fussing behind her shoulder. She was probably in her forties, efficient in a wax coat, jeans and wellingtons, carrying a huge black bag. The woman nodded at Bisto and Len.

'Well done. You did exactly the right thing. With luck, you might have saved the foal. I'll take over from here, shall I?'

Bisto grinned. 'It's to be hoped the foal's fallen back into position.' He patted Ruby's long nose. 'If not, I suppose it's a C-section for you, Ruby, girl. Well. Good luck with it all, Gary.'

Gary turned his back and moved closer to the vet, breathing deeply, his fists clenched. Jill Maynard opened her bag and busied herself with attending to Ruby. Pauline turned to Len.

'Shall we step outside and leave them to it?'

They emerged into the bright sunlight, Barbara pale, with her arms folded, Bisto in his white vest and pink shorts, Pauline holding the apple pie, serene in butter-yellow floral dress and Len, towering over them all, rubbing his whiskers with dirty hands.

Pauline spoke first, offering an encouraging grin. 'I came to bring you this pie for lunch, Len.' She met his eyes steadily and took a breath. 'We haven't seen much of you recently.'

Len shuffled his feet. 'Been busy. Farm. Sheep. Tractor.' He glanced over his shoulder at the stables. 'Mare.'

Barbara's voice boomed. 'I hope you're not too busy to eat the apple pie. My sister made it specially. She spent all morning cutting apple shapes out of pastry and fussing to make the edges all even.'

Len took the pie. Pauline's cheeks were pink. She murmured, 'Don't be a stranger, Len.'

The farmer glanced over his shoulder and then down at the apple pie that he was cradling in his arms. 'No. Right. Well. Nice pie, Pauline. Thanking you.'

Pauline turned. 'We should be going. I hope all is well with Ruby. Let me know, won't you?' She waited for him to speak, but he merely nodded assent. 'Take care, Len.'

As they walked to the car, Barbara glanced at Bisto. 'Well, that was a strange episode. You're not a secret vet, are you?'

Bisto shook his head. 'No, for sure, I'm just Irish. You know the stereotype. We Irish know a thing or two about horses. My brothers worked with them. I own a couple.'

Barbara's voice conveyed her disbelief. 'Well, it was truly miraculous, what you did with the mare. I mean, I thought it was going to die. Its bottom looked terrible.'

Bisto shrugged. 'It was just a mare having a foal. Quite normal, I suppose. The vet will see she's all right now.'

Pauline was quiet, lost in her thoughts as she opened the car door and slid into the driver's seat. Bisto hobbled around the other side, clambered into the back seat, stretching out his ankle. Barbara climbed in beside her sister and Pauline started the engine, feeling the weight of sadness settle on her shoulders.

She wondered what would happen next. Len had taken the pie, her peace offering, and she wondered if he'd think of her as he was eating a slice. She doubted that he'd add a dollop of cream or some custard. But she'd reached out to him in a gesture of friendship, an apology for her harsh words over Bisto. She'd leave things now. The ball was in his court and he could make the next move. She wondered how long it would take, if he'd be round the next day, knocking on the front door with an armful of fresh vegetables, scratching his whiskers.

As she steered the car in a half circle away from the farm, she glanced into the rear-view mirror. Len was standing still watching them leave, clutching the pie, as Gary ran excitedly from the stable waving his arms and began to yell at his father.

17

As Bisto walked into the dimly-lit bar of the Sheep Dip that evening, Oskar had a pint of Murphy's at the ready and as he handed it to Bisto, the barman grinned.

'Well, you're a dark horse. I hear you sorted out the new arrival, Bisto. A foal over at Bottom Farm. You didn't tell anyone you knew all about horses.'

Bisto peered into the gloom. There were faces he recognised: Justina was picking up empty glasses from a table where Yvonne and Chrissie had just installed themselves to share a bottle of wine. Bisto winked over at them. One table away, Kostas was by himself, sprawled across a chair, his curls pushed back by sunglasses perched on the top of his head. He was wearing a tight black vest and cut-off jeans, sipping white wine. There were several other faces Bisto recognised from the cricket match: the Priddy cousins waved and he grinned in their direction. Kevin Carter lumbered over and clapped Bisto on the back.

'We all heard the news. Would you believe it? You saved the mare and the foal. Len Chatfield must be pleased, although he'll have a huge vet's bill. But what about you, Bisto? I bet you have a mysterious past back in Ireland, eh? What were you there? A jockey, I should think?' Kevin ruffled the little man's white curls.

Bisto slurped the top from his glass. 'I've several horses back at the château, a couple of mares. I'd seen something like it before. Ruby's all right now, is she?'

Kevin jerked his thumb in the direction of the corner, his ginger tresses in his eyes. 'You should ask Gary Chatfield. He's over there, where he usually sits. Been there for a couple of hours. He told everybody what you did.'

'A pint of whatever Gary drinks, Oskar,' Bisto swivelled back to the bar, fumbling in his pink shorts pocket for a pair of ten-pound notes and thrusting them at the barman. 'And another pint for Kevin and one for your good self.'

Bisto moved towards the shadowy corner, nodding at people he knew as he went, then he plonked the glass of cider on the wooden table in front of Gary and slumped in a chair, stretching out his foot. The walk down from Pauline's house on the outskirts of Winsley had made the joint ache a bit. Kevin scraped back the chair next to him and sat down heavily, muttering, 'All right, Gary?'

Gary had been examining his hands. He glanced up slowly and gave a brief nod. 'Kevin.' His eyes moved slowly to Bisto. 'All right?'

'Pint of best cider for you there,' Bisto beamed, pleased with himself, and took a mouthful of beer.

Gary grunted. 'Very grateful about Ruby.'

He stared into the distance and then back to Bisto. He wiped his forehead, paused and then nodded. 'It went well after you left. Vet said foal slipped back into the right position.' He noticed the glass, reached out shaking fingers and lifted the cider to his mouth. 'It came out, natural. Ruby's fine. Foal's doing well.'

Bisto's face shone. 'That's good news. So, what are you calling it, the little foal?'

Gary swallowed more cider and then rubbed a grimy fist over

his chin. Bisto smiled: it was the same gesture Len used to rub his whiskers.

Gary mumbled. 'Think you should choose the name. You being the one who helped out and all.'

'It's a lucky little foal, for sure.' Bisto thought for a moment, caught Kevin's eye and winked. 'Why not call it Shamrock?'

Gary frowned. 'Shamrock it is then, as you say.' He drained his cider. 'Never been a fan of foaling time. Fair turns my stomach, birthing. Same with sheep, cows, anything that has babies. Gives me the willies, to be honest.'

Kevin shrugged. 'I was there when my daughter was born. It was an odd experience. Truth be known, I wasn't much use to the missus.' He swallowed best bitter and pulled a face. 'I'm more comfortable hacking hedges than I am dealing with women's business.'

Bisto gave a short laugh. 'Your bit stops at the conception, does it, eh? You'd leave all the rest to the poor women to sort out?' He glanced at Gary. 'Or the mare?'

Gary's face darkened. Kevin nodded. 'That's about it, if the truth's told.' He frowned. 'You got kids, Bisto? Wife?'

Bisto raised his beer. 'A son, Barney. A couple of grandchildren, and a lovely daughter-in-law.'

'Where are they now?'

'Back where I live in France, keeping things ticking over for me. Phoned my lad just this morning. He's busy as hell.' He thought for a moment over a mouthful of Murphy's. 'I'll go back in a while, when I've finished here. Pauline's been very kind, letting me stay.'

Kevin gulped his pint and wiped the froth from his ginger stubble. 'You flying back from Bristol?'

'No, I don't fly now.' Bisto squeezed his eyes closed. 'I used to love it. But I gave it up. I had a bad experience. It put me off. I'll take the boat and the train, for sure, now.' He raised his eyebrows. 'Can I get you another pint, Kev? Gary?'

Gary stood up. 'Better get home. Father working late tonight. I'll sort out some bread and cheese for when he's in and take a look at Ruby and the foal.' He eyed Bisto. 'Shamrock. Like I said, I'm grateful.'

He eased himself to his feet, stared around the bar, nodded at Oskar and shuffled away. Bisto watched him go. 'He seems like a nice enough fella...'

Kevin agreed. 'He is. A bit shy, I think. It was hard for him, losing his mother. He and Len are loyal to each other, they keep the farm going well but I don't think there's much conversation in the house.' He finished the dregs in his glass. 'A man needs a good woman for that sort of thing – conversation, warmth, love.'

Bisto stood up. 'Same again?'

'My round.' Kevin protested, about to stand, but Bisto placed a hand on his shoulder.

'You get the next ones, eh, Kevin?'

Bisto ambled to the bar. He passed a small table where Dr Natalie and her husband Dr Mario were sharing a drink together. She was leaning back in her seat, her feet raised on the opposite chair, her hands over the protruding bump. Bisto grinned at her.

'I see you're drinking orange juice. How are you keeping?'

Natalie looked up at Bisto. 'Good. Not bad at all. I'll be glad when it's all over, though.'

Mario picked up his own glass of orange juice. 'Me too. I promised I wouldn't have a single tipple until Nat's had the baby. I'm trying to show solidarity.'

'It's all babies and foals in this place...' Bisto mused.

'Pardon?' Mario smoothed his beard.

'Babies. Motherhood. Can't be easy with the warm weather – I expect it's hard to get comfy the nights?' Bisto chortled. 'When's it due?'

Natalie rolled her eyes. 'The beginning of September.'

'First babby's always the most worrying.'

Natalie reached for her glass and Mario took her hand, bringing it to his lips. She gazed at her husband with anxious eyes. 'I'll take care of her.' He exhaled a professional breath and turned to Bisto. 'How's the counselling going? Joe Parry's a nice chap.'

Bisto nodded. 'He is. It's helped me a bit, but I was thinking – I won't go again.'

'Your choice, Bisto.' Mario was still holding his wife's hand in his. 'Hope it's all going well at Pauline's.'

'Just grand,' Bisto beamed. 'Well, I'll be getting along to the bar for some more of these.'

He raised the empty glasses and resumed his stroll towards Oskar, who was serving Tilly Hardy at the bar. She had her arm linked through the crook of a young man's elbow. He was no older than twenty. Bisto noticed he was dressed completely in black: leather jacket, skinny jeans, even his hair was jet black, hanging over his ears in shiny tendrils, almost to his shoulders. Tilly was leaning against him, a wide smile on her face, her fluffy grey curls still damp, presumably from the shower. Bisto gave her a short salute.

'How are you, Tilly? How's the novel coming along?'

She giggled. 'Oh, it's finished. I'm going to London next week to meet my publisher. It's all going well. Out soon. You'd love it, Bisto.' Oskar handed her a bottle of bubbly and two glasses and she chuckled again. 'Will you have a glass with us?' She indicated the young man, hugging closer to him. 'This is my son, Fabian. He's home from his gap year.'

Fabian turned to Bisto, offering him a slight smile. Bisto met his eyes. 'Good to meet you, Fabian.'

Fabian's expression didn't change. 'Yeah. Cool.'

Bisto turned to Oskar. 'Tilly's bottle's on me, Osk. And I'll have a half of the usual and a pint of best for Kevin. Oh, and give the doctors a couple more orange juices – I'm sure the Vitamin C will help them both.'

Tilly stroked Bisto's shoulder. 'That's so kind of you, Bisto.'

Fabian closed his eyes. 'Bisto? You're Irish. Cool.'

Bisto paid for the drinks, gathered up two glasses expertly and turned to go. Fabian murmured, 'Cheers, man.'

'Ah, you're grand,' Bisto muttered, focusing on not spilling the drink.

'Oh, by the way,' Tilly cooed. 'Have you heard about what's happened to one half of the Feral Peril?'

Bisto paused. 'Dulcie's cats? No. Everything all right, is it?'

Tilly was pouring sparkling wine into two glasses. 'One's gone missing. The one with the white paws. Dulcie hasn't seen it for three days. She's out of her mind with worry.'

Bisto moved away. 'Clive? Ah, I'm sure he'll be back home when he's hungry.'

He moved precariously to the table where Kevin was sitting, stretching out long legs ending in huge ankle boots. He put the glasses down carefully, trying to ignore the image that had crept into his mind: the hard eyes, frowning face and the tight-lipped expression of Dulcie's neighbour Phyllis as she stared down the barrel of an air rifle.

* * *

It was half past ten as Bisto sauntered home. He sang a little lilting song as he walked, keeping perfect time with his swaying gait. In the kitchen, Pauline and Barbara were sitting at the table, finishing mugs of hot chocolate.

Pauline stood up immediately. 'We were chatting and waiting up for you. Would you like a hot drink, Bisto?'

'I wasn't waiting. I was finishing my drink.' Barbara glanced at him sourly. 'He looks like black coffee would be most suitable.' She narrowed her eyes. 'Or a stomach pump.'

Bisto laughed and plonked himself next to her, tapping her elbow. 'I only had the one and then two halves. You should have come down the pub with me, Babs. We had a grand time.'

Barbara sniffed loudly, probably due to the alcohol on his breath. 'You are incapable of having a grand time, as you put it, without the added benefits of alcohol to make you pleasant.'

Pauline was cutting a slice of fruit cake. 'That's not really true, Barbara. Have some cake, Bisto. I just made it this afternoon.'

'Don't mind if I do, Pauline. I'm thirsty after all the work on the new garden room today, and hungry after the beer.' He grinned at Pauline as she put the plate down and lifted the slice of cake, biting off a mouthful and making a contented sound. 'Delicious.'

He noticed Barbara watching him steadily. He slurped the creamy top of the hot chocolate she'd just placed in front of him. He winked at her.

'You're thinking what a good-looking fella, am I right, Babs?'

She wrinkled her nose. 'You wouldn't be my type. I was just thinking about how you've bashed all the wood down from the old conservatory and all the dust seems to have collected everywhere.'

'Don't worry,' Pauline sighed. 'I'll have it cleared up tomorrow.'

'And I was wondering about your family, Bisto. I mean, if you have a son, there must be a wife...'

Pauline turned to her sister; her face alarmed. 'I don't think we should ask questions, Barbara.'

'Why not? He's living here, under your roof. He's always in the pub. We find out he's a bit of a horse whisperer or whatever you call those traveller people who are good with animals and it occurs to me, Bisto, that we don't really know each other well at all.'

Pauline offered a warning glance. 'Barbara, I don't think...'

'She has a point, Pauline.' Bisto leaned forward in his seat. The Murphy's and the conviviality in the pub had made him bold, cheerful, and his natural caution was blurring at the edges. 'I tell you what – you can ask me a question and I'll ask you one. Is that okay, Babs? Sort of a getting-to-know-each-other game.'

Barbara folded her arms. 'I've certainly nothing to hide.'

Bisto winked at Pauline and shovelled cake into his mouth. He was enjoying himself. 'All right, you first – ask away.'

Barbara's voice boomed. 'Very well – who are you and why are you here?'

'That's two questions, but I don't mind.' Bisto leaned back in his seat on two legs. 'Righto. I'm Bisto Mulligan. I'm seventy-six years old and I own a château in France, in the Loire.'

Barbara bit her lip. 'I don't believe you – you're making it up. It's – what do you call it? Irish blarney.'

Bisto held his hand up. 'Ah, let me finish. I know I looked terrible when I arrived – I'd been through a lot. I came over to Ireland for a family funeral. I don't fly. I took the boat back to Liverpool, lost my wallet and you know the rest. I'm on my way back to France. I've been married twice. Divorced, then died, as Henry VIII might have said. I moved to France after my second wife passed away.' Bisto thought for a moment, his eyes staring into space. 'I was in a bad place, so I quit my job, and started over again.' He examined his fingers, reached for his mug of hot chocolate and gazed at the liquid thoughtfully. 'I'm in good health now, apart from a once-dodgy ankle that's well on the mend, and I like a small tipple now and again, as you know. My philosophy on life is I won't always be here, but while I am, I intend to make the most of it.'

Pauline's eyes were examining his face. 'It's hard to move forward after bereavement, isn't it?'

She was thinking of Douglas, how quiet the house had been since he died. She had spent so many lonely evenings listening to the wind creak in the eaves. Now her evenings were spent chattering convivially and sharing anecdotes. She sighed contentedly.

Bisto closed his eyes. 'At the time, I wanted everything to stop. There was no reason to...' His voice trailed off, and he was lost in thought. He sat upright and gave a cheery smile. 'Ah, but isn't life a blessing. We move forward.'

Pauline nodded. 'Douglas' death took me by surprise, totally. Grief became all I had for a while. My life was filled with sorrow and I had nothing else. But gradually you learn to live with the pain. It doesn't go away. But you build a new life around everything you have, including the memories and the sadness.'

Bisto sighed. For some reason his vision was clouding; tears had brimmed in his eyes. He wiped his face on his wrist and swallowed more hot chocolate.

'An occasional drop of the black stuff helps, though. And I do as I please now I don't work. That's a blessing.'

Barbara leaned forward. 'But it must be difficult, on your own? I mean, if your wife died, you must be lonely sometimes. Is that why you drink beer? Do you miss her? And which member of your family died in Dublin? You say you went home for a funeral. Who died? Was it a close relative?'

Bisto's face cracked in a smile immediately, his eyes twinkling. 'This is turning into an interrogation, Babs. Besides, it's my turn to ask you. So, we agreed, one question each.'

Barbara sat upright, put her hands in her lap, secretary-efficient. 'All right. Go ahead. One question.'

Bisto chuckled. 'Right. This is it. How come a good-looking woman like you has never been married?'

Barbara felt her skin freeze. She lifted her hands from her lap, waved them and attempted a laugh. 'Oh, I'm not good-looking...'

'Sure you are, the both of yous.' Bisto turned to Pauline. 'There's Pauline, beautiful, blonde, voluptuous...'

'My hair is silver,' Pauline giggled, covering her mouth.

'And you, Babs – you have a body of the woman half your age, lovely eyes, and a grand smile when you let it come out.'

Barbara's shoulders had started to climb towards her ears. 'I'm seventy-seven, for goodness sake. I'm hardly a looker. I mean, I was all right once, but...'

'So, I'm not wrong, am I? It's your turn to answer the question. How come a lovely woman like you never married?'

Pauline's voice was a whisper. She put an encouraging hand on her sister's shoulder.

'I often wondered...'

Barbara's breath was rising and falling in her chest. Her face had become hot.

'Well, I almost did. Well, no, I didn't. I mean, I could have. But no, I couldn't have, I mean, he wasn't able to...'

She thought of Robert, how much she had loved him, all those years she had waited, hoping that one day he'd be free to say the word and invite her to share his life forever.

'There was someone once, someone special...'

Her voice had become strangled in her throat and she couldn't say any more. She was whisked back to a time, in her bedsit, hunched on the end of the bed, when Robert had blurted it out, how he loved her, how he wanted to be with her more than anything in the world but he couldn't. The price was too high. They would have to make the ultimate sacrifice. Their love affair was over and there was no other way. A sob choked in her throat as it had stopped her words all those years ago in her twenties.

'No. No, nothing. There was nobody. I don't do love. It only ends in disappointment and misery...'

She stood up, staring wildly at Bisto. Her eyes met Pauline's and they shone with tears. She gasped, mumbling something about being tired, and rushed from the room.

Pauline breathed out and turned her gaze to Bisto, her hands out, her shoulders raised in a shrug. She wondered whether to go after her sister, but wisdom suggested that she give Barbara time and space. It was becoming clear that Barbara was more complex than she'd given her credit for. More sensitive, too. Bisto was still staring at the open door where Barbara had made a fleeing exit.

'For sure,' he muttered. 'And there's a woman who knows how it feels to have her heart broken.'

18

Barbara hadn't fallen asleep until gone one o'clock and her dreams had been fitful. She remembered Robert, tall and blond, a handsome cleft in his chin, the spread of his shoulders beneath his shirt, the green eyes that twinkled. It was so many years ago, but in her dreams she was losing him again. He was telling her it was all over, his words the mere scratchy echoes of a long-playing record, that he had to make an honourable choice, the most difficult choice of his life, and Barbara held her breath as her heart was being wrenched into pieces. Her sleep was ragged, damp, like tattered memories; her thoughts were filled with snatches of words of love, the tearing pain of tears and loss.

When she woke, it was almost ten o'clock, and Bisto's words came back to her. He'd told her she had the body of a woman half her age. Barbara made a low scoffing noise. He was full of Irish blarney, that Bisto. She ran her hands over the nightie, feeling the softness of her body beneath the voluminous thin material. Her waist was still slim, her hip bones sturdy. She moved her fingers over muscly thighs and wondered what a man might make of her now. She pushed thoughts of Robert away. He would be in his eighties, if he was still alive. She hadn't heard from him in fifty years. But she was strong, still relatively fit; the country air was doing her good and the dizziness that put her into hospital hadn't returned. And Bisto had said she had a lovely smile.

Barbara slid out of bed. The red curtains were drawn and the room had a hazy dimness, the sunshine filtered like setting honey. She padded in bare feet over to the wardrobe mirror and stared at herself. Her hair had grown a little; it was steel grey, but not so severe now. The curls had loosened. But her eyes held fierceness, and there was a permanent frown creased in between her brows. She practised a smile and the frown seemed to fade. She beamed again, a wide grin and fluffed her hair with long fingers.

Barbara stared at the image smiling back at her. It was a cold old lady pulling a distorted face. But it didn't have to be. She stood back and posed, turning sideways and then back, smiling again. She looked happier. Her skin was tanned, her face a deep brown contrasting with the paler laughter lines around her eyes that the sun had missed. She was even quite attractive.

Barbara took a breath in and held it. Then in one swift movement, she hauled the night dress over her head and threw it to one side, attempting the practised swish of a stripper. She was naked, her skin pleated in places, imperfect: her shoulders were bony, her thighs too wide, her calves too skinny, her breasts too small.

'No, I don't have to see myself negatively. I just have to *think* myself beautiful, and I *am*,' she said aloud and stood tall, proud, thrusting out her chest, moving her feet, and suddenly she was striding around the room.

Barbara marched up and down the rug, its softness between her toes, and she placed her hands on her hips, swaying so that her backside rocked. So, is this how it feels to be sexy, she wondered. Suddenly, she was smiling. A tune had come to her and she was humming it. A familiar tune, a saxophone or trumpet, sleazy, too loud, with confidence, with abandon: 'The Stripper'. She began to sing loudly 'Dah-dah-dah, da-da-da dah...'

She strutted across the room, sauntering into the sliver of sunlight which seeped from between the curtains and back again. She smiled, threw her head back, ran long fingers through her hair, and kicked out a leg, waggled a buttock. Barbara was in full stride. She was alive, sexy, independent.

She sang louder, the tune building to a climactic flourish, and she sashayed across the bedroom, her arms waving languidly over her head, ending with a final display in front of the curtains, wiggling every part of her body, imagining a black feather boa around her neck, an audience of rapt males cheering, clapping and gazing at her with lascivious eyes. The daft thought made her giggle. She pranced towards the curtains and, her lips pursed in a red kiss, Monroe-style, she swished back the drapes and leaned forward, her face shining, baring all in a centrefold pose.

She shrieked, a too high screech of shock. Barbara was staring straight into the wide eyes of a handsome curly-haired man holding a chamois leather in his fist. Kostas gave the window a leisurely smear, winked, rubbed a bead of perspiration from his brow and began to climb down the ladder. The windowpane was sparkling clean except for a descending drizzle of foam. Barbara clapped both arms around her naked chest and shivered. The smile had gone from her face; it was at once replaced by a familiar anxious frown.

Below, Dizzy rushed into the kitchen and hugged Pauline, leaping up and down on the spot, her cheeks flushed a deep pink.

'I asked him, like I said I would. Oh, Pauline, I just came out with it and he agreed.'

Pauline put a gentle hand on Dizzy's shoulder. 'You asked who? What?'

'Kostas. You said he was doing your windows. So I sidled up to his ladder and...' Dizzy took a step back, made a cute little bow with her lips and blinked her eyelashes. 'So I said "Hi, Kostas. You look busy..."'

'And then...?'

'He didn't look busy at all. He just stood there, his shirt unbuttoned, a bucket in his hand and said, "Hi. It's nice to meet you." So polite and charming with a sexy voice. Oh my goodness, my heart fluttered and I nearly fell over...'

'This is Kostas you're talking about? While he's doing my windows?'

'Keep up, Pauline.' Dizzy fanned herself with her fingers. 'Imagine. He's there, gazing at me with those huge serious eyes. So I just said it. "Would you like to have supper with me, at my home? On Friday night?" And he looked at me and licked his lips, slowly, just like a cat with cream.'

Pauline rolled her eyes. 'Isn't he a bit young for you, Dizzy?'

'He could be in his early thirties. Ten years between us, at the most.' Dizzy blew air from her mouth. 'If it's more, well I don't care – I'll be a cougar. Whatever it takes. Anyway, as I said, he has the most gorgeous brown eyes – long lashes, to die for. And he said... he said...' Dizzy put on a deep voice and an accent that definitely came from nowhere near Greece. "Is hokay, Friday I ham free." And so I gave him my address and he'll be round at seven. So, Pauline, thanks for telling me you'd booked him to come here.' She gave a little bounce and her eyes shone. 'Now I have a date. I mean, an actual date with Kostas. Oh my goodness me.' She leapt up and down again, waving her fingers.

Pauline grinned. 'That's great. What will you dish up? For supper, I mean?'

Dizzy burst into giggles. 'Me, on a plate. I have this plunging neckline dress. And it's all thanks to you – telling me he was coming here to do the window cleaning.'

Pauline's face was baffled. 'I didn't know you were going to ask...'

'No, really – I'm totally grateful. It was much easier – I could talk to him here, away from prying eyes, just him and me. So – let me make it up to you now, Pauline. Let me do your hair for you. I have my kit in my bag. I'm on my way to do a cut and blow dry in Thorpe.'

Pauline closed her eyes. 'All right.' She recalled last night, when Bisto had called her a good-looking woman. A blonde. Hadn't he said voluptuous? Even now, she could still be beautiful. She felt a new confidence thrill like icy water across her skin. She always took care of herself but here was a chance to make the most of what nature had given her. After all, being seventy-five might put her in the older age bracket, but she could still feel sexy, desirable. Why not? She met Dizzy's eyes.

'Yes, just a trim, but make it look a bit more up-to-date. Sleek. And maybe a subtle change of colour, more blonde than silver?'

Dizzy lifted up her bags containing the tools of her trade. 'I've always wanted to do your hair. Platinum highlights – and I can make it really glossy and swishy.'

'Not too different, though, Dizzy. I don't want to look like someone else.'

Pauline perched on a chair as Dizzy wrapped a transparent plastic apron around her neck. 'I haven't calmed down yet. I can hardly believe it. I have a date with Kostas – he's coming over to my house, it'll be just me and him. Isn't it wonderful? Pauline, don't you think he's good-looking?'

'Not my type,' Pauline sighed. 'But I can see that he's attractive. He's dark-haired, good-looking, a sexy man, with a lot of James Dean's insouciance about him.'

Dizzy wrinkled her nose. 'What does that mean when it's at home? Insouciance?'

'Indifference.'

A resolute voice came from the doorway, and both women stared at Barbara who was standing with her arms folded, her face disgruntled.

'Perhaps he couldn't care less about anything. Except himself.' She saw the optimism drain from Dizzy's face as she narrowed her eyes. 'I think you're making a mistake. Some people are only capable of self-interest. All good-looking men are the same. Narcissists. Believe me, I've met them.'

Barbara looked from Dizzy to Pauline and back to the hairdresser, delivering her killer blow through thin lips. 'If you ask me, most women would be best advised to stay at home and share a supper with their dog. They'd be safer. At least there would be more chance of a little honest and reciprocal affection.'

* * *

Bisto's ankle hadn't bothered him at all on the walk up to Dulcie's house. She appeared at the door seconds after he had knocked, her small face drawn and anxious. Bisto put his arm around her and they strolled into the bright sunlight of her garden. She patted his shoulder.

'It was good of you to come all this way to see me. But I'm so upset. I've no idea where Clive is. It's been days now – it's not like him.' She stared sharply at Phyllis' caravan in the next garden. 'I bet *she's* got him tied up in there.'

Bisto shook his head. 'I'm sure he'll be back home soon, Dulcie. But will I pop next door for you and have a small chat with Phyllis? Just to see if she hasn't noticed Clive around her place?'

Dulcie's red eyes glistened. 'Oh, would you, Bisto? That'd be kind of you.'

Bisto grinned at her, gave her a hug and walked steadily in the direction of Phyllis' hedge that was stuffed with the roll of barbed wire, past the wooden warning sign, around the blaze of blossoming flowers to where Phyllis was sitting outside, sprawled in a battered rose chenille armchair. Her dress was tucked around her thighs, allowing the cool air to circulate between her knees, and her brown stockings were in rolls around her ankles. She held a plastic cup in one hand and a pitcher in the other, filled with damson liquid. As Bisto approached, she raised it to him.

'Just having a tipple before lunch. Want to share one with me?'

Bisto grinned. 'Don't mind if I do. What do you have in the decanter, Phyllis?'

'Sloe gin, homemade: 2016. Proper vintage stuff.' She grinned. 'I got blackberry brandy too. And some cucumber vodka I made this summer. That's got a kick to it like a mule's back leg. What's your poison?'

Bisto moved a plastic chair next to Phyllis and eased himself into a sitting position. 'The sloe gin looks grand. I'll have what you're having.'

Phyllis walked slowly, easing herself up the steps into the caravan and Bisto surveyed the garden, the neat clusters of blooms, and the ordered vegetable plot. Phyllis emerged from the caravan and dragged herself carefully down the steps, clutching a small goblet in one hand.

'Best crystal. My only piece,' she muttered, pouring a huge measure of the burgundy liquid. 'I don't normally have guests. Here – cheers.'

They chimed their drinks together, Bisto's glass with a large fragment chipped from the lip, and Phyllis' plastic cup.

'*Sláinte*, Phyllis.' Bisto took a swig and allowed the sweet syrup to fill his mouth. 'Ah, but this is good.' He closed his lids for a moment, feeling the sun's warmth on his face. When he opened his eyes, Phyllis was staring at him.

'It's nice to see you, Bisto. But I expect she's sent you – the old witch next door. I heard her screeching out for her cat. Ridiculous name for an animal – Clive.'

Bisto swigged the sloe gin and examined Phyllis' face for guilt. 'You haven't seen Clive, though, Phyllis?'

'I haven't. If I did, he'd get my foot up his feral arse. But no, I wouldn't harm him. Even though I loathe the woman, I wouldn't shoot her cat. I bet she's telling everyone that's what I've done though.'

Bisto shook his head. 'She misses him. I expect she's worried.' He closed one eye and peeped at Phyllis through the other. 'So why do you two lovely women not get along? You're neighbours. You're always six of one and half a dozen of the other with your arguments.'

The air was still for a moment. Phyllis was drinking, deep in thought. Then she patted her tightly curled white hair.

'She's a horrible woman. Have you smelled her? She passes wind all the time. She eats nothing but beans and lentils. It's a wonder the cat has stayed as long as it has. She must stink the house out.'

'You should give her some of this delicious sloe gin.' Bisto lifted his glass and Phyllis filled it again.

'We go back a long way, me and Dulcie. We were best friends once. Then, of course, it all changed.'

'And why is that, Phyllis?'

Phyllis cackled. 'Men. What else would it be?'

Bisto frowned. 'And what have we all done now?'

'It was a long time ago. We were nineteen, I think – not much more. There was this lovely man, Albie Matthews was his name. Handsome as anything. Soldier. Dulcie was stepping out with him. Then one day she came round to my house, screaming the place down, her face all red – said I'd stolen him off her.'

Bisto grinned. The sloe gin had made him feel sleepy, and he stretched out his legs; the warmth of the sun on his cheeks was good. 'And did you, Phyllis? Steal him from her?'

Phyllis snorted and swigged from her tumbler. 'I might've.' She winked at Bisto. 'She'd said they were engaged. But I didn't care. Albie preferred me. I was hot stuff then, Bisto. Figure like Betty Grable, I had.'

'The American actress from the wartime,' Bisto muttered. 'It was the long legs she had, wasn't it?'

Phyllis sighed. 'Mine were just the same then – everyone admired my legs. I drew the lines on stockings, in eyebrow pencil down the back. Now look at them.' She stared down at her legs, pink and mottled with veins, stretched out in front of her. 'Useless. They ache so much now I wish the doctors would cut them off sometimes.'

Bisto reached out and filled her mug. 'What happened to your man, the soldier, Albie Matthews?'

'Neither of us had him in the end.' Phyllis sniffed. 'Shot in Malaya, he was.' She finished her drink and reached for the decanter. 'And that was that, really.'

Bisto held out his glass. 'Love, Phyllis. It makes clowns of us all.'

Phyllis poured to the top. 'It certainly does, Bisto.' She took a mouthful of sloe gin and thought for a moment. 'Are you in love with Pauline Pye?'

Bisto shook his head. 'Ah, but she'd be a good catch. Lovely woman. No, Phyllis, but I'm not really looking for love. Not now.'

Phyllis' eyes narrowed. 'You have a broken heart too, then. Like I do.' She shifted the position of her body in the tattered armchair. 'They don't mend, broken hearts.'

Bisto sighed. 'Especially when we don't take the chances, we had to say the right things.'

'What happened, Bisto?'

The drink sweetened his tongue and he eased himself back in the seat to remember. He was quiet for a moment. 'Nisha was the love of my life. I told her that every day. No, I miss her, but I don't regret a thing except that she's gone from me now.'

'Who, then?' Phyllis leaned forward. Bisto's eyes were closed. 'Who did you neglect to say the right words to?'

Bisto sipped from the chipped crystal glass. 'Ah, it was my own mammy. I've just been to her funeral a few weeks back, in Dublin.'

Bisto sat up and looked into Phyllis' face. She held out the decanter and he proffered his glass.

'She was in her nineties. We'd had many fallings out. I just let things slip, moved away, didn't see her for a few years, too many. Then she died and we hadn't made things right. I went to her funeral anyway. To be honest with you, it messed with my head a bit, the fact that she'd gone and I'd never told her how much she'd meant to me. That's how it all started to go wrong, how I ended up here.'

The sloe gin glugged in the delicate glass as Phyllis poured. 'I'm sure your mammy loved you, Bisto.'

'She loved the other kiddies more, my brothers and sisters. And she was right. I never was the sort of son she wanted. She disliked everything I did – the way I read too many books, the way I played music all night, the way I was always thinking about my job, the way I didn't keep regular hours like my Da and my brothers who worked in Dublin on the railway or with the horses. I never gave her enough time.'

'What instruments do you play?'

Bisto shook his head. 'My mammy could play the spoons, lovely, so could my brother Pat. I like the string instruments myself.'

Phyllis tapped his hand with her pudgy fingers. 'And what did you do? For your job?'

He sighed. 'Ah, it's all water under the bridge now, Phyllis. Too much work, too much time spent on helping others and neglecting the ones I loved. I didn't think about it at the time, it just came naturally. But her funeral brought it all back to me. And then after it was all over, I took the boat to Liverpool, drank Guinness, lost my wallet and luggage, hitchhiked, fell over in the ice and the mud, and all I could think of was what Mammy would say: "You'll never come to any good, Bisto Mulligan, you mark my words." You know, she was right there.'

Phyllis drained her drink, leaned over and patted his knee. 'I think you're a nice sort of bloke, Bisto.' She tipped the last of the sloe gin into his glass. 'A lot of folks in Winsley think the same. You should stay here with us. Settle down. Marry Pauline Pye. Set up a home here. You'd be happy.'

Bisto brought the glass to his lips and sighed. The sunshine seemed to cocoon him in warmth and soft buttery light, and he leaned back in the plastic seat and sighed again.

'I'm not sure what to do, Phyllis. Not yet.' His mouth was filled with soft sweet gin. 'I have a lot of things to be thinking about. But you never know what will happen. Who can say?' A smile twitched across his lips. 'But watch this space, eh? There may be one last-ditch shot at love for Bisto Mulligan before too long. Who knows? Certainly not me.'

19

A week passed and Barbara spent most of it resting in a deckchair in the garden, watching Bisto in his pink shorts and grubby white vest moving rubble from the old conservatory. He seemed to have broken a lot of bricks and glass and created piles of rotten wood but not much more. By Saturday morning, he was still lifting the broken bits of the conservatory into piles and shovelling dust. As she frowned in his direction, he turned to her with a grin on his face and called across, 'Don't worry, boss. It'll all be grand. I've done this all before.'

Barbara lowered the book she was reading, an interesting non-fiction about how to be popular and likeable. She scowled. 'So, what was your job before you became a professional drinker? Did you work on a building site?'

He winked at her. 'Ah, trust me, but I know how to deliver the goods, Babs. Last thing I rebuilt was a turret on my château.'

'I'm sure the last thing you built was a big bar bill.' She drew her lips into a straight line. 'When will this garden room start to look like anything but a recycling centre?'

Bisto lifted some rotten timber and piled it into a wheelbarrow. 'For sure, by next week you'll see it starting to take shape.'

'It's the beginning of July. Will it be finished this summer, do you think?'

'I always keep my word, boss. It'll be the dandiest garden room you ever saw. And Pauline will just love it.'

Barbara put her book in front of her face and closed her eyes. Everything seemed to be about Pauline. Not that she was jealous – she'd started to see her sister in a new light. Pauline wasn't as fretful or as needy as Barbara had imagined. In fact, she was kind-hearted and good fun. People liked her. Dizzy had been around first thing to talk to her and ask for advice, proclaiming that she was now dating Kostas after their supper at her house. Barbara had given her opinion: it was hardly dating. He'd had a meal with Dizzy, listened to her babble about herself for several hours, left without even giving her a kiss and he'd politely offered to reciprocate with a snack at his lodgings in Milton Rogus. However, no date had been set.

Dizzy was ridiculously excited, and Barbara had thought it only wise to point out that Kostas could have no interest in a middle-aged woman who was far too needy and had lurid hair, otherwise he'd have contacted her already. Barbara was dismayed to see tears form like glass bulbs in Dizzy's eyes, and Pauline had quickly suggested that Dizzy contact Kostas and remind him that he'd invited her to sample his mezze and she would be delighted to pop over. Barbara resolved to try to be more encouraging, like her sister.

Barbara glanced at the pages of her book about learning to be popular. She'd picked it up in Taunton, hoping that she could understand Pauline's secret, her way of being magnetic, drawing people into her warmth. Surely it wasn't just about baking apple pies and biscuits for people. Barbara sighed – the whiskery farmer had not even brought the plate back from the pie Pauline made over a week ago. There was gratitude for you. People like Pauline were easily taken advantage of, all the time. Yet she didn't seem to care. She was in control, she oozed confidence, and everyone admired her. But the book Barbara was reading puzzled her: she couldn't understand why her sister was so popular and yet no one found her very interesting. The answer hadn't become clear.

Everyone liked Pauline so much, especially Bisto. His eyes were always shining in her direction. She'd started to look glamorous recently; she'd taken to wearing pretty summer dresses and her hair was shiny and stylish. Barbara fingered her own curls. She lifted her eyes from the new chapter she'd begun, entitled 'The Power of Being Positive' and glanced across the narrow track towards the neighbour's garden.

The young man was there again, the boy with black hair and clothes, hanging around the daughter. Barbara supposed she'd finished revising for A levels and had spare time on her hands. She could hear fragments of chatter; the girl's voice raised in laughter. They'd been together for the last few days, every day, and it had started to irritate Barbara for some reason. She screwed her eyes small and watched as they moved around the garden. She recalled that the boy's name was Fabian. Ava Darby was cavorting in a crop top and shorts in a most unseemly way. Barbara thought Fabian must feel hot in the black leather jacket and jeans. The temperature was already rising and it wasn't yet noon.

Barbara glanced over to where the old conservatory had been. Bisto was busy piling filthy panes of glass into a wheelbarrow, so she raised her voice to make sure he heard her.

'I do wish those young people would give it a rest. They've been courting all morning. It's the third time this week. Can't they go for a walk somewhere and give me a bit of peace?'

Bisto guffawed. 'It's Tilly's son, Fabian, just arrived back from his gap year. He's a pleasant young fella. I met him in the pub. It's nice that the young ones are having a good time.' He lifted another piece of glass carefully placing it on the pile. 'We aren't young for long, that's for sure.'

'Who'd want to be young?' Barbara's voice was insistent. 'Seeing young people frolicking all over each other is just nauseating, isn't it? It'll end in tears for one or other of them, if not both.'

Bisto stood up straight. 'But wouldn't we all like a chance to do it over, to be young again and have some fun?'

'No, I certainly wouldn't.'

'And why's that, Babs?'

'Oh,' Barbara yawned, pretending boredom. 'It's all too much trouble, having relationships, trying to keep it all going.'

He scratched his white curls. 'Ah, what's the alternative, Babs? Being sad and lonely for the rest of your days?'

The shock was instant. For a moment, she didn't know what to say. She threw the book on the grass and stood up, pushing the deck chair backwards. 'Don't be so rude, Bisto. It's really none of your business.'

His blue eyes met hers and she couldn't pull her gaze away. He put his hands on his hips and leaned towards her, his expression unusually serious.

'Perhaps it's time to let the past go, Babs. Maybe it's still holding you back.'

The air came straight from her lungs, and at first she couldn't speak. Her heart had started to thump. Then her breath returned.

'How dare you.'

She heard the tremor in her voice and hoped she wouldn't cry. She was determined to hang onto her dignity, and that meant showing that she was offended, outraged, and he had overstepped the mark.

'You have no right...'

'Babs, I know how you must feel – really I do. It's not something I talk about much either, grief. My own wife died years ago and it went hard with me. Then I lost my mammy a few weeks ago. It's not been easy at all – I'm not proud of how I reacted to it all. But we have to live with the sorrow, and we try to move forward.'

Barbara stood as tall as she could. Her throat constricted and tears blurred her vision. When her voice came out, it was weak and too high.

'Are you counselling me? You? You live the life of a vagrant…'

Bisto took two steps towards her. 'It's all right to lean on someone once in a while. I know it's easy to hit out, to be angry, believe me. I've been hitting out at myself for months, years. Life isn't fair. But…'

Barbara gasped: her shoulders were shaking and her cheeks were wet. She couldn't remember a time when someone had been kind to her, had told her it was acceptable to feel hurt. She didn't know quite how to react, but she felt herself crumbling, weak. She swallowed tears. Bisto put his hands on her shoulders. Barbara could smell the sweat on his body from working in the heat: it wasn't unpleasant, a thick, manly smell. She breathed him in. His voice was soft, close to her ear as he approached.

'You're a good woman, Babs, for sure you are. One of the best.'

Despite Bisto being some five inches shorter than her, Barbara leaned her head on his shoulder. For a moment, she wanted to cave in, to let all the tears out, to sob freely in his arms. His hand was on her back, patting her gently. It felt safe and good to have another person so close to her, so reassuring. But it was not something she was used to, being comforted, held. She swallowed air sharply, forced away her feeling of vulnerability and pulled back.

'I'm fine. Thank you. I'm all right now. It was a moment's stupidity.'

His eyes stayed on her face; his expression concerned. Barbara dabbed at her cheeks with her fingers, smeared the streaks of wetness from her face. Bisto bent over and handed her the book, title up: *How to Be More Popular*. His expression was serious and he seemed to shake his head slightly. Barbara forced a laugh.

'Silly me. I'm fine now. Really. Bisto – ah – well – can I get you something to drink? I mean, the weather is very hot. Water, perhaps?'

He was still staring at her. Seconds ticked, heavy on the air, then the light chatter of voices came from the kitchen. Pauline was talking to someone, a woman.

'Let's take the tea outside, shall we?'

Barbara turned sharply and saw her sister coming towards her. She jerked away, her body stiff, and turned her back to Bisto. Pauline was wearing a pretty blue dress and carrying a tray with four teacups, a tea pot and a plate of biscuits. She beamed at Bisto, her face shining, her hair silky soft.

'I've brought tea, refreshments for us all. I thought it would be nice outside, in the sunshine, all together. And look who's come round to see us. What a treat.'

'Hello, Bisto, Barbara. Nice to see you both.'

The cheery voice came from Chrissie Drake, the vicar, who was beaming at them. Her cascade of dark curls had been drawn back into a top knot tied with a red bow. She was smiling, dressed in dark trousers, a red top and a smart dark jacket. She was wearing red lipstick. Barbara thought she was overdressed – she'd surely melt on such a hot day, but the vicar smoothed the greying hair on her temples, beamed and extended a cool hand.

'Barbara. How are you? So glad you're still staying here with us in Winsley.' She noticed the book. 'Oh, I've read that one. Yes, it's very interesting, isn't it, the way the author focuses on the power of positive thinking and makes it a commonplace practice in our lives?' Chrissie turned to Bisto. 'Well, you've been busy, doing a fabulous job for Pauline here. Shall we all stop for a cup of tea and a chat? I have rather good news.'

They sat together at the little bistro table round the side of the house which overlooked the neighbours' garden. As Pauline poured tea, they could hear Fabian's voice, a steady drawl, interspersed with Ava's giggles of laughter.

Bisto helped himself to a ginger biscuit and dunked it in his tea. 'Nice to see you, Chrissie. How's life over at the church? Is God behaving himself?'

Chrissie was thoughtful for a moment, then she offered a confident smile. 'God is as wonderful as ever. Look at this fabulous weather, this delightful cup of tea, the joyous company.' She sipped from her teacup. 'That's why I'm here, really.'

Barbara pulled a face. 'Because of God? I hope we're not expected to go to church on Sunday and increase the congregation?'

Chrissie smiled, a cat with the cream. 'Something far more sinful, I'm afraid. But just as enjoyable.'

'It's really exciting.' Pauline offered the plate of biscuits. 'There's a play on this evening on the green in Winsley.'

'I'm not keen on plays.' Barbara wrinkled her nose. 'I can't see the point of making things up. There's too much invented rubbish – why can't we just stick with what's real?'

Chrissie pressed her arm. 'It's Shakespeare, Barbara.' Her voice conveyed pure admiration. 'And I have tickets for us all.'

'Tilly Hardy's friend is the director. He has a touring company and they come each year to perform to the villages.' Pauline rubbed her hands together. 'They are doing *A Midsummer Night's Dream*.'

Chrissie nodded. 'They started in Cornwall on 21 June, of course, but they are touring through Somerset and Devon in July and we have them here this evening. Everyone will be there. We must go.'

Barbara rolled her eyes, unimpressed. Pauline's face was soft with excitement.

'We'll take a picnic and rugs. Sandwiches, rolls, quiches, salad, little cakes, a flask.'

'A drink or two maybe.' Bisto sat upright, suddenly keen. 'We can pop over to the Sheep Dip for a bit of light refreshment between the acts.'

'Then it's settled. We'll all go.' Pauline grinned. She was thoughtful for a moment, imagining all the villagers assembled to watch the play. Everyone would be there.

Chrissie purred. 'I'm so looking forward to it.'

Barbara sipped her tea and listened for sounds of the young couple across the lane, her ears straining for their voices. It was silent but she knew they were still there. They would be kissing, cuddling each other. Of course, it would all end badly. Barbara stared at the dregs in the bottom of her cup and sighed. The tealeaves had formed a distinct heart shape. Barbara suddenly felt depressed. *A Midsummer Night's Dream* was a romantic comedy, wasn't it? And she had no time for comedies – or romance.

20

Pauline was walking arm in arm with Bisto in the centre, his other arm precariously looped through Barbara's, who had insisted on carrying the picnic basket. She was smiling; she thought they resembled the three characters in *The Wizard of Oz*. Bisto unshaven, in the middle, swaggering, his jacket too big in the body, his curls unbrushed, was the Scarecrow – she thought this affectionately, the desire to ruffle the wayward curls uppermost in her mind.

Barbara was the Tin Man, walking upright, stoical, staring into the distance in front of her, hard-hearted, determined not to enjoy the day. She was saying, 'We'll only be going there in order to come back. And as for sitting on the damp ground – doesn't that give you piles?'

Pauline was feeling a new affection starting to kindle for her sister; she'd always just believed their lives were poles apart. Barbara had never really liked her as a child; later, she'd never liked Douglas and, when Jessica was born, she'd kept her distance, proclaiming loudly over the phone, 'I don't do children.' But Pauline was beginning to understand her – behind the cold, hard, tin exterior, there was a kindness, honesty, a heart of gold.

And she, Pauline, in an orange dress, the lion who'd lost a bit of her courage after Douglas died, needed a reason to be bold. But she felt new warmth stirring in her heart, a new beginning. She was becoming the old Pauline again: positive, cheerful, full of energy. She could even love again, she knew it. She linked her arm through Bisto's; he pushed his wrist through the crook in Barbara's arm and they sauntered along together. Pauline was humming the tune of *Follow the Yellow Brick Road* as she walked, doing a little skip with each alternate note, then she heard the loud murmuring sound of a tractor approaching and suddenly there was Len Chatfield, aloft in his cab.

Pauline pressed her lips together, determined she would not let him pass without a word this time. She lifted an arm, not to wave, but she held it upright and with a playful pretend voice of authority, she called, 'Halt.'

Len slowed his tractor, allowing the vehicle to idle, and Pauline slithered her arm from Bisto's and approached the cab. 'Hello, Len.'

He nodded briefly. 'Pauline.' His eyes moved to Bisto, then Barbara, and back to Pauline's orange checked dress.

'It's lovely to see you. How are things up at Bottom Farm?'

He chewed his lip thoughtfully for a moment. 'Same, I reckon.'

'We're going to see the play, Len. On the village green. It's *A Midsummer Night's Dream*. Shakespeare. We have a picnic too.' She smiled at him hopefully. 'Why don't you come and join us?'

He paused for a moment, saying nothing, so she met his gaze and giggled. 'It would be really fun.'

Len looked away, glowered at Bisto, and gazed back at Pauline's orange frock. 'Too much to do. No time for plays and stuff.' He rubbed his whiskers.

Pauline shrugged and gave her shoulders a small swing. 'Well, if you change your mind, Len, there's plenty of food. And we've got some cider...'

Bisto chimed out from a few feet away. 'And there's plenty more to be had in the Sheep Dip.' He waved an arm. 'Come and join us, Lennie boy. It'll be good craic.'

Len frowned. 'I don't know that I want any crack.' The engine revved. 'Or no plays. Too busy.' He narrowed his eyes. 'Farm. Tractor. Land. No, I have no time for plays.'

The tractor edged forward and away, Pauline raising her hand to wave. She watched him go, thinking about how hard it had been for Len to meet her eyes. She felt sad for a moment that he was still distant, and then a new strength filled her heart. If Len couldn't become more sociable, she would have to help him. Pauline was sure she could find a way. It just needed a bit of patience and some planning. She rejoined Bisto, who had taken the basket from Barbara, and sighed.

'Len needs more fun in his life.'

Barbara grunted. 'He wouldn't know fun if it grew teeth and bit his backside. He's a miserable man, that one.'

Bisto grinned at her. 'Ah, but he's not a bad sort. Just a case of being too busy in his work. It can do that to a man, you know. A woman too. Sucks out your soul, too much work.'

'I don't agree.' Barbara's voice was firm. 'I worked as a secretary in the Royal Air Force for years. They couldn't have done without me. And I loved my job. I was indispensable. I brought order to everything I touched.'

'I'm sure you did, Babs.' Bisto winked at Pauline. 'Onwards and upwards now, ladies. There's a play to be seen and a picnic to be drunk...'

As they arrived at the village green, there was a swarm of activity by the huge canopy which had been erected in the centre of the square, in front of the pub. The canopy was bright orange and several men and women in black t-shirts and jeans had built a stage from rostra blocks and were creating a set of lurid green trees, bushes and a huge backdrop. A smiling sun and a pale moon hung down at the back and the whole canopy was decked in twinkling lights, even though it was early evening and the sun was still beating down. Pauline looked around for a good place to sit, close to the play and not too far from the pub: Bisto might need a refill or two. Barbara stood next to her; her arms folded. Pauline heard her mutter, 'The grass is so dry, it's turned brown. We'll still need a nice rug to sit on. I hope there's one packed, Pauline.'

'Hello, there. So nice to see you all.'

Pauline turned and met the eyes of a blond gentleman in his thirties. He was cleanly shaven, wearing a light blue sports jacket, a cream coloured shirt, a red bow tie and smart jeans. Barbara patted her curls. Hugo Garrett hesitated for a moment, then hugged Pauline, embraced a blushing Barbara, and shook Bisto's hand. 'Perfect weather for some outdoor theatre, isn't it?'

'Lovely to see you, Hugo,' Pauline smiled. 'Have you brought a picnic?'

Hugo offered his charming smile. 'I'm afraid not – I'll have a bite to eat later. I have to dash off to London straight after the show. I don't drink and drive – I'd be lethal.'

'Do you have a place of your own in London?' Bisto asked.

'I do – a little flat, very cosy. I have to have a pad there really – I have business in London, so I go up a lot.'

'You know how to live the perfect life,' Bisto mused. 'Country residence, London bolt hole. It must be great.'

Hugo's brow creased. 'Sometimes. It has its ups and downs.' He glanced at Barbara and her blush deepened. 'Good to see you are both still here, enjoying life in Winsley. When I'm back from this little jaunt in London, you must all come up to have dinner at the manor with me. Would that be okay?'

'Oh, yes...' Barbara caught her breath. She felt silly, reddening again, but Hugo reminded her so much of the man she'd known and loved, many years ago, and it brought back sensations and feelings she'd been determined to keep hidden. She took out her handkerchief and pretended to wipe her nose.

'That'd be lovely, Hugo,' Pauline smiled easily, resting her hand on Hugo's forearm.

'I'll be looking forward to it,' Bisto added, licking his lips. Pauline wondered if he was thinking of the food or the fine wines they might sample.

'I'll be in touch when I'm back.' Hugo glanced over his shoulder. 'Oh, do excuse me. There's Tamsin and baby Harley. I must pop across and see how the little one is doing.'

Pauline watched him move away, elegant and assured. Barbara gave a silent sigh, then leaned over and whispered, 'Didn't your friend Dizzy say he could be the father of Tamsin's baby?' She patted her sister's shoulder. 'I wonder – do you think it could be his?'

Pauline giggled, filled with warmth for her sister. She couldn't resist a little joke. 'You're settling in well, Barbara – you're learning to gossip like one of the locals...'

'Oh no, not at all – I only meant—'

'Let's sit over there, near the front.' Bisto pointed to a spot near the stage. 'There's your friend Dizzy and that Yvonne one from the Post Office.'

They weaved through the seated audience members, Pauline tugged out a rolled up rug from the bottom of the basket and arranged it on the ground next to Dizzy, plonking herself down. Bisto sat in the middle and Barbara perched on the edge, smoothing her jeans and picking off a blade of dry grass from the material. Dizzy was all smiles and waving hands.

'So I said to him, "Well, what about Sunday night?" and he said "Yes, you can come round to the little bedsit in Milton Rogus." So – that's all settled – I'm on for tomorrow night. With Kostas. A second date. He's making mezze and we're going to drink ouzo. He's so sweet and so funny. And I think he likes me too. I'm so excited. Oh, Pauline, do you think I should take an overnight bag? Just in case?'

Yvonne giggled, patting her blonde hair. 'Kostas is going to be a lucky man.'

'Perhaps you should play it cool in the early dates, Dizzy – keep him guessing.' Pauline suggested. Bisto was rooting around in the picnic basket, pulling out a bottle of Guinness.

'I thought I'd wear hot pants,' Dizzy giggled. 'A little crop top. What do you think?'

'Mutton dressed as lamb – to the slaughter,' Barbara grumbled.

'You'll look a treat,' Bisto murmured into the neck of the bottle he'd just opened.

Barbara looked around her. 'Oh, I can see Chrissie, the vicar, with Dr Natalie. And there's Tilly the novelist, chattering to a man with a funny ponytail – they're over there, by the stage. Look, there's her son, the boy who's dating the girl from across the lane – but he's with someone else. That's Claudia he's talking to, the daughter of Oskar and Justina from the pub, isn't it?'

Pauline leaned over and touched her sister's shoulder gently. 'Claudia, yes – she's talking to Fabian. I can't see Ava Darby, or Julia, or her husband Peter.'

Barbara blew air from her lungs. 'Do you think he's cheating on Ava? There could be a scene...'

Bisto sucked beer from the bottle. 'He was a good cricket player, Peter Darby. Not sure his wife likes me since I urinated on her flowers. I wonder if Kevin Carter's here. I owe him a pint...'

Yvonne shrugged. 'Your neighbours don't get out much, Pauline. The Darbys. We don't see them socialising much in the village. He seems all right, though, the husband, Peter – he comes in the Post Office for a paper most mornings – he reads the *Guardian*. I've never seen his wife call in at all – not sure I've even met her.'

Dizzy breathed out. 'I popped round to their house about a week ago to offer my services. I introduced myself to Julia Darby, said I'd do her a good cut, neighbours' rates, but she stopped me mid-sentence and told me she had a regular hairdresser in Bath and wouldn't be interested in hiring a local amateur to mess about with her hair. The cheek of it.'

Barbara was turning her head, surveying the people sitting on the green. 'The two old ladies aren't here. Phyllis and Dulcie.' She turned a shocked face to Pauline. 'You don't think Phyllis has shot her with that air rifle, do you?'

Pauline smiled. 'They'll be here soon. The play doesn't start for twenty minutes. There's still time.'

Yvonne leaned forward. 'Dulcie still hasn't found Clive. It's been weeks now. She's out of her mind with worry.'

'Dead in a hedge, no doubt,' Barbara sniffed. 'I'm surprised your friend Kevin hasn't found it with a bullet hole through its head, Bisto.'

Bisto finished the beer, up-ending the last of the dregs into his mouth. 'Ah, you know what cats are like. Clive's probably off hunting near the pig farms, filling his belly with rats and mice. He'll be back as soon as the weather changes, no doubt.'

'Poor Dulcie.' Pauline lifted out a plate of cucumber sandwiches from under a tea towel. 'She adores those two cats.' She offered the plate to Dizzy, who helped herself to two white bread triangles, then she held out the sandwiches to Barbara, but her sister was still gaping into the distance.

'Who's that waving at us? It's the mad writer woman, isn't it?'

Bisto waved his arm. 'It's Tilly Hardy. She's coming over here.' He winked at Pauline and started to rummage in the picnic basket. 'Perhaps it's my body she's after.'

'I'm not sure even medical science could find a use for it,'

Barbara scoffed, but Bisto was busy tugging the lid from a bottle of cider.

Tilly Hardy rushed towards them, pulling a man by the arm; he was lagging behind, his expression unhappy. Her grey curls blew around her head like a soft rain cloud. She was wearing a long patchwork skirt which came to her ankles and a rainbow t-shirt embellished with a peace sign. Her feet were bare. The man with her was in his fifties; he was very slim, with a slightly receding hairline, although his long ponytail of brown dreadlocks hung almost to his waist. He was pale, anxious looking and wore round metal glasses, a faded t-shirt and black jeans. Tilly pushed him forward.

'This is Bo-Bo. He's the director of *A Midsummer Night's Dream.*' She crouched down next to Pauline, and Bo-Bo joined her, nodding at the little group. His forehead was creased with deep lines of concern.

Bisto took a sip of cider. 'We're looking forward to the play. One of my favourites it is, *A Midsummer Night's Dream.*'

'We're all very excited,' Pauline added.

'The thing is...' Tilly tugged at Bo-Bo's arm. 'Well, Bo-Bo and I go back a long way, don't we, Bo? We were at the same uni – we were even an item for a while, weren't we, Bo?' Bo-Bo nodded. His face was very serious.

'We meet up every year – I help to organise the theatre-on-the-green project, and we invite the players here annually. Bo-Bo's very good. He's directed all kinds of alternative theatre in Berlin and Budapest.'

Dizzy gazed at Bo-Bo. 'I've never met a real director before.'

'Thing is, guys,' Bo-Bo's voice was soft, almost a whisper. 'We have a problem. I'm not sure we can even do the show now. We might have to cancel. One of our musicians is unwell.'

Barbara folded her arms. 'A musician isn't that important, surely. It's a play, not a musical, for goodness sake.'

Bo-Bo sighed. 'This is serious. It affects the whole production, the impact of it on the audience.'

'It is serious,' Tilly repeated emphatically. 'Without music, *The Dream* has no ambiance.'

'Ambiance?' Barbara was unsure. 'When I saw it, it was just a load of fairies prancing about.'

'But that's the point.' Bo-Bo's eyes flashed behind his glasses. 'It can't look like prancing fairies. The music creates the ethereal atmosphere; it's a semiotic, part of the magical metaphor – it suggests the transition between reality and dream, between fairy-land and humankind. Without the music, the play just won't work.'

Barbara shrugged, unconcerned. 'That's a pity.'

'How can we help?' Pauline asked.

Tilly's eyes were wide. 'Aren't you a musician, Bisto? When I was playing my guitar at the May Day Fair, I distinctly remember you saying you have some musical skills. I mean, I'd play the guitar for Bo-Bo, but it needs something stronger, more emphatic and persistent.'

Bo-Bo turned his spectacled gaze on Bisto and his voice was thick with concern. 'Can you save the day, man? I mean, I'd pay. What instruments can you play? I need to convey the evocative sense of the otherworld, the wraithlike presence of the fairies, the mischief and the mayhem.'

'I can do a fair turn on the violin for you.'

Bo-Bo grabbed his shoulder, his expression desperate. 'Do you know the play? Are you familiar with *The Dream*?'

'I know it very well, Bo-Bo. In my days at university in Dublin, I played Bottom in an amateur production. It was good craic.'

'I'll pay you fifty pounds for the gig. Can you do it? I need violin music between each act and some improvisation to symbolise that the magic is happening. Can you do that?'

'I can, of course, no trouble. But I'd rather you paid me in kind.'

Tilly chuckled. 'Of course. We can set up a free tab at the bar for you.'

'And the ladies too?' Bisto indicated the four women on the rug.

'It's a deal,' Bo-Bo breathed out with relief, holding out his palm for Bisto to shake.

'You've saved the day, Bisto,' Tilly clapped her hands.

Bo-Bo stood up, turning to the stage. 'Come on then. I have an old violin backstage. We'll have to tune up, sort out cues, practise with the accordion player and the djembes – so many important things. There's no time to waste.'

Bisto winked at Pauline and struggled to his feet, taking the half- empty bottle of cider with him as he and Tilly scuttled after Bo-Bo, who was clearly a man with a mission now, surging forward. Pauline turned to Barbara. 'This should be interesting.'

Barbara raised her eyebrows. 'Interesting? Do you think so? You know what Bisto is like, with his stories. I mean, does he actually play an instrument at all? Pauline, this could be a complete disaster. And that's looking on the bright side...'

21

The play opened with a single drawn-out note from the violin, and then a sweet simple melody hung on the air as sprites swirled nimbly across the stage, weaving long streamers in the branches of the luridly painted trees and bushes of the set. Then the fairies, green-faced and clad in mottled colours of the forest, giggled playfully and hid among two-dimensional trees, invisible, as the imperious Duke of Athens appeared on stage, tugging the ferocious Queen of the Amazons who was handcuffed. Barbara was not really paying attention: she was deep in thought. She was aware that there was an argument on the stage, that a young woman did not want to marry the man her aged father had ordered her to wed, that she was prepared to 'die the death' rather than to lose her true love. But Barbara was thinking about herself; she was more concerned with reality.

The book she'd been reading, about how to become popular, was filling her thoughts. There had been a lot of discussion in the chapters about forming reciprocal relationships, about showing yourself to be an empathic person. Barbara had never really understood empathy. She knew how to be polite, how to say please and thank you, or how are you today, but she'd never really listened properly to others' responses. They had never really mattered. What had been important to her was order, organisation. She had been proud of her work in the Royal Air Force. She was always commended for her skills, duties that fell within the realm of her job. She was efficient on the phone and stood for no time-wasting from callers. She knew clearly which phone calls to pass on to the person it was intended for and which to deflect. But her abilities – to file things in an orderly way, to type business letters, to meet deadlines and to furnish her bosses with the information exactly as and when they needed it – were second to none. She had been an excellent secretary.

A little sprite called Puck was on stage now, frolicking and chattering to Oberon, the Fairy King. Off stage, a melodic violin tune became tempestuous, powerful, as Oberon appeared from the bough of a tree and raised his magical fist. But Barbara was thinking about when she first met Robert, how her life had been lifted on a whirlwind. Of course, she'd still been efficient in the office, an exemplary secretary. Her work had never suffered because of her private life, although in the daytime her head had often been filled with the excitement of the evening, and what would happen when Robert would arrive. Often, he wouldn't be there on time. Sometimes he would be very late; sometimes he wouldn't turn up at all. It couldn't be helped. She knew the reason why. Then he'd arrive days later with flowers, chocolates, profuse apologises and so many kisses. Barbara understood about his other commitment. It still hurt her; it still made her heart ache and her imagination filled with the rattling of a film strip: the scenes of her beloved Robert elsewhere, with someone else. But he'd promised her it wouldn't always be like that. They would be together soon, for always. And of course, she'd believed him. And she couldn't turn back – she couldn't stop her feelings being so strong.

The violin played an Irish jig from the wings as Bottom and the Players cavorted on the stage. Then the fiddle became an eerie air, as Puck approached to listen. Barbara swallowed hard. By the time Robert had told her the truth, about his 'situation', it was too late. She loved him. It was the only time in her life she'd truly felt empathy. She hung on his every word. She met his passion with a passion of her own; his deep kisses were returned and doubled. And when he let her down in the evening, or when he left her in the morning, as they both put on their uniforms and promised to meet soon, she knew the ache of separation and the agony of jealousy. That was what happened to you when you felt empathy.

The violin moaned, a poignant off stage note that filled the air as the two pairs of misguided lovers followed each other in the forest. Barbara's thoughts drifted back to the book she was reading. She'd had few friends in her life, no one really who understood her or cared about her. Yet here she was in Winsley Green, surrounded by villagers who seemed to like her, who liked Pauline a lot and eagerly included her sister in their lives, enfolded her in day-to-day activities and made her feel important. And Barbara had found she was in no hurry to return to Cambridge.

The truth was that she'd started to care about the villagers: the two feuding old ladies, the lost cat, Clive. Barbara was actually concerned about them all, despite the sharp words that came out of her mouth before she'd considered how someone might react. She liked Chrissie, the sweet, mad, caring vicar who was so kind to everyone. She was worried about Ava Darby and whether Tilly's son Fabian had rejected her for Claudia. Barbara knew how Ava would feel if she was being two-timed – jealousy consumed people totally, Barbara knew that.

Then there was Julia Darby – she might be lonely, all by herself in the house across the lane. Barbara was fretful about Dizzy too – she may have ridiculous hair and laugh too loudly, but she was throwing herself at Kostas in a desperate way and that could only result in a broken heart. Barbara knew how that would feel. She was actually experiencing empathy and it felt strange, warm, fuzzy, and something else – she felt vulnerable; she could even have her feelings hurt. That's what happened if you trusted people, empathised with them, came to care for them. Then her thoughts turned to Bisto. She had thought him a tramp, a vagrant, a drunkard. But he was warm, kind, funny, and full of goodness. He was clever too, well read. And he was building a proper garden room for Pauline. He clearly liked Pauline. But he had hugged her, Barbara, and she had felt something she hadn't allowed herself to feel in a long time. A connection, the stirring of a different kind of warmth. Something, an emotion, long since buried, twanged inside her heart like a violin string; a note so strong it made her feel both excited and afraid. She stared at the stage, lost in thought.

Titania, the fairy queen, wearing a transparent costume like a butterfly's skin, her golden hair down to her waist and a crown of white flowers over her brow, crooned, 'What angel wakes me from my flow'ry bed?' Bottom, now magically transformed, had sat upright in her bed and his head was the head of a donkey. Barbara blinked. The fairy queen was fondling the donkey's ears, calling her fairy handmaidens to shower attention on him. Bottom was demanding that his ears were scratched and Peaseblossom, Moth and Cobweb, three dainty fairies in translucent costumes, were dancing prettily around him, fawning and caressing his ass head. Then Bottom called, 'Where's Mustardseed?'

A gentle violin tune came from off stage and Bisto appeared, leaping onto the stage. Arms aloft, instrument in one hand and bow in the other, he cavorted in a comic pirouette and then curtseyed. The ankle was clearly much better now. He was wearing a yellow tutu and vest, the top badly concealing his hairy chest. He wore a blue wig, the shiny synthetic hair falling across his shoulders and as he waved the arm holding the bow, the light shifted on his fluorescent pink wings. The audience roared with laughter as Bisto yelled a falsetto, 'Ready!'

Barbara couldn't help it. She began to laugh uncontrollably. Tears sprang to her eyes, rolled down her cheeks and she covered her face, she was laughing so hard. Next to her, Pauline was howling in hysterics too. Dizzy's face was pink, her eyes crinkled, her mouth wide and Yvonne slapped Barbara on the shoulder, spluttering, 'I don't believe it. Oh, just look at him.'

Then the audience began to stand up, one by one. Barbara recognised Kevin Carter, the hedger, with his wife and little auburn-haired daughter. He was the first to clamber to his feet and clap his hands. Then Chrissie was upright, then Hugo Garrett, cheering and calling, 'Hoorah!' Barbara leaped to her feet, pounding her hands together so hard that it hurt.

Pauline scrambled up next to her, then Dizzy was up and yelling. Everyone was shouting, cheering, calling out Bisto's name. The little man turned to the audience and gave a low curtsey and the applause became so loud Barbara's ears buzzed. He curtseyed again, waving his violin and bow in the air and the crowd whooped. He bowed, his head almost touching the stage, and as he swept forward, his electric blue wig promptly fell off, exposing his white curls. When he looked up again, his bright green face was creased with a wide smile.

As the light faded and the moon rose, a crescent hook into the darkness, villagers stayed on the grass, drinking, chattering and laughing softly. They all agreed that the play had been the best ever, a great success, and Bo-Bo and Tilly were surrounded by a throng of people offering praise and compliments. Bisto's glass was full at all times and he moved from group to group, laughing with neighbours who had now become friends. He was still wearing the yellow tutu, but his face was almost devoid of green makeup and the blue wig was now squashed on the top of Kevin Carter's ginger head. Fairy lights twinkled; a magical spray of colour that kept the dream-like enchantment of the play alive. The doors of the Sheep Dip Inn were thrown wide, and inside glasses clinked and laughter bubbled softly, interspersed with occasional affable roars of enjoyment.

Pauline sipped a warm mulled cider and glanced around. Dizzy's eyes were constantly roving, searching every new arrival's face, but Kostas was nowhere to be seen tonight. Gary Chatfield had arrived by himself, staring down into a glass, watching others enjoy themselves. Pauline noticed his eyes on Tamsin, Yvonne's daughter, who had brought the baby and was now talking to Andy Priddy, his arm round her. Ava Darby had arrived too and she was holding Fabian's hand, both of them wearing dark clothes, an expression of self-absorption on their faces. Pauline wondered if Gary was lonely. He was in his thirties and still broodingly handsome, but he rarely socialised except for the times he drank cider in the pub, preferring to spend his time working on the farm with his father.

Pauline closed her eyes and considered Len. He'd always been jovial, helpful, but of late he'd been withdrawn and distant, even more reclusive, shunning company. Pauline suspected she knew why that was and she smiled sadly; it was easy to sympathise with Len and his son: they had seemed so uncomfortable in Bisto's company. To both of them happy-go-lucky Bisto, so well-travelled, so worldly-wise and spontaneous in social situations, must be diffi-cult to accept into the routine of their lives. Bisto was popular in the village now, easy-going, without responsibilities, and Len must feel that his life was all hard work and no fun. It wasn't surprising, Pauline thought, that Len might feel a little jealous.

The mulled cider was warm and syrupy on her tongue. Pauline's eyes moved to Barbara. Her sister was talking animatedly to Dizzy, a hand gently resting on her arm, and Pauline could hear her voice, insistent, murmuring, 'You won't get him to love you by throwing yourself at him. A woman needs to be mysterious, distant – a prize a man wants to win for himself.'

Pauline smiled. She had no idea where Barbara's opinions had come from. She didn't read romantic novels and, to the best of her knowledge, Barbara had not been in many relationships. Pauline knew there had been someone in Barbara's life during her twenties, but she had never met him. She'd even wondered at times if Barbara had made him up, but Pauline had been busy with her own life. There had been boyfriends, broken hearts, and then her first fiancé, Jeff. That hadn't ended well: Jeff had been great fun at first, but later unreliable to such an extent that he met another woman and moved to Saudi Arabia with her, leaving Pauline alone with a cheap diamond ring and the determination to find a sensible match. Then Douglas had come into her life; he was honest, funny and he clearly adored her. She had little time to think of Barbara in Cambridge, whose routine revolved around uniforms and duties and a career. She was too busy falling in love, marrying, and being a mother.

'It's Pauline, isn't it? Hello.' Pauline swivelled round and stared into the face of a man who was in his forties, clean shaven, with neat dark hair and black-framed glasses. 'We haven't spoken properly yet. It's been very remiss of me. I'm Peter Darby – your neighbour.'

Pauline took his outstretched hand and smiled easily. 'Hello, Peter. I've spoken to Julia and met I met your daughter Ava but we don't seem to have crossed paths yet.'

Peter nodded and grinned, showing even teeth. 'I work a lot – away from home sometimes. But I believe you've been very kind to Julia. I remember her telling me about the incident with the cat and the headless rabbit – poor Julia was quite horrified.'

'I'm used to Dulcie's cats,' Pauline explained. 'Things like that happen a lot here.'

'So I believe. We've moved from Bath. It's a bit of a culture shock for Julia.'

'I hope she'll settle soon. Isn't she here tonight, to see the play?'

'She has another one of her headaches, unfortunately.' Peter cleared his throat. 'I've come to pick up Ava and walk her home but it appears she has her own escort.' He stared across to a kissing couple in black, leaning against a tree at the edge of the green. 'The novelist's son, I believe. I haven't been introduced yet.'

Pauline grinned. 'They seem to be getting on well.'

'Pauline...' Peter adjusted his glasses. 'I'm glad I bumped into you. I'm taking Julia away for a few days. Paris. I'm hoping it'll cheer her up a bit. It's her birthday tomorrow and I know she'll love the museums, the galleries, city life.'

'I hope so.'

'I just wanted to let you know we'll be away. Ava isn't coming with us. Her A levels are over now, and she probably won't get out of bed until after midday, but I wonder if you could just keep an eye...'

'Of course, Peter. That's no problem.'

Peter glanced at Bisto, some yards away, who held a glass to his mouth, laughed loudly then continued a conversation with Dr Natalie and Dr Mario. 'Your partner was a success on stage this evening, I believe.'

Pauline giggled. 'Bisto's not my partner; he's my house guest, Peter. He's staying for a short while, rebuilding the conservatory, making a garden room.' She met his eyes. 'You and Julia must come over one evening and meet him properly.'

Her eyes strayed to Bisto, whose glass was almost empty. He was patting Dr Natalie's hand, no doubt talking about her expected baby. Dr Natalie was very pregnant now. She had developed the habit of rubbing her belly gently every so often, leaving a comforting hand on the roundness. And Dr Mario had a protective arm on her shoulder, standing close by. Pauline smiled. Even doctors were anxious about a first baby.

Suddenly a yell made her turn her head sharply. Dulcie was rushing towards Bisto, waving her hands. Bisto had turned and held out an arm to the old lady. Without thinking, Pauline hurried forward to Bisto and took a position on the other side of Dulcie who was panting and gasping, her face a mask of panic.

'Dulcie, what is it?' Pauline's voice was thick with concern.

Bisto held her arm gently, supporting her elbow. 'Take a deep breath now, Dulcie. It'll all be fine.'

'Doctor...' Dulcie stared from Dr Mario to Dr Natalie. 'It's an emergency. It's Phyllis.'

'What about Phyllis?' Bisto's brow creased. 'Is she all right?'

'She's fallen. I ran here to tell you. She slipped on the steps of her caravan. We were arguing about Clive – I'd just called her a morbid murderous bitch and she came for me, then she tripped.'

'You should have called an ambulance,' Dr Mario suggested.

'I've no phone. Nor has she.' Dulcie's grey hair had tumbled across a damply crumpled brow. 'But you need to come now. Now.'

'My car is in The Sheep Dip car park.' Dr Mario rubbed his beard, his eyes alert. 'Pauline, will you wait here with Natalie?'

Pauline nodded, extending an arm to touch Natalie's elbow.

Bisto turned to Dr Mario. 'I'll come with you.'

* * *

'We'd better be quick,' Dulcie moaned. 'It's serious. I shouted at her and she fell down the steps and didn't move. It wasn't my fault but I might have killed her. I think she's dead.'

22

The rain had been drizzling for two days without pausing. It was late afternoon and the skies were dishwater grey as Barbara stared out of the kitchen window. She could see where the conservatory had been, now mounds of wet rubble and stone. Bisto had done very little work on the new garden room due to the downpour: piles of grubby glass, edged with mould, and damp wood were stacked outside. He was in Taunton visiting Phyllis, who was in hospital, resting her sore hip. Chrissie had given him a lift in her Fiat, which he'd referred to as the little God-mobile. Dulcie had refused to accompany them; even though she was visibly relieved that her neighbour was not dead and, in fact, was alive and well and yelling at the nurses in Primrose Ward to let her come home because her flowers needed tending and her nasty neighbour might take the opportunity to let her cat pee on them, Dulcie said she couldn't visit.

'I can't look at the woman. She's probably roasted Clive alive and eaten him. I can't forgive her for that.' She'd folded her arms and passed wind. 'I just wouldn't want to see her dead, that's all.'

Barbara gazed at the rain and turned back to the kitchen table where Dizzy was laughing, chattering non-stop, holding court with Pauline, their mugs of coffee now empty. Barbara was bored. They were talking about love again. Dizzy had been at it for an hour now – she had been on another date with Kostas and she couldn't understand why he hadn't responded to her obvious ploys to lure him into the bedroom.

'He is so gorgeous, though, Pauline. I mean, when I arrived at his house, he was wearing denim cut-offs and an open-necked white shirt, showing his entire chest. If that's not a come-and-get-me sign, I don't know what is.'

Barbara made a low sound through her lips. 'Perhaps he was just warm. I mean, it's mid-July. He's bound to be sweaty, isn't he? He's a man.'

Dizzy leaned forward, extended her hand and patted Pauline's. 'It wasn't that I didn't give him lots of encouragement. I said to him, "Ooh, Kostas, these seats are so hard." We were sitting at the table on wooden benches, and I said, "Don't you have anywhere more comfortable where my back won't ache so much?" And he just grinned at me and said, "Anything for my friend Dizzy," and he brought me a cushion.'

'Perhaps he respects you as a woman?' Pauline offered gently. 'It's early days.'

'I wondered if his English wasn't good enough to understand the clues I was dishing out,' Dizzy moaned. 'I mean, I took off my jacket – I had on a little halter top, and I said, "I'm feeling so hot, Kostas," and I thought he'd take the hint but he just nodded and brought me a glass of water.'

Barbara grunted. 'Perhaps he doesn't fancy you. After all, you're years older than him. Maybe he sees you as a big sister. Or a mother substitute?'

Dizzy's face was horrified. 'Do you think so, Pauline?'

Pauline went over to the Aga, settled the kettle on the hot plate and reached for the jar of coffee. 'I doubt it. He'd be mad not to be interested.' She thought for a moment and gave a low chuckle. 'I don't really understand men. I mean, after all these years, I still find them unpredictable and peculiar.'

Dizzy narrowed her eyes. 'Well, I can tell you this. Bisto definitely has the hots for you, Pauline.' She turned her gaze on Barbara. 'You must have noticed it, Barb?'

'I can't say that I have.' Barbara was disconcerted by the feeling of uneasiness that was spreading through her body. She knew that Bisto was fond of Pauline. She'd noticed the way he smiled at her, how affectionately he patted her arm. Dizzy was probably right. But Barbara was shocked by how much the thought didn't please her at all.

Pauline shook her head. 'Bisto? Oh, I don't think so, Dizzy.'

'Anyone can see he's in love with you,' Dizzy beamed. 'And why wouldn't he be? You look great. The sun has brought out the blue of your eyes, and your skin is so tanned. He'd do anything for you. Why do you think he's still here, refusing to leave?' She swivelled around in her chair and met Barbara's anxious gaze. 'Maybe we need to find you a bloke, Barb? You've never been married, have you? But there's still time. What about...' She chewed her lip, thinking. 'What about old Len Chatfield? He's on his own. I dare say he could use a woman up there at the farm.'

Barbara put her hands on her hips. 'Use a woman?' Her face was pink. 'I'm not that sort of person. I won't let anyone use me.' She puffed out warm air between her lips. 'Those days are over. I'm not interested in whiskery Len, or any other man.'

Dizzy accepted the coffee Pauline was holding out and gulped down a mouthful. 'Are you a lesbian, Barbara? Perhaps we could find you a nice woman, someone you could share your life with?

There's a lady over in Milton Rogus whose hair I do. I'm sure she's gay. I can usually tell if people are. She's called Jennifer; she's blonde, really pretty, a little younger than you. She rides a moped, so she'd have transport.'

'Just stop it.' Barbara's eyes glinted. 'No, I'm not a lesbian, although if I were, it would be none of your business. I don't want any relationship, not with Jennifer with the moped, not with the rude farmer, not even...'

She stopped herself and forced a grin, although she was sure both women were staring at her with surprise and pity in their eyes. The only way out, Barbara decided, was to show empathy and positivity.

'I don't need anyone in my life. I don't like love. But I could do with another coffee, Pauline.' She forced a giggle. 'A good cuppa's more reliable than most men. It's hot, strong and bitter. Just like me.' Barbara was suddenly pleased with herself. She had made a joke.

Pauline blinked at her for a moment, and then scraped her chair back. 'Sorry, of course I'll make you one – I didn't notice you'd finished...' She turned to Dizzy. 'This talk of romance has made me hungry. Will you stay for supper, Dizzy? Bisto should be back soon. I can make us a salad and I have some new potatoes and quiche.'

Dizzy sat upright. 'Oh, I'd love to, Pauline. After all, Bisto's a man. Maybe he can throw some light on how I can get Kostas in the sack.'

Barbara murmured under her breath 'I don't think Bisto is interested in anything other than his next glass of beer.' But at least she'd said it quietly – she was trying her hardest to be sweet and considerate, like Pauline.

A few hours later, the four of them sat down to a pleasant supper with a bottle of wine and a glass of elderflower lemonade for Barbara, who was seated next to Dizzy. The conversation was mostly about Phyllis, who seemed on the road to recovery and enjoying having someone serve her up the hospital meals. She had befriended a woman in the next bed who had just had a hip replacement and was off her food, so Phyllis was eating double helpings. Pauline was passing the potatoes to Bisto when Dizzy said, 'Do you think I'm unattractive?'

Bisto's fork was in mid-air, a chunk of quiche in his mouth; Pauline raised her eyebrows and shook her head but Barbara managed to speak first.

'Well you're no oil painting, Dizzy. The crazy hair colour doesn't help. I mean, if you dressed a little more sensibly and dyed your hair brown, then you'd look just like everybody else...' Barbara met Pauline's eyes to check if her remark had been helpful. Pauline shook her head, almost imperceptibly.

Bisto leaned forward. 'What Babs means is...' He waved his fork. 'That you're a very striking woman – bubbly, sensual, warm. But not everyone has the same taste in people, do they now? And thank goodness they don't, or I'd have been a very lonely man all my life.'

Pauline smiled at him and piled more potatoes onto his plate. 'I think you look lovely, Bisto.' She turned to Dizzy. 'And so do you. The hair colour suits you. It's vibrant, just like you. Not everyone likes to be dull all the time, Barbara.'

Barbara jerked her head, stunned. Pauline bit her lip – her comment had come out all wrong. She didn't mean to imply that her sister was dull, but she saw Barbara's cheeks flush pink and both sisters suddenly looked uncomfortable.

Dizzy didn't notice. 'The thing is, though, this business with Kostas. I mean, we've been together on dates and we seem to get on well, but I don't know if he really likes me.'

Barbara was staring at her knees. Pauline sat down uneasily and muttered, 'He must like you. He's dating you.'

'But he's never kissed me. I mean, I've given him plenty of

opportunity. Perhaps I'm being silly and he sees me as a friend. I don't know what to do. I don't want my heart broken again.'

Bisto glanced from Dizzy to Pauline. 'But isn't it what we all do? Run the risk of a broken heart, every time we take a chance? Isn't that what love's journey is all about?'

'Love's journey. That sounds so nice.' Dizzy leaned her cheek against her palm. 'But there's nothing as wretched and painful as being dumped. It makes you feel so low, so pointless. Like you shouldn't even exist.'

Barbara's face was still tinged pink; she had pushed her food away and was staring out of the window.

Pauline sighed. 'You're a lovely woman, Dizzy. But sometimes, if someone doesn't want us, it's love's way of saying they're not the right person. I had a fiancé, Jeff. I was so in love with him. But he went off with another woman and I thought I'd never love again.'

Barbara turned her head, her face suddenly softer. 'I didn't know that, Pud.'

Pauline ignored the nickname; she decided she'd put it down to sisterly affection. 'I got over it in time. Then I met Douglas.'

Dizzy sighed. 'I'm forty-three. I haven't had a proper relationship in ages. After what happened last time, I...'

Barbara's brow creased. 'What happened?'

'A man I loved – we were together for several years. He's married now; he has a much younger wife, very pretty, and a child...' Dizzy reached for her glass of wine and gulped two mouthfuls. 'And so I was hoping that this thing with Kostas might...'

Bisto scratched his curls. 'You're a head-turner for sure, Dizzy. But more importantly, you're a lovely woman, bright and warm and funny and great to be with.'

'But that's not what men want, is it, Bisto?' Dizzy opened her eyes wide. 'Men want... oh, I don't know what it is that they want, but they don't seem to want me.'

'Then they aren't the right one,' Barbara said emphatically.

Dizzy waved her hands. 'After... after my last relationship fell apart, I thought, right. I'll be cheerful, happy. I'll be me – I'll find out who I really am, after being part of a couple for so long. I'll do my hair how I want – he was always saying let it grow long, don't wear this, wear something else, so I thought now I'm by myself, I'm going to celebrate who I am.' Dizzy threw her arms wide. 'But nobody wants to celebrate who I am with me.'

She stifled a sob and Barbara reached out and put a hand on her shoulder without thinking. Her words came quickly, from the heart.

'You be who you want to be. Losing someone you love like that is so hard to get over. It's like you've lost a piece of yourself.'

Pauline nodded. 'I agree. After Douglas died, the house was so quiet. I mean, he wasn't here much but without him, every corner just seemed to hold silence and loneliness still inside it.'

'I know what you mean, Pauline...' Bisto was staring into his wine glass. 'I was so miserable when Nisha died. I came very close to doing something I'd have regretted.'

The three women were staring at him. Bisto looked from one face to another: Pauline's soft eyes, Dizzy's open mouth, Barbara's expression of sadness as she muttered, 'Bisto?'

'Ah, it doesn't matter now. Those days have gone.'

Barbara strained forward. 'What did you do? Nearly?'

Bisto shook his head. 'I had a hobby before; I used to do it a lot... in between working. I worked hard and Nisha thought it would help me to relax and get away from all the day-to-day pressure... and it did. I loved it; I'd wind down...' He was quiet for a moment, thinking. 'Then, without her, I didn't see the point in carrying on all by myself, so I was out doing... what I did... and I almost ended it all there and then. But when I thought about it, at the last minute, I knew Nisha wouldn't want me to do anything to harm myself – she'd want me to go on...'

'I'm so glad you didn't do anything dreadful,' Pauline breathed.

Bisto's smile was crooked. 'I lost touch with reality for a while. But I'm all right now.' He filled up his wine glass, and then Pauline's and Dizzy's. 'I gave up the hobby straight after. But I still haven't given up on love.'

'Really, Bisto, you're still expecting to find someone to love? You're seventy something.' Dizzy's laughter burst like a bubble.

'So that means we're all past hope then, does it now?' Bisto chuckled. 'Well for my part, I haven't given up hope of finding myself a good woman.' He winked at Pauline. 'One who'll share my heart and lust after my body?'

'I agree, Bisto,' Pauline giggled, her fingers over her lips. 'There might just be a man out there for me one of these days – who knows?'

'Well then, here's to romance in the future for us all.' Dizzy held her glass high and Pauline and Bisto chinked theirs against hers. Barbara scraped back her chair.

'I need a breath of fresh air.'

'It's dark outside, Barbara... it's well past ten o'clock,' Pauline murmured, but Barbara hauled open the back door and breathed in the cool night. She wandered out into the garden, smelling the sweet richness of night-scented stock, and gazed up at the sky. It was crammed with stars, bright twinkling jewels of light against black, and she stood quietly for a moment. The wind wrapped itself around her shoulders and she shivered, but she was not ready to go back inside. She felt suddenly very alone.

She heard a clattering noise, not unlike raucous music. From the house across the lane came the thump-thumping of bass guitar and drums. The front door had been opened briefly and the volume had increased; the rattle of voices lifted on the breeze.

Barbara listened for a moment and glanced over the hedge at the Darby's house. There was soft light from several of the windows and waves of laughter and loud music filled her ears.

Then she heard the anxiety in her voice as she called out.

'Pauline, can you come out here? Didn't you say the Darbys were away? I think there's somebody in their house.'

23

'I'll stay here,' Dizzy's eyes opened wide. 'Who knows what's going on over there?'

'It'll just be the young ones enjoying themselves.' Bisto set off towards the road, Pauline and Barbara at each elbow.

'I did promise Peter I'd keep an eye out for Ava,' Pauline murmured, pulling a small torch from her pocket and shining the light into the darkness in front of them. 'She probably has some friends over, a dinner party or something.'

'It sounds more like an orgy,' Barbara grunted. 'They've probably got a rock festival going on.'

Bisto patted her shoulder. 'I'd like to go to the sort of orgies you go to, Babs – it sounds great fun.'

'Oh no – not me – I've never been to an orgy.' Barbara rolled her eyes. 'But I've seen them on television. Naked bodies cavorting everywhere and drugs and wife-swapping.'

Bisto grinned. 'I'm sure the young ones next door are just dancing and having a drink and the like.'

They crossed the dark road, shadows lurking in the hedges, and turned onto the path that led to Julia's house. The lights were merely a dim glow upstairs. In one room downstairs, coloured lights flashed. As they approached, the rumble of music became louder; even outside, they had to raise their voices.

'I expect Ava's having some friends round,' Bisto shrugged. 'There's nothing like young ones' parties to raise the roof. I bet they're all locked already.' He beamed at Pauline. 'With a bit of luck, they might offer us a gargle, eh?'

Pauline noticed two silhouettes locked in an embrace over by the hedge. A voice called over. 'Hello, Pauline.'

'It's Claudia,' Pauline smiled as Oskar and Justina's daughter emerged into the light, her hand clasped in that of a young man with longish hair who greeted them in a chirpy voice.

'Hello there, Pauline. And it's Bisto isn't it, and Barbara.' It was Jack Priddy, Andy Priddy's cousin. He was slender in jeans and a Motörhead t-shirt, not seeming to feel the night chill at all.

'Is Ava having a party?' Pauline's voice was soft.

Claudia made an anxious face. 'Yes, Fabian invited us the other night at the play.' She turned to Pauline apologetically. 'Oh, you're her nearest neighbours, aren't you? We must have disturbed your evening. I'm so sorry.'

'Not at all.' Pauline smiled at Claudia. 'Nice to see you have a night off from working in the pub. I didn't know you two were an item.'

'Oh yes.' Claudia snuggled up to Jack. 'We've been together for two years. I'm off to uni in September. Jack will be able to come up at weekends.'

'What a great couple you make.' Pauline turned to look over her shoulder at the low rumbling noise of an idling engine at the gate and her expression showed concern. 'Oh dear.'

Barbara caught her breath as she stared at the panda car. 'It's the police. I wonder if Dizzy called them.'

Pauline gave a little laugh. 'It's just Gavin from Milton Rogus. I'll go and have a word with him.'

Bisto grasped Barbara's elbow. 'Right. We'll go into the house ahead of you, will we, Pauline?'

'That might be a good idea.'

As she and Bisto approached the house, Barbara heard Pauline's friendly tone calling softly, 'Hello, Gavin. How are you? How are Ruth and the children?' Then she felt Bisto's fingers on her arm, rushing her forwards. She leaned over to him.

'Why don't we just let the police...?'

'Ah, maybe it's best if we have a quick word with the young ones first.'

He pushed the front door, which sagged wide. There were lights on in both rooms off the hallway, fairy lights twinkling from the room on their right. Bisto gently manoeuvred Barbara behind him and walked into the room, where music was booming so loud the floors vibrated. Inside, three figures were dancing wildly in the semi darkness, the soft light illuminating ecstatic faces and writhing limbs.

Bisto nodded and led Barbara to the room on the other side of the hallway. The light inside was a soft red glow and half a dozen young men were huddled in a group together. There was a heavy smell, like burning wood or incense. Barbara noticed one young man was strumming a guitar; another bearded man had just passed his cigarette to his friend who wore glasses. Bisto approached gently and patted the bespectacled young man on the shoulder who turned to him, grinned and offered him a puff of the cigarette. Bisto crouched down and whispered something in his ear. Immediately the young man came to life, moving quickly to extinguish the cigarette and, seconds later, his friends suddenly developed the urge to open the windows, clean the ashtrays and tidy the room.

Bisto smiled at Barbara and they walked into the kitchen, which was lit by small candles in jam jars. A dozen young people were crowded into a small space around the work top where there were many open wine bottles and cans of beer. Bisto greeted a young man softly.

'Hello there. Do you know where I can find Ava?'

The young man had the beginnings of facial hair and a mischievous grin. He laughed in Bisto's direction. 'Are you her grandad?'

Bisto leaned forward, a gentle hand on his shoulder and whispered something. The young man moved backwards; his face alarmed.

'Outside? Are we being raided?'

Bisto spoke calmly. 'No, I think it's just one gentleman of the law. I popped in to let Ava know.'

The young man shrugged and brought a beer can to his mouth. 'She's upstairs, I think, mate. With Fabian.'

Bisto turned and led the way to the staircase. On the bottom step, a young man and woman were sitting, bent over with their heads down. Bisto squeezed past them and Barbara followed, her eyes taking in the shape of a girl on the top step in a flimsy frock, swaying against the banister. Barbara reached out a hand to steady her.

'Are you all right?'

The young woman turned to Barbara, flashing heavily mascaraed eyes and gave a peal of laughter. Barbara could smell the strong alcohol on her breath, and something else, something bitter and rank. 'Can I help?'

She helped the young girl to sit down on the top step and watched her flop forward like a rag doll. She put her hand on the girl's soft curly hair and it felt damp. 'Have you drunk too much?'

The girl bared her teeth. 'Wine... and gin.' She giggled helplessly.

Barbara shook her head, taking in the sloping shoulders, the way her body sagged. 'You should go home, really.'

The girl sniffed. 'Don't really care...' Her body keeled over to one side. Barbara helped her sit straight and she immediately slouched the other way, leaning against the banister.

'Wait here a moment. Don't move, there's a dear.'

Barbara stood up, quickly following Bisto, who had already charged into one bedroom, muttered, 'Ah, sorry,' and reversed out again.

They rushed into the next room, thrusting the door wide, and Ava looked up from the bed with anxious eyes. She was sitting next to Fabian, her legs curled beneath her. They were both wearing dark clothes and Fabian was holding his guitar, watching his fingers move nimbly across the fret. Ava's face took on a moody expression. 'It's the people from next door. What do you want?'

Fabian raised a hand. 'Bisto. Stay for a drink, man.'

'I just popped round to let you know,' Bisto offered. 'There's a police car outside so it might be an idea to sort things out a bit downstairs. I think there's a little of the wacky baccy floating about.'

'We're not doing anything wrong.' Ava knit her brows. 'It's just a party.'

Fabian met his eyes. 'Yeah, you're right. Thanks, man.' He put down his guitar and wriggled from the bed. 'You won't tell Ava's mother, will you, Bisto?' Fabian frowned. 'She's been bit low lately.'

Bisto grinned. 'I think you'd better call it a day, Fabian – get all your friends off home and we'll tell the policeman at the door that everything's fine. I think Pauline's talking to him now, but he'll be here at any minute.'

'Thanks man. You're a dude.'

Barbara looked from Ava to Fabian. 'There's a young girl sitting on the steps. She's very drunk. I'm sure she can't be eighteen. Can one of you call a taxi or something? I'd like to get her home safely.'

'I'll do it.' Bisto pulled his phone from his pocket.

Barbara turned quickly, rushing back to the girl who was still on the top step, flopping like rubber, precariously bending forward. Barbara took her arm. 'What's your name?'

'Saffy.' The girl hardly opened her mouth. 'Saffy Dyer.'

'Saffy, I'm Barbara. How are you feeling?'

Saffy seemed to notice Barbara for the first time. 'Bad. Horrible. Sick.' She leaned against Barbara's shoulder. 'You're nice. Like my gran. But she died.'

'How old are you, Saffy?'

A sniff, then her voice came softly. 'Sixteen.'

Barbara slipped a hand around her back. 'Right, I'm going to get you home. Where do you live?'

'Yarbury Huish.' Saffy shrugged and slumped forwards. 'I'll be in big trouble.' She sniffed and her shoulders started to shake. Barbara rubbed her back gently.

'It's all right, Saffy.'

Tears rolled down her face, dark smudges of mascara on her cheeks, and her brow puckered. 'I've got no money left – I spent it on wine. My mum will go mad. I'm supposed to be grounded because of my school report last term. And I feel sick.'

Barbara felt Bisto's hand on her shoulder. 'I've called a cab, Barbara. It'll be outside in five minutes. We'll get this young one in it and on her way home, will we?'

'I'm going in the cab with her, Bisto.' Barbara's eyes blazed. 'I want to make sure she gets back safely, not leave her in a taxi by herself. She might be sick. And I want to talk to her parents, make sure she's not in any trouble. Poor thing. Look at her. She's clearly upset and ill and has no one to look after her.' Barbara breathed out. 'It's the least I can do.'

Saffy, wide-eyed, stared from Barbara to Bisto and back to

Barbara. She wiped her hand across her nose and it came away damp with tears and a string of mucus from her mouth.

'Thank you, Barbara. You're my friend...' Saffy started to giggle, then her face contorted, more tears followed and her shoulders shook. Barbara placed a firm hand on her shoulder.

'Come on, Saffy. Let's get you safely home. Bisto, can you give me a hand?'

Barbara stood up firmly and heaved Saffy to her feet, helping her stagger down one step at a time. Saffy sniggered, belched and the sobs came again. Barbara held on to her firmly. 'You just hold on. We'll get you outside and the cool air will bring you round. I'm taking you home in a taxi.'

At the bottom step, Bisto patted Barbara's hand. 'I think the taxi's just arrived outside. Will I come along with you?'

'No, it's fine, Bisto. I'll take it from here.'

Bisto glanced at her. 'Here's my wallet, Babs. It should cover your fare back home too.'

Barbara smiled at him, reached out a hand and took the wallet before edging forward a step at a time, Saffy leaning against her, her head forward, her curls damp. Bisto watched her go, noticing the way she clutched the girl close to her and chatted to her, offering encouraging words in her ear. Bisto scratched his white curls.

'Well, I'll say this for you, Babs. For a woman who thinks she needs to read books on empathy, you've a hell of a good heart on you.'

He watched her pause at the doorway, stare out into the cold night air and wrap an arm around Saffy, helping her to take a tentative pace down each step. He realised he was grinning. Then he caught Pauline's eye as she came in with Gavin, the local police constable, and he waved his hand in her direction. Ava would be all right now.

24

The days heated like a pressure cooker, each one hotter than the one before, turning up another degree each day. But despite the heatwave, the residents of Winsley Green and the surrounding villages could be seen on the village green and in their gardens warming up, stretching loose limbs and then practising hurling footwear as far as possible, following up each throw with careful studied measurements and shaking of heads. The following Saturday, 3 August, the excitement reached its pinnacle: it was the day of the Annual Welly Throwing competition between all the local villagers, and rivalry was as combustible as the weather.

Pauline drove Bisto and Barbara in the little VW Beetle to a field on the outskirts of Winsley Green. It was a fallow field at the end of Bottom Farm, belonging to Len Chatfield, but for the day it had been decorated with bunting and bales of hay designating the parking spaces and the throwing arena. As Pauline drove in, she noticed a brightly painted sign which proclaimed *Welly Wanging Competition Here Today*. The background was yellow and there was a simple drawing of a green wellington boot. Below the sign was another that read:

1. Pay a fiver

2. Wang a welly

3. Measure your throw.

All proceeds to local charity.

Barbara sighed from the back seat. 'At least it's all for charity.'

Pauline glanced through the driver's mirror and noticed her sister's unhappy face. She offered a wide grin.

'You'll love it, Barbara. It's great fun. Kevin Carter wins the men's section every year. Last year, Yvonne won the ladies' competition although the landlady from the pub in Milton Rogus said it was a fix. I thought there were going to be fisticuffs. But afterwards we all have a drink together—'

'There's a bar, then, is there?' Bisto sat upright, his eyes alert. The little car jolted over the uneven ground as Pauline turned into the makeshift car park and brought the Beetle to a standstill.

'Festivities during and afterwards. Usually, Justina and Oskar put up a tent with drinks and snacks.' Pauline reached for her bag and turned to Barbara. 'I only stayed for half an hour last year. I just chatted to Dizzy and Yvonne and had an orange juice, but this year I'll stay until the end, now I have you both with me.' She beamed. 'And I might just throw a welly.'

'But you won't be able to have a gargle with the rest of us,' Bisto sighed. 'That's a shame, Pauline.'

'Wish I'd learned to drive,' Barbara muttered. 'I never needed to in Cambridge – public transport was always so much simpler.'

'You could still learn,' Pauline piped up. 'I could teach you.'

Barbara shook her head. 'I'd have rather stayed in the house today. Bisto was doing so well with the new garden room – you can almost imagine how it'll look now. It's a shame to disrupt work for something as silly as throwing a boot around.'

'Welly wanging,' Pauline insisted. 'It's big locally. Everyone takes it very seriously. It'll become very competitive; you watch.'

'Well I'm not wanging any wellies,' Barbara grunted.

'Is there a prize?' Bisto clicked his seat belt and wriggled out of the car.

Pauline glanced at him, standing in the field in his new green Ireland t-shirt and his pink shorts. 'How's the ankle now, Bisto?'

His face creased in a smile. 'As good as it'll ever be. I can walk, dance, wang a few wellies. I'm grand.'

A huge blue refreshments tent took up one corner of the field; chairs surrounded a makeshift arena with a few hay bales and a white line had been painted on the grass. Hugo Garrett was standing on top of a low pile of hay bales, talking into a microphone, his arm around Len Chatfield's shoulder. They were surrounded by a throng of villagers, some sixty people at least, who made a loud rippling noise as they clapped their hands.

'... pleasure to say thank you to Len Chatfield, for allowing us to use his field again.' Len rubbed his whiskers and Hugo shook him by the hand. There was more applause. 'It's always a spectacular day, and I look forward to some friendly rivalry and some records being broken.'

A male voice shouted out, 'Somebody better beat Kevin Carter this year...' and there was a loud hoot of laughter from one section of the crowd.

Hugo smiled. 'As usual, I will remind you all of the rules before the competition commences. First and most important, since this is fundraising for charities, entries cost £5 for adults and £1 for the under-thirteens.'

Hugo paused and consulted the piece of paper in his hand. 'The rules state that at least some part of the wanged welly must land inside the marked area in order to count as a bona fide throw. The marked area is ten feet wide and the tape is part of the marked area.'

Barbara glanced around her: each face was serious, brows

knitted in concentration. She breathed out slowly. It would be a long afternoon.

Hugo cleared his throat. 'Each competitor in the four categories – male, female and boy and girl under thirteen – must wang from behind the wanging line. Stepping over the wanging line will automatically invalidate the wang.'

Barbara noticed a man shake his head and tut, as if such an action would be unthinkable, intolerable. All eyes were on Hugo.

'A sensible run up is permitted as long as wanging isn't held up or delayed by the practice. Only wellies provided by the organiser, size nine Dunlops, will be used. The welly may be wanged by any non-artificial means, and it must be in contact with the wanger's body, whether it be hands, feet, teeth, whatever, at the moment of wanging. At the end of the competition, the longest wanger in each category will be pronounced the winner. I will be here to present trophies to the winner of the male adults category, who will then be crowned as "Master Wanger" and the winner of the female adults category who will be crowned "Mistress Wanger."'

A voice from the crowd that sounded like Gary Chatfield's called out, 'They'll be a pair of wangers then.'

A single voice laughed. Hugo smiled into the crowd. 'And to start proceedings off this afternoon, I will wang the first welly for the male adults' category.' A polite trickle of applause rippled through the crowd and Tilly Hardy pushed her way to the front, held out an arm to Hugo and clambered up beside him. She was wearing a tie-dyed vest and a denim skirt and her hair was tied with red ribbons in two loose plaits. She waved to the crowd. Hugo offered her his cheek and she kissed it, then he grinned at her.

'You all know Tilly Hardy, our local celebrity novelist. She has a brand-new novel coming out this month...'

Tilly jumped up and down excitedly. 'You'll all have to buy it. It's very steamy...'

Hugo offered his professional laugh with a nod of his head. 'Tilly will kindly be wanging the first welly for the ladies' competition.' Again there was applause and a few shrill whistles. Tilly giggled and shook her plaits.

Barbara glanced at Pauline, who was clapping. Bisto had disappeared. Barbara mouthed, 'Where's Bisto?' to her sister over the roar of applause and Pauline mouthed back, 'Gone to see Oskar,' and nodded her head towards the blue tent.

Barbara watched as Hugo took his place on the starting line, walked back several paces and then ran forward, hurling the welly into the air. It made a low arc and landed with a heavy thud several feet away. Hugo and Len walked to the welly with serious expressions: they were going to measure the throw. Pauline jogged her arm with an elbow.

'Barbara, look – there's Dizzy.'

A couple were approaching, a man with tanned skin and dark curly hair, wearing a pair of denim shorts and a t-shirt in a pale peach shade, and Dizzy, with newly coloured pink and burgundy streaks in her hair and an orange mini dress. Dizzy had her arm linked through Kostas' and she was smiling and waving. Pauline rushed over to meet them. Dizzy immediately began chattering and Barbara saw Kostas' eyes drift to the welly throwing, where Hugo had completed his turn. She thought for a moment: here was an opportunity for her to talk to the villagers by herself, to try to be a little more independent and to practise being friendlier. She walked over to Hugo and touched his arm in the way she'd seen Pauline do, although she wasn't sure whether it was a gesture of friendliness or a way of making someone stop and listen to you. She smiled.

'Hello, Hugo. Was it a good wang?'

He stared at her for a moment, his face puzzled. Then he beamed. 'Pauline's sister, of course – oh, do excuse me...'

'Barbara,' she said, to help him out. That was what empathic people did.

'Barbara, yes, hello.' He glanced over her shoulder, checking faces in the crowd. 'Yes, it was an average throw, but it's not my forte, sport. I've never been good at it. Bit of rowing, a bit of rugby at school, and that was it. I preferred maths and Latin.'

Barbara waited for him to speak again, but he was peeking over her shoulder to watch the next competitor. Tilly was taking the first ladies' throw. She chucked the boot aimlessly and it landed a yard away from her feet. There was a trickle of applause and a single wolf-whistle as she rubbed her hands together and strutted away while Len did the measuring. Barbara tried again, remembering that the book suggested encouraging someone to talk about themselves. She took a breath. 'Were you ever in the Forces, Hugo? I was a secretary in the Royal Air Force.'

He shrugged. 'Not me. I'm happier with my business in London. My brother Jeremy's just retired from the RAF after twenty-five years. He's a few years older than me – he's in his forties. I'm the youngster of three boys.'

Barbara beamed, thrilled with the success of being an engaging conversationalist. 'Does he live locally, your brother Jeremiah?'

'Jeremy. In fact, he is looking at buying a place in Thorpe. He went through rather a messy divorce a few years ago and I think he'd like to live locally.' He gazed at Barbara and she nodded encouragingly. The book had suggested that doing this was a signal to prompt the speaker to continue. Hugo smiled briefly. 'Jeremy keeps his plane in my barn. Perhaps he'll have his own space for it soon.' He glanced at his watch. 'Oh goodness, is that the time?'

Barbara grasped his arm. 'A plane? How exciting. Are you a pilot too?'

Hugo pulled a face. 'No, it's Jeremy's – well, it was my grandfather's old Tiger Moth. Jeremy takes it for a spin at weekends. Not my sort of thing at all. If you'll excuse me...' His bright blue eyes met Barbara's. 'I ought to mingle with the villagers... I'm afraid those are my duties today. I'm sort of the host of it all.'

'Oh, of course – I'm sorry.'

He pressed a hand against Barbara's shoulder briefly. 'I'll be in touch with Pauline when I'm back. I had meant to invite her and Bisto to dinner – you too, of course. I must work out a mutually suitable time...'

Barbara sighed and watched Hugo rush past her and away. He reminded her so much of Robert, all those years ago. Barbara remembered sadly that she'd seen a lot of Robert's back view too, as he walked away from her so frequently, leaving her alone and aching for more of his company. Hugo had stopped to talk to Kostas, and they were laughing together. Barbara glanced over at Pauline, who was chattering to Dizzy. Yvonne from the Post Office had joined them; she was carrying baby Harley in her arms and the three of them were engrossed in conversation.

Barbara wondered what to do. She considered the possibilities. Bisto would be up in the beer tent: she could go and talk to him. She noticed Kevin Carter leaving the beer tent, approaching the arena to take his throw. A crowd had gathered around him. Barbara wondered how it felt to be so easily popular. She wondered if Dulcie might arrive, or if Phyllis was out of hospital. They might talk to her. Or Dr Natalie: Barbara wondered how she might ask her how the pregnancy was going: as she knew nothing herself about the experience, she'd need to choose her words carefully. Then she felt light pressure on her arm and turned to look into the smiling eyes of Chrissie Drake.

'I was hoping I'd find you, Barbara.'

Her heart sank. She hoped Chrissie wasn't recruiting for her church congregation. But the vicar seemed relaxed, even off-duty in a light cream top and a pair of khaki shorts. Chrissie offered Barbara her most encouraging smile.

'I wanted to find you and say thank you and well done. I heard about what you did at the impromptu party the other night.'

Barbara frowned. She had no idea what Chrissie was talking about. The vicar's eyes shone.

'I was speaking to one of my parishioners, Shona Dyer. She told me after church the other day how you'd brought her daughter, young Saffy, home in a taxi, how you wouldn't stay for a coffee, insisted on paying for the ride, and how you kept poor Saffy safe. I knew it was you as soon as Shona described you. It was such a Christian act. That's so wonderful.'

Barbara shrugged. 'I just wanted to see her home safely. All sorts of things can happen to a young girl...'

'You are an inspiration, Barbara. Saffy's very young, at a vulnerable age, and a little rebellious. Who knows what might have happened to her? I'm sure God looked down on such a good act and was pleased.'

Barbara pressed her lips together. 'I'm not sure God is remotely bothered about me.'

It occurred to her that she should be nicer to Chrissie, but she didn't recall anything about how to talk to vicars in the non-fiction book. They had so much empathy for others, she supposed it wouldn't matter if you didn't show them any back.

Chrissie was persistent. She linked her arm through Barbara's affectionately. 'Right. You and I have a competition to do. We're going to wang a welly.'

'Oh no.' Barbara's face was horrified. 'I don't do wanging wellies. I've never wanged one in my life.'

Chrissie chuckled. 'Well now is a good time to start, Barbara. Let's show Winsley Green what you're made of, shall we?'

25

Pauline watched Dizzy rush over to claim Kostas from Hugo, smiling up into his face, and she turned to Yvonne. 'So, are they an item now?'

'Apparently not.' Yvonne's eyes met Pauline's with a meaningful expression. 'He pecks her on the cheek every now and then, but it seems they are still at the "good friends" stage.'

'Poor Dizzy.' Pauline frowned, gazing into the crowd. 'Where's Barbara?'

Yvonne lifted baby Harley higher onto her shoulder and pointed across to the arena by the hay bales. Pauline turned around and stared, hardly able to believe the spectacle she was looking at. Len was indicating the point of the starting line to two women. Barbara and Chrissie had picked up a wellington each, Chrissie waving hers energetically through the air and Barbara carrying hers at arm's length as if it was filled with lead and still smelled of manure.

Meanwhile, Bisto wandered out of the beer tent, feeling much happier with a half of Guinness inside him. He was ready to do a bit of welly wanging himself now, and he'd promised Kevin Carter he'd follow him onto the field after he'd finished his jar. He glanced over the grass to where a woman was standing, holding a green wellington in both hands. Bisto narrowed his eyes. He recognised the clean jeans, the neat blouse, the soft curls, and the hesitant stance. He shook his head to clear his vision. It was definitely Barbara and she was definitely about to wang a welly. He smiled and eased his way through the crowd to the front.

Chrissie threw her welly expertly and Len rushed over to measure it. It was a good throw, apparently – Len nodded to Chrissie and put up his thumb. She breathed out. 'Well, it looks like I've beaten my last year's throw. I came fifth last year. Maybe I'm in with the chance of a place this year.' She rolled her eyes to the skies and whispered. 'Sorry – I can't help being a little competitive.'

Barbara was unsure whether Chrissie was addressing her or the Almighty. She stared all around herself awkwardly – she didn't want to be hovering on the starting line, holding a sweaty boot in her palms. Len gestured to her and rubbed his whiskers with a huge hand.

'You're up next, Barbara.' He waved a hand. 'Welly. Wang it. Hard as you can.'

Barbara turned to Chrissie; her face pinched. 'What do I do?' She saw the crowd on three sides of her, leaning forward, all eyes intent. 'I'll make a fool of myself and hit someone on the head. I'll look silly, won't I?'

Chrissie moved to stand behind Barbara and put a hand on her shoulder, whispering in her ear. 'Don't just throw it, Barbara.'

'What do you mean?'

Chrissie's voice was low. 'Think of this as a clearing opportunity. Imagine something you've carried with you for a long time. Something that weighs heavily on your shoulders. Imagine a problem, a burden, something you want to get rid of for good. Imagine it clearly and think of it now.'

Barbara imagined Robert. She thought of his charming smile, the sound of his voice, persuasive and full of charisma. She recalled his neat blond hair, his strong embrace. After all these years, she could still remember each detail picture-perfectly. She nodded. 'Yes. I'm thinking of it.'

'Right,' Chrissie whispered. 'Now transfer that problem to the wellington boot. Imagine the boot is that problem. Fill it to the top with something that has bothered you for far too long.'

Barbara imagined Robert, stuffed inside the boot, his head and the top of his uniform protruding through the leg. She imagined him saying that he was sorry, that he loved her, that he would never forget her and, although it hurt him, he had responsibilities to his wife and to the child they were now expecting. It was over, for ever. Barbara gripped the boot tightly, squeezing Robert's neck.

'Right,' breathed Chrissie. 'Now I want you to hurl that boot, Barbara. And when you hurl the boot, you throw that entire problem away forever. Got it.'

Barbara gritted her teeth. 'Got it.'

'Right,' Chrissie yelled. 'Now wang that welly, girl.'

Barbara took a few steps back, ran hard and hurled the boot with all her might. She saw it take to the air and propel itself forward. It seemed to carry the desperate force of her throw, the desire to push away pain that had held her still for years. The boot surged forward through the air and landed with a dull thud. There was a hush then someone in the crowd gasped. Len ran to measure the distance. Barbara thought she heard the crowd breathe out in unison and a single voice shouted, 'Well done, Babs.'

Chrissie had an arm around her as Barbara bent forwards. The throw had exhausted her. She had hurled away much more than the boot and she was suddenly drained. She stared at the grass for a few seconds, and when she stood up straight again, she felt a little light-headed. She saw Len holding up the tape measure, his face flushed with admiration.

'Twenty yards, two feet and eight inches,' he yelled. 'Good throw. Well done, Barbara.'

She turned to Chrissie. 'Is that all right?'

Chrissie grinned. 'Very impressive. You must have needed to rid yourself of a big old problem there.'

Barbara thought about it for a moment. 'Yes, I think I did.'

Then Bisto was by her side. He hugged her, kissed her cheek and shouted, 'It's a drink you'll be wanting after such a deadly launch, Babs. It seems you're in the lead.'

Barbara stared at him for a moment. His eyes sparkled, brimming with mischief. She took in his stocky shape, his strong arms and broad shoulders beneath the Ireland t-shirt, his white curls, and she smiled. Suddenly she felt happy, lighter, and she rubbed a hand along his bicep affectionately.

'Thanks Bisto – yes, perhaps a small glass of something is in order. After the wang I've just done, I do feel a little thirsty.'

Pauline was next to her, an arm around her waist. 'I always knew you were athletic, Barbara. Right.' She met Len's eyes, and smiled warmly. 'Let's see if welly wanging runs in the family. I'm next please, Len.'

Len glanced at Bisto, then away for a moment, then at his boots before recovering his composure. He raised his voice professionally.

'Right you are, Mrs Pye. Your turn.'

'Thank you, Len.' Pauline stared at him deliberately, almost provocatively. Then she lifted the welly from his hands and strutted towards the white line. She raised it in the air, her mouth set, determined. Len's eyes were on her, she knew it; he was watching her every move. She would talk to him later; she would explain that she was sorry she'd offended him but she was simply not going to put up with his stubbornness. But for now, she was going to show him that his silly behaviour meant nothing to her. She swung the welly behind her and launched it forward into the air, momentarily wishing she was aiming it at his head.

Bisto's voice came from behind her. 'I'll take my turn after you, Pauline. And after that I think we should all go up to the tent and say hello to Oskar. You too, of course, vicar. The first round is on me.'

Len was measuring the throw. It wasn't a good one. Pauline turned away and sashayed towards Bisto without a look back. She wouldn't talk to Len Chatfield, not today. She'd make him wait.

Inside the cool shade of the beer tent, Oskar handed over a half of Guinness to Bisto, tonic water for Chrissie and lemonade for Pauline. Barbara decided to try a white wine spritzer, which she sipped anxiously. They sat around a table and were quickly joined by Kevin Carter, his wife Melanie and his auburn-haired daughter, Olivia. The little girl was almost asleep in her mother's lap and Melanie seemed tired, waving a beer coaster in front of her pink cheeks. Kevin was excited about the competition. He was in the lead and determined to win the trophy again this year.

Bisto was convinced his own throw should have stood: Len had disqualified him for having his foot over the line. His ankle had let him down again, he laughed. But Barbara was glowing; she was the centre of attention, everyone congratulating her on her magnificent throw. Justina had offered her a complimentary plate of nibbles, served by an enthusiastic Claudia. Yvonne had taken a selfie with her, threatening to send it to the local press, hailing her as the best woman wanger in years. Chrissie was busy telling everyone that she had coached Barbara's magnificent throw. Pauline was so proud of her sister: despite her own efforts, Pauline's welly had only travelled ten yards, but she didn't care.

Dizzy and Kostas called in to the tent for a drink. Pauline waved them over, but Dizzy glanced at the group, shook her head and led her beau out into the bright sunlight. Then Dr Mario arrived, his arm around Dr Natalie, who was moving slowly now. Bisto offered her his chair and went to the bar to ask Oskar for two orange juices. Barbara reached over to Natalie and tried to say something flattering and kind.

'You look positively glowing. I expect you're really feeling well.'

Natalie shook her head. 'It's only a few weeks away now. I can hardly wait until the baby's born. I can't sleep at night. The weather's so hot and the baby seems to be really active when I'm lying down.'

Mario laughed. 'If Natalie doesn't sleep, then I don't sleep. The baby kicks me too, especially in the early hours.'

Barbara pulled a face. She didn't really understand pregnancy, but she was trying to be kind. 'Must be painful.'

Bisto sat down, placing a glass of fruit juice in front of each of the doctors and supping the frothy top from another half of Guinness. Pauline leaned over to Natalie.

'I have a lovely shawl, hand crocheted, an antique-style beautiful thing. It was made by my mother when I was expecting Jessica. Would you like it for the baby?'

Natalie shook her head. 'I'd love it. But I can't take it from you, Pauline.'

'I won't use it now. Jessica will never use it – she's in New Zealand and her three children won't want an old shawl. But it's so soft and such a nice piece. I have it wrapped in tissue paper.' Pauline seemed unhappy for a moment. 'I'd be really glad for you to have it.'

Natalie breathed out. 'That's so kind.'

'Shall I drop it in at the surgery?'

Natalie put a hand to her dark hair and pushed a hand over the beads of perspiration on her brow. 'I'll pop round, if I may. Next week sometime? To be honest, I'd be glad to get out of the house.'

Barbara held up a finger. 'Listen. Isn't that someone talking on the loudspeaker outside?'

Mario nodded. 'You have excellent hearing, Barbara. It's Len. I expect he's about to announce the results.'

Chrissie pushed back her chair, lifting her glass of tonic water, which was still full. 'Shall we go? It will be the presentation.'

Kevin stood upright, lifting the sleeping Olivia from Melanie's arms. 'Must be six o'clock. Right. Onwards and upwards. This trophy has my name on it.'

They arrived at the hay bales to see Len aloft, microphone in his hand. Tilly Hardy was next to him, smiling, a box containing two trophies at her feet. A boy around twelve years of age was waving a small trophy in the air and the crowd were cheering. Len scratched his whiskers and beamed.

'Well done young Freddie. Good wanging. Now next, we have Mistress Wanger. Close call this year. Third place, our own reverend, Chrissie Drake.'

Chrissie hooted and flapped her arms. Barbara thought that she hadn't known vicars could be so enthusiastic. She reflected she'd never really met a vicar before, but she liked Chrissie and decided it was for the best that she was exuberant. It went with her passion for religion. Barbara glanced at Len, who was smiling. She had never seen him smile or, for that matter, heard him speak so many words in succession. She thought he was quite amiable; he was clearly much more comfortable when he was in a professional role, talking about welly wanging. Around Pauline he seemed incapable of putting a full sentence together.

'And in second place, our Winsley Green Post Lady, Yvonne Norris.'

Barbara studied Yvonne, who hugged Pauline and then Chrissie. She was surprised by their excitement and all the fuss:

they'd only thrown a wellington boot, for goodness sake. Len spoke softly into the microphone.

'This year, we have a new winner. Someone who I believe is a novice to welly wanging but her throw beat all the rest. We're delighted to have her in our community for the summer. And, with an impressive throw of twenty yards, two feet and eight inches...'

The crowd held a single breath. Barbara suddenly felt uneasy. Her heart had started to thud far too hard.

'Our new Mistress Wanger is Miss Barbara Harvey.'

The crowd clapped, whooped and cheered. Len caught Barbara's eye.

'Come up here and receive your trophy, Barbara. Well done.'

She felt Bisto's hand on her back, his voice next to her. 'Go on, Babs. You're a winner.'

Then somehow she'd clambered up on the hay bales, and Tilly had pressed a gold coloured trophy into her hands and hugged her. Len put his arm around her and kissed her cheek. She felt the scratchy rub of his whiskers, and he smelled of sweet hay. It was very pleasant. Barbara suddenly, without planning it, threw her arms into the air, holding the trophy high, and the crowd roared and cheered her name. She had no idea what had come over her. It was like her heart had become a bird and was soaring somewhere over her head, then it flew up into the skies. She felt Len take her arm and help her down to the ground below and Bisto manoeuvred her back to their little group. He squeezed her arm.

'Mistress Wanger, eh? You're very impressive, Babs.'

She was giddy, holding the gold trophy against her chest in clammy hands. Len spoke into the microphone. 'Now for the men's prize. It's been a close thing again this year, with a lot of rivalry between the local villages.'

A shout went up of, 'Milton Rogus.' Then someone booed. Barbara gazed around the crowd. She could see Dizzy and Kostas, standing next to each other. Dizzy threaded her wrist under Kostas' immobile arm. Claudia had left the beer tent and was holding Jack Priddy's hand. Next to them, Andy Priddy was embracing Tamsin, who had reclaimed baby Harley, asleep on her shoulder. Both men were in shorts and t-shirts. Jack was leaning forward hopefully. Len coughed.

'In third place, we have Gary Chatfield.'

The crowd applauded and a shout went up. 'Fix! Keep it in the family, Len!' followed by good humoured laughter.

Len grinned. 'In second place, we have last year's winner, our master hedger, Kevin Carter.'

Applause was strong and a little laughter trickled. Kevin was at the front, looking around him in disbelief. Len nodded. 'But this year, we have a new winner, someone I'm happy to welcome to Winsley Green.'

A whisper went through the crowd, and then there was silence, everyone listening, their faces puzzled. 'With a great throw of thirty-one feet and six inches, our new Master Wanger is...'

Everyone stared over their shoulder. Dizzy prodded Kostas and he shrugged. Bisto shuffled his feet. The Priddy cousins stared at each other, Kevin Carter's face had taken on a disgruntled pout as he lifted his tousle-haired child from his wife's arms.

'Peter Darby.'

People looked over their shoulders as Peter and Julia Darby pushed through the throng to the front. Peter, in glasses, shorts and a cycling top, was assured and athletic. Julia was slender and pallid in a black lace wrap, her dark hair in a chignon, and she was wearing a large pair of sunglasses. She paused and allowed her husband to move forward to the hay bales, watching him leap up and receive his golden trophy from a simpering Tilly.

Yvonne whispered, 'Julia Darby looks like a vampire. Won't she turn to dust, outside the house?'

Pauline put a finger against her lips and smiled. 'Shhh.'

'Well done. Peter, our winning Master Wanger,' Len bellowed and Peter held his trophy up amid raging applause.

'We would now like our Master and Mistress Wanger to stand together on the stage and take our congratulations as we all raise a toast to them,' Len announced.

Barbara felt hands propelling her forward. Then she was aloft, balanced on hay bales next to Peter Darby who had his arm around her and kissed her briefly on the cheek. A sea of faces rolled before her, grinning, yelling, and raising glasses.

Barbara smiled and closed her eyes for a second. Before today, she hadn't been kissed since her twenties. Now she'd thrown a wellington, won a wanging competition and had been kissed by three men in one day. She broke into a wide grin. Life could be very perplexing, but it was also starting to be great fun.

26

It had been Barbara's idea to go shopping and now that they'd almost finished buying new summer clothes, she'd offered to treat them both to lunch in a little café. Barbara had been very cheerful since she'd become Mistress Wanger last Saturday. Even now, five days later, it was as if she'd developed more warmth, more compassion: she certainly felt accepted as one of the villagers now. She hadn't stopped talking about how many men had kissed her cheek that day.

Pauline had noticed a gleam in her eye when she'd commented that Len Chatfield wasn't such a bad man after all, in fact he had been quite charming, but not quite as charming as Hugo Garrett who'd told her his brother had just left the RAF. She wondered if her sister was developing a fondness for the farmer.

Barbara glanced at the menu and then up at a young waiter. 'We'll have a bowl of carrot and coriander soup and a wholemeal roll, please. We have to keep ourselves in good condition at our age.'

Pauline grinned. 'Also, if we only have soup, perhaps we can indulge in a nice cake and a cup of coffee later.' She watched Barbara straighten the napkin and adjust the cutlery on her side of the table and was surprised by the rush of affection she felt towards her sister. She reached out and squeezed her hand. 'Do you know, Barbara, it's funny, but I don't feel seventy-five at all.'

Barbara nodded. 'I couldn't agree more, Pud. It's the country air that does us good, I think.'

'Pauline.' It was a gentle reminder. 'Pud reminds me of when we were teenagers and I always thought that you were hinting that I was fat.'

'Really?' The waiter placed two bowls of soup on the table and a basket of bread. Barbara broke a roll, dipped it into the orange liquid and licked her lips. 'You were always the pretty one, the one Dad preferred. No, I never thought you were plump, just vivacious and sweet. You were the one everyone liked. I felt skinny, a bean-pole with frizzy hair.'

Pauline inspected the roll and stared at her sister. 'I always admired you for being so slim. My hair wouldn't curl and yours was so nice. And you were good at hockey and I could never play sports well.'

'I saw the way boys looked at you, and how you had so many friends. I was the scrawny one that no one liked.'

'But you were always so strong, Barbara – so organised and in control. I was such an air-head.'

Barbara shrugged. 'I'm not sure I liked you much as a child. You were Dad's favourite. I was quite jealous and a bit cross all the time. So I kept myself to myself.'

Pauline reached over and touched her sister's fingers. 'It's so sad that we haven't talked like this before.'

'I had my life in Cambridge and you had yours in Somerset. We were poles apart.'

'I know. And time flies by so quickly and it's easy to get set in your ways.'

The sisters ate in silence for a few moments then Pauline

coughed lightly. 'Are you looking forward to going back to Cambridge?'

'Do you know, I've hardly thought about it? I suppose I ought to check my house is all right. The neighbour next door, Mrs Beveridge, knows where I am if there's a problem – she has my mobile number, although I hardly ever use the thing. It's ridiculous, though. I only came to stay with you for a week or two and it's been over four months. This summer's just flown by.'

Pauline sighed. 'I'm glad I asked you to stay. I wasn't sure at first but now I'm getting used to having you around. And Bisto too. He's been such a catalyst.'

'How do you mean?' Barbara leaned forward, suddenly even more interested. 'He's certainly a reformed character.'

'Everyone in the village loves him. I've got to know some people even better since he's been here.' Pauline took a deep breath. 'I'll miss him when he goes back to France.'

Barbara thought about her sister's words for a moment and nodded. 'Yes, I'll miss him too.' Her eyes met Pauline's. 'And you – it's been good spending time together. It's been really... pleasant.'

Pauline smiled. 'It has been wonderful.' She pushed her empty bowl away. 'Barbara... I want to ask you something.'

Barbara leaned forward and smiled, basking in her new-found empathy. 'Anything at all.'

'Well, I know you had a serious relationship for a while, when you were in your twenties. It was just things you put in your letters, the sense of planning a future with... you know, *the* one. But I never really knew anything about him. What happened?'

'Ah, him, *the* one. Yes. Robert. Group Captain Robert Nicholson.' Barbara pressed her lips together. 'We were together for four years.'

'Why did you split up?'

'His wife became pregnant.' Barbara's tone was grim. 'He'd told me for years that he was going to leave her, that he didn't love her, that he loved me.' She swallowed, thinking for a moment. 'I believed him. I shouldn't have. He kept me waiting and hoping and then, in the end, he did the right thing and stayed with her.' Barbara breathed out, a single heavy breath. 'She was pregnant with their first child. He gave me a long speech about being honourable. It was an excuse, I think. He'd never have left her. It broke my heart. But I'm over it.'

She thought about the wellington boot she had hurled away, carrying the last remains of her clinging painful memories. 'Yes, I'm fine now. There are other fish...'

Pauline smiled. 'Plenty more of them in the sea...'

Barbara and Pauline scrutinised each other steadily for a moment, each wondering about the other, each asking herself if it was possible that her sister might have feelings for someone, perhaps even a certain short man with white curly hair and a strong sense of mischief. Then Pauline smiled, a thought coming into her head.

'Tilly's book is out today. Shall we go into Waterstones and buy a copy before we go home?'

'What's the title?'

'I'm not sure. But Tilly writes under her own name, so it won't be hard to find it. We should go and pick a copy up.'

Barbara nodded. 'Definitely. I'm done with non-fiction. Tilly's book is just what I need. Do you know, Pauline, a bit of romance might even do me good.'

* * *

Bisto surveyed his handiwork and smiled. It was beginning to look like a garden room now, the foundations built and the shape more defined, the framework showing where the glass would be fitted and columns for the huge sliding doors. It would be magnificent. Pauline would love it. It would be finished in two weeks, maybe three. He put his hands on his hips and sighed. Pauline. She was a lovely woman. He'd miss her: the warmth, the smile, the cooking, the easy-going nature. He thought about her sister, Barbara, the frosty-knickered one who'd become softer, more considerate. She was an enigma, Babs, and not at all as he'd thought at first. No, he decided, Babs was all right; she was certainly a one off.

He wondered about buying them each a present before he went back to France. A little keepsake, perhaps a piece of jewellery. He hadn't really thought about going back at all. He'd need to take something for Barney, whom he'd spoken to on the phone earlier. His son had done well, running the business in his absence – they'd had plenty of guests and Barney had said he and Marie-Ange had been run ragged, changing towels, keeping the garden nice and washing bedding. Bisto thought he'd take something back for the girls too, although he'd no idea what to buy them – they were young women now. Emilie was fourteen, Giselle sixteen. He grinned. It would be wonderful to see them all again.

Bisto hummed to himself quietly and wondered whether to resume his work on the garden room or get himself a drink. A cool glass of water would be best – he was parched in the haze of the early afternoon sun. A voice rattled in his ears and he turned his head and saw a young woman pushing the gate open. She waved and called out, 'Hi Bisto.' He frowned: it was the young one from across the lane, Ava Darby, looking surprisingly friendly.

He waved back. 'Hello there.'

She was next to him, in shorts and a t-shirt, smiling. Bisto thought she seemed awkward, embarrassed, so he said, 'Pauline's not in. I'm guessing it's a cup of sugar your mammy's after?'

Ava giggled, covering her mouth with slender fingers. 'No, Mum's indoors. She's turning the spare room into a studio or something. She's busy. It's you I wanted to see, Bisto. I wanted to say thanks.'

Bisto shrugged. 'It's no problem. What did I do?'

'You helped me out when I had the party. It was Fabian's idea and, of course, I thought it'd be great, what with Mum and Dad being away, but so many people turned up from all over, people I've never met before and then the policeman arrived and Pauline chatted to him and distracted him while you came in and sorted it out.' She breathed out heavily. 'Imagine if the policeman had found cannabis in the house. Dad would've killed me. I'm so grateful, Bisto. I wanted to say thanks. And you didn't say anything to my parents when they came back, which was just so cool.'

Bisto shook his head. 'I think your Da asked Pauline if everything was all right and she just told him what a great girl you are.' He chuckled. 'We all do things that are a little bit mad at times. And Fabian's a nice lad. No need to upset your mother, eh?'

'Thanks, Bisto.' Ava pushed a hand through her hair. 'Fabian said he'd buy you a pint in the Dip.'

'I think he owes me for a few already.' Bisto chuckled, and his eyes moved to the lane. A small car had stopped by the gate and a woman was easing herself out of the driver's door. 'We have a visitor.'

Ava frowned. 'It's Dr Natalie.'

Natalie approached them slowly, her clothes wafting in front of her, her belly moving like the bow of a sailing ship. She was very heavily pregnant now and Bisto noticed little drops of perspiration on her forehead. She stopped in front of him, breathing lightly and smiling.

'I hope Pauline's in.'

'She'll be back any time now. How are you, Natalie?'

'Oh, the usual. Back pain all morning. Baby's not due for three weeks but I was going crazy at home trying to get comfortable. I had to get out. Mario is in London at a conference and I was so achy this morning, I got up at six and I tidied the whole house, even the nursery.' She beamed at Bisto. 'I called round because Pauline offered me an antique shawl. I said I'd come round to collect it this week. It'll look lovely in the newly decorated nursery – it's painted buttery yellow, like liquid sunshine…'

Bisto was staring at her. He patted her arm. 'Pauline will be here in a moment. Will you come in for a cup of tea?'

Natalie thought for a moment. 'Do you know, I'd love one? I'm parched. It's so hot. And it might do me some good to sit down for a bit. Even my legs ache.'

Ava's face lit up. 'Shall I come in and make the tea, Bisto? I owe you a favour. And I know Pauline has such nice biscuits, the home-made ones she keeps in a tin.'

Bisto nodded and they trooped indoors and sat in the kitchen. The Rayburn was turned down to the lowest setting, so Bisto filled the electric kettle as Ava pulled three mugs from the hooks beneath the cupboard. She watched Natalie settle herself into a wooden chair and asked, 'Tea or coffee? Milk? Sugar?'

'Black coffee for me,' Bisto grinned.

'Anything herbal, please. Something calming.' Natalie's hand moved to her bump and she caressed the mound thoughtfully. 'The baby's been quiet today but it's nice to sit down. I've been feeling a bit odd. I've had terrible lower back pain, going all the way round to the front.'

Bisto put Pauline's cake tin on the table, crammed as ever with biscuits, and muttered to himself. 'It's the Braxton Hicks, maybe?'

'What's that?' Ava wrinkled her nose. 'Sounds like a rock band.'

'Early days, the preliminary contractions,' Bisto murmured. 'Nothing to worry about.'

'Of course it's Braxton Hicks. I've had it solidly for two days now.

It's been excruciating, to tell the truth.' Natalie's face became serious. 'You have children, don't you, Bisto?'

'A son, Barney. He's almost fifty now. But yes, I remember being with his mother, Maeve, when he was born.' He breathed out. 'It's a special time, the first baby.'

Natalie accepted the herbal tea Ava had given to her and stared into the liquid. Ava moved to the cake tin and took out a brownie, biting into the soft chocolate topping.

'Tell Pauline these are delicious, Bisto.' She chewed for a moment; her eyes closed. 'I decided long ago, I'm never having kids.' Ava eyed Natalie's dress, the folds around her middle and her deep-set eyes, which seemed to sparkle beneath a frown. 'Thank goodness for birth control, I say. I mean, by the time I'm your age, Natalie, I might have changed my mind but...'

Bisto sat down softly in the chair opposite the doctor, watching her as she sipped her herbal tea. She was holding her cup in the air, staring blankly ahead, her mouth open. His cup of black coffee was untouched. Ava poured herself a glass of water.

'I'm off to uni later in the autumn, I hope. My results are out in a few days. Fabian has been talking about coming with me. He's had his gap year and he was hoping that if I get into Manchester he could try a late entry or he might apply for a place next year and we could get a flat together up there. Manchester is a great city. I'm going to do Music. Fabian's a musician too. He plays guitar. I'm more classical but...'

Natalie gave a little moan from deep in her throat. Ava wondered if she was bored so she tried again. 'I suppose you went to uni years ago, Natalie. Did you just do medicine? I suppose you did. Did you always want to be a doctor?'

Natalie was gripping her mug with pale knuckles. Bisto stood up slowly.

Ava shrugged. 'Did you go to uni, Bisto? Or were you a brick-layer? The building outside is going well...'

She stopped. Bisto was ignoring her. He was out of his seat and moving over to Natalie. Then, all of a sudden, the doctor keeled forward, the herbal tea splashing out of the overturned mug, dripping across the edge of the table and on to the tiled floor. There was a loud groan, like a cow lowing, and Natalie raised her head from her arms.

'It's started, Bisto. My waters have just broken...'

Bisto was next to her, his hands on her shoulders. Natalie threw her head back, her face distorted with pain, and whimpered. She stared wildly at Bisto.

'I need Mario here.'

Bisto patted her hand. 'If he's in London, we'd better call him now. You're in labour, Natalie. We'd better take you in to hospital.'

Natalie fell forward and groaned again. 'It's happening now, Bisto, now – the baby's coming.'

Bisto shook his head. 'Ah, the first one's never quick...'

Natalie's face contorted as she stared at him. 'It's not my first baby. Bisto, I'm having it now, here. I can feel it.' She panted, groaned again and grasped his hand in desperation. 'Help me. I'm so scared. I can't lose this one.'

Bisto took her wrist gently. He smiled at Ava.

'Now, Ava, you're going to have to be my assistant here. Upstairs in the bathroom cupboard, there are clean towels. Put the kettle on first then go and get them, as many as you can find. And a duvet. While you're at it, take out your mobile and ring the surgery – ask them to contact Mario and the midwife urgently.' As a wide-eyed Ava clattered at the sink and then scampered away, he knelt down next to Natalie. 'Right, let's get you comfortable and then we'll get busy. If this little one is on its way into the world, there's nothing to be done but what's totally natural.'

Natalie grasped Bisto's sleeve. 'I can't have it here. But what am I going to do? It's like the birth last time, I know it – I need to push. But what if it goes wrong again, what if...'

Bisto took her elbow. 'Natalie, I'll let you into a secret. I've been here before when mothers have brought children into the world. Plenty of times. I mean, I didn't do the routine deliveries myself, but I'm a bit of an expert when it comes to babies and mothers. And if there's anything complicated, then I'm your man. You're going to be fine. You're in safe hands. Come along now, let's get everything ready. Then we can say hello to your little one...'

Natalie stood, turned to Bisto and leaned against him, panting. She pushed her face into his shoulder and let out a long low growl. Bisto placed a hand on her lower back.

'You're going to be just grand now, Natalie.'

He glanced over his shoulder. Ava was in the doorway, her face pale beneath her tan, clutching a pile of towels and dragging the duvet from Barbara's room. He winked across at her.

'Right then, Nurse Ava. Stand by. We're going to support Natalie to have her baby right here – on the kitchen floor. It's a lucky thing Pauline keeps the place spotless. I'll just scrub up.'

* * *

'Isn't that Natalie's car, Barbara?' Pauline lifted the shopping from the boot. 'It looks like we have company.'

'I expect Bisto's chatting away to her indoors. He's certainly not working on the garden room.' Barbara lifted a small package from her bag. 'I can't wait to show him Tilly's new book.' She grinned. 'I love the blurb. "*Great Sexpectations* by Tilly Hardy. The raunchy new sequel to *Of Vice and Men.* Trendy Wendy Whiplash returns – each page crammed with wicked frolicking – read it and don't spare the blushes." Who'd have thought she'd write erotic romance? Oh, I can't wait to read this one.'

Pauline chuckled. 'I'll ask her to sign it for us, shall I? Perhaps we'll learn something new.'

The sisters opened the front door and Pauline stopped and frowned.

'What can I smell? Is it disinfectant? TCP?' She raised her voice. 'Bisto? Are you here? Have you injured yourself?'

Bisto's voice came from the living room, light and cheery. 'In here, ladies. Quiet now, though – we don't want the babby woken up.'

Pauline and Barbara exchanged glances and then moved to the lounge door, their two heads peering around the corner. Inside, Ava was tidying towels into a perfectly folded heap. Bisto was in an arm chair, drinking coffee from a mug, and on the sofa, Natalie was lying down, propped up with cushions, her legs covered by the Buddha duvet, smiling at a bundle in her arms, a tiny baby peeping from the folds of an antique crocheted shawl. Natalie half-closed her eyes and beamed.

'Hello Pauline, Barbara. Nice to see you. I'm sorry I used your home as a makeshift delivery room. But I'd like you to meet my son, Matteo Daniel Silva.'

27

Pauline pressed her nose against the glass. 'August the eleventh and it's bucketing down outside. It's been relentless for two days. Is it ever going to stop?'

The evening sky was murky, grey as a tossed ocean; the rain battered the kitchen window as the wind blew in gusts. Pauline was deep in thought, her mind on Bisto and how heroic he had been. She was thinking about the incident with the mare recalling Bisto's calmness and helpful suggestions when the foal went into labour. He'd said he had horses at the château in France, but it was clear now that birthing didn't faze him: he was always calm and in control.

Then her mind moved to Len. She hadn't seen him for a while, not since the welly wanging. She couldn't take him another apple pie. There had to be other ways to talk to him. And she was ready to say her piece to him now. She had even rehearsed it to herself on more than one occasion.

Barbara didn't notice. She was engrossed in Tilly's book. Pauline was talking to herself, clattering about, searching for something in the kitchen cupboard, making a cake and a casserole for their supper for when Bisto came home, but Barbara was fascinated by how Wendy Whiplash's life could be so hectic.

'I expect Bisto will be back by eight o' clock. He was just going to have a couple of drinks with Mario. To wet the baby's head.'

'I don't understand that,' Barbara muttered. 'The poor woman has the baby and the men celebrate. It's all wrong...'

She went back to *Great Sexpectations*. Two pages ago, Trendy Wendy was being given 'the whole can of beans' by Jasper the Grocer and now, an hour or two later, she was bending over the hay bales while Farmer Thomas offered her 'a belly full of marrow'. Barbara was puzzled. She had thought the act of love was a silent moment of tenderness between the sheets, whispered endearments and promises, but Wendy Whiplash was entirely capable of screaming her thoughts out loud. And what candid thoughts she had.

'I wonder if we should invite Dizzy and Kostas round sometime,' Pauline mused. She was sifting flour for a sponge cake. 'For supper? We might help Dizzy out a bit. We could invite a few local people...'

'Are they still an item?' Barbara's eyes were glued to the page. Wendy had covered her bottom with chocolate ice cream and a young milkman called Frederick was helping her to clean it off.

'They see each other once a week, on a Friday.' Pauline cracked eggs into a bowl. 'But it's not leading to anything very romantic. Poor Dizzy is desperate to seduce him, but he's slow to take a hint.'

'Perhaps she should put ice cream on her backside?'

Pauline paused for a moment, raised her eyebrows then began to weigh sugar. Barbara turned a page. Trendy Wendy had now met a lifeguard called Sally Anne who'd invited her to her beach house for a 'Prosecco pants-off dance-off'.

Barbara was perplexed by Wendy's ready enthusiasm. She'd thought sex was simply something special between two people and here was Wendy frantically notching up new lovers on every second page. Barbara's careful reading was interrupted by someone banging on the front door. Pauline glanced up from her baking.

'Can you see who that is, Barbara?'

Barbara scraped back her chair, still holding the book open between her fingers as she trudged through the hall. She tugged open the front door and stared at Len Chatfield, water dripping from the peak of his cap. He nodded at her.

'Hello Barbara.'

'Len.' She gazed from his bushy whiskers, his sun-bronzed face with paler crinkles around his bright blue eyes, to the plastic bag he held up in his huge paw of a hand.

'I got these for Pauline. Vegetables. Kale, leeks, carrots, some potatoes.'

Barbara nodded. 'She's inside cooking. Bisto's due back in a couple of hours.' She gazed at his expressionless face and tried harder. 'He's out with Dr Mario celebrating. They're wetting the baby's head. Although I think the idea is ridiculous with poor Natalie at home nursing little Matteo while the men are out having fun.'

Len met her gaze and said nothing. 'So, she's making his dinner?' He held out the bag of vegetables. 'Maybe she can use these for tomorrow. Nice in a good rabbit stew. I could bring her one if she wants...'

Barbara wrinkled her nose. 'I'm not sure I like dead rabbits.'

She recalled the one Derek had brought into Julia Darby's kitchen a while ago and she wondered how Phyllis was feeling now she was out of hospital, and what had happened to Clive. The cat must surely be dead: it was weeks since he disappeared. She heard the rain hammering on his coat and hat and remembered Len was standing at the door. She gave him her best smile.

'Would you like to come in for a cup of tea?'

Len thought about it for a moment. 'No. Things to do at the farm.'

Barbara nodded to show that she understood. 'Sheep? Tractor? Manure?' she suggested hopefully.

Len sighed. 'He turned out to be a doctor then, Pauline's Irishman? Delivered the baby right there in the kitchen, I heard?'

'Obstetrician, before he retired.' Barbara lifted her hand and waved Tilly's book. 'He's surprised us all. Apparently poor Natalie and Mario lost their first child and so the second one was a real worry to her. Bisto said it all happened really fast. It was a good job he was on hand to save the day.'

'I see.'

Barbara frowned for a moment, remembering how he had helped Tamsin. Bisto had advised her to treat baby Harley's colic with gripe water. He was clearly sympathetic to mothers and babies and was used to caring about their wellbeing. She pressed her lips together. There was so much she didn't know about Bisto – so much she'd misjudged. Len was muttering something to himself. Barbara met his eyes.

'Pardon?'

'Well, he's a good bloke, that Bisto, I reckon.'

Barbara had an idea. 'He's down the Sheep Dip Inn right now with Mario and a few of the others – Kevin Carter and Peter from next door, probably the Priddy boys, having some drinks. Why don't you go down and join them?'

'No time for drink. Lots to do on the farm.'

Barbara agreed. 'You're a busy man, Len.' He was staring at her. 'Well, thanks for the bag full of veg. Pauline will be delighted.'

Len bowed his head to gaze at her hand. Water shook from the peak of his cap and fell in a shower of rivulets across his ruddy face.

'What's that? Book?'

'Tilly Hardy's latest romance. It's just out this week. It's really good.' Barbara's voice was too high.

Len knotted his brows. 'I heard it was all a bit racy.'

'It is.' Barbara giggled. 'I've just got to the bit where Wendy Whiplash is dancing on the bed with her panties in one hand and a glass of Prosecco in the other.' She noticed Len's eyes were large, so she added, 'I could lend it to you if you like. Except I think Pauline wants to read it first. But you're welcome to have it after we've both finished.'

Len's head moved from side to side. 'No time for books.' His eyes met Barbara's and suddenly his face was even more serious. 'You and your sister, you're modern women, I reckon.' He hesitated, his eyes round. 'I mean, you're reading all this sexy stuff. You're both women of the world, then?'

'We are, Len.' Her laughter trilled. 'I'm hoping it'll give us a few new ideas.'

Len jerked back, turned half away, lifting the collar of his jacket. He muttered something about the farm and the sheep and pushed away into the driving wind towards the gate where his Land Rover was parked, his step hurried.

Barbara breathed out. Men were strange creatures. She lifted the bag of vegetables and closed the door firmly. She'd have time to read a few more chapters before Bisto arrived back for supper.

* * *

'Sorry I'm a little late.' Bisto removed his coat, which wasn't damp at all. The rain had stopped its clattering an hour ago, just before eight o'clock. He handed over two bottles of bubbly. 'Here – one's from

Mario to say thanks for allowing Natalie to give birth on your kitchen floor. The other's from me to say thanks for making supper.'

Pauline was ladling a casserole with dumplings and rich gravy into bowls. Steam rose in a curl, as if from Aladdin's lamp. She smiled and pointed to an open bottle of Merlot.

'I have a nice red wine that will go perfectly with supper.'

Barbara sat down at the table and picked up one of the bottles. 'Prosecco?' She thought of Wendy Whiplash and her abandoned dance without underwear. 'I think I'd like to try some of this.' She met his eyes and smiled. 'Thanks, Bisto.'

'So, who was in the Sheep Dip?' Pauline made herself comfortable in the chair opposite Barbara, at Bisto's side, and picked up a fork.

Bisto was tipping fizzing Prosecco into a crystal glass for Barbara as Pauline was pouring Merlot into two more. He chuckled. 'Everyone. You should have been there, Pauline. We'd have had a grand time together. You too, Babs.' He turned his attention to his food. 'Kevin was there, Gary Chatfield, Yvonne from the Post Office, Tamsin and Andy Priddy, Peter from next door, Ava and Fabian.'

Pauline furrowed her brow. 'Not Julia?'

'She's busy painting at home. Oil landscapes, Peter said – she's made the spare room into a studio. But young Ava was full of it all, telling everyone about the way she helped with the childbirth.' He grinned. 'Although when Natalie was crowning, I thought the poor young one might pass out. But she did very well, Ava, considering she had never seen a placenta before. I bought her a drink anyway.'

'Sounds like it was all...' Barbara thought for a moment. 'Good craic.'

'Oh, and it was. And Kostas was there. But not Dizzy. He had a friend from Milton Rogus with him, a young man called Bernie Richards. A nice young fella – he bought me a pint. And Hugo Garrett was there too – he gave me a lift home. He seemed a bit worried – he has a big business meeting in London tomorrow. Make or break, he said it was. I felt a little bit sorry for him. His fingers were dithering all night, and he'd had a whisky so maybe he shouldn't have been driving in his car. I kept an eye out for him. He's invited all three of us round to his house when he gets back from the city though – for dinner, on the sixteenth. It's a Friday. I said we'd all go.'

Barbara sipped her Prosecco. It was sweet and yet dry at the same time and tickled her tongue and the roof of her mouth. It made her think of Wendy Whiplash – bubbly and fun and a little bit dangerous. She beamed at Bisto.

'Was Tilly Hardy there?'

'Oh yes, I think she'd had a few drinks. She was celebrating her novel just being out with several bottles of champagne.' Bisto scratched his head. 'She kept trying to kiss me. I'm not sure what had come over her. She kept saying how doctors made good lovers in her experience.'

Barbara swallowed more Prosecco. 'I haven't come to that part in the book yet... the bit where Wendy meets a doctor, but I expect she will, and no doubt he's going to do something inappropriate with his stethoscope,' she giggled.

Bisto frowned. 'Tilly stood up on the tables and made a speech about how she loved everyone in the village. She was tipsy, I think. Yvonne took her home. I hope she'll be all right in the morning.'

Pauline covered a smile. 'Perhaps it's the eternal romantic attraction between a woman and a caring medical man? I remember being very fond of Dr Kildare when I was young.'

Bisto breathed out deeply. 'The attraction thing didn't seem to work well for me at all. My first wife was angry that I was never home. It caused us problems. And my mammy used to say I was just wasting time, playing at doctors and nurses. She hated what I was doing, said it was just me seeking attention, like I'd always done, wanting to be the big "I am". She wanted me to work on the railway like my Da. My two brothers worked with horses – my Mammy loved that.' His fork was in the air. 'It was only when I met Nisha that a woman understood why I worked so hard at it. It was a vocation, a calling. I had to give it everything.'

He sighed. 'Until then, until Nisha, it was like I had two lives – I was Dr Mulligan in the hospital and then I was the empty man who was tired out at home and had little to say for myself.'

Barbara refilled her glass with Prosecco. 'Is that why you didn't mention your life before you came, Bisto? That you were an obstetrician?'

He shrugged. 'Well, I'd wanted to tell you all about it. It was a big part of who I was. But by fifty-five I was almost burned out and then, after Nisha died, I'd started to drink a bit too much. I almost lost it that time. And I'd fallen out with my mother in Ireland, so I retired from working in the hospital in Swindon, took off to France, bought a château and renovated it. I put all my hours into doing it up, to stop me falling off the wagon, and then I invited Barney, my son, to help me manage a gîte business there. He met a French girl, married her – they took on most of the work and that was that. I was a free man. I'd just sit in the sun all day reading books, sipping a glass of wine.'

Pauline giggled. 'Sounds lovely.'

'But I neglected my mammy. And she never wrote or phoned – she was always a stubborn one. Then I heard she'd died. A neighbour rang. I went back to Dublin for the funeral and realised I'd blown the chance to tell her I loved her, to patch things up. I'd put my head in the sand again. So I went on a big bender. You know what happened with my tickets and my wallet, how I lost them on the ferry. It was my own fault. I ended up in Swindon and went round to see Nisha's brother, Randeep, who was a doctor too; we'd been close during my time in the hospital there. And then I'd found out he'd passed away too. I'd just let things slip. Time had come and gone and beaten the wind out of me. I was deflated, devastated. It threw me, and I was back to where I'd been when I lost Nisha, reeling with the grief again and drinking to numb the pain. Until I met you two.'

'We found you,' Pauline smiled. 'Or rather, I knocked you down with the car. How is the ankle?'

Bisto stuck a muscular leg onto the table, tanned and hairy beneath the pink shorts. 'It's grand now. It'll never be any better than this, but I can still do a jig if you'd like me to.'

'We thought you were a tramp when we first picked you up,' Barbara chuckled. 'But then you did look awful, and you smelled horrible.'

Bisto leaned forward. 'But you both let me stay here without judgement and gave me the time to heal, and I'll be forever grateful for that, I will.' He raised his glass. 'You're the best of women, for sure. So to you both. *Sláinte*. To my two lovely women, Pauline and Barbara – I love the pair of yous.'

Pauline held up her glass of wine. 'And you too, Bisto. I'll miss you when you go.'

'Likewise.' Bisto nodded. 'But I suppose I'll have to be moving on. Things to do back at the château.'

'Bisto...' Barbara considered her question as she glugged her Prosecco. 'I wonder. Do you have a woman back in France – you know, an *amour*?'

Pauline turned her head sharply to look at her sister and Barbara felt the heat rising in her neck and cheeks. She probably shouldn't have asked. Perhaps they'd think she was interested in Bisto for herself, and she couldn't allow anyone to think that. Bisto chuckled.

'No. Nobody loves me, Barbara. Perhaps I'm a bit too old for getting myself a fancy woman. What do you think?'

Barbara held the chilled glass to her face, then swallowed the last of the Prosecco in a swig.

'I don't think age has anything to do with it. I mean, we might be in our seventies but we still have – you know – feelings.' She became aware that Pauline was watching her, so she said the first thing that popped into her head. 'I mean, Len Chatfield was here at the door this afternoon. He's a fine figure of a man. And he's available. And he said we were racy women, modern women, you and me. Perhaps he has a thing for one of us. Or both. What do you think, Pauline?'

Pauline shrugged and looked away. She wished she'd answered the door earlier when the farmer visited: it was time to talk to Len now, to make amends. 'He's a nice man.'

Barbara wondered if she had embarrassed her sister – Pauline certainly seemed flustered, so she tried a lighter note. 'Or there's Bisto. Maybe we could all be a threesome.' They were staring at her. She put both hands to her face; her cheeks were hot. 'Oh, I don't mean like in Tilly's book. I mean, well, we live together and we are happy, we're good friends, we get on well. That's all I meant. It's not like he's, you know – a prospective love interest or anything...'

Silence hung in the room for a moment, close and unavoidable. Bisto glanced at Pauline.

'So what about yourself? Would you see yourself with another fella, Pauline? Or are you happy to be single and intend to stay that way?'

Pauline nibbled the end of a finger. 'I'm not sure, Bisto. If the right man came along and asked me... well, I certainly wouldn't rule it out.' She reached for her glass and drank the last dregs thirstily.

Bisto leaned back in his seat and surveyed Barbara, who was breaking open the second bottle of Prosecco. The cork popped and she filled up all three glasses, the fizzing froth dribbling over the top and onto the table into a scintillating pool.

'And what about you, Babs? Is there a Mr Right out there for you, do you think?'

He was staring at her across the table. Pauline had her eyes fixed on her sister's face. Barbara gazed from Bisto to Pauline and her thoughts raced. The truth was, Bisto was clearly in love with Pauline. She could see it in his expression. And Farmer Len loved her too, with a smouldering passion. Pauline had two men who adored her and she, Barbara, was out in the cold again, alone and unwanted. It was just like the old times. Pauline was the sweet honeycomb surrounded by buzzing kissing bees and she was the stale reject, the odd one whom no one ever noticed.

Barbara lifted her drink and knocked back the Prosecco in three gulps, setting the empty glass down on the table with a dull thud. Her eyes sparkled.

'To tell you the truth, Bisto,' she boomed. 'I'm done with men. I mean, why would I ever give up my independence to sleep in a bed with a sweaty old slob? Oh no. If a man wanted a chance with me now, he'd have to run naked through the streets with ... with my name tattooed across his bottom before I'd take any notice of him.'

She was aware that Pauline and Bisto were staring at her, both with their mouths open, their glasses in their hands, poised like statues with stunned faces. Barbara wondered what Wendy Whiplash would do in this situation, or what she might say to rescue her from the embarrassment of being the centre of everyone's gaze. Wendy probably wouldn't mind – she'd make the most of it. Barbara laughed out loud, triumphant. She'd show she didn't care, that it didn't matter that no one loved her. Although she secretly knew that it did – it mattered a lot. But she needed to regain her poise, to keep her feelings hidden and safe, as safe as would be possible now.

She refilled her glass with a flourish and laughed again, even louder.

'Yes, a man would have to be naked and have *Barbara* tattooed across his buttocks.' She brayed again, wildly. 'And he'd have to throw himself at my feet, desperate for my love. Otherwise, I'm on my own and much better off with my own company and a full glass of Prosecco.' She beamed and swallowed the entire contents of the glass in one mouthful. 'And that, as they say, is that.'

28

Barbara was staring into the blackness, wide awake. Alone and drowning, she thought, like a fish stuck in the bottom of a swirling inky pond. The red figures on the digital clock told her that it was past three, but she couldn't sleep. To escape the warmth of the duvet, she pushed her long legs out of the bottom of the bed, feeling the cool air bite at her ankles and numb her toes. It wasn't altogether an unpleasant sensation – at least it relieved the turmoil in her head. Her thoughts were jumping like lemmings, leaping hopelessly into an abyss below. The only answer to the buzzing in her head was that she must be completely in love with him.

Her thoughts went back to the Prosecco moment at supper, when she'd bravely proclaimed her independence for ever. She'd noticed Bisto's quizzical expression when she said all the stuff about never loving again and how any man would have to proclaim his love to her in the nude. No wonder he'd looked surprised. She had made a fool of herself. He was clearly sorry for her. And she'd noticed Pauline's sidelong glance at Bisto. Pauline was too nice to mock her sister outwardly, but it was definitely a look of pity. Or perhaps Pauline had exchanged a moment's empathy with Bisto. They clearly had deep feelings for each other.

Perhaps Pauline was being apologetic, as if she was saying: *I'm so glad you've chosen me, Bisto – despite my crazy sister's outbursts that clearly come from her long-term loneliness and the fact that she is a little unpredictable and completely mad.* And Bisto's kind eyes as he smiled at her, the good nature, his embarrassment at Barbara's tipsy explosion. He must have thought: *Barbara, having to reject a man? I doubt if any man would want such a mad ould woman. I've picked the right sister for myself, to be sure.*

Barbara could hear their voices whispering in her head, kind voices, but ones that secretly knew that three was a crowd, that Barbara should go back to Cambridge and leave them alone to develop their passion for each other. Barbara wondered if that's what she should do tomorrow – today, now. Should she go home?

She pictured Bisto, asleep in the next room. How easy would it be to sneak in to observe him. She had seen women do this in films and it was always so romantic. The woman invariably had a misty expression, smouldering eyes, as she padded into the bedroom and watched the man for a moment as he slept softly. The camera would close in on the woman's expression, heavy-lidded, the parted lips, the lust and the clear intention to show her feelings, to act impulsively on them. Then she would remove her night dress, a skimpy thing, pulling it over her head and, lithe and naked, she would slide in next to the slumbering prince and his eyelids would flicker; he would smile, turn to her and pull her into his arms.

Barbara replayed the scene, with herself as the leading lady in her blue winceyette nightie, struggling out of the folds, the sleeves snagging over her wrists, and then she'd be cold, exposed, goosepimpled and bare-bodied, desperately snuggling in next to Bisto, and he would be snoring, wearing his vest, the white hairs on his chest damp with sleep. Perhaps he would stay asleep, or murmur one single soft word – 'Pauline...' Or perhaps he'd wake and turn to her and say, 'Is it cold that you are, Babs? Shall I get you a hot water bottle?' Or he'd laugh aloud and call out, 'Did you walk into the wrong room by mistake?' Or he'd simply frown with disgust and say, 'Go back to your own room, you mad ould woman. It's your sister I've the hots for, not you.'

Barbara gulped hard. She wanted to cry. She should pack her things; she should go back to Cambridge with the last shred of her dignity intact. She was making a mistake; it was a ridiculous thing at her age, after all this time, falling in love, and with Bisto Mulligan of all people. Her thoughts raced, cannoning into each other. When did she first start to have such strong emotions for him? She'd believed he was a tramp. She'd found him repulsive. Now that she knew he had been an obstetrician, a professional man of some importance, who could deliver a baby on the kitchen floor, he was a man whom she could admire, like she had admired Robert.

But that wasn't it. That wasn't why the feelings had started and snowballed into a passion, merely because Bisto was respectable now. A cine film played in her head: Bisto on stage in a blue fairy wig and costume, cavorting and playing the violin; Bisto pluckily Morris dancing with his painful ankle; Bisto gently helping Ava and Fabian sort out the potential problems at their party; Bisto, so devoted to his mother and his ex-wife that it drove him to feel a yearning that involved drinking too much and losing his way for a while. Bisto. She thought about him fondly – that smile, that warmth, that unique wonderful person who'd entered their lives by falling under the bumper of Pauline's car and Barbara had grimly pronounced him dead. She sighed. She had loved him for a very long time.

And Robert, whose memory she had hurled away like an old rubber boot: she had wasted so many years, believing love was not for her, that she was safer to immerse herself in work and order and routine, to avoid emotional connection. Tears filled her eyes as the thought shocked her to the core: the droplets had been dripping steadily from her tank of time for so long – how many years did she have left? And she'd wasted the chance of finding love because she was too afraid of the powerlessness of a strong feeling, and now it was here, and she had all this emotion bursting in her heart, she'd have to watch her sister grab the spoils and land the man for whom she felt so much tenderness, who would surely offer his love eagerly to her sweeter, much nicer sister.

Barbara felt a tear trickle onto her cheek. What did she have to offer a man? What was she, compared to her sister? Pauline was homely, generous – a wonderful cook. Barbara could just about prepare a meal from tins and packets – she'd never really bothered about food much. Pauline was easy-going, warm, and friendly. Barbara was starchy, stuffy, without the social graces of her pretty sister. Pauline was attractive, sexy, full-figured; Barbara's body was a string of sinew and bones; she was knobbly-kneed, plain, frizzy haired.

Bisto had always been nice to her, generous; he'd tease her with his good-natured banter, he'd be affectionate. But Barbara knew it was just a form of pity. He was a kind man and he was being thoughtful, and she was a stupid old woman who had made a complete fool of herself by hoping someone so sweet and popular and intelligent and pleasant could ever have any other feelings for her other than simple tolerance.

A sob heaved from her lungs, followed by another, a raw gasp and she rolled over, clutched the pillow and howled. She was a fool, lonely, unwanted, completely ridiculous. This was what happened when you allowed yourself to feel, to be sensitive to others. Before she could stop herself, she was sobbing into the pillow, dampening the fabric, burying her face in the folds. Her heart ached; her whole body was ravaged by a pain she hadn't allowed herself to feel in many years. Barbara cried hard, painful tears and although she desperately wanted to stop, the agony was overpowering. As she stuffed her face into the soft cotton and wept, an idea cemented itself in her head. It was the only way out. Tomorrow, she would pack her suitcase and go home. It would be for the best.

* * *

She lugged her case downstairs at nine thirty into an empty kitchen. A mug was on the worktop, containing a tea bag, propping up a note in Pauline's handwriting. *Help yourself to breakfast. Bisto and I have popped over to see how Phyllis is.* Barbara let the case fall from her fingers. *Bisto and I.* How easily it had flowed from her pen. Of course. Barbara heaved a deep sigh from the pit of her chest and picked up the case. She didn't want breakfast. She turned to go and looked straight into an anxious face peering at her through the kitchen window.

'Dizzy?'

Dizzy pushed open the kitchen door and ran straight at Barbara, throwing her arms around her neck.

'Oh, Barbara. I knocked at the front and no one heard me, so I came round the back. I'm so glad you're here.'

Barbara let the case drop with a thud onto the floor tiles. 'Pauline's out. With Bisto.'

Dizzy glanced up. Her face was red, her mascara blotched. She'd clearly been crying. 'Please, Barbara – I need sympathy. And tea.'

Barbara drew a breath and reached for the kettle and the mug containing a tea bag. 'I'm hardly the best person...'

'Oh, but you are. You're wise and strong and I know you'll give me the best advice. You're a really modern woman...'

Barbara made an *oomph* noise and handed Dizzy the mug of tea.

Dizzy scraped a chair back and plonked herself down at the kitchen table. Barbara glanced at her watch and sat down with reluctance and the hope that it wouldn't take too long. She folded her arms.

'What's he done then, Dizzy?'

Dizzy burst into tears, her face reddening into blotches. When her voice came, it was strangled in her throat. 'It's Kostas.'

'I didn't think it would be the invisible man. What about Kostas? I thought you two were an item.'

Dizzy grasped her mug for support. 'I thought we were. I've been to his flat, he's been to supper with me half a dozen times, we've been out shopping together, and we've chatted over coffee into the early hours.'

Barbara pressed her lips together. 'But you haven't slept with him? He's not smitten then?'

'No, he's not. He likes someone else.' Dizzy's tears started again. 'He told me last night. He even asked for my advice about how to get someone he liked to notice him. He said, "Dizzy, I need you as my best friend to tell me how can I...?" Oh, Barbara, he doesn't love me – what shall I do?'

Barbara patted her hand. 'It's not the end of the world, Dizzy. He's just a man.'

She watched Dizzy as she sniffled and pulled a paper tissue from her sleeve and dabbed at her eyes. Barbara took a deep breath. Here she was advising Dizzy about love and she was the one who needed counsel herself. She blurted out the first words that came to her.

'They break our hearts, these men. But we'll get over it.'

Dizzy's wails became louder. Barbara slid from her chair and moved behind Dizzy, resting her hands on the shaking shoulders, moving her mouth close to Dizzy's ear. It was clear now. Barbara's tone was low.

'Kostas is gay, isn't he?'

Dizzy nodded, frantically. 'He loves me as a friend. He said so. But he's met a man he likes, Bernie Richards from Milton Rogus, and he's besotted with him. Of course, I think Bernie is straight. Poor Kostas. Now we're both unhappy.'

Barbara pressed her fingers against Dizzy's shoulders, massaging tense muscles.

'Think of it this way, Dizzy.' She stared into the distance. 'Kostas is a good friend. You'll always have that. A friend is worth so much more than a passing fancy. And you're free to find someone else, for yourself. You'll find the right man. You're young, good-looking, bubbly. You can have your choice of men... and Kostas too.'

Dizzy swivelled round, her face aghast. 'Oh, Barbara, do you really think so? Do you?'

Barbara nodded. 'Of course. Be yourself. Just be the bright bubble of fun that you are. Love will find you in time.'

Dizzy sniffed, wiped her eyes. 'You know Kevin Carter broke my heart? Years ago. I thought he was the one – we were together for ages – then suddenly he met someone else and that was the end of it.'

'I thought as much.' Barbara patted Dizzy's hair. 'He's not the right one for you either, Kevin.' She smiled. 'Not empathic enough.' Dizzy was staring at her. 'Seriously, Dizzy – enjoy a friendship with Kostas. He's a lovely man and he clearly cares about you, but not in a romantic way. Look for love together, but separately, and help each other. I'm sure it will work out. Trust me.'

Dizzy stood up and wiped her eyes, spun round and hugged Barbara. 'Oh, thank you so much. You're so kind. That's made me feel so much better.'

Barbara smiled. Dizzy grinned back, and sniffed once. She seemed decidedly more cheerful. Barbara thought of her bulging suitcase, the long journey home and how much she would miss

Bisto. She didn't feel cheerful at all. Dizzy was chattering and Barbara's attention was pulled back to reality.

'...when I first met you and you said I was named after a potato I thought you were really stuck up and cold. But now, I think you're amazing, Barb. You're so wise. I'll do that, just as you said – make the most of being friends with Kostas. He's really cool. And I will, I'll find someone else, the man of my dreams. You're right, I'm still young. I can still find my soulmate...'

Barbara picked up her case. 'Good. Now I have to be going, Dizzy – if you'll excuse me... Just leave your empty mug on the side when you've finished your tea.'

'Thanks. I will. You know what's funny – I don't understand, Barb...' Dizzy gulped her tea. 'Why you're all alone and single. I mean, you're so nice. I wish you'd let me do your hair. It's much softer now you've let it grow. I could put a dark rinse through it, something to make it shine. I mean, you're positively glowing now you have the sun on your skin. There must be a man out there for you—'

Barbara put a hand out to stop her chattering. 'Sorry, Dizzy – I'm running late. Let yourself out – just pull the door closed when you go – everyone leaves their houses unlocked round here, I've no idea why...'

'There are plenty of nice single men your age. What about the farmer, Len Chatfield? He likes you, I'm sure. At the welly wanging competition, I'm positive that he was eyeing you up...'

Barbara turned, her hand on the doorknob. 'Dizzy, I really have to go.'

She stepped out into the sunshine and her heart was beating hard, knocking in her throat. Suddenly she felt light-headed, weak, tired. She'd walk into Winsley Green; take a bus to Taunton and then a train to Cambridge. She gulped in a deep breath and strode forwards to the gate, gripping the handle of her case. In the next-door garden, Julia Darby was painting at an easel, a large-brimmed hat on her head. She waved to Barbara and shouted a light greeting. Barbara kept her eyes on the path and clenched her teeth. Dizzy was calling to her from the doorway of the house, yelling her heartfelt thanks, but Barbara would not turn around to listen. It was too late to turn back or to rethink her plans.

She had to be strong. She was going back to Cambridge. She knew what she had to do. She had to return home, to keep herself safe, to stop her heart from being broken again. She couldn't give herself good advice as she'd given Dizzy. Her situation was hopeless. She was too far gone now. She'd return to her little terraced house in Cambridge and begin her own life again. Of course, things would not be the same as they were before. Something fundamental had changed in her, something that could never be reversed. A new feeling, one she knew from long ago. She knew the signs, the aches, and she knew its name. It was called love and it meant that she was hopelessly sunk.

But she had to fight back, to move forward, fast, and not look back or she'd change her mind. Barbara set her jaw, turned the corner and heaved the case in front of her as she walked forwards, her head down. That was it now. It was behind her; it was all over. She'd never see Bisto again.

29

Pauline pulled up the little VW Beetle in front of the two adjacent cottages, Bisto peering out of the passenger's window. The first house, Dulcie's, had the curtains drawn in the upstairs and downstairs windows and everything was dark and very quiet. Beyond the fence and the sign that demanded 'KEEP YORE FILTHEY ANIMALS OF THIS PROPPERTY' there was a garden crammed with blooms of all colours, a sweet-scented paradise. Outside the caravan, Phyllis was sitting on her pink chenille armchair at the table, her stockings rolled down to her ankles, clutching a glass of dark liquid. One pale leg was raised up on a bucket, the thigh and knee bandaged. She turned to Bisto and Pauline waving a glass decanter and beamed, 'Hello – come and have a sloe gin.'

Pauline perched on a chair at the end of the table and accepted the drink. Bits of black peel were floating in the bottom – presumably sloes, although Pauline thought they might be spiders. Bisto took a glug of the gin. 'How are you feeling now, Phyllis?'

She leaned forward. Her face had become thinner, a little more drawn, but she banged the table with a pudgy fist and barked a laugh.

'Is that Dr Bisto asking? I hear you've been delivering babies.'

'Just the one baby, Phyllis. Matteo Silva, the little one is called. But it's good to see you out of hospital now.'

'Oh, it was lovely. Just like a five-star hotel. Three good meals a day, wonderful people in there – except for the poor old dear in the bed opposite with her mouth open day and night, who never spoke a word for five days then passed on. Other than that, it was just like a holiday. People took such good care of me – they were so nice. Besides...' Phyllis pointed a dagger-finger at Dulcie's cottage. 'It was good to get away from *her* in there. The wicked witch with her evil cats.'

Pauline furrowed her brow. 'Is Clive back then?'

'Dead in a ditch, I hope.' Phyllis spat on the ground. 'Where's your nice sister?'

'Resting,' Pauline offered.

'Same as me.' Phyllis indicated her leg. 'They've told me I have to do as little as possible on account of my hip. A nurse comes here every day – she's practising, she said, although I did ask for a proper one. She wants me to move back into the house but I do like the caravan in summer time. It's cooler and bright and it lets in fresh air, not stuffy, like in the cottage.' She topped up her glass and Bisto's. Pauline's was still full. 'So, Bisto. You've not left us then? Aren't you going back to France or somewhere soon?'

'The Loire, yes, in a couple of weeks I expect. When I've finished building Pauline's garden room. It's not far off now – just needs a roof and we're all done.'

Phyllis narrowed her eyes in Pauline's direction. 'I reckon you'll be missing this one when he's gone, girl? A man like this will be hard to replace.'

Pauline stared at the swirling skin at the bottom of her drink. 'Yes, we'll all miss him.' She glanced up and smiled. 'But you can always pay us a visit, any time you want, Bisto.'

Bisto waved his beaker. 'And you can visit me in my château. You could meet Barney and Marie-Ange and the girls, see the horses, and I'd show you the local sights, the local wine. That'd be nice. A little reunion, it'll be, perhaps?'

The three of them sat quietly for a moment at the plastic table, gazing into their glasses as if trying to read the bits of sloe and discern a future. The silence was broken by a wild shriek from just a few feet away.

'I thought it was you two. I heard your voices from my kitchen window, laughing and drinking and having fun with that dreadful woman while I'm next door, all alone by myself and feeling sad.'

Bisto glanced over his shoulder. 'Dulcie. Come and join us, will you?'

Dulcie stood still, glowering, her hands rounded into hard fists, her elbows crooked for a fight. 'I'd rather eat cat shit. And when it comes to it, I've only one cat. And that's all because of her. She killed my Clive.' Dulcie turned eyes of burning coal on Phyllis. 'So you're out of hospital then, Phyllis? I hoped you'd have died while you were there and never come back.'

Phyllis leaned forward in her chair, her back stiffening. 'You're a hateful old bitch, Dulcie Brimicombe. You've always had it in for me, ever since I took Albie Matthews off you. Because he preferred me to you.'

'He did not.'

'Oh, he did, Dulcie. He told me you were all over him. You parted with your gifts easy, is what he said to me. I was always hard to get.'

'Oh no, you weren't. You were the village bike even then, Phyllis Hammer, and you know it.'

Phyllis heaved herself to her feet, leaning dangerously over the table. 'You're a lying cow.'

Dulcie moved forward, her fists raised, dodging like a boxer. 'And you were ugly. Butt ugly. But men said it was all the same to them, once they got you in the dark and pretended you were Betty Grable.'

Pauline shook her head sternly. 'That's a horrible thing for them to say. That's taking advantage of a woman's—'

'You're a lying witch.' Phyllis grasped the glass decanter, raising it high in the air. 'You take that back now, Dulcie.'

Dulcie edged closer. 'Truth hurts, doesn't it, Phyllis? The truth of you being a loose woman. The truth of Albie loving me, not you, but you seduced him. And the truth about my Clive – you killed him, didn't you? I bet you fried him up in that filthy caravan of yours and ate him out of spite.'

'Liar.' Phyllis' mouth opened so wide it almost filled her reddening face. Then she lifted her arm behind her and threw the decanter. It whizzed through the air, just missing Dulcie's head. Dulcie screeched, a banshee wail, and flung herself forward at the table, knocking it over and grasping at Phyllis' hair. Phyllis snatched at Dulcie's dress, ripping the fabric and exposing a bony shoulder. Bisto nodded at Pauline.

'I think it's time we helped out a little bit here, Pauline. You grab Dulcie and I'll get her neighbour.'

Pauline wound her arms around Dulcie's waist and tugged, but the little woman was holding on fast to Phyllis' hair. Bisto took up position behind Phyllis, prising her arms away from Dulcie, but as soon as he pulled one claw away, she heaved a fist towards Dulcie's face. Pauline leaned back, using her full weight to prise the smaller woman away and Bisto attached himself to Phyllis, gently trying to lever her from Dulcie without harming her hip. The four of them grunted, panted and heaved, then an engine revved up beside them and they froze, still as a tug o' war statue. A Land Rover came to a standstill, dust clouding beneath the heavy tyres, and a blonde woman slipped from the driver's seat, her hair tied back in a ponytail. She was wearing jeans, wellingtons and a wax coat. She frowned. Her voice was crisp and to the point.

'Does Dulcie Brimicombe live here?'

Dulcie let her hands drop from Phyllis' hair. 'I'm Miss Brimicombe. Who are you?'

'Jill Maynard, the vet from Yarbury Huish. Have you lost a cat?'

For a moment, the world was still. Then Dulcie's little voice croaked, 'Clive? My Clive? Have you found him?'

'I think I have.' Jill folded her arms. 'He's been hanging around my place for several weeks now, looking for food. I couldn't grab him. He's a slippery customer. But today, I managed to get him in a cage and I checked his chip. It seems he's yours.'

Dulcie's hands fluttered in front of her face. 'Clive? Black with white paws? Is he all right?'

'I'll get him now.' Jill leaned over and pulled a cat basket from the passenger seat. Inside, a small shape wriggled and shifted. A low growl came from the depths.

'Clive!' Dulcie's voice trembled. 'Oh, I wonder how he got all the way to Yarbury Huish?'

Jill put the cat basket on the ground and pressed her lips together.

'I have a theory. I was up at Len Chatfield's, at Bottom Farm a while ago, delivering a foal. He may have scrambled into the Land Rover and hidden there, then leaped out at my place. He's not particularly friendly.' Jill examined a scratch on her wrist. 'He was hell to catch...'

Dulcie opened the basket and Clive leaped out, looking cautiously around him. He had put on weight, his stomach rotund and his eyes bright. 'Clive.' Her voice was a whimper. 'Clive. Come to Mummy.'

She bent over and picked the cat up and he rubbed his whiskers against her face, purring. 'Oh Clive, Clivey. You're home.'

Pauline plonked herself into a plastic chair and sighed. She saw a dark shadow slip from the bushes and Derek had joined them, eyes closed, rubbing against Dulcie's legs.

'Well that's a miracle, for sure,' Bisto marvelled.

Phyllis sank down onto her chair and reached for the dregs of sloe gin in her glass.

'Well, I'm glad your cat's alive, Dulcie. I'll say that.'

Dulcie glanced at her and her eyes were filled with tears. Her voice was a whisper.

'Thank you, Phyllis.'

Phyllis laughed. 'I'd offer you a drink to celebrate the wanderer's return but...'

'You threw it at me,' Dulcie attempted a smile.

Phyllis considered her hopefully. 'I have some raspberry vodka in the caravan.'

Dulcie kissed the top of Clive's head before putting him gently on the ground. Clive and Derek rubbed noses, sniffed each other and then ran off chasing into the flowerbed. Dulcie coughed. 'A small glass of the vodka'd be very nice.'

'Pauline, would you fetch it for me?' Phyllis pulled a pained face. 'My hip is playing me up something terrible...'

Pauline smiled. 'Of course I will, Phyllis. But then Bisto and I had better be going. I have so much to do at home.'

'Besides,' Bisto stood up and stretched his limbs. 'I want to be finishing off that garden room. And it'd be nice to see Babs too.'

* * *

Pauline drove through Winsley Green, her eyes on the road but her mind wasn't on Phyllis and Dulcie and the reunion with Clive. She was hoping to meet a tractor coming in the other direction. She tugged her mind away from thoughts of her disagreement with Len and listened to Bisto offering his theory on how everything works out for the best if you just let it run its course.

'A positive attitude counts for so much in this life, Pauline. Nisha used to say it was what made people healthy. She was a psychologist.' He was quiet for a moment, thinking. 'She was so positive, a source of total happiness, my Nisha. It didn't help with her health much. I guess she was unlucky.'

Pauline nodded. 'You must miss her so much, Bisto.'

He let out a long breath. 'At first it was terrible, after she'd gone. I was close to ending it. I wanted to give up. I thought I was managing all right in France for all that time, keeping myself busy, then there was that business with Mammy's funeral in Dublin and my brother-in-law in Swindon.' He turned to Pauline. 'But I've you to thank and your sister. The time I've spent with you has been really wonderful. I fell on my feet when you knocked me over, Pauline.'

She grinned. 'I'll miss you when you've gone, Bisto. We've had a great time, haven't we?'

'We have indeed.' He ruffled his white hair. 'And I feel like a new man. And Babs. She's a new woman, I'm sure.'

'It's been lovely having her to stay. Do you know, Bisto, it's taken all this time for me to understand what a gem of a sister I have in her. I hardly knew her before. And you've helped by being there. You've brought us together.'

'You're right, she is a gem. And I was thinking perhaps she might like...' Bisto sat up straight. 'Oh, now will you look at that, Pauline? It's the vicar, Chrissie Drake, by the side of the road, and she's waving her arms and shouting. Do you think we'll stop and ask her what's bothering her?'

Pauline glanced in the driver's mirror. They had passed Chrissie and she was flapping both arms in the air and leaping out into the road. Pauline stopped the Beetle and put the gears into reverse.

'I think we should.'

Chrissie rushed to Pauline's window; her face flushed.

'I just wanted to say, Pauline – I just wanted to say what a pity it was I never got to say goodbye properly to your sister.' Chrissie paused a moment to regain her breath. 'She was so nice. Even though she didn't make it to church, I thought of her as one of my flock. We'll miss her, won't we?'

'Whatever do you mean?' Pauline frowned. 'Barbara's at home, isn't she?'

'No, no, not at all. I just saw her, about twenty minutes ago.' Chrissie's brow was perspiring. 'She had a huge suitcase. She was getting on a bus to Taunton. I tried to get her attention, but she just took a seat on the bus. She was definitely leaving.'

Pauline looked at Bisto. 'I don't understand.'

He frowned. 'What would be at Taunton? Why would she take a case?'

'I've no idea.' Pauline was baffled.

'She was definitely concentrating on going somewhere.' Chrissie leaned forward into the window to make her point. 'She didn't see me, although I yelled after her, shouting in the street like a harridan.'

Bisto put his hand on Pauline's arm. 'Do you think we should take a drive into Taunton? Maybe check out the station, see if she's gone there?'

Pauline caught her breath. She felt a little flustered, anxious. 'Yes, I think we should, Bisto. I can't think why she'd leave, though.'

Bisto wrinkled his brow. 'She had a drink of the Prosecco last night, and I thought she seemed a bit – well – unsettled. I was a little bit worried about her myself then.'

'We'll find her.' Pauline set her mouth in a determined line.

Bisto sighed. 'I hope we'll be there in time. It would be terrible if she'd left us and gone back home without saying goodbye.'

Pauline shifted the car into first gear, gave Chrissie a wave and urged the Beetle forwards. A frown settled between her eyes. She wouldn't allow Barbara to leave: she would miss her sister now in a way she'd never thought possible before.

30

The disposable cup was piping hot; it burned her fingers and Barbara carefully transferred it from one hand to the other. She lifted off the lid and brought the foamy topping to her mouth, sipping it precariously. She hadn't had milky coffee since she'd been a teenager, and this one was flavoured with vanilla, creamy and sweet. She needed the comfort. A cold wind blew along the platform, chilling her shoulders and making her shiver. Barbara wondered why train stations were cold places, even during the hottest month of the year.

A muffled voice proclaimed that the train would arrive at platform three shortly. Barbara glanced down at her case and worked out that she'd need to lug it onto the train carefully, avoiding bashing her ankles, not becoming stuck in the aisle between the seats, not thumping it into other passengers. She'd be glad when she was settled in the quiet carriage and she could rest her eyes. Her lids were heavy. Her heart felt heavy too, lumpen and aching, but she was focused on the journey home.

There were a lot of other passengers waiting for the train, many of them single travellers, like Barbara. She wondered if they had someone to go home to. A woman in her forties, her hair greying at the temples, made her recall the kind vicar, Chrissie Drake. There was a man and a woman standing close together with a small baby in a carrier. Barbara wondered how little Matteo was doing, just days old. And who was the father of Tamsin's baby, Harley? She would never know now. She wondered about Dizzy. She had grown to like Dizzy or, at least, to appreciate her carefree, bubbly personality. And she had genuinely felt sorry for her, the way she had been infatuated over Kostas. She hoped Dizzy would find someone more suitable and that she and Kostas could remain friends. He seemed like a nice man, and he appeared to value Dizzy. Barbara wondered if Kostas would find someone to love. So many people, she sighed, all disappointed, all feeling the pangs of heartache.

Over by the café, there was a man probably in his forties, tall, bespectacled, brisk looking. He looked a bit like Peter Darby. Barbara imagined his wife would be an artist too, a landscape painter. She recalled Julia Darby in the garden next door, with her brushes and easel, a straw hat on her head. She wondered how Julia's paintings were coming along. She'd like to see one, maybe even buy a nice framed picture of the colourful troupe of Morris dancers or the cricket players on the green in their white kit. Barbara thought of Bisto playing cricket, his remarkable catch, and she knew that she would miss Winsley Green, the friendly people, the fun, the social interaction. And, of course, she'd miss Pauline terribly. She had grown so fond of her, more than she could have imagined. But most of all she'd miss...

She put it all out of her head and stared at the railway line, gazing into the distance where a signal shone a green light. The train was shuffling closer. She bent down to grasp the handle of her case, tears in her eyes, as a nasal voice over the speakers announced that it was the train to London Paddington. She'd be in London in no time at all; she'd take the tube to King's Cross, then board the train to Cambridge. She'd be home in four hours. The word *home* jarred in her heart and she wondered how she'd ever settle for her little terraced house again.

* * *

They were outside the station in Taunton. Pauline had pulled into a parking space and the engine was idling. Bisto unfastened his seatbelt and glanced at her. 'I'll just run in quickly, will I?'

Pauline clutched the wheel. 'Yes, go on, fast as you can. I'll wait here. Be quick though or I'll have to buy a parking ticket.'

'Right.' Bisto wriggled out of the car and was on his way at a fast pace.

Pauline watched him go, then she reached into the glove compartment and pulled out a wrapped toffee, popping it into her mouth. The smooth sugary taste was soothing as she thought about Barbara, how they had so little in common, how at first she had been anxious about her sister staying with her. Now all she could think of was how much warmer and softer her sister had become; how much she enjoyed being with Barbara; how much she'd miss her if she'd gone back to Cambridge.

Bisto thought fleetingly that his ankle hardly hurt at all now. He was moving quickly towards the double doors, hoping that he'd reach Barbara in time before her train left. He launched himself down a small flight of steps and on to the platform. He gazed around wildly, noticing a woman with a child, a young man who looked like a student, a couple holding hands. His eyes searched for the information board, and he saw one further down the platform, near the café, so he hurried towards it. He read each word quickly: there was a train to Exeter due to arrive shortly; in ten minutes, the Penzance to Edinburgh train would pass through, calling at dozens of northern stations including Newcastle-on-

Tyne. Bisto bit his lip. There was no mention of a train to Southampton.

He whirled round; there was another platform over the bridge. He'd try there next, in case Barbara was waiting on the other side. Bisto shuddered, aware of the chilly wind funnelling down the track. It occurred to him that, if Barbara had returned to Cambridge, if her train had already left, he'd suggest to Pauline that he caught the next train and follow her there. He was sure he could convince her to come back. He'd find the right words. He'd make a joke about how he needed her to be his boss. Then another thought came to him. He'd tell her that he and Pauline wanted her to stay on a little longer, to see the summer out: after all, they'd been having such fun together.

Bisto spun around and was on his way immediately, then he saw a grey-haired man wearing a high-visibility jacket. Bisto stopped him, stared into a pair of authoritative eyes and gasped, 'Has it left yet, the train that goes to Cambridge?'

The railway assistant frowned. 'The London train pulled out eight minutes ago. I'm afraid you've missed it.'

'When's the next one?'

'There will be one in two hours: Cambridge, change at London Paddington.'

The man sniffed. Bisto noticed the tip of his nose was red. The railway worker clearly had a cold, or was feeling the effects of the funnelling wind that blew along the tracks.

'If you need to call at the ticket office...' He waved an arm in the direction behind Bisto. 'You have plenty of time. The café's open.'

'Thanks.' Bisto stood still a moment and scratched his curls. He was suddenly filled with emptiness. Barbara had gone. She would be on her way back to Cambridge now: he'd arrived too late. He decided he'd wander back to Pauline, sit with her in the parked car and discuss his next move. He was already formulating a plan as he gave a deep sigh and shuffled dejectedly forwards.

He felt someone behind him, the sense of being watched. He whirled round and saw a tall woman standing by the café, holding a suitcase. Her eyes met his.

'Barbara!' He rushed over and clutched her wrist. She turned and stared into his blue eyes. 'Babs – did you miss your train?'

She gazed at him for a moment, then she twisted her neck to look at the railway lines, the length of track coiling away into the distance and then she looked into his eyes again. 'I didn't get on...'

He was speaking without thinking about the words. 'What happened to make you want to leave? What made you stay?'

Her tongue stuck itself to the roof of her mouth. She gaped wildly at him, and then she turned her gaze away, appearing to watch an approaching train. A voice crackled through the speakers: it was the train to Exeter. She said nothing as it slowed and came to a halt. Doors were thrown open and people stared to clamber out. She shook her head.

'I don't know. I was going back to Cambridge. Then I just didn't get on the train. I couldn't.' She was gabbling now. 'The ticket's still in my purse.'

Bisto shoved his hands in his shorts pockets and gazed at his feet, then he met her eyes. 'Come home with us, Babs. Don't go away.'

'I don't know what to do...'

She watched people moving forwards, taking their places in carriages. She didn't know why she missed her train. She hadn't thought about what she would do next. She'd only known that her feet wouldn't carry her forward; she couldn't leave. She had watched the train pull away while she clutched her case in her hand and stared blankly. She shrugged.

'I was going to leave. I'm in the way. With you and Pauline.'

He frowned, a confused knitting of his brows, then he laughed, one short surprised bark. 'Me and Pauline? No.' His fingers closed around her wrist. 'Please. Come back with me. Pauline has the Beetle outside in the car park. She's waiting. I came in to fetch you back.'

A guard had started to slam doors shut. An announcement echoed: the Exeter train was about to depart, calling at St David's and Exeter Central. Barbara didn't know why she was holding her breath. Bisto's eyes met hers: he was earnest, honest.

'Please come back to Pauline's. Will we all finish this summer together, eh, Babs?' He tugged at her wrist. 'Pauline wants you to stay. I want you to stay.'

She sighed. The Exeter train was pulling away. Bisto lifted her case in one hand and put the other palm-flat against her spine, resting it on her back, shepherding her away from the platform. 'Let's go home now, will we?'

She let him manoeuvre her towards the exit, past the few people who were milling around, looking at the station announcements, holding bags and cases. Barbara sighed again, more deeply. The decision had been made for her. She was going back to Winsley Green. But she had no idea what she'd do now, or how she'd feel.

Dizzy clapped her hands excitedly. 'All the results are in. Claudia got two As and a B. She's going to do languages at Bristol. Justina and Oskar are thrilled, but they'll miss her in the bar. Kostas is thinking about getting a bit of part-time work there. And I heard that your neighbour's girl got an A for Music and she's off to Manchester and Tilly's son is going with her. And Tilly's been on a radio station, talking about her book and she's having a fling with the radio presenter.'

She sighed and took a sip of lemonade. 'I expect she's researching her next book. Seems like everyone is pairing up. Except me. And Kostas. Bernie Richards wasn't interested in him – I knew he wouldn't be. But Kostas has bounced back. He says there's someone in the village he really likes. But he won't tell me who.'

Barbara was trying to listen but her mind kept straying. The snip-snip of the scissors above her head and the warm shaft of sunlight from the kitchen window had made her drowsy. Dizzy directed her attention to Pauline.

'You're up next for a trim, Pauline. What do you think of this style on Barbara? It's all loose curls now but I've shaped it to frame her face.'

'You look lovely, Barbara,' Pauline murmured as she bent to lift a tray of cupcakes from the Aga.

Dizzy gasped. 'Oh, they smell gorgeous. Can we have one in a moment with a cuppa?'

Pauline nodded. 'Let them cool down and I'll ice them first. I'm practising for the fête up at the manor house. I'm determined to win the cupcake section, if it's the last thing I do.'

Barbara wriggled uncomfortably. 'What fête?'

'It's in eight days' time, so people are preparing already. It's an annual thing.' Dizzy sprayed something on Barbara's hair. It smelled strong and floral and caught in her throat. 'Everyone goes mad at the fête. It's at Hugo Garrett's big manor house and there are competitions. Len judges the vegetables and everyone enters eggs, vegetables, flowers, cakes and there's a Miss Winsley Green. It's Yvonne's daughter Tamsin this year. And there's a tug o' war rope pulling competition. And Oskar puts up a big cider tent.'

Pauline chuckled. 'Bisto will be all right then.'

Barbara closed her eyes for a moment. Bisto was outside in the sunshine, working on the garden room. It was almost completed. Barbara had managed to avoid him for the last three days, being

silent or busy when she was in his company. He'd been quiet too –
helping around the house and chatting softly to Pauline, but mostly
spending his time on finishing the garden room. They'd been alone
for a few hours yesterday while Pauline was out at yoga and shopping in Taunton so Barbara had claimed she had a headache and
gone to lie down. She'd spent the time in her bedroom reading the
last chapter of *Great Sexpectations*. She had predicted the ending –
Trendy Wendy really did get her men, all six of them at the same
time. Barbara felt a failure: she couldn't even land one.

The sunlight through the kitchen window made her eyelids
throb. Barbara counted in her head. Ten days' time. After that, Bisto
would be going home, back to France. And she'd be going back to
Cambridge. Then it would be all over. She became aware that Dizzy
was speaking to her. She looked up and blinked.

'Pardon?'

'You're all done – the hair is finished. You look fabulous.' Dizzy
chuckled. 'So where is it you're all off to tonight?'

Barbara sighed. She wasn't sure that she was looking forward to
the meal, with the three of them and Hugo Garrett, but they had
been invited and Bisto had accepted on their behalf.

Pauline giggled. 'Dinner at the manor house at eight sharp,
apparently. There will be the four of us. It will be a real treat. Hugo
invited Bisto ages ago, then he bumped into him in the Sheep Dip
two days ago and asked us round tonight. I'm going to dig out my
poshest frock.'

Barbara gazed at her hands. She didn't have a frock, let alone
anything posh. She'd go in clean jeans and a blouse. It wouldn't
matter: no one would be looking at her. She took the mirror that
Dizzy was proffering and stared at her reflection, her face framed
with soft curls, dark hair mixed with slate grey. She nodded briefly.

'Thanks, Dizzy.'

'Fab, isn't it? You know, both of you look much younger than you are. I hope I'm so fit when I'm your age. I was saying to Yvonne yesterday how great a time you two are having up here with Bisto.'

Barbara stood up awkwardly and Pauline took her place on the kitchen chair, grinning up at Dizzy.

'Okay, work your magic.'

Dizzy lifted her scissors. 'A light trim, some more highlights and you'll be stunning.' She giggled. 'Honestly, Pauline, you're positively glowing these days. Anyone would think you had a man to impress.'

Pauline caught Barbara's eye and winked. 'I just might have. Who knows?'

Barbara sighed and looked away. 'I think I'll go up for a rest. Just for an hour, so I have plenty of energy tonight.'

Pauline nodded. 'Okay, but I ought to tell you I've left something on your bed. I bought it yesterday. A sort of present. A "thanks for being here" gift.'

Pauline took in Barbara's perplexed expression and couldn't help the smile that spread across her face. It felt so good to have her sister back. And the present she'd bought was perfect. It was upstairs in her room, wrapped in soft tissue paper; Pauline sensed her sister was uneasy about something and she hoped it would make Barbara feel happier again.

* * *

Barbara held it up and stared into the mirror. She did like it – it was beautiful. Pauline's taste was exquisite. Barbara wondered how much her sister had paid for the dress – too much, of course. Barbara was almost afraid to try it on, a pale green tea dress in a silky material, embroidered in a Chinese pattern with delicate little rosebud flowers. It'd suit her perfectly and it would be ideal for the dinner at Hugo's. She ought to try it on. Barbara asked herself why she wasn't looking forward to the meal at the manor. She knew why straight away: Bisto would be thrilling company, Hugo would remind her of Robert, with his impeccable style and manners, and Pauline would be relaxed, enjoying herself. But Barbara would be on edge the whole time.

Barbara reminded herself that she was over Robert. But she wasn't over Bisto and it could be excruciating, watching his easy conversation and warm humour while Pauline scintillated opposite him and she, Barbara, would be quiet and invisible. She gazed at herself holding up the dress and decided that she needed to be more positive now – she'd have a great evening. She had a new dress, her hair looked good and she was dining at the manor.

Barbara nodded at her reflection and spoke to it aloud, clenching her fists in determination. 'You'll be fine, Barbara. Better than that, you'll really enjoy yourself. You can shine at the dinner tonight. You'll show everyone.'

She practised a smile in the mirror, and another broader one, as if she was really enjoying herself, and swung the dress a little in front of her, as if she was happy and glamorous, the centre of attention.

'I can do this, and I will,' she muttered to herself as she slipped her blouse off, pulling the pale green dress over her head and down over her jeans. She nodded, determined, catching a glimpse of her reflection in the mirror. She was lean and elegant in the dress. 'I can do better than pretend. I have this lovely frock; I'm with my sister and she's happy. That will be enough: I'll concentrate on myself, on enjoying myself, just for me.'

* * *

Pauline parked the VW Beetle in the driveway of the manor house and slid out of the driver's door, her heels sinking between the stones on the gravel drive. She gazed up at the square shaped house, at the huge windows with heavy lace blinds, an imposing building at the end of a vast green lawn, with its pale Bath stone frontage and the magnificent double-pillared arched doorway. She breathed out. She hadn't seen the manor from the front before – she'd been to the summer fête twice but had accessed the gardens around the back from the car park in a rear paddock. From the front, the house was very elegant and sophisticated. She imagined how it would look inside – high ceilings, white walls, oak beams, red carpets, chandeliers.

The three of them picked their way across the lawn to the grand entrance. Bisto offered a crooked elbow to the sisters and they each slipped an arm through. He chuckled. 'Well, don't we look every inch the swanky guests?'

Pauline nodded: they had scrubbed up well. Bisto had bought himself a dark jacket and trousers, a white shirt and a green bow tie, and he sauntered along with a confident swagger. Pauline had chosen a long shimmering dress in pale grey, with a low neckline, a pearl necklace and a dark lace shawl. But Barbara stole the show in her silk tea dress, which came to her calves and was set off with an emerald green wrap she'd borrowed from Pauline. Barbara had a special aura about her this evening, Pauline thought – with her soft curls and her pretty dress, her flirtatious laughter and a show of new confidence, Pauline could tell her sister was determined to shine, launching herself enthusiastically into the party mood, quipping and giggling. Pauline thought she appeared transformed. Barbara lifted the brass knocker and rapped it against the heavy wooden door.

They waited. Bisto chuckled. 'I'm wondering if a butler might come to the door any minute, an ould man in a stiff black suit with a pale miserable face and a tea towel over his arm?'

Barbara chortled. 'Or a majestic woman with a diamond tiara

and a long satin dress? A double chin and a fur stole and an ostrich feather fan? His mother, perhaps?'

'Or a little maid all in black with a frilly white apron and a cap?' Pauline wondered. Barbara knocked again.

'Or maybe Hugo in his nightshirt and one of those Rip Van Winkle caps? Maybe he's having a nap – he's forgotten we're coming.'

Barbara banged the knocker again. Bisto went over to a square window and peered inside. He called over, 'There's a formal dining table in there, silver candelabras, but no plates or glasses or anything. Lots of rugs and wooden furniture. And it's very dark.'

'Perhaps we're eating in the servants' quarters?' Barbara suggested, fluffing her curls.

Bisto padded back over the grass. 'I think we'll go round the back and have a look there, will we? Maybe Hugo's by his swimming pool, enjoying a small cocktail before dinner?'

'A cocktail would be nice,' Pauline suggested.

Barbara recalled the cocktails in Tilly Hardy's novel, the aphrodisiac ones Trendy Wendy consumed with the suggestive names about sex and beaches and screws. She thought it might be interesting to try one herself, purely as an experiment. It would proclaim her new status: confident, independent, poised. Even if Bisto and Pauline didn't take their eyes off each other all night, even if Hugo was most dashing and charming, Barbara knew she'd survive. She'd do better than that: she was comfortable in her own skin. She'd be fine. And she was wearing a dress that proved it.

The three of them wandered around the back of the manor, arm in arm. There was a terraced garden, statues, a fountain and, at the bottom of stone steps, a perfect blue kidney-shaped swimming pool surrounded by sunbeds. Beyond the pool, they passed through a neat flower garden and stopped in front of some outbuildings, large stone barns opening onto a field.

Bisto strolled to one of the buildings and peered through the window and called out excitedly. 'He's got some lovely old cars in here. Several. An Aston Martin, an old Porsche. Some beautiful classic bangers. There's his Jag. And isn't that a Bentley?'

Pauline joined him. Barbara moved to the next barn. A door was loosely open, and she tugged it ajar.

'Oh, look at this. It's an ancient aeroplane – a Tiger Moth.' Bisto and Pauline were at her side. 'I remember Hugo telling me about this. It's his brother Jeremy's.'

They stared at the large yellow biplane, which was extremely well cared for, the gleaming wings and nose protruding under dust covers.

'It's lovely,' Bisto mused. 'I've flown one of these myself.'

Pauline stared at him. 'Really? You're a pilot too? You're full of surprises, Bisto.'

He shrugged. 'Nisha bought me a pilot training course for a birthday. I got my licence. Oh, I loved it, being up in the sky. Took away all the stress of work, to be sure. Best present I ever had. Ah, but they are lovely little things to fly, Tiger Moths.'

Barbara elbowed him mischievously. 'Well, here's your chance, Bisto. Go on – have a go.'

He sighed, looked out at the field of close-cropped grass and he shook his head. 'No, I won't fly now. Not at all.'

'No?' Barbara's face shone with interest. 'Why not?'

'It's a very long story.' Bisto scratched his curls. 'Not a nice one to tell, not really.'

A voice yelled, a single cry, from a distance and the three of them jerked their heads to look at Hugo Garrett, who was running towards them, dressed in a checked jacket, dark jeans and a cloth cap. He waved his arms and called out.

'I'm so sorry. It's off. We'll have to call it off.'

When he jogged level with them, the smell of alcohol was strong on his breath. His face was pale.

'Look, Bisto – Pauline – ladies, I have to be somewhere else now.' He held up a set of car keys to prove his point. He was perspiring beneath the cloth cap. 'Something's come up. Dinner will have to be another time. I'm afraid there's been a bit of a – crisis.'

Bisto frowned. 'How can we help, Hugo?'

'You can't.' Hugo's voice was clipped, strained. 'I have to go now. To London. To sort it out.'

He set off at a pace in the direction of the barn with the cars, thrusting open the large door and disappearing into the darkness. Bisto called after him, 'I don't think you should be driving, Hugo.' There was a moment's pause, then the sound of a rumbling engine. Seconds later, the green Jaguar lurched from the barn and came to a halt in front of them, the driver's window open.

Hugo called out, 'We'll do dinner another time, eh?'

Bisto put his hand through the window and grasped Hugo's sleeve. 'Hugo, how much have you had to drink?'

Hugo rubbed a hand over his face. 'I just had the news. I wasn't expecting to have to go out. I had a few whiskys. It's been a difficult few days, and now this...'

Bisto spoke quietly. 'You can't drive, Hugo.'

'I have to...' Hugo's brow creased as if he might cry. 'I have to get to London. I have to speak to someone, to change their mind. It's important – it can't wait.' He revved the engine.

Bisto rushed around the front of the car and pulled open the passenger door. 'Then I'll come with you. You're not safe to drive by yourself...'

The Jaguar jerked away before the door had closed and Bisto's voice was lost in the revving of the engine as the car disappeared between the high gateposts leading to the road. Barbara grabbed

Pauline's arm. 'Can we follow them in the Beetle? We should try to get him to change his mind.'

Pauline had stared to run, her heels sinking into the soft ground. 'Bisto will be doing that. But we should be there, to help. They'll be heading for the M5 if Hugo's driving to London. He'll have to go through two villages and some narrow lanes. It'll be difficult to catch them...'

Barbara had sprinted ahead, her voice trailing behind her as she pelted past the kidney-shaped swimming pool and up the steps.

'Come on, Pauline. We have to. You saw the state of Hugo. He's tense and tipsy. And he's got Bisto with him.'

31

'Drive faster, Pauline. We'll never reach them once they're on the motorway.'

'The sign says thirty miles an hour. Didn't you see back there? It says "Please drive carefully through Milton Rogus".'

'But you're doing twenty-eight. You could go faster. Do thirty-five at least. You know the local policeman, Gavin – it'll be fine.'

'All right, Barbara, I'll put my foot down. Once we're past Thorpe, there will be no chance of catching them...'

The little VW took the corners at speed as the road narrowed. One side of the road was spattered with pretty cottages. They passed a corner shop. Barbara leaned forward.

'I wonder why Hugo had to go to London right now.'

'He has business there...'

Barbara shook her head. 'But it's late – past half past eight. Do you think he has money troubles? He said something about changing someone's mind. Perhaps he's gone bankrupt?'

Pauline gripped the wheel. 'I hope we can stop him.'

The car turned a sharp bend and chugged up a hill. She pulled out sharply to avoid two cyclists who were in the centre of the narrow road. One of them turned and showed her a scowling face.

'Sorry – emergency,' she shouted.

The road was muddy, trees either side of them, and there were fields full of pigs.

Barbara wrinkled her nose. 'What a horrible smell.'

'We're near the silo. We should be in Thorpe round the next corner. After that we drive for a couple of miles and turn onto the main road. If Hugo's reached the Taunton road already, we'll miss him. Oh, I hope we don't meet anything coming the other way.'

Barbara's eyes brightened. 'I just had a thought. I'll text Bisto. I'll get him to make Hugo stop until we get there.' She fiddled with her mobile, searching clumsily through a list of ten names. 'Here he is. Oh goodness – I don't think there's any phone reception...'

'I'm not surprised,' Pauline offered grimly. 'We're out in the sticks. And I'm sure Bisto is out there trying his best to stop Hugo. That's why he went with him.'

Barbara was still pressing a button on her phone. 'Bisto was very brave.'

Pauline shot her a glance, negotiating a bend as the road widened and a simple sign welcomed them to Thorpe. There were houses again, a small church, a riding stables, a single post box. She gazed momentarily at Barbara, who was fiddling with her phone, then she couldn't help laughing out loud.

'Do you know, Barbara – I know we're in a race against time, but I'm quite enjoying this.'

Barbara glanced up. 'Enjoying what?'

'Me and you, doing things together with each other, for each other. It's really lovely.'

Barbara nodded. 'We're like those men who've all been to the same school. They help each other because they're linked together for life.'

Pauline grinned. 'The old boys' network?'

'That's it.' Barbara chuckled. 'We're here for each other now, you and I. We're the old girls' network.'

'That's exactly what we are, Barbara,' Pauline whooped. 'I'm so glad you came to stay.'

The Beetle climbed a hill as the road narrowed again and Pauline groaned as she saw a four-by-four approaching her at speed. 'I'll have to pull in.'

'Can't they let us through? It's an emergency.'

Pauline puffed out air as she stopped the car, pushed the gears into reverse and backed up. The boot of the VW was in a hedge. The four-by-four rushed past, the driver a silver-haired woman in a wax jacket who was glowering over the top of the steering wheel. Pauline made the Beetle lurch forward, accelerating.

Barbara grumbled. 'What a rude driver.'

Pauline smiled and glued her gaze on the road ahead. They had reached the top of a hill, past fields and pylons, and turned into an even narrower lane with grass growing in the middle. It was only just wide enough for one car, and the hedges at either side were high. Despite the hot weather, there was mud by the side of the road. Barbara was pushing buttons on her phone again.

'I think I have reception now...'

'We're a mile from the main road.' Pauline rounded a bend and saw something that made her sit up straight. 'Barbara, look – what's that?'

Barbara jerked up her head. In the distance was a green car on the other side of the road, the rear end poking out from a five-bar gate where it had stopped. She narrowed her eyes. It was definitely the Jaguar and it had crashed headlong into the entrance to a field. A tall man was leaning awkwardly against the side of the car.

She yelled out, 'Stop, Pauline. It's them – it's Bisto.'

Pauline pulled into the opposite side of the road and pressed her foot sharply on the brake pedal, pulling hard on the handbrake. She swung her legs out of the driver's side, lifting her long dress and putting her feet down carefully, but Barbara was already out of the car. They rushed over to Hugo, who slumped against the side of the Jag, the driver's door hanging open. His face was pallid, his brow damp, and there was blood coming from a cut above his eyebrow. The front of the Jaguar had smashed against the gate and there was steam hissing, rising from the engine in a misty billow. Barbara grabbed Hugo's arm.

'Are you all right? Where's Bisto?'

'I'm here, Babs – we're all fine.' Bisto emerged from the passenger side of the vehicle, waving his phone. 'We're all grand here.'

Barbara hurried over to him, putting her hand to his face. 'You've cut your lip.'

'I must've bitten it when we hit the gate. But Hugo's car won't start now. The engine's stoved in – the radiator's had it, I think.'

Pauline had taken a tissue from a box in the car and was mopping blood from Hugo's brow. 'How are you feeling?' she asked him, gently pressing against the wound.

'Pretty foolish, to tell the truth,' Hugo mumbled, his words a confused slur. 'We're in a mess now and I'm entirely to blame.'

'I'll call an ambulance,' Pauline suggested.

Bisto shook his head. 'No, no, don't do that, Pauline.' He glanced at Barbara and winked. 'We're not damaged, only the car. An ambulance might bring the police out and there'd be a breathalyser test and it won't be much good for Hugo, will it? No one's been hurt and I've checked him over just now. He'll be dandy.'

Hugo nodded. 'I'd rather just get home. Bisto was about to phone my brother who's staying in a hotel in Taunton at the moment. But I don't know how Jeremy could be of use. His two-seater Morgan couldn't tug us out of here.'

Pauline caught her breath as an opportunity filled her head. 'I know exactly who can help us.' She moved away a few paces and pulled out her phone, searching for Len Chatfield's number. 'I'll just give him a call.'

Bisto wiped a smudge of blood from his mouth.

'It's good to see you, Babs.' He grinned. 'Let's get everyone back home and safe, will we? Then maybe we could all have a stiff drink.'

Hugo's eyebrows shot up. 'I could use one, definitely. I'm shaking like a leaf. And I won't make it to London tonight.'

He sighed and flopped back against the Jaguar. He smelled sharply, of sweat and alcohol. Blood had begun to seep from his head wound again. Barbara took Pauline's hanky from his hand and held it against the cut.

'Have you got business problems in London, Hugo?'

He shook his head slightly. 'My businesses take care of themselves. They're all fine.'

Barbara frowned. 'But you said your business was in London. You're always going there. I thought that's why you'd rushed off. I was worried you might be bankrupt.'

Hugo smiled sadly. 'Different kind of business. Romance. It's all failed, I'm afraid. It's all over.'

'But you don't need to drive to London. Can't you just talk about it over the phone and make up?' Barbara examined the handkerchief and returned it to Hugo's brow.

A sigh shuddered from Hugo's chest. 'We've been together for eight years. I knew it would come to this eventually.' He blinked hard. 'This week, it all came to a head. I've been dumped, and there's nothing I can do about it.'

Barbara stared at him. 'After so long? That's horrible. Did she say why?'

'He. Dominic.' Hugo closed his eyes for a moment. 'And yes. He's married – always has been, since I met him. And now he's going to stay with his wife and concentrate on his young family. That means there's no room for me in Dom's life now. But I'd always hoped...'

'Of course – he's led you a proper dance, hasn't he?' Barbara's eyes flashed as they met Hugo's. 'I know the type. You hang on to a shred of hope year after year and you make yourself believe that it will be all right, that he loves you and his promises to leave his wife will really happen one day. You carry on believing, because he's so wonderful and nice to you and you think he's such a good person and although he doesn't love his wife, he doesn't want to hurt her. But you know it'll end in heartbreak.'

Hugo was staring at her. 'Yes...'

'Hugo.' Barbara's voice took on the lecturing tone of a teacher. 'You have to let him go. You can't waste your entire life wondering what might have been and wishing it had been you he'd chosen, and not his wife. Believe me, clinging onto scraps of feelings like that is a waste of your time. You have to put yourself first, love yourself most. He's gone now. But you're still here and you're a handsome man and you are what's most important. Yes, it will hurt for a while, like a bruise on your heart. But bruises fade, and then they disappear, and you'll be fine. You'll move on and find someone else to love and you'll forget this man and how he lied to you and you'll find happiness somewhere else.'

Barbara's face was determined, her chin thrust out. Hugo took a deep breath and murmured, 'Thank you.' Barbara removed the hanky: the bleeding had stopped; the cut wasn't so deep. Hugo nodded at her. 'That's wise advice, Barbara. I can see that now, after I've been so foolish for years and then tonight I drank a whisky or two and chased after Dom and nearly caused a bad accident. And yes, yes, you're so right – I will find someone else maybe, one day.'

Barbara patted his arm. 'I know I'm right. This Dominic was the wrong person for you. The right one is out there – for all of us. Believe me, I know.'

She turned her head to see Bisto staring at her. His top lip was swollen but his eyes were clear and full of admiration. Barbara glanced at her sister as she heard the sound of a rumbling noise in the distance.

'Pauline – what's happening?'

Pauline looked back from the roadside where she was waving her arms to someone in the distance.

'He's here,' she called. 'Len's here – and he's brought a huge piece of farm machinery to tow us home.'

Len turned the corner, driving some sort of wide digger which he brought to a stop just behind the Jaguar. He jumped down from the driver's seat and stared at Pauline, then nodded.

'You look nice, Pauline. Dress. Shoes. Very pretty.' He then turned to Hugo. 'I've got rope. I'll pull the Jag out and tow her home.'

Pauline smiled. 'Thanks so much for helping out, Len.' She watched him unwind a huge coil of rope as thick as her arm.

Len raised his eyebrows in agreement. Bisto waved his mobile. 'I've contacted your brother Jeremy, Hugo. He'll meet you there, at your place.'

Len was busy wrapping a huge knot of rope around the tow hook on the bumper of the Jaguar. His huge frame hunched over, keeping his eyes on his work. Pauline patted his enormous shoulder.

'You're a guardian angel, Len.'

He glanced up; his lip curled. 'Least I can do to help Hugo, Mrs Pye. Seems your evening has been interrupted though, seeing as you're all dressed up nice and out for a good time with your gentleman friend.' He glanced at Bisto, scratched his whiskers and stared away.

Hugo gave a brief cough. 'It's very good of you, Len. When we get back, I must give you a little something for your kindness.'

Len grunted. 'No charge for being neighbourly, Hugo. Least I can do for a local gent.' His eyes fell on Bisto again then, his knot completed, he slunk back to climb up into the driver's cab.

'I'll follow you, shall I, Len?' Pauline called.

'No need. I'll take Hugo back.' Len didn't meet her eyes. He nodded once and started the engine. Slowly, the tall farm machine edged forward, and the Jag was eased out of the gateway and steadily onto the road. Hugo clambered up next to him.

'Shall we get in the Beetle then?' Barbara gazed at her sister's face. Pauline's jaw was set, her face frozen in an expression of annoyance. She was staring after Len as he pulled the green car securely away. She had her hands on her hips, she was breathing heavily and her eyes sparkled.

'He's being such a foolish man.'

Barbara frowned. 'I thought you liked him. I thought you two got on well.'

'He's behaving ridiculously,' Pauline repeated, staring after him. 'This won't do. I'm not putting up with it. You can expect a word or two from me very soon, Mr Len Chatfield, you wait and see.'

Barbara was puzzled. She gazed over her shoulder. Bisto was installing himself in the back of the VW. She breathed out with relief and waited for her sister.

Pauline was still standing statue-like, her face flushed and angry. She had been the practical one in a moment of crisis, finding help for Hugo. Len was the right man for the job, as ever, always dependable and steadfast. It had been convenient too; she'd had an ulterior motive; she'd hoped Len would have taken a moment to talk to her and she could have made amends. But now, as far as Pauline was concerned, as far as matters of their friendship which she cherished and valued, things weren't going well. She thought, as her heart thumped hard, that she and Len needed urgently to communicate properly, to speak about their feelings, but he was out of practice in such matters. He was clearly piqued with her; she had hurt him and only she could put it right. As she clenched her fists together, a plan was already forming. She knew what she would do next. If she could just persuade him to call round...

Barbara muttered to herself beneath her breath. Pauline was clearly fuming despite Len being kind enough to rescue Hugo and his car. Barbara couldn't work out why she was so annoyed with him, but her instinct told her it was best not to say anything.

32

Pauline was feeling nervous. She knew she shouldn't be – she'd looked forward to her celebration lunch all week. She had bought a lovely oak table for the centre of the garden room – it was her new formal dining room with a pleasant sitting area. There was a stunning view through vast glass windows onto the garden which was bursting with colour from the flowerbeds. The ceiling and the sides were huge knotted oak beams supporting glass windows on three sides. Bisto had done a wonderful job. There were blooms in vases on the windowsills, three new cream armchairs around a small coffee table, and two simple Moroccan floor lamps stood in opposite corners. It was truly magnificent.

It was one o'clock and the garden room and kitchen were full of guests. Dizzy had arrived first, then Chrissie Drake, both helping Pauline to cover the table with nibbles, quiches, breads and various salads and to set out wine, lemonade and glasses. Then Justina and Oskar arrived with a barrel of cider. Natalie and Mario turned up with champagne and little Matteo in the shawl, and Yvonne brought nibbles and wine. Others had arrived in quick succession, bringing bottles: Andy Priddy and Tamsin with baby Harley, Tilly

Hardy with a signed copy of *Great Sexpectations* and a bottle of Prosecco, Kevin Carter and his family and several bottles of local scrumpy.

Bisto and Barbara were both in their element, shaking hands, kissing cheeks and welcoming the guests as if it was their own home. Barbara had the green tea dress on again and Pauline thought her skin had taken on a healthy sheen. She was a different person from the tense sister who had arrived in April – she was now gregarious, confident, with a new poise and a welcoming smile. Bisto was his usual self, chattering and joking with everyone and basking in the compliments from people stunned by his handiwork. Mario asked him if he'd be available to do some work on his house but Bisto said cheerfully that he was going back home on Monday morning. Today was Friday, the fête was tomorrow, and Pauline knew she'd miss Bisto. But that wasn't the reason for her heart thumping in her throat or the gnawing sadness.

Pauline squeezed the stem of her bubbly glass in her fist and offered her best party smile. But her heart was drumming, and it was hard to keep her mind on the people around her. Yvonne was saying something about Tamsin and Andy and how good he was with the baby but Pauline was finding it hard to listen. A loud knock at the front door made her leap and she smiled at Yvonne.

'Another guest. I must answer the door – sorry, Yvonne. I'll be back in a minute.'

As she rushed past the hall mirror, she checked her reflection. Her lipstick wasn't smudged, her hair shone and swished round her face. She grasped the doorknob and pulled it open, her mouth already in a smile. Her neighbours, Julia and Peter Darby, filled the porch. They held out a bottle of champagne.

Pauline gasped, trying not to show the disappointment that immediately filled her heart. 'Julia. Peter. How nice to see you.'

'Sadly, we can't stay, Pauline,' Peter made an apologetic face.

'Julia has a meeting with a local artists' guild in half an hour in Taunton. They've seen her paintings...'

'I've completed four now – I'm on my fifth. All local landscapes in oil, all light and shade studies. And people really like them. I'm so excited.' Julia beamed and Pauline wondered if it was the first time she had seen her neighbour smile. She looked very different, her skin a warm golden brown, her dark hair loose around her face. 'It was the trip to Paris,' Julia enthused, hugging Peter. 'It got me thinking about being creative. And now I can't stop painting again. I just love it.'

'That's wonderful news.' Pauline smiled. She was gazing over Julia's shoulder. A vehicle had just stopped outside the gate and she craned her neck to look.

Peter thrust the champagne bottle in Pauline's hands. 'Ava and Fabian are on their way – they'll be over in a few minutes. We must catch up soon. You'll have to come to dinner.'

Julia giggled. 'Tell Bisto my roses need watering.'

Pauline's face lit up. 'Dinner would be lovely.'

She knew she ought to mention that Bisto was leaving next week, Barbara too, but her eyes were focusing on a figure sliding out of a car parked by her gate. She narrowed her eyes but couldn't make out who it was. It seemed like a tall man. Perhaps two of them – she wasn't sure. But it wasn't Len. Pauline sighed.

'You'll be at the fête tomorrow at the manor house, though?' Julia suggested. 'I'll be there – I'm doing a mini exhibition of my paintings.'

'Yes, well, that's wonderful – I'll see you then.'

Pauline raised a hand as they turned to walk away. As Julia and Peter neared the gate, they stopped to greet the two men. One of them was blond, wearing a tweed jacket; the other was in jeans and a black jacket, a red-haired man. Pauline felt her heart grow heavy again, but she offered a welcoming smile as the men approached and she held out a welcoming hand.

'Hugo. Lovely to see you.'

Hugo beamed. The cut over his brow was now just a thin red line. He indicated the red-haired man next to him, a pleasant freckle-faced man in his forties with red stubble and a wide smile.

'This is my brother, Jeremy. Jem, this is Pauline – one of my local guardian angels.'

Pauline was about to shake his hand but Jeremy hugged her. He smelled of sweet aftershave, a mixture of leather and cinnamon. He grinned.

'So pleased to meet you, Pauline. And thanks for all you did for my brother. '

Hugo shrugged. 'I didn't behave well. It's embarrassing really... but if it hadn't been for Pauline and Bisto and Barbara and Len...'

'Len's not here.' Pauline was instantly cross with herself for drawing attention to the farmer's absence. She forced a giggle. 'But everyone else is inside. Do come in.'

Jeremy proffered two bottles of champagne. 'It's a lovely place you have here. And I can't wait to meet everyone. I've just bought a house in Thorpe, so you are all my neighbours, in a manner of speaking.'

Pauline led them inside. The garden room was buzzing with conversation. Barbara was quizzing Tilly about her next book. Chrissie was enthusing about christening arrangements with the doctors, squeezing little Matteo in her arms. Bisto, Oskar, Hugo and Kevin were arguing about the best types of cider, Bisto inviting them all to the Loire château and Oskar offering to bring some new cider over for him to sample. Andy and Tamsin were sitting in the soft armchairs, holding hands, and Pauline watched as Dizzy chatted to Jeremy, both laughing too loud at a mutual joke before they stepped out into the garden together, Jeremy carrying a bottle of champagne and two glasses.

Pauline sighed. It was almost three o'clock: Len wouldn't come now, although she'd made a point of inviting him, once by text and then again by phone. He'd been abrupt, of course. 'I might be busy, Pauline. Sheep. Farm. Digger.' But she'd hoped he would come; she'd set her heart on it.

'He's a lovely man, though,' she muttered beneath her breath, then she was filled with a sense of regret and sadness; Barbara rushed up with a plate of mini samosas and chuckled.

'Try these, Pauline. They are exceptional. Really spicy. Yvonne made them.'

Pauline took one and bit through the pastry, deciding that she'd find another opportunity to have a word with Len. After all, it wasn't Len's fault: she had upset him and she would make amends. He'd be at the fête tomorrow, judging the flowers and vegetables. She'd put on something special and go. And this time she wouldn't miss the chance to speak her mind.

* * *

As they queued up to enter the fête, Pauline felt the thud of her heart hammering in her chest. She offered a brave face, smiling at Chrissie, who had set up a small desk in the gateway and was busily taking a pound from every visitor, destined for a worthy charity. Pauline had dressed carefully too, so that she appeared nonchalant, as if making no effort, but she'd left a button on the emerald silk blouse undone, revealing an amethyst necklace, and she'd worn her favourite black jeans, the ones that hugged her hips and accentuated her waist. She wasn't feeling confident though, as she gazed at the manor house, this time from a completely different angle, from the paddock that looked onto the outbuildings where Hugo kept his cars and Jeremy's

Tiger Moth. Pauline suddenly remembered the tray of cupcakes she'd made for the competition: they were still on the kitchen table.

Barbara was oblivious to her sister's anxiety, chattering to Bisto as he put a gentle hand on her shoulder and inclined his head forward to listen to her. The two of them had spent a lot of time together over the last few days. Pauline thought she knew why. It was because they would both be leaving in two days' time, going their separate ways. Pauline knew they had become firm friends; she felt a pang of regret at the thought of the three of them being apart after such an eventful summer. She would miss Bisto's cheery banter and Barbara's now-gentle retorts. But that wasn't foremost in her mind now: another emotion was in the way, an emotion that wriggled and bit at her skin like ants and left her stung and on edge. She was determined to resolve things this afternoon, once and for all.

Bisto was chuckling. 'Oh, and I had a good time in Taunton this morning, shopping. I bought a few things I needed to take back with me to the château.'

Barbara slapped his arm playfully. 'I've never known men to go shopping together before.'

Bisto shrugged. 'Kevin gave me a lift there and back. He had some business and his bank closed at noon, so I had just enough time to pop in for my provisions. I let him into my little shopping secret...'

Pauline dragged herself from her thoughts. 'What did you buy, Bisto?'

'A few presents for Barney and Marie-Ange and the girls.' He tapped his nose with his finger. 'And something else – a little something for you both and, well, a surprise.'

'What surprise?' Barbara folded her arms. 'I hate surprises.'

Bisto chuckled. 'And it'll be a surprise like one you've never had before. But it has to be said, Babs, it's something I know you'll find interesting, to say the least.' His eyes twinkled as he paid Chrissie with a five pound note and told her to keep the change, complimenting her on the huge straw hat she wore to keep the sun from her head.

They walked into the grounds to the spread of marquees, set up like a huge encampment. There were all sorts of stalls, competitions to be entered, raffles to be won and, in the centre of the ring of tents and brightly coloured gazebos was a wide grassy space designated for the tug o' war. There was even an art tent. Pauline waved to Julia Darby who was inside, surrounded by other artists, her hair done up in a bright knotted scarf, wearing a flowery dress. She waved back, clearly animated.

The noon sun gave the marquees a vibrant sheen, the canvases golden yellow, and the grass was soft and luxurious underfoot. Bisto's eyes were swivelling around the displays, presumably keeping his eye out for Justina and Oskar's refreshment tent. Pauline gazed at the various attractions; she had already noted where the judging was, inside a vast grey tent. Len would be in there now, selecting the best blooms and measuring marrows. Pauline felt her breathing become restricted in her throat. She was already dreaming up excuses to leave the group, but the makeshift toilets were in the opposite direction.

Two figures turned the corner and a familiar voice called, 'Yoo-hoo, Pauline.'

Dizzy was wearing a blue mini dress and her hand was clasped firmly in that of a tall red-haired man with freckles and a broad grin. He waved his free arm and the pair rushed over.

'Well, you two made quick work of getting together,' Barbara grunted.

'How could I not?' Jeremy beamed. 'Desiree is almost a neighbour. And I have to say, she is wonderful company and has been very welcoming.'

Barbara raised an eyebrow. Dizzy giggled. 'Jem and I came here in his Morgan, the two-seater. It's lovely. And, oh, Pauline, you should see his house in Thorpe. It's beautiful. It has six bedrooms.'

'Seven,' Jeremy murmured, with a squeeze of her hand that didn't go unnoticed by Barbara.

'And it's just brilliant.' Dizzy was so excited that she almost pivoted on the spot. 'Jem and I are having dinner here at Hugo's tonight. We're double dating with – oh, guess who.' She paused and glanced at the confused faces in front of her. 'Kostas, that's who. He and Hugo are, well, becoming very good friends, shall we say?'

Jeremy grinned. 'I think I'm going to enjoy living around here.'

Dizzy snuggled up to Jeremy, kissing his cheek in a way Barbara thought a little too eager. She decided to change the subject for everyone's sake.

'Jeremy, I've seen your Tiger Moth in Hugo's barn. It's lovely, beautifully kept.'

'It is,' Jeremy agreed. 'And now I'm living around here, I must get out in it regularly.'

'Bisto has flown one before,' Barbara nudged the little man next to her, who was shaking his head vigorously. 'Bisto's a pilot.'

Jeremy nodded. 'Come by any time. Give her a whirl. I leave the barn open. You'd always be very welcome.'

'Ah, I don't fly now,' Bisto shrugged. 'But thanks anyway.'

Dizzy pulled at Jeremy's arm. 'Well, we'd better move on. Jem is going to be in the tug o' war and I want to visit the fortune teller.' She snuggled up to Jeremy, hugging his arm. 'Who knows what she might tell us about the future?'

They strolled away, Dizzy laughing softly. Barbara watched them go, her brows knitted. 'Fortune teller?' She grinned at Bisto.

'It's Hayley, the woman who teaches yoga, dressed in a long skirt. Pauline told me...'

Bisto gave her shoulder a squeeze. 'Oh, will you excuse me a minute, Babs. There's Kevin, going to Justina and Oskar's tent. I just need to go and have a word with him about – something. The tug o' war and – some other things he needs to help me with.'

Barbara watched him scuttle away; the bob of the white curls and the mischief-laden roll of his gait making her heart feel warm. She smiled sadly.

'We'll miss him, won't we, Pauline?'

She turned to gauge her sister's reaction, but Pauline was not there. Barbara frowned. 'Well, she's slipped away suddenly. That's very strange. I wonder what Pauline's up to.'

33

There was no one in the tent except Len. Pauline stood in the entrance, conscious that she was breathing hard. She observed him, notepad in his hand, moving between the covered trestle tables with displays of bright flowers. He had on a cloth cap, his tartan shirt rolled at the sleeves, his blue jeans tucked into wellingtons, and he looked strong and authoritative. Pauline watched him scratch his whiskers as he wrote something down. She remained rooted to the spot, taking in every detail, waiting for the right moment. He shuffled forward to the next display, now just feet away, and scribbled, tearing off the sheet of paper carefully and pushing it under the display. Pauline took a breath. Len's gaze moved up from the flowers. He was staring directly at her.

'Pauline.'

She took a step forward.

'Len.'

He shook his head. 'You shouldn't be in here. No one is allowed in the judging tent while adjudication is in progress.'

Pauline moved forward, taking the notepad out of his hand. She studied the writing. 'You've finished.'

He met her eyes. 'I have.' Then his gaze swivelled around to the displays of flowers and vegetables. 'All done now. Onions. Carrots. Marrows. Blooms. House plants.'

'Good.' Pauline moved closer to him, close enough to rest a hand on his shoulder. 'Because we need to talk.'

She stared into his eyes, at the laughter lines, the deep-set brows, the moody gaze; she examined the ruddy face, the long whiskers, the full lips. There were things she needed to say. She raised an eyebrow.

'You haven't been very nice to me recently, Len. I thought we were friends.'

He scowled. 'I thought we were, good friends. But that's before you got yourself that Irishman...'

'Bisto,' Pauline sighed.

'Living in your house. With his modern ways. Delivering babies and helping with foals and making friends in the village so quick and building you a garden room.' His glare was almost vicious. 'I can't compete with that.'

She put a finger on his lips, not so much to silence him as to touch his mouth. 'You don't need to compete, Len.' She traced the curve of his cheek. 'You're the one. It's always been you, no one else.'

Len frowned, pulling back from her touch. 'Don't play with me, Pauline.'

Pauline touched his wrist. 'I'm not playing games.'

'I lost my wife, Lizzie, years ago.' His eyes were wide, startled, like a trapped animal. 'Since then, there hasn't been anybody. I've been alone. It was best that way. But then you...'

Pauline put both hands on his shoulders. She could feel his breathing, irregular and troubled. 'Then I what, Len?'

'You were there, a widow, but too beautiful for the likes of me. I wanted... I wanted to talk to you, but the best way was to bring you logs, to clear the path, to help you out. I just hoped you might like me a bit, you might want to...'

'I like you a lot, Len. More than like you. And I do want to...' She kissed his lips, a slow meeting of mouths. When she drew back, Len was staring at her.

'I won't be trifled with, Pauline. I'm a man who means business. I won't be hurt again.'

'I don't want to hurt you,' Pauline murmured and kissed him again. Len stood stiffly at first, his body tense, then she felt him relax and he wrapped both arms around her and pulled her to him in a determined bear hug. They kissed once more. His rough fingers touched her cheek.

'Do you mean it, Pauline Pye? Can you love a simple farmer man like me?'

She pulled him close. 'I can, Len, and I do.'

She was about to kiss him again, but there was the rattle of approaching voices, the volume increasing.

'Quick, someone's coming,' Pauline giggled, tugging his sleeve and they scuttled under the trestle table, hiding beneath the long cotton covers. Her eyes shone as she peered out and saw a pair of skinny legs approaching. She recognised the voice instantly.

'The judging's been done. I'll show you who's best in the village, Phyllis Hammer.'

Pauline grasped Len's huge hand with hers, placing the other over her mouth to stop herself from sniggering. The skinny legs were joined by a larger pair, leaning on a stick, the brown stockings rolled to the ankles. Pauline held her breath.

'I don't know why you think you can win any competitions, Dulcie Brimicombe. Your place is a filthy mess. You don't even have any flowers in your bog of a garden.'

There was a pause. Pauline could hear someone moving the

blooms on the table above her. Then Dulcie's voice was high with triumph.

'Look. First prize. Miss D. Brimicombe. That's me. I've won the first prize for Winsley's best blooms.'

Phyllis' voice was low. 'They are *my* blooms, out of *my* garden. You've stolen them. You thieving witch!'

'You can't prove it, Phyllis. I grew those marigolds fair and square.'

'They aren't marigolds. They are begonias. You don't even know the names of them.'

'I did grow them. They are mine. What's my prize? A bottle of whisky. There, it says so, next to my name.'

'If you had any flowers in your garden, Dulcie, your cats would have piddled on them and killed them. Your place stinks.'

'You're jealous.'

'Jealous? Of you? You stole my blooms.'

'Well, you stole my boyfriend, Phyllis. Albie Matthews was mine, not yours.'

'No, he was not.'

Pauline watched as the legs turned away. Still arguing, the two women moved to the exit. Pauline heard a few choice expletives and a sound that might have been fabric ripping or the passing of wind before Phyllis suggested they visit the cider tent to discuss it further. Pauline turned to Len and whispered.

'Well, they've gone. The coast is clear.'

Len crouched motionless and scratched his chin. His eyes were serious, deep-set. 'What shall we do now, Pauline?'

He leaned forward and kissed the tip of her nose. She breathed in the sweet scent of him, hay and perspiration and something fragrant from the flowers. She felt dizzy, like a teenager. She giggled, leaned forward and put her lips next to his ear.

'Well we could go back to my place. There will be no one

around for hours.' She pinched his cheek playfully. 'You know what I'm thinking about, Len? Tea. Cupcakes. Bedroom.'

* * *

Barbara was sitting in a deck chair, next to Tilly Hardy. Her legs sprawled in front of her and she was holding a glass of lemonade. Tilly was gushing about the craft of writing an erotic romance. She held her glass of bubbly up.

'Of course, I'm done with Wendy Whiplash now – I'm thinking of bringing my stories a little closer to the originals. I could write the tale of a sweet virgin maid and a darkly handsome man called Mr Arsey. I'll call it *Prude and Prejudice*. And another one about pirates, sex on the high seas – jaunty cabin girl Jackie Hawkins and Long John Silvertongue jolly-rogering in *Pleasure Island*. I have enough ideas to keep me going for years.'

Barbara was watching the activity in front of her, on the cleared patch of grass where the tournament was about to take place. Kevin Carter and Andy Priddy were examining a length of thick rope.

'Looks like the tug o' war will be happening soon. I wonder where Bisto is. And Pauline.'

'Oh, I expect they're enjoying the fête.' Tilly sipped her champagne from a tall glass. Bubbles rose around the tiny strawberry at the bottom. 'I have a new man in my life, DJ Johnny, so there's plenty of opportunity for research.' Tilly winked at Barbara. 'Now look at all these hunks preparing for battle.'

She nodded to a group of men who were stripping off their shirts, passing a length of the rope to each other, exchanging serious glances. Barbara recognised the Priddy brothers and Kostas on the Milton Rogus team, although it appeared that the Greek god was intending to pull for Winsley Green, as he took his place next to Hugo. Jeremy whispered something in his ear and he nodded, still in sunshades, sauntering to stand behind Jack Priddy. Peter Darby arrived, athletic in cycling shorts, waving at his wife Julia and Ava, who was arm in arm with Fabian. In his black clothes and shades, Tilly's son seemed far too cool to tug a rope. Dr Mario jogged to meet the men, turning to wave at Natalie and the baby who were sitting under the shelter of a tree. Oskar joined them, still in his jeans and t-shirt. Gary Chatfield sauntered over, a little unsteady on his feet, a glass of cider in his hand, waiting for instructions. Bisto appeared, grinning at everyone around him, and took the end of the rope.

Tamsin, in tiara and a shiny Miss Winsley Green sash, approached to start the proceedings. She was glamorous, her long hair smooth, a floor-length cream gown shimmering in the sunlight. She paused, waiting for the men to organise themselves into a line. Gary swigged from his glass and said something to her, and she looked away. Kevin glanced over his shoulder and noticed Gary finishing his drink. He let go of his part of the rope and went over, touching Gary's shoulder.

'Get to your place now, Gary. You're in front of Bisto.'

Gary sneered and glanced across at Tamsin. 'She won't talk to me. Stuck up now – that's what her problem is.' He threw his plastic cup on the ground. Kevin picked it up.

'You've been drinking. Do you want to sit this one out?'

Gary waved his arms. His handsome face took on a surly expression. 'Why won't she talk to me? What's wrong with her?'

Tamsin glanced at Gary and turned her back. Kevin gripped Gary's arm. 'Maybe you should go home?'

Gary snarled. 'She won't speak to me.' He wrenched away from Kevin's grip and writhed closer to Tamsin. 'You won't speak now, Tamsin. You're too good for the likes of me. Is that it?'

Andy Priddy took a step forward. His cousin Jack gripped his bicep, tugging him back. Tamsin lifted the corner of her gown and swept several steps away. Kevin put a sturdy hand on Gary's shoulder.

'Get on home now, Gary. Where's your dad? He'll give you a lift.'

'Tamsin.' Gary's face was red. He was bawling her name, his brow a knot of anger. 'You weren't ignoring me last year, were you? In the stables up at Bottom Farm? Now you got baby Harley and you don't want me near him. You think you're too good for me now, don't you? All stuck up in your white dress.'

Andy's face flushed and his fists became balls of rock. Tamsin took a pace forwards and stared at Gary; her brow imperious.

'Go away, Gary. How many times do I have to tell you to go away? It's over. The baby and I don't need you. Just go away and leave us alone.'

Tilly nudged Barbara. 'Look! The plot is at the point of climax and dénouement. I'll put all this in a novel. How exciting!'

Barbara felt sorry for both Tamsin and Gary, embroiled in a public display, their lives bared for all to see. She was about to push herself up from the comfy deck chair and go and comfort one or other of them, but Yvonne had reached her daughter and was patting her hand and Hugo had escorted Gary to a waiting Oskar, who led him back to the tent. Barbara arched an eyebrow.

'Winsley only have six – they are two men short.' She glanced across at Bisto, in his green Ireland t-shirt and pink shorts, as he raised a thumb to her. Miss Winsley Green displayed her cool exterior and raised a red handkerchief, about to declare the tug o' war ready to begin.

Suddenly, Andy Priddy shouted, 'Heave away,' and the contest had started. At first no one seemed to move, then there was a tugging back and forth, the men grunting and growling, their bodies bent like battling bulls. Kevin threw back his head and roared, heaving the rope backwards, his heels stuck in the grass. For a moment, there was stalemate: no one moved, then the

Priddy boys launched a forceful attack, jerking Kevin forwards. The Winsley team staggered behind him. For a split second, they were off balance, then there was a loud yell from Kevin and they pulled as one. Kostas tumbled forward, his sunglasses launched from his head, and the Milton Rogus team collapsed like a house of cards. A triumphant roar went up from the Winsley lads. Kostas picked himself up, grinned at the crowd, shook the dust from his denim cut-offs and jogged back to join Hugo. The Priddy cousins stared at each other in disbelief. Barbara leaned over to Tilly.

'I hope they aren't doing a women's tug o' war. I'm certainly not taking part in any of that nonsense.'

'Oh, there was a women's competition earlier. You must have missed it. Chrissie led the Winsley women against Milton Rogus but we lost.' Tilly shrugged. 'But what's happening now? What's Kevin Carter up to?'

Kevin had taken centre position on the grass arena and was holding up his hands. Some of the tug o' war contestants had flopped down on the ground. Kevin called out, 'Your attention, ladies and gentlemen.' He grinned and waved his arms again. The crowd became silent.

'Ah,' Kevin began. 'You all know our friend Bisto is leaving us next week to return to foreign lands. Well, ah, he has something he'd like to – er – get off his chest before he goes. In a manner of speaking.'

Bisto stood up, grinning at the crowd. He had an audience and he was clearly ready to perform. Kevin raised his voice.

'Now, what's about to happen here is not for the delicate or the easily offended. It might be a good idea for parents to take their little ones away for some sweeties or lemonade.'

A few people shuffled away, but most eyes were glued on Bisto. He was gazing cheerfully around him, his lips curved in satisfaction. Then his eyes met Barbara's and he winked. She frowned back: she had no idea what was about to happen. Kevin continued.

'Bisto has something he'd like to say. Something special. So – let's take it away for Mr Mulligan, lads.'

From nowhere, the tug o' war teams on both sides struck up a tune, singing loudly with one voice. Barbara recognised it immediately. It was 'The Stripper'.

Bisto stood proudly in the centre of the men and whisked off his green t-shirt, twirling it around his head, exposing his chest of curly white hairs, pale flesh against a tanned neck and arms. Then he bent down, stood up again, wiggled his hips and thrust his fingers down the front elastic of the pink shorts.

The volume increased. 'Dah dah-dah, da-da dah dah...'

Barbara frowned. 'Whatever is he doing?'

Tilly leaned forward to get a better look. Bisto pulled down the shorts to his ankles, tugged out one bare leg, kicked them into the air with a flourish and caught them. He whirled the shorts above his head. Barbara gasped. He wasn't wearing ordinary underpants. He had on a thong. A leopard print, silky, shiny thong. Barbara leaned forward next to Tilly so that she could see well.

Then Bisto yelled. 'And this is all for you, just as you asked for, darlin',' and he turned around, wiggling his bottom.

The back of the thong was nothing but a thin string that seemed to lodge itself between the cheeks of Bisto's pale backside. Barbara leaned even further forward and stared. There was something written on his buttocks, in black writing from a felt-tip marker. She narrowed her eyes. At first she couldn't believe it, but it was there, indelibly, in capital letters. Tilly was nudging her. The whole crowd were staring at her and some people were chortling. The men had stopped singing and were clapping, a huge round of applause. There it was, on Bisto's left bottom cheek: BAR. And on his right buttock, BARA. She put her hand to her face to cool the warmth of the beating blood that was making her blush.

'I don't understand,' Tilly whispered.

'I told him,' Barbara groaned. 'I said I wasn't interested in love. I said a man would have to be naked with my name on his buttocks before I'd...' Her voice trailed off and she was suddenly overcome. Everyone seemed to be cheering and clapping.

Tilly was shoving Barbara to her feet, propelling her towards Bisto. Before others pushed her forward into the arms of the almost-naked little man, Barbara heard the novelist murmur, 'This is priceless. It's definitely going to feature in my next best seller.'

34

'I've never been so embarrassed,' Barbara grinned. 'All those people watching and cheering. And you kissing me like that.'

Bisto took her hand as they turned the corner into the lane that led to Pauline's cottage. He was dressed in the Ireland t-shirt and pink shorts again, but he pulled a face of exaggerated discomfort. 'These thong things aren't all they're cracked up to be. My mickey's packed tight in a hammock.'

Barbara stared into his eyes, enjoying the china blue twinkle. 'I thought it was all very fetching, Bisto.'

He shrugged, cradling his hand in hers. 'I'd been planning it since that night, the one where you drank the Prosecco and said a man would have to run naked. Of course, I couldn't do the full shebang – there'd be kiddies watching.'

'I'd no idea you even liked me...'

'It must be a semantic pragmatic syndrome...' Bisto grinned as Barbara frowned at him. 'You didn't get my signals.'

'I thought Pauline loved you...'

'I don't think so,' Bisto chuckled. 'She has another man in her heart. And he has the big hots for her.'

He wrapped his arm around her, and Barbara grinned. She towered over him by at least five inches. She draped an arm over his shoulder. It felt very nice indeed. They had arrived at Pauline's gate. Barbara sighed.

'Do you think Pauline will be upset? About us two, I mean. She'll be surprised.'

'No, I think she might have her mind on other things right now.' Bisto had noticed the Land Rover parked in the lane. 'Will we go in?'

They walked up to the path together. The front door was ajar, as if someone had entered in a hurry and not bothered to close it. Barbara muttered, 'No one ever closes their doors around here. Do you think that's neighbourly? Or just tempting the burglars?'

Bisto grinned. 'It's a wicked sense of humour you have on you, Babs. I've grown very fond of it.'

Barbara smiled at him and wondered if he was teasing her. She hadn't intended to make a joke at all. They crept into the hallway, past the mirror and into the kitchen. Barbara stared at the table. There was a tea pot, two half-empty cups of tea that hadn't been washed. But the thing that surprised her most was Pauline's precious cupcakes that she had made so carefully for the competition. One or two had been eaten – there were some empty paper cases on the dish – but others had been scattered across the table and two were on the floor, squashed. Barbara made a low humming noise of disapproval.

'I wonder if the Feral Peril have been in here.'

She looked around. Pauline's blouse was discarded on the tiled floor next to a tartan shirt, a huge belted pair of jeans, two over-turned wellington boots. Barbara's perplexed gaze met Bisto's twinkling eyes.

There was a scuttling sound on the stairs, footsteps hurriedly descending, and Pauline came into the kitchen, stopping wide-eyed to stare at them. At first, Barbara thought her sister was shocked because she and Bisto were holding hands. But Pauline was dripping and dishevelled, her hair in wet strands over her face, wearing a dressing gown tied at the middle and hanging loosely, gaping open at the top. She had nothing on underneath.

Pauline's hand flew to her neck and she hoisted the dressing gown around her, pulling the belt tight. She giggled.

'Barbara. Bisto. You're back – already. I – I was in the shower. Has the fête finished?'

Bisto grinned. 'I think the fun has just started, Pauline.'

He could hear the clomping footfall behind her and suddenly Len Chatfield was in the room. His hair was damp, his face flushed and smiling. He was wearing Barbara's blue winceyette nightie, which hugged his huge frame very snugly.

'Pauline, love, you said there was a dressing gown in the other bedroom but I couldn't find it...' He stood still as stone.

'My nightie seems to be very popular with the men,' Barbara observed. 'I remember you looking particularly fetching in it too, Bisto.'

Pauline put a hand to her mouth and giggled. Len turned away, the nightie riding up over his sturdy thighs, then he changed his mind and moved back to Pauline, putting his arms around her and leaning a whiskery chin gently on the top of her head. He nodded across the room twice.

'Barbara. Bisto.'

Bisto gazed from one flushed face to the other. He squeezed Barbara's hand. 'Babs and I just popped back to tell you that we were off out for a while and we'd see you both later.' He grinned hopefully at Len. 'We'll be back just before dark.'

Barbara nodded, picking up the hint. 'Oh yes, there's dancing and drinking down at the fête until late. Bisto and I are going to have some fun.' She paused. *Bisto and I*. She'd said it aloud for the first time – and it sounded wonderful. 'So we'll be back later.' She gazed at her sister and their eyes met, then Barbara offered her the coup de grace – she winked. Pauline giggled, put her hand to her mouth, and winked back.

'Ah, right, well. I'm sure Len and I have plenty to occupy us.'

Len put strong arms around her waist. 'Talking. Planning.' He thought for a moment. 'Kissing.'

Pauline glanced at Bisto and Barbara, taking in their clasped hands, their bodies close together. 'Can you be back just after nine? I'll make us a late supper and we can open a bottle of wine. It looks like we all have something to celebrate.'

Bisto wrapped an arm around Barbara's waist. 'Okay, sounds like we have a plan. Come on, Babs. We'll see you later. Pauline, Len.'

Pauline beamed at them and gazed up at Len. She rested her head against his chest. It felt right to her, her face against the steady thud of his heart; she felt calm and relaxed, as if she had come home.

Len pulled at the neckline of his nightie, which had opened up to expose a nipple. 'Supper would be very nice,' he said to Barbara and then, glancing at Bisto, he smiled and said 'I'm looking forward to it. It'll be – what d'you call it? – a good craic.'

* * *

Back in the paddock at the manor house, festivities were underway. A band was playing on a makeshift stage and there was dancing on the grass where the tug o' war had taken place. The space was full of people cavorting in groups, around handbags, and couples smooching. Julia and Peter Darby were in each other's arms, smiling at each other. Andy Priddy was swaying slowly, Miss Winsley Green's head on his shoulder, her eyes closed; Jack Priddy was smooching with Claudia, and Fabian and Ava were by the speakers, holding hands. A few feet away, under a tree, Tilly Hardy was cuddling her DJ and, in the shadows, two old ladies were arguing over a bottle of whisky.

Chrissie was in the centre of the dance floor, wearing a long blue dress, dancing energetically with Gary Chatfield who moved awkwardly, staring at his feet as if he was learning the steps. Barbara put her mouth close to Bisto's ear. 'Do you think she's converted him?'

Bisto grinned. 'It won't do him any harm.' He stared around, his eyes seeking out Justina and Oskar's temporary bar.

Barbara squeezed his arm. 'Do you want a pint or two of the black stuff, Bisto?'

He turned and his eyes twinkled. 'No, not right now, Babs. There's something on my mind more pressing than the drink.' He winked at her. 'Will we take a walk across the field, maybe go up to the manor, and enjoy some time together? I'm not in the mood for drinking with the lads, to tell the truth.' He gazed into her eyes. 'I want to spend my last few days here with you.'

They moved away quietly, leaving the booming of bass and drums and the tinkle of laughter behind them. They crossed the paddock, picking their way across dusty dry grass towards the manor house. Bisto held Barbara's hand firmly, swinging it a little as they walked. She glanced at him.

'Do you want to call in and say hello to Hugo?'

Bisto shook his head. 'Ah, no. Hugo and Jeremy are having the big romantic dinner, aren't they? With Dizzy and Kostas.'

They had reached the barns and he looked around for somewhere to sit. There were some old tyres heaped on the ground. He perched on the end of a pile of three tyres and patted the space next to him.

'I want it to be just you and me. If that's all right with you too.'

She sat down next to him. 'It's more than all right.'

He wrapped an arm around her, and she put her head on his shoulder. They were quiet for a while. Then he murmured, 'I'm fond of you, Babs. You know that now.'

She sighed. 'Yes, I do. But we've left it too late.'

Bisto considered her words. 'I'm only seventy-six. Sure, we could have another twenty years.'

'I mean the summer's over. Now you have to go back to your château. I have to go back to Cambridge.'

He planted a kiss on her head. 'Distance never stopped love, though.'

'But you've been married twice. I'm just an old spinster – I'm crotchety and set in my ways.' Barbara gazed up at him.

He grinned and kissed her lips. 'You're lovely. And we'll be just grand.'

Barbara was silent, thinking for a while. Then she muttered, 'Bisto – I have two questions.'

He hugged her to him. 'Fire away.'

'Well, first, it's just that... Nisha, your wife. She was the love of your life. I mean, I can't compete...' The words stuck in her throat.

'She was,' Bisto sighed. 'But *was* is in the past. I'm in the now, Babs, with you. Nisha was a wonderful woman. But so are you. And she'd want me to be happy.' He kissed Barbara's lips, the merest brush of skin on skin. 'I had my heart broken and it's taken time to mend. But you saved me. You brought fun and laughter to my life.' He chuckled. 'I'd never met anyone like you, Babs. And I fell in love.'

Barbara squeezed her eyes shut. His words were pure honey, a sweetness she'd never expected. She breathed out.

'Well, that's good.'

Bisto raised his eyebrows. 'And what's the other one?'

'Other?'

'You had two questions.'

'Oh yes – I do.' Barbara pinched his arm playfully. 'You said Bisto was the nickname your mother gave you. But you must have a real name. What is it? I don't even know.'

His face brightened. 'Manus. Manus Mulligan. At your service.' He snuggled closer to her, his face taking on a mischievous expression. 'But I'd like it if you'd call me Bisto. Especially later on, when I creep into your bedroom at midnight.'

'Creep into my bedroom at midnight indeed?' Barbara's voice was mock-indignant. 'I expect you to climb in with me first thing, when I go to bed.' She raised an eyebrow. 'I need something to keep my feet warm.'

He leaned over and pulled her close, kissing her. When they pulled apart, he said, 'Will you come to France? Next week, after you've been to Cambridge and checked your house. Come and stay with me.'

Barbara frowned. 'For a holiday?'

'If you like.' He took both her hands in his. 'You could stay as long as you wanted. You could stay forever.'

'I could,' Barbara smiled. 'Yes, perhaps I would like to visit your château.'

Bisto fumbled in his pocket. 'I have a gift for you – it's only a little thing.' He handed her a piece of tissue paper and Barbara unwrapped it slowly, pulling out a small silver pin brooch in the shape of a little man in a hat.

'Thank you, Bisto. It's lovely.'

'It's a leprechaun.' He took it from her fingers and fastened it on her blouse. 'There. You'll be carrying the image of me wherever you go.'

'It's lucky. I'm lucky now. I have you.'

Bisto breathed in deeply. 'I bought a little one for Pauline too. A shamrock. Hopefully it'll bring her luck with the farmer.'

'She seemed quite lucky, back at the house,' Barbara giggled. Then her face became serious. 'Bisto – there is another thing I'd like. Another sort of present...'

'You've had a little fancy brooch and my declaration of undying love.' He raised surprised eyebrows, grinning at her playfully. 'What else can I do for you, my darlin'? Just name it.'

She took a deep breath. 'Why don't you fly any more? Why didn't you fly from Dublin to France? What happened? You said it was a long story. I'd like to hear it.'

Bisto nodded slowly. 'I told you I have a pilot's licence, my PPL. Nisha bought it for me, the training, so that I got the licence and I loved it, the flying, the freedom away from the daily grind. I flew most free weekends, and I took her with me sometimes. Oh, it was lovely, just the two of us up in the heavens and miles below us was the ground, all little square patches of fields and the sky up above like an upside down ocean. I loved being up there in the skies. If I'd believed in God, I'd have felt closer to him in a plane.'

'So why did you stop flying?'

'I put the little plane into a dive. Two days after Nisha died. I tried to crash, deliberately. Then for some reason I pulled out at the last minute. It shook me to the core. I could have done it, so easily, stopped my life, dead, just like that. And I said to myself, "Well, Bisto, that's it. You've had it with the flying now Nisha's gone." I promised myself I wouldn't get into a plane again. No more flying.'

'Never?' Barbara sighed. She gazed at Bisto and then moved her eyes to the barn where Jeremy's Tiger Moth was housed. 'Not ever?'

Bisto gazed at his hands, twiddled the thumbs together for a moment. His voice was quiet. 'I think you're asking me to prove that I love you, is that right, Babs?'

'Maybe I am.' Barbara thought carefully for a moment. 'Maybe I want to know that you're ready to move forward with me. That the past is behind you now.'

Bisto stood up and took her hand, pulling her to her feet. They walked steadily to the barn, pulling the door open. The Tiger Moth gleamed, canary yellow, the bright wings, the shiny black propeller. Jeremy had looked after it well. Bisto clambered up into the cockpit and held Barbara's arm so that she could climb up to the seat in front of him.

There were two pairs of goggles on the seats, a few blankets in a pile. Bisto put on his goggles and Barbara copied, covering her lap with the blankets he passed to her. She adjusted her safety harness as Bisto started the engine.

'This is about trust, isn't it, Babs?' His voice came from behind her 'Proof that I won't let you down.' The propeller whirred; the engine growled but she thought she heard him say, 'And I won't. Me and you, Babs, and the ride of our lives.'

She shouted, laughing, 'I remember you saying once that you wouldn't ride me even if I had pedals.'

She twisted round to see Bisto pointing to his eye, then his heart, then to Barbara. Suddenly, the biplane was moving out of the barn, accelerating into the open field ahead. Barbara caught her breath. The plane began to lift, the nose pointing to the sky and she was at the front looking out. She felt a rush in her stomach, a feeling of thrill and fear and panic not unlike love. She thought she might scream.

Then they were in the air, the engine grumbling and the wind making a low eerie sound. Barbara's heart pounded, but it wasn't the throbbing irregular beat that had landed her in hospital months ago, in the springtime: this was the strong thrum of excitement. Bisto tapped her shoulder, raising his eyebrows behind the goggles. She held up a thumb, indicating that she was fine. In his goggles, his white curls ruffled in the wind, he looked lovely. And he had been right; as the plane tilted to one side, Barbara saw the tiny patchwork of fields, some ploughed, some green, some mustard yellow. They were heading for the moors, hills rising below them and above an endless blue sky, a scattering of thin cloud. Then Bisto turned the plane into the sun and the wings gleamed pink as if illuminated by a magic wand. In the distance, the sun was sinking over the peaks, melting undiluted orange crush into the valleys, streaking the ground with crimson, mixing with the deepest blue.

The bright yellow of the plane shone gold and the wing tips took on the tangerine reflection of the sunset. Barbara stared over her shoulder. Bisto and the Tiger Moth were bathed in a shimmering glow. Everything was almost blinding, an iridescent tinge, the sunset colours seeping into every corner of the plane and illuminating Bisto's face, his goggles, his smile. As the plane flew above the craggy rocks, its wings and cockpit the colour of fire, the world below was lost in the glare of the vermillion sunset. In the plane, Barbara was encased in a bubble of candy-coloured warmth that gave her a feeling of complete serenity, perpetual safety, and she felt completely at peace. The biplane hovered in the air, almost still for a second. Then it swung round towards home.

Barbara glanced back at Bisto. He was smiling, and she knew that they were thinking the same thing. They had started a journey into the future. The sun had not set yet on their lives and they were bathed in warmth and the knowledge that this was their time, their moment, and they would enjoy every second of the thrill of being lifted on the air, the earth waiting below. It felt good.

ACKNOWLEDGMENTS

Thanks to my agent, Kiran Kataria, for her kindness, support, wisdom and integrity.

Thanks to Sarah Ritherdon, Nia Beynon and all at Boldwood Books who work so hard: it is a privilege to be part of such an inspirational team.

Thanks to everyone who continues to give me so much encouragement on my writing journey. You know who you are. But, just to clarify, love and thanks to Erika, Rich, Shaz, Frank, Ian, Susie, Chrissie, Kathy N, Julie and Martin, Rach and Jeff, Nick, Rog, Jan, Jan M, Ken, Trish, Bill, Kay, Pete O', Sarah E, Sarah and Jim, Mart, Cat, Beau, Zach J, Matt B, Casey B, Dianne, Jali, Sorry Suso, Ruchi, Slawka, Shaz K, Nik, Katie H, Stephanie, Ingrid, Helen and Jonno.

Heart-felt thanks to the NAC community past and present and to all those lovely people who shared a special year with me at Falmouth. Thanks to Helen, Susy, Jane, Mark, Tom, and Kris for being great tutors.

Thanks to Ivor at Deep Studios for the creativity, camaraderie and the videos.

A special mention for Peter Blaker and the Solitary Writers, whose friendship and talents I value beyond words. Thanks to the splendid Dorset Chapter of the RNA.

Thanks to my family always: Irene and Tosh, Tony and Kim, Liam. Cait, Maddie, Joey, Ellen, Angela and Norman.

Special thanks to Big G who is the source of it all.

Also, thanks to my neighbours whose warm spirit has inspired this book: Martin Wurzel, Lindsay, Kitty, Ian, Jackie, Nina, James, David and Margaret. Thanks also to Jenny, Claire and Paul who keep the local community well-fed and smiling.

Finally to anyone, wherever you are, who has taken the time to read something I've written and smiled: thank you all.

MORE FROM JUDY LEIGH

We hope you enjoyed reading *The Old Girls' Network*. If you did, please leave a review.

If you'd like to gift a copy, this book is also available as an ebook, digital audio download and audiobook CD.

Sign up to Judy Leigh's mailing list for news, competitions and updates on future books:

http://bit.ly/JudyLeighNewsletter

Five French Hens, another fun, uplifting read from Judy Leigh, is available to buy now.

ABOUT THE AUTHOR

Judy Leigh is the bestselling author of *A Grand Old Time* and *Five French Hens* and the doyenne of the 'it's never too late' genre of women's fiction. She has lived all over the UK from Liverpool to Cornwall, but currently resides in Somerset.

Visit Judy's website: https://judyleigh.com

Follow Judy on social media:

facebook.com/judyleighuk

twitter.com/judyleighwriter

instagram.com/judyrleigh

bookbub.com/authors/judy-leigh

ABOUT BOLDWOOD BOOKS

Boldwood Books is a fiction publishing company seeking out the best stories from around the world.

Find out more at www.boldwoodbooks.com

Sign up to the Book and Tonic newsletter for news, offers and competitions from Boldwood Books!

http://www.bit.ly/bookandtonic

We'd love to hear from you, follow us on social media:

facebook.com/BookandTonic

twitter.com/BoldwoodBooks

instagram.com/BookandTonic